P9-CNB-662

MUSKOKA LAKES PUBLIC LIBRARY
P.O. BOX 189; 69 JOSEPH STREET
PORT CARLING, ON P0B 1J0
705-765-5650 pclib@muskoka.com
www.muskoka.com/library

ALSO BY ANNE EASTER SMITH

A Rose for the Crown
Daughter of York
The King's Grace
Queen by Right

ROYAL MISTRESS

ANNE EASTER SMITH

A TOUCHSTONE BOOK
PUBLISHED BY SIMON & SCHUSTER
NEW YORK LONDON TORONTO SYDNEY NEW DELHI

Touchstone
A Division of Simon & Schuster, Inc.
1230 Avenue of the Americas
New York, NY 10020

This book is a work of fiction. Names, characters, places, and incidents either are products of the author's imagination or are used fictitiously. Any resemblance to actual events or locales or persons, living or dead, is entirely coincidental.

Copyright © 2013 by Anne Easter Smith

All rights reserved, including the right to reproduce this book or portions thereof in any form whatsoever. For information, address Touchstone Subsidiary Rights Department, 1230 Avenue of the Americas, New York, NY 10020.

First Touchstone trade paperback edition May 2013

TOUCHSTONE and colophon are registered trademarks of Simon & Schuster, Inc.

For information about special discounts for bulk purchases, please contact Simon & Schuster Special Sales at 1-866-506-1949 or business@simonandschuster.com.

The Simon & Schuster Speakers Bureau can bring authors to your live event. For more information or to book an event, contact the Simon & Schuster Speakers Bureau at 1-866-248-3049 or visit our website at www.simonspeakers.com.

Designed by Akasha Archer

Manufactured in the United States of America

10 9 8 7 6 5 4 3 2 1

Library of Congress Cataloging-in-Publication Data is available.

ISBN 978-1-4516-4862-1
ISBN 978-1-4516-4863-8 (ebook)

For my dear friend Reniera,
who has seen me through thick and thin for more than forty years

Contents

The House of York in 1475

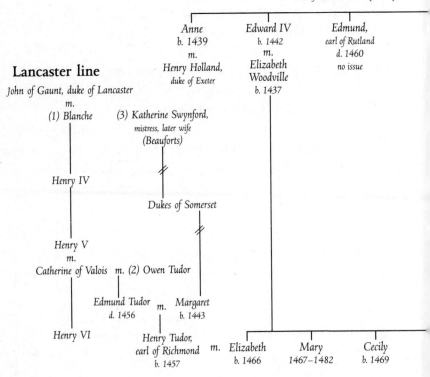

Richard
d. 1460, duke of York,
son of Richard, earl of Cambridge, and
Anne Mortimer, descended from the 4ᵗʰ &
2ⁿᵈ sons of Edward III, respectively

Anne
b. 1439
m.
Henry Holland,
duke of Exeter

Edward IV
b. 1442
m.
Elizabeth
Woodville
b. 1437

Edmund,
earl of Rutland
d. 1460
no issue

Lancaster line

John of Gaunt, duke of Lancaster
m.
(1) Blanche   (3) Katherine Swynford,
                        mistress, later wife
                        (Beauforts)

Henry IV

Dukes of Somerset

Henry V
m.
Catherine of Valois m. (2) Owen Tudor

Edmund Tudor m. Margaret
d. 1456   b. 1443

Henry VI

Henry Tudor,   m. Elizabeth   Mary   Cecily
earl of Richmond   b. 1466   1467–1482   b. 1469
b. 1457

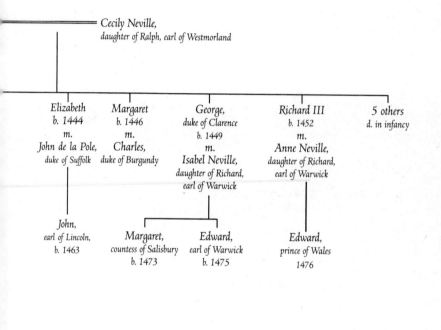

Cecily Neville,
daughter of Ralph, earl of Westmorland

Elizabeth
b. 1444
m.
John de la Pole,
duke of Suffolk

Margaret
b. 1446
m.
Charles,
duke of Burgundy

George,
duke of Clarence
b. 1449
m.
Isabel Neville,
*daughter of Richard,
earl of Warwick*

Richard III
b. 1452
m.
Anne Neville,
*daughter of Richard,
earl of Warwick*

5 others
d. in infancy

John,
earl of Lincoln,
b. 1463

Margaret,
countess of Salisbury
b. 1473

Edward,
earl of Warwick
b. 1475

Edward,
prince of Wales
1476

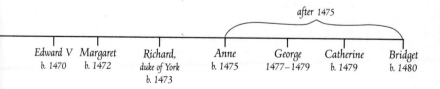

after 1475

Edward V
b. 1470

Margaret
b. 1472

Richard,
duke of York
b. 1473

Anne
b. 1475

George
1477–1479

Catherine
b. 1479

Bridget
b. 1480

ACKNOWLEDGMENTS

Jane Shore was a mercer's daughter and wife of another mercer, and thus the first place I needed to have access to was the archive belonging to the Mercers' Company or guild in London. You cannot merely walk into the Mercers' Hall and ask to poke about in their basement. You have to have an introduction. Thank goodness for my sister, Jill Phillips. If she doesn't know the right person to contact, then she has a friend who does. It was through her good friends Sue and Tim Powell that I was put in touch with David Vermont, a past Master of the Mercers' Company. David kindly set up the introduction with Archivist Jane Ruddell and her assistant Donna Marshall, who spent hours helping me ferret out what I could about Jane's father, John Lambert, as well as Jane's first husband, William Shore. It was a fascinating day at a fascinating place in the heart of the city. (The mercers have had a guild or mysterie since 1304.) Many thanks to them all for their invaluable help. As always, Jill was my host during my research in London, and I cannot say enough about her generosity.

Thanks also to the Eton College staffer who sent me a copy of the important article by Nicholas Barker about Jane that appeared in a 1972 edition of *Etonia,* the school's scholarly magazine. This is the most comprehensive account of Jane Shore's life, including new research that revealed Jane was not the only daughter of a Thomas Wainstead, as previously thought, but one of several children born to John Lambert and his wife, Amy. I was grateful to Anne Coward, Visits Office Assistant at Eton College, who took me on a private tour of that famous boys' school. My old flatmate from Gloucester Road in the Swinging Sixties, Patricia Triggs Atherton, was kind enough to host me in Henley and drive me to Eton for the day.

Also due thanks is my friend and nurse midwife, Maryann Long, who from her home in Australia talked me through Jane's complicated birth scene.

Sadly in 2010, before *Royal Mistress* was conceived, I lost my former agent, Kirsten Manges, to motherly duties. However, I gained a new champion in Jennifer Weltz of the Jean V. Naggar Literacy Agency, and she has been very helpful during another difficult transition in the life of an author: a change of editor. The wonderful Trish Todd originally signed me to write *Royal Mistress* for her, but she has moved on and up in Simon & Schuster, and I am now in the delightful hands of Heather Lazare. I hope to continue this new relationship for at least as long as I did with Trish. Heather was brave enough to take me on midway into this project and has gently seen me through.

Once again, I must thank my husband, Scott, who gets as excited as I do at each new book and cheers me on until it is completed. Finally, without my unflagging and eagle-eyed "reader," Catherine Thibedeau, this book would not be the book it is. Apparently, I am the master of the dangling modifier, and yet she never complains.

DRAMATIS PERSONAE

Historical characters

Elizabeth (Jane) Lambert

John Lambert, *her father, a mercer of London*

Amy Lambert, *her mother*

Isabel (Bella) Lambert, *her sister*

Edward IV, *first Yorkist king of England*

Elizabeth Woodville (Bessie), *Edward's queen*

Thomas Grey (Tom), marquess of Dorset, *her son by her first husband, John Grey*

Sir Richard Grey, *his brother*

Edward (Ned) and Richard (Dickon), *Edward and Elizabeth's sons*

Elizabeth of York (Bess), *Edward and Elizabeth's oldest daughter*

William, Lord Hastings (Will), *Edward's lord chamberlain, Tom's stepfather-in-law*

Katherine Neville Hastings, *his second wife, Tom's mother-in-law*

George, duke of Clarence, *Edward's younger brother*

Richard, duke of Gloucester, *Edward's youngest brother*

Anne Neville, duchess of Gloucester, *his wife*

John (Jack), Lord Howard and later duke of Norfolk, *a councilor*

Margaret Howard, *his second wife*

Thomas Howard, later earl of Surrey, *John Howard's son*

Elizabeth Howard, *his wife*

Henry Stafford (Harry), duke of Buckingham, *Edward's second cousin*

William Shore, *a mercer of London*

Thomas Lyneham, *Richard of Gloucester's solicitor*

Sir John Norrys, *one of Edward's esquires of the body*

Sir Walter Hungerford, *another esquire of the body*

Sir Francis Lovell, *Richard of Gloucester's friend*

William Catesby, *a lawyer*

Roger Ree, *Edward's deputy chamberlain*

John Etwelle, *a mercer and former apprentice of John Lambert*

Dean Reynking, *dean of Arches at St. Mary-le-Bow*

Dr. John Argentine, *Ned's physician*

Dr. Domenico de Serigo, *Queen Elizabeth's physician*

Isabel Thomson, *servant to Thomas Lyneham*

Jehan LeSage, *Edward's jester*

Fictional characters

Sophia Vandersand, *a silkwoman and Jane's friend*

Jehan Vandersand, *a weaver and Sophie's husband*

Janneke Vandersand, *a silkwoman and their daughter*

Pieter Vandersand, *their son*

Ankarette Tyler, *Jane's maidservant*

Matthew, *John Lambert's apprentice*

Wat, *William Shore's apprentice*

Martin, *Jane's steward*

Kate Haute, *Richard of Gloucester's former mistress*

Betty, Master Davies, and Anne, *fellow inmates of Jane's in Ludgate gaol*

PART ONE

1475-1476

Of noble blood I cannot boast my birth,
For I was made out of the meanest mould,
Mine heritage but seven foot of the earth,
Fortune ne'er gave to me the gifts of gold,
But I could brag of nature if I would,
Who filled my face with favour fresh and fair
Whose beauty shone like Phoebus in the air.

Thomas Churchyard, "Shore's Wife," 1562

ONE

London, Winter 1475

Wrapped in warm woolen cloaks, their faces and animated conversation hidden in the folds of capacious hoods, Jane and Sophia rounded the corner of Soper Lane and the Chepe and collided with a man equally cocooned against the bitter January wind.

"God's teeth, look where you are treading, sirrah!" Tom Grey barked, his hand on his dagger. But upon realizing he had almost been knocked down by two young women, he immediately bowed. "My pardon, ladies. It was I, Tom Grey, who was at fault," he apologized. His practiced eyes roved from one face to the other and settled without hesitation on the prettier of the two. "Are you hurt?"

Jane Lambert met his admiring stare with the certainty of one used to attracting male attention and was struck by his youthful good looks. While Sophia bent to pick up the silks that had fallen from her basket, Jane was left to assure the young man the fault was entirely theirs. "I am afraid our chatter was too lively," she said, hoping he had not heard her describing her latest conquest as a puling brat. "We were not paying attention. However, Master Grey, if we have done you no hurt, we must go on our way to the cordwainer."

"Allow me to accompany you, mistresses," Tom answered, his eagerness telling Jane that he was serious about the offer.

Sophia began to protest, but Jane dug her elbow into her friend's ribs and thanked the young knight—for certes, from the cut of his cloth he must be gently born, she decided. Smiling, she took his proffered arm. "We accept with pleasure." Without thinking to ask her companion, she told Sophia to take the other. The timid Sophia touched Tom's arm as if it were on fire but did not demur.

And thus the trio made their way down the cobbled street to Cordwainer's Row, Jane having no inhibitions about engaging Master Grey in conversation. Sophia, on the other hand, glanced warily right and left, hoping no one she knew would tell her husband she was on the arm of another man. Jealous Jehan Vandersand could be abusive for no good reason whenever he returned from the Pope's Head, and here she was, on her way to deliver some of the silks she had spun to the weaver and should only be about her business. She rued allowing Jane to be so bold. Although she had admired Jane's fearlessness from the first day they had met as children, it had got the two friends into more trouble than Sophia had ever anticipated over the years. She began to count the steps to the weaver's work-shop, where she could safely make her escape.

"My father's establishment is behind us in the Mercery, Master Grey," Jane was saying, avoiding a puddle of drying piss from the contents of a chamber pot thrown earlier from an upstairs window. "He has the finest Venetian silk in London, does he not, Sophie?"

Sophia nodded, and Tom laughed. "I do not think Mistress Sophia approves of me."

"Sourface Sophie!" Jane cried, grinning at her friend. "That's the name I gave her when we were girls," she explained while Sophia blushed. "I was always the naughty one, and she was always try-ing to save me from landing in hot soup." Seeing Sophia was now mortified, Jane hurried on, "But we are the best of friends, and I cannot think of life without Sophie in it, even though she is mar-ried now and must be a dutiful wife and mother."

Tom smiled encouragement at prim Sophia, her long Flemish features offering no hope of beauty, and turning back to Jane, he could not imagine his luck. He had left his mother at her town house not an hour earlier in search of a tavern after arguing with her over how little time he had spent with his wife in their six months of marriage. He had stormed out, determined to wash down his woes with strong ale in the anonymity of a city drinking establishment, when he had encountered Jane and her companion. Now he was drinking in the sensual beauty of the young woman beside him, which was every bit as intoxicating to the hedonistic young man as any cup of ale. And even more titillating was seeing the young woman return his interest.

"Good day to you, Master Grey," Sophia said, withdrawing her arm and bobbing a curtsey. "Jane," she said meaningfully, "do not forget your errand. Your father needs his shoes." With relief, she crossed to the conduit in the middle of the Chepe, then to the other side of the busy thoroughfare and disappeared through the doorway of the weaver's house as the couple watched.

Without Sophia as chaperone, Jane suddenly felt exposed. "Forgive me, sir, but Mistress Vandersand is right. I must attend to my errand or my father will have yet another reason to chastise me." She reluctantly reclaimed her hand, which Tom had taken to his lips, and she tucked it into her coney-lined muff. "May God give you a good day, and my thanks for your escort."

"But, mistress, you have not told me your name."

"'Tis plain Jane, sir," Jane said with a twinkle. "Although I was christened Elizabeth. And I work at my father's shop under the Maiden's Head." She laughed when his eyebrows rose in astonishment. "He is a mercer, sir, as I told you. John Lambert is his name, and you would know the guild's insignia is the head of a maiden if you lived in London. She is well known in the city; you'll see her swinging from every mercery. Ah, perchance you are from the provinces?"

Tom nodded but chose not to take her hint and reveal any of his personal information. Let her think he was Master Tom Grey and not Sir Thomas Grey, marquess of Dorset, oldest son of Queen Elizabeth and her first husband; he was enjoying himself. "And are you always so bold, mistress?" He laughed. He was determined to see this engaging, sensual young woman again; she was such a pleasant change from his dull, though young and very rich, wife.

"Until we meet again, Jane Lambert," he said, pulling up his hood and covering his thick chestnut hair. "For I am certain we shall." He turned and walked back the way they had come.

Jane felt as though she was floating down Bread Street. She wondered if Tom Grey had experienced the same exciting rush as she had when he had kissed her hand. This man was different from all the others she had dallied with, she was certain.

Later in the early darkening of the day, Jane was on her way down to the kitchen when she heard her father's voice say her name from the spacious solar on the second floor. The door was ajar, and she could not resist eavesdropping. Then she wished she had not.

"She was seen walking arm in arm with a complete stranger this morning—albeit a well-dressed stranger," her father complained. "She does not seem to care about her reputation. I will have to punish her yet again, wife. Does she think when she walks abroad that people in the Chepe will not know who she is? Or does she forget she is my eldest daughter and I have my good name and business to protect? Why can Jane not comport herself like dear Isabel?"

Jane grimaced and leaned heavily against the wall in the passage. Always Isabel, she thought bitterly; she can do no wrong. Was it just ill luck that invariably caused Jane to be found out? She knew Bella was no paragon, but nothing her sister did ever chafed at her father's temper as Jane's transgressions did. To be fair, Jane mused, there was no reason to resent her eighteen-year-old sister: after all, she knew Bella would never be a rival to her beauty and intelligence, but she was jealous of her all the same. Bella was their father's adored favorite, his obedient and diligent daughter who warranted fatherly embraces, whereas Jane seemed only to incite him to the occasional slap or tirades about insolence and sloth.

"'Tis no wonder we cannot find a husband for her. And God knows, I have tried," John went on to his placid wife, Amy.

"There, there, my dear," Amy soothed. She often found herself defending her willful, passionate daughter, perhaps because Amy recognized her own nature in Jane's. She hoped John would never discover Jane flirting, as Amy had on more than one occasion, and was thankful her daughter had intelligence and good breeding enough to resist losing her maidenhead to some amorous young apprentice. "She has beauty on her side, never fear. And she knows the mercery trade as well as any. She will find someone, mark my words."

John patted his pretty wife's hand. "It cannot be too soon for me, my love," he said, and Jane was glad to hear a softening in his tone. "I suppose I must call her down and show her that I will not tolerate such imprudent behavior."

Jane tried to leave her hiding place and race down the stairs to avoid being seen, but her fine woolen skirt snagged on a nail, and she was caught red-faced when her father flung wide the door.

"Just the person I wanted to see." John's tone took on its familiar impatience. "Come in and explain your conduct in the street today." He stood aside to let her pass in front of him into the warm, fire-lit room. "Who was the man you were seen walking alone with so cozily?"

Jane could not help retorting, "But we were not alone!" And then she hung her head. "His name is Master Grey, Father," she said and cast a pleading look at her mother, whose eyes remained fixed on her mending project.

Amy did not dare give Jane any sympathy, as much as she longed to. She hated these scenes, and knowing well John's violent temper, she did not interfere, unwittingly giving Jane more cause to be disappointed in her. Her mother's apparent subservience had only made Jane more determined never to be governed completely by a man, despite her understanding of a woman's lot in society.

Jane was not privy to the many times Amy had attempted to stand up for herself during the first few years of her marriage, but after many beratings and several beatings, Amy had learned to be the stoic, dutiful wife she was now.

"What else do you know about him, pray?" Her father stood in front of his daughter, his fists clenched. Jane raised her eyes to his angry blue ones and shook her head. "I know nothing, Father. I promise you that Sophia was with us until the very last minute, when she had to cross the street. I left him almost immediately—"

"Not soon enough for a clatterer to see you, my girl," he cut in, shouting now. "It was all about the Chepe in minutes, how little you think of your good name and mine. Take this for behaving like a harlot," he said, and he struck her face hard with the back of his hand. "Leave us, and forgo your supper. You disgust me."

Jane let out a sharp cry of pain and ran from her father as fast as her bulky skirts would allow up to her room, where she flung herself on the bed and wept.

"I hate it here," she moaned into the snowy white pillow. "I wish I were dead."

Tom Grey looked up at the maiden's head sign swinging over the door to John Lambert's mercery and smiled at the memory of Jane's remark of a few days earlier. He had not been able to get the buxom, green-eyed young woman out of his mind. He was twenty years old and confident in his good looks, and what he had liked about Jane was that she, too, knew she was comely. They were well matched, he thought as he had walked away that first morning, and if he did have the chance of seeing her again, he might tell her so. His confidence had been gained by watching and aping the seduction techniques of his stepfather, the king, and his stepfather's best friend, Lord Hastings, who, much to the frustration of his mother, began to take Tom with them when they enjoyed a rollicking evening in the taverns and stews of London as soon as the youth was old enough. His mother had hoped they would have given her pleasure-seeking oldest son sage paternal counsel on behaving like a gentleman instead.

Thus it was with more than three years of wenching experience tied up in his codpiece that Tom now clicked open the latch on the sturdy wooden door that led into John Lambert's flourishing mercery. Shelf upon shelf was weighted down by bolt upon bolt of magnificent silk, satin, damask, cloth of gold, silver cloth of gold, wool, velvet, sarcenet, scarlet, grosgrain, kersey and cambray, and in one corner, looking like delicate, magnified snowflakes, lengths of lace from Venice, Antwerp, and Bruges vied for a customer's discerning eye. Gorgeous tapestries hung on the walls and fine lawn bed linens were cleverly displayed on a long table, where two women were fingering the quality and discussing the price with a sturdy middle-aged man whom Tom took to be Mercer Lambert. The wide window along the front, which in more clement weather would have been opened to the air to facilitate customers' viewing, gave adequate light through its leaded glass panes, but the back of the shop was only lit by a wheel chandelier of wrought iron hung high from a sturdy beam. One carelessly dropped taper and John Lambert's fortune could disappear in a fireball that would light up London. As he searched the premises for Jane, he noticed the mercer paid a small boy to sit close and watch, alerting an apprentice when a candle got near the end of its wick.

Tom ducked behind a gaudy display of velvets and saw his quarry entering from the small garden at the back of the shop. Jane spied him instantly, and her heart raced; she could not believe he had actually sought her out. Checking that her father was still in deep conversation with the shilly-shallying buyers, she beckoned to Tom to join her in a less conspicuous corner. One of her father's apprentices, who was fond of Jane, turned his back as Tom sidled past him to Jane's side.

"Master Grey, may I help you?" Jane said pertly, already intoxicated by his scent of leather and musk.

Tom merely raised her hand to his lips, his eyes alight with humor.

"You know full well why I am here, mistress," he told her. "I had to see you again, 'tis all."

Jane raised her voice and pulled her hand away. "A short mantle for the summer, you say, sir? Let me show you the lightest of wools we have."

"Good day to you, sir." John Lambert's voice behind him made Tom swing round to face the unsuspecting father of the alluring target of his visit. "Is my daughter serving your needs? She knows as much about our wares as any of my apprentices—if not me."

Tom saw John appraise his customer's apparel and knew by the genuine smile that the mercer had discerned from the fashionable gown that Tom was a man of means. Mercer Lambert was deferent with members of the gentry, Tom was relieved to note; the man had not guessed the real purpose of his visit.

"You are kind, Master Lambert—if I have the pleasure of speaking to the owner of all this," he gushed, and he airily waved his hand to encompass the shop, "but I had only just stated my business. I did not know this young lady was your daughter. Mistress Lambert, your servant," he said, nodding to her. "I would be happy to see the worsted you recommend."

"Then I shall leave you to Jane," John said, bowing and rubbing his hands, which always made Jane cringe. When her father anticipated a worthwhile sale, the gesture never failed to annoy her. She hurried past Tom toward the shelf of wools. "And thank you for choosing my humble shop, Master . . ." John raised a questioning eyebrow, expecting the man to give him a name, but Tom merely nodded in acknowledgment and quickly followed Jane.

"Thank you for not saying your name, Master Grey," she said as they fingered three different bolts of blue cloth. "I was seen in your company the other day, and 'twas reported to my father, you see. He was not kind." And she lowered her eyes to the cloth, her hand going protectively to her ill-used cheek. "What do you want of me, sir?"

"I know not why, Jane, but I cannot get you out of my head. If you tell me where you live, I can send a message there to arrange another meeting."

"In truth it cannot be here or Father will suspect," Jane replied, titillated by the notion of a secret tryst. "Our house is the largest on the east side of Hosier Lane before Watling Street, anyone can tell you which. Mayhap somewhere quiet, like"—she thought quickly back to other times when she had allowed an ardent young man to kiss her and rumple her bodice, and made up her mind—"like the churchyard behind St. Paul's." It was quiet, and the buttresses created shadowy shelters for young lovers. "Send me a message with but the day and time and I shall be there."

She took a deep breath to calm herself; she could not believe she was arranging a rendezvous with this stranger and under her father's rather long nose. But it seemed that God had answered her nightly prayer for the love of a handsome young man and had sent Tom to her. Perhaps now she might know the delights of the romantic love depicted in the old poems. Secrecy was of the essence, she knew; she would worry about the more mundane aspects of courtship, like obtaining her father's permission, once she and Tom had expressed their love for each other.

She felt more alive than she had in several months, and as she counted out three ells of the midnight blue wool for him upon a tacit agreement that he must buy something, her palms were sweating and her mouth felt dry.

Tom grinned, delighted he had secured an assignation so easily. He took the measured cloth and walked boldly up to John, who was now seated on a high stool, working on his accounts. "How much do I owe you for three ells of this worsted, Master Lambert?"

he asked pleasantly, undoing the pouch at his belt and jingling the coins. "And how much for your daughter?" was on the tip of his tongue to add, but he buried the mischievous urge.

Not a week later, the cloak on his spare six-foot frame running with rain, William Shore, a mercer from Coleman Street, stood on the same spot as Tom Grey had and heard the creaking of the wooden sign above him in the gale. He noted the fine carving on the door to Mercer Lambert's shop before pushing it open and stepping into a far more lavish establishment than his own. Hanging his dripping cloak on a peg near the door, he smirked as he estimated the wealth of his fellow mercer spread before him in the colors of an exotic eastern bazaar he had heard about on his travels to Burgundy. If Lambert's daughter might inherit even a fourth of this, he thought, she would be worth taking under my roof. Then the familiar knot in his belly interfered with his mercenary thoughts; he had carefully avoided the unpleasant duty of husband for all of his eight and thirty years. However, when John had approached him about the possibility of marriage with his eldest daughter—together with a handsome dowry and the promise of inheritance—the temptation to add to his already burgeoning business was too great, and so he ignored his gut. As well, John Lambert had impressive credentials: he had once been elected as a city alderman, been appointed sheriff, and had once served as master of the mercers' guild.

And so, here William was to inspect the goods—all of them—and make a decision. He saw John examining a bill of lading and walked over to him.

Jane had been helping an elderly matron and her reticent son choose a damask for the son's presentation at court when she heard the door open and saw the middle-aged, lanky man enter the shop. His face would not set any maid's heart aflutter, Jane thought, although he was pleasant-enough looking. She watched as he went to speak to her father, his long hair limping damply to his shoulders from under his close-fitting cap, and she recognized the same mercer's murrey livery that her father wore. She only half listened to her customer's efforts to decide which patterned satin to choose and instead eyed the two men, who kept looking her way while in earnest conversation.

"I think the brown, do you not, Mistress Lambert?" the woman asked, and Jane quickly refocused her attention on the sale. The son was gazing at Jane with admiration, and she gave him a quick smile. It never hurts a sale to flirt a little, she told herself, enjoying the male attention as she always did.

"Aye, my lady, I believe the blue would inadvisedly draw all eyes to your son, and I hear the king does not like competition," Jane said. As his mother turned to hold the fabric up to the light, Jane added with a wink, "Your good looks should garner you enough favor with the ladies, in truth." The young man beamed at the compliment. "Now I shall have Matthew measure you, sir, and I thank you for your patronage." She waved at the apprentice, watching at a discreet distance, who hurried to take charge.

"Come here, daughter," John Lambert called to her when he saw Jane was free. "I wish to present you to a fellow guild member, Master William Shore."

Jane had to look up a long way to her father's friend. At a little under five feet, she was used to craning her neck to talk to men, but it seemed to Jane that Master Shore was uncommonly tall. He stared down at the comely young woman and was disconcerted by her unabashedly curious gaze. Had William been at all interested in women, he might have noticed the almond shape of those green-gray eyes, or the way her generous mouth appeared ready to laugh and how her nose came to an upswept end, making her look younger than her twenty-two years. Instead he cringed at her forthrightness as immodest and regarded her beauty as Satan's bait. But as a businessman in search of an advantageous marital match, he inclined his head graciously and gave a suitably agreeable response.

Jane, unaware of the man's disapproval—or indeed intent—began cheerfully enough: "Master Shore, I give you God's greeting. Is your business with me or with my father?" Noting the man's unusual disinterest in her looks, she became more businesslike. "I doubt not that I can help you find something, if that is what you have in mind, but you may have to wait if my present customer has a question of me."

"Certes, Master Shore's business is with *me*, Jane," John snapped. "Do not be impertinent."

"But, Father . . ." Jane said, indignant; after all, he had summoned her. But seeing both men's disapproval clearly written on their faces, she held her tongue. God's truth, now what had she said to anger her father?

"I wanted Master Shore to know you better, 'tis all," John Lambert answered, not troubling to give her an explanation. He peered up at William, hoping Jane had not already disheartened the sober suitor.

Had she known William before? she wondered. But as she was certain she had not, she was puzzled. Gripping her hands together, she inclined her head in William's direction. "Forgive me, sir, if my forwardness offended," she apologized, giving him a reluctant curtsey, "'twas not my intent."

"You may leave us and attend to Lady Margaret," John said, pleased with his daughter's deference. "Come, Shore, we can talk privately in my office."

Jane had noted her father seemed a little more unctuous with the guest mercer than he was wont to be with those he considered inferior, arousing her natural inquisitiveness. Did her father owe the man money? She could not think so, for hadn't John lent the king a large sum recently for Edward's great venture to fight the French? Was William perhaps part of a council that was able to reinstate her father as alderman? But nay, that unpleasant incident had been more than ten years ago, and John's legendary temper would not be put to the test again by the city fathers. So, who was this man to her father? She did not have time to contemplate further as at that moment the candle boy slipped a note into her hand and then sidled back to his perch. Jane looked at the small wad of wet paper and then at the boy and raised an eyebrow, but the boy turned up his hands and said, "A man give it to me when I went to take a piss outside." He chose not to show the shiny farthing the man had given him in exchange for being a messenger, but he could feel it tucked into his grubby, damp shirt.

Friday at nones was all that was written in the bold hand, but Jane felt her stomach turn over and gooseflesh prickle her arms. She gave the boy a quick smile, stuffed the note down her bodice, and went back to see how her customers were doing with Matthew.

When William Shore left the shop half an hour later, he was surprised—and gratified—to receive a nod and a smile from the young woman who might one day be his wife.

"You will obey me in this, Jane," her father said at supper that night and was relieved that Jane appeared acquiescent for once. "Master Shore has excellent prospects, and you will treat him with respect when he calls courting. You will not toss this one aside, do you hear?" Jane toyed with her fingers in her lap as she remembered how she had managed to rid herself of two other unappealing suitors, once by feigning madness, she recalled, suppressing a smile. "Your mother and I believe it is the only chance you will have to wed, and we need to be thinking about Isabel." He gave his younger daughter a kindly smile.

But Jane's silence caused Amy to reach over and shake her daughter's arm. The half-eaten serving of fish pie lay on Jane's trencher, and she appeared intent on shredding a hunk of bread crumb by crumb.

"You must thank your father, Jane," Amy said, not unkindly. "What? Would you rather remain here as a spinster for the rest of your life?" Jane did look up then, and her mother was horrified to see two large tears spill down her cheeks and onto her spotless linen napkin. "Tears!" Amy exclaimed in surprise as John downed his wine, angrily pushed his chair back from the table, and strode from the room. "I thought you would be pleased. I know how long you have wanted to escape from here," Amy confided.

Jane stared in awe at her mother and wiped her tears. "You do?" she said. "But, Mother, am I not to have any say-so in this decision?" She blew her nose and asked Bella to leave, which the girl did with sulky reluctance. Then Amy pulled her stool around to Jane's and poured them both another cup of wine.

"Your father is not an ogre, Jane, although I know you imagine him one. He does care about you, although 'tis true he favors Bella. I have tried to compensate, but you do not make it easy. My dear, you remind me very much of myself when I was young. Aye"—she nodded when Jane's eyes questioned—"I was as rebellious as you, but I settled into marriage because it was expected and because I wanted my own household and children. We have been blessed with six . . . seven if you count poor little Meg, may she rest in peace . . . and I am proud of you all. Your father wants you settled, and I want you happy. Perhaps William Shore can provide both. Now promise me you will give the man a fair chance."

Jane's eyes stung again, but she did not dare tell her mother she desired someone else—someone else whom she had just met and who, with time, would surely declare himself. Now was not the moment, however, but as soon as Tom came forward, surely his suit would be considered as good as William's. It was plain he was gently born, and surely her father would be ecstatic if she raised the Lamberts up to the gentry or perhaps even the nobility. There was an air about Tom, although perhaps it was because he was already a prince to her. How she would gloat when Tom came to ask her father's permission to woo her. Now, knowing her mother was waiting, she shifted in her seat and promised to walk out with William, and Amy was satisfied.

"You'll see, my dear. Once you get used to a man, you can love him and be a good wife. And then you will have the gift of children. 'Tis they who bring a woman the greatest joy."

"Aye, Mother," Jane acquiesced, imagining a son she might have with Tom Grey and not Master Shore. "I dream of holding my own babe, 'tis true, and I pray for it nightly . . . with whomever I wed."

The next few weeks were as confusing as they were titillating for Jane, believing she had two men vying for her hand. To placate her father, she allowed William to come courting and hoped that, before the slow-moving, deliberate mercer signed the formal contract, Tom Grey would declare his intentions.

It was not long before William came to Hosier Lane and sat with Amy Lambert and her daughter as he struggled to find common ground for conversation. All he knew was his trade, and he had never sought much female company in his almost forty years. Growing up, he had found his several younger sisters foolish and had chosen to escape the wilds of Derby as soon as his long, narrow feet could take him to London. There he had worked hard for the customary seven years as an apprentice to Mercer Reynkyn and received the freedom of the city when he was in his mid-twenties. As a guild member, William had associated with many of the most prosperous merchants in Europe, and his shop in the Coleman Street ward, although not as extensive as John Lambert's, was making him a comfortable profit. Even his forays to Antwerp and Bruges had been all about business, and if the truth be told, he had never paid much attention to his surroundings and was able to offer the two women but minimal details of those cities. Aye, he was good at conversing about all things commercial, but in front of Jane and her mother he was quite at a loss for words.

In fact, he was uncharacteristically nervous and was annoyed to see his hand shaking as he picked up his cup of wine. He saw Amy confide something to Jane, and so anxious was he they were talking about him that when Jane suddenly laughed at Amy's innocent joke, he started abruptly and spilled wine all over his fine grosgrain gown.

"God's truth," he mumbled, brushing off the tawny liquid with the back of his hand as his neck flushed red around the fur of his collar. "Your pardon, Dame Lambert, so clumsy of me."

He would have been surprised to know that his moment of humiliation actually caused Jane to feel sympathy for him. It made this rather stiff, unemotional man seem human, and she quickly went to help him. When he saw her concern for him, his mind was eased and he smiled his thanks. Jane was gratified to see that the smile made the man's normally sober expression almost handsome. Mayhap he is not so bad, she told herself, unconvincingly.

"I understand your business in Coleman Street is beneath your accommodations, Master Shore," Amy said, also trying to lessen the discomfort of her guest and make genial conversation. "Do you have two or three stories?"

William, taking measure of the Lambert's solar in his mind, said that he did indeed have three stories and that his parlor was only slightly smaller. "It lacks a woman's touch, I regret to say, Dame Lambert. 'Tis not so well appointed as this, but it could be." He was pleased with his hint that perhaps Jane might be the woman whose touch it lacked. Amy tittered and looked coyly at Jane.

Sweet Jesu, Jane thought, taking a bite of sugar wafer, they had her wedded to him already. The bell for sext sent a tingle through her body. In two hours, it would ring for nones, and, if sweet St. Elizabeth had heard her plea, she would soon be with Tom Grey.

The bell reminded William he had business elsewhere, and he gratefully took his leave, first kissing Amy's hand in an exaggerated show of courtesy and then giving Jane an elegant bow. "Shall we walk to mass together soon, Mistress Jane? If it please your father and mother, perhaps I could escort you on Sunday."

Jane wanted to say, "Nay, it is too soon," but did not dare when Amy agreed to his company with alacrity. The two women watched him stride toward Chepeside, his long legs and splayed feet teetering on his wooden pattens.

"Your father will be pleased to know how well you behaved," Amy said, cheerfully. "I think Master Shore is smitten."

Jane took her cloak from a peg and hid her smile in it, winding the soft stuff around herself and pulling up the fur-lined hood. "I am going to see Sophie, Mother. I promised to help her with the children this afternoon." Amy reminded her to stop in the Poultry and buy a chicken for tomorrow's dinner as Jane strapped on her pattens to keep her feet out of the mud. Amy was pleased with her, and although there was mending Jane could be doing, she let her daughter go and visit her dearest friend. Jane was devoted to the little ones, she knew. She needs her own babes, Amy thought, consoling herself that Jane would have them soon enough with Master Shore.

A few minutes later, Jane had disappeared around the corner of Watling Street as if she were going to the Vandersands' house a few minutes away in St. Sithe's Lane. But as soon as she guessed her mother had closed the door and retreated into the kitchen to see to tomorrow's main meal, she turned and hurried in the opposite direction toward St. Paul's. When she had dressed to greet Master Shore that morning, she had really chosen her wardrobe for Master Grey. Her mother had approved and even commented on her apple green damask gown, commending her for dressing to attract the prospective bridegroom.

Jane felt for her purse and checked to see she had enough money for a chicken at the more expensive poulterer on Carter Lane, and she set off eagerly for her assignation with Tom. She would buy the chicken later, and God help her if there were none left.

A little while later, the rain was letting up when Jane reached St. Augustine's Gate, which led into St. Paul's yard. The market in front of the south door of the cathedral was all but over, but not wanting to risk being recognized, she skirted the back of the building where the high free-standing pulpit of Paul's Cross stood. Today, with no announcements or sermons to be heard, there were no spectators gathered around it, and except for a gravedigger busy with a bucket of bones near the charnel house, the rain was keeping other visitors away.

She huddled in the lee of a buttress along the north side of the church, pulled up her hood against the drizzle, and waited on the cold seat. She was early, she knew, and she whiled away the interminable minutes thinking about William's visit. It did seem to her that the man was determined to have her, but this was not the first time John Lambert had attempted to marry off his eldest daughter, and so Jane convinced herself that she could turn Master Shore away.

Her practiced fingers fondled the soft silk woven into her belt as she ruminated on her future, feeling a flaw in the weaving that made her look down at it with critical eyes. She and Bella had learned at an early age the art of working silk into elaborate fringes and tassels that were so fashionable at court as adornments on bodices, sleeves, and hats. Bella's dexterity put Jane's to shame, and Jane decided her talent lay in the less complicated weaving of belts, ribbons, and colorful garters for hose and in attracting customers; the irony that her father was not above using her beauty for the latter did not escape Jane. Bella, on the other hand, was allowed to work at home, under the kinder eye of their mother, but Jane spent much of her week at the Mercery, employing her lap loom when the shop was quiet. For all she was lazy at her loom, Jane had discovered she had a talent with the pen, and she liked nothing more than amusing her mother and sister on quiet evenings with her clever verses.

Jane's reverie was interrupted by a group of monks chanting their way to nones along the path through the churchyard to the cathedral. Jane signed herself and intoned an ave, her eyes following them past the stone pulpit until they disappeared. It briefly crossed her mind that the choice of sacred ground for an illicit meeting might open up a rocky road to hell, but she dismissed the idea with a "pah!" and a smothered giggle and thus failed to see Thomas until he startled her with his first words.

"You did not expect me, Mistress Lambert?" he teased, catching her hand and pressing it to his lips. "Do you have such little faith in me?"

The bells above them clanged for nones and her embarrassed stammer, "N-nay, T-Tom, I mean, Master Grey," was thankfully lost in the din.

Tom curled her arm in his and joined her on the stone seat. It was out of the wind and drizzle, and she had been right about the privacy. He made sure there was no one about as he indulged himself in the first kiss of this new affair. She smelled of rosemary and citron, and her lips were hungry and warm. His instinct that Jane was versed in the art of flirtation had not failed him, and he could sense she wanted more, so he kissed her again.

"Your eyes are the color of the sea, Jane," he told her, holding her perfect oval face in his fingers. "I cannot make up my mind if they are green or gray."

His kiss stoked a fire in her that left her wanting more, but she knew what she must do in this dance of courtly love. Had she not read it over and over in her books: she must chastise him for his compliment. "You are impertinent, sir. You do not know me well enough to kiss me thus."

She expected that more high-flown prose or even poetry would continue the dance, but instead he said boldly, "Then forgive me, sweetheart, is this better?" And his lips were again on hers and this time she could feel his tongue seeking an entry. She pushed him away despite how much she longed to kiss him back in the same way; she did not want to forget the lessons that kept a real love like this burning brightly, even though he seemed to have waived his courtly manners. There was a rule that pertained to this moment, was there not, she thought. Ah, aye, rule number fourteen:

The easy attainment of love makes it of little value; difficulty of attainment makes it prized.

Jane smiled. "Perhaps I do not understand the conventions of courtly love well enough, Tom. Do I not deserve some poetry? I am sure you are not supposed to kiss me so . . . so soon."

Tom raised an eyebrow. "You are a tease, Jane. But I will try." He pulled a wayward strand of hair from her coif and wound it around his finger. "Your tresses are like the sand on the seashore," he said, studying it. "I am no poet, in truth. Where have you heard this . . . ?" He wanted to say "nonsense" but he indulged her.

"My tutor let me read an old book in Latin about romance. I think he was besotted by me when I was but thirteen." She smiled at the memory. "It was by one Master Capellanus, and I made poor Master Cook translate much of it. Latin was not my strength, I am afraid."

"You learned Latin? I thought girls learned but the rudiments of reading and writing."

"Pish," Jane retorted. "Not only do my sister and I know Latin, but we speak some French, too, Maître Gris. But you have cleverly changed the subject. We were talking about love. True love between a man and a woman."

She leaned into him eagerly and willed him to declare his love, too, but he sank back against the wall and carefully unraveled her hair from his finger. His reticence made her impulsive.

"There is a mercer who is seeking my hand," she began a little desperately, "and my father is anxious to be rid of me, but I cannot go to another when the only man I wish to be with is you." She stared anxiously at his face, but his expression caused her to rush on. "If my father knew you, too, wished to court me, he would not gainsay you. 'Tis plain you are gently born, Tom. You are, are you not? Speak to me, I cannot bear your silence. You are looking at me strangely. What does it mean?"

What does it mean, Tom thought, disconsolate. It meant he must drop this promising affair like a burning brand. For once in his young and vigorous life he would have to spurn one of the most tantalizing prospects for a mistress he had ever met. Had he misread her flirtations? Her eagerness to meet with him in secret; her nervousness at his nearness at the shop; her presence here at his first suggestion of a tryst; and her very experienced kiss had suggested she was as ready for a tumble as he was, he had felt certain. But what was all this about true love? He was aware of the idea of courtly love, but it was out of fashion now—something troubadours warbled about centuries ago.

He had difficulty concealing his disappointment and got up impatiently, leaving her dejected on her cold stone seat. In other situations, he would have walked off, never given a backward glance, and sought out new prey. But this time was different, and he did not know why. He looked back at her, huddled in her cloak, her beautiful eyes imploring him to come back and take her in his arms, and her sincerity made him search his own heart. And he realized for the first time in his life that Jane had stirred something new in him. Was his heart engaged? Nay, he told himself, they hardly knew each other. But what he did know was those very things that had drawn her to him—her honesty and willingness to risk danger—were now making this awkward, he thought sadly: she thought she was in love and thought he was, too. Aye, he was truly attracted to this provocative woman. In truth, he had not expected that his emotions upon seeing her sitting alone against the soaring buttress of the cathedral wall would have provoked such swift action. He should have waited to kiss her; he should have wooed her more, she was right. But he also wanted to take what she was so clearly offering and not have to compromise himself. For all her flirtatiousness, Jane Lambert was a virtuous young woman, he realized with chagrin. He must choose his words carefully. Dear God, but women were a trial.

"I am not who you think I am, Jane. You must believe me when I say I understood our liaison to be a flirtation only. I did not mean to mislead you, but I was misled by your eager response to my overtures. I confess I wanted to bed you, but I now see you are a woman of virtue, and I will bother you no further. I am not worthy of you." It was feeble, but it was the best he could do, and he hoped he had quelled the unfortunate subject of marriage.

He expected tears and indeed her face was wet, but her eyes were defiant, and he saw the tears were simply raindrops. By now Jane was on her feet, repeatedly clenching her fists. "Not worthy of me? What is meant by that, pray tell? I can see by the cut of your cloth you are worthy of John Lambert's daughter. I was so certain we both felt love on that first day we met. You only wished to bed and not woo me? In that case, 'tis *I* you thought unworthy, is it not?" Her accusations came at him like annoying houseflies, and when he turned up his hands wondering how to respond, she backed away from him. "Farewell, Tom Grey," she told him. "I hope you know you have broken my heart this day. You are fortunate I did not break your nose."

It took every inch of will not to laugh. Instead Tom honored her by kneeling in the muddy grass, and, finding one of her cold hands, he held it to his cheek. "I did not say I *could* not love you, Jane. I said I must not. God go with you." She snatched the hand away, and he watched her run along the church wall and around the corner before he picked up his soggy bonnet and wandered back to his mother's house, hoping to avoid one of her lectures. He was in no mood for her censure, too. For the first time in his life, he understood he had hurt someone, and he did not care for the feeling one bit.

He could not know that Jane had only reached the other side of the cathedral before she had given way to sobbing. After thumping the ancient stone of a buttress several times, her sobs began to subside; her pride would not allow her to be seen in such distress, and so she used her wet cloak to clean her face before turning toward home. She could not stop thinking back on the scene and Tom's sudden change of heart. She heard again his words: "I did not say I could not love you; I said I must not." What could he mean? It was possible he was promised to another, but perhaps he did not love his betrothed and would return to her. A tiny ray of hope crept into her heart. Perhaps all is not lost, she thought; perhaps he needs time.

Jane's head went up as her confidence increased, and she did not see a fat hen in her path until it ran squawking from underfoot. "The chicken!" she suddenly exclaimed, turning back and hurrying toward the poulterer. "I almost forgot the chicken."

TWO

LONDON, SUMMER 1475

Jane flung open the shutters of the bedchamber she shared with Bella and willed the day to dawn. The moon was retreating, and as the first shaft of the June sunrise shimmered off the towering spire of St. Paul's, she looked out at the familiar view with a mixture of regret and excitement. What would her eye fall upon this time tomorrow, she wondered, feeling her heart beat a little faster while her fingers clutched the windowsill. She did not want to leave the safety of the house on Hosier Lane, but she wanted to be free of the twenty-two stifling years under her authoritarian father's roof. And today she would get her wish.

It was her wedding day, and as the dawn's rays turned the sky from purple to ruby rose and orange, she quoted: "*Red sky in the morning, shepherd's warning.* Oh no, we shall have rain before long." She raised her eyes heavenward, hoping it was not a portent. The thought of rain sent her thoughts back to the damp day and Tom Grey, and she could not help letting out a moan of pleasure when she again imagined his mouth on hers.

Disturbed by the noise, Bella turned in her sleep, but she settled back without waking, and Jane looked at her in their shared bed with a modicum of guilt. Certes, she would miss her mother and probably Bella for a little while, but she would not miss her sister's jealous nature. Jane had never been able to confide her unhappiness to Bella, who had no complaints about their father.

Aye, she had no regrets about leaving the Lambert hearth, she decided. She saw her marriage as an escape from her uncomfortable familial relationship and into the freedom of her own household. Growing up on the streets of England's largest city, she was wiser than her counterparts living pampered but lonely lives behind the high, thick walls of their fathers' castles. She had thwarted many a youth intent on claiming her maidenhead, and had done it with a swift kick and clever retort, followed by a sympathetic smile. She had witnessed cutpurses run off with their prizes and drunkards brawl outside a tavern; pelted unfortunates at the pillory who had cheated on their customers; twice escaped the humiliation of the cucking chair for her ready tongue; had felt compassion for the grotesquely formed beggars vying for every prominent street corner; and she had seen her fair share of death, both young and old. Aye, Jane was no innocent, and she now idly wondered why she had guarded her virginity so vehemently. Sophie was married these past seven years, and Jane had eked out as much confidential information as her friend was willing to divulge about marriage and the business of bedding. Jane had been envious of Sophie's wifely status, but her friend had also confided that her duty between the sheets was nothing more than that: a duty, to be borne whenever her husband desired. The only good thing about it, she had told Jane, were the children that followed; in truth, it was Sophie's motherhood that Jane envied the most.

Listening to the bells for matins ring out, she watched as people more faithful than she hurried up the street to St. Mary-le-Bow on the corner. Up until four months ago, she was resigned to being a spinster of the parish, and at twenty-two, she was older than most brides, but now she was about to embark on a new life.

Tom Grey's face intruded on her thoughts again, and she felt the familiar tugging in her heart as she had every day since she had met him. "I did not say I could not love you, Jane." She heard his words running through her mind for the thousandth time. Aye, Tom, but you dissembled.

A few days after the disastrous tryst at St. Paul's, she had received another message, this time delivered by the apprentice Matthew, who gave it to her upon his return to Hosier Lane, where he shared a room under the eaves with two other of John's apprentices.

The Swan at Newgate, Monday at four o'clock, Tom had written, and Jane's spirits had soared. He has come to his senses, she had congratulated herself on that chilly February day. She remembered slipping out of the house as the late-winter sun hung low in front of her on her way along Watling Street, having once again invented a visit to Sophie as the reason for her absence.

The Swan was an imposing inn hard by the Newgate, and she shivered when she looked up at that part of the city wall and the gate that housed a gaol, imagining the poor creatures huddled for warmth behind the barred windows. The tavern door stood open, and a welcoming light from the fire in the wide hearth had cheered her as she walked boldly through into the large taproom, the smell of ale and roasting meat making her mouth water. She had immediately seen Tom sitting alone at a small table, and he rose to greet her, his face serious but his words kind.

"Mistress Lambert, I am pleased to see you come. I was afraid you would not." He led her to the table and called for a cup of ale for her. He pulled up another stool opposite and asked about her health. Jane had noticed he had not touched her, not even taken her hand to kiss or to help her onto the stool. Being impatient to hear what he had to say, she had dismissed the omission and leaned in, anticipating a declaration of love, or at least of affection.

"I have not stopped thinking about you since our meeting," he began, and Jane's pulse had quickened. "I was certain your regard for me was lost forever, and I must confess my conscience has been pricking me."

"As it should, Tom Grey," Jane retorted. She smiled seductively at him. "And you are telling me that you have changed your mind." She saw by his wide eyes that she had again surprised him and so gladly spoke her mind. "I do not require much of you to be happy, in truth. Not a fortune or a mansion. Nay," she assured him, "I just want to be with you always and know what real love is between a man and a woman." She wanted to reach out and touch his hand that was fingering his cup. "So, Master Grey, do you wish to court me?"

Tom instantly regretted the meeting. Aye, he had had feelings for this woman, but only in the rarest of circumstances did people of his rank find love in a marriage contract. He had lost one child-wife and had no feeling for his second, and he was still only twenty. Jane could have been his lover and consolation. He tried to let her down gently: "Do you remember that I said I *must* not love you, Jane?" He saw her nod, but her face clouded. He plunged on, hoping she had understood. "You have guessed the reason, have you not?" he implored her, with his look saying the words for him. But she was silent. He took a deep breath. "I swear I did not lie to you, although I confess I was a coward not to tell you why then. The simple truth is, I am not free to love you as you believed, because . . . because I am a married man." He turned up his hands helplessly. "And there is naught I can do about it. You would not have me unless I asked for your hand, so I had to withdraw my attention. But, please believe me when I say I was drawn to you, Jane."

Jane sat perfectly still. She watched him fidget with the ribbon tie of his gipon, his eyes avoiding hers while her stomach heaved and her heart constricted. She wanted to throw the remains of her ale in his face, spit in his eye, kick over his stool, run out into the cold evening air and scream. Instead a familiar children's rhyme fell unbidden from her lips: *"Tom, Tom the whoreson, Stole a heart and away he run,"* she improvised bitterly. "You took me for a harlot, Tom, while I offered you my heart." Her eyes glittered now like sun on the sea. "And if you understand nothing else, you should understand that a woman's heart is not your plaything. You have sat here this evening and once again allowed me to reveal my heart, and then you rebuffed me—again. Dear God, how could I have been so foolish." And she had run from the warm tavern all the way home.

Aye, how could she have been so foolish, she thought now on her wedding day, looking out over London. And yet she knew if she had it to do over again, she would have given herself to Tom Grey—wed or unwed—and risked the consequences for love.

A long stone's throw over the city wall from The Swan, Tom Grey, staring out of the solar window of his mother's residence, was still regretting Jane's loss three months later.

"Are your thoughts worth a groat, my son?" Tom's mother teased him after failing to attract his attention on her arrival in his chambers. "You appear distracted of late. Is there anything troubling you?"

Tom swung around and smiled at his mother. Going to her and bowing over her hand, he thought she must be the most beautiful woman in England. "Nay, Mother, nothing that should worry you. I was anticipating my journey to Lancashire, 'tis all. My lady wife has need of me."

"And when do you leave, Thomas? The king has asked that you escort me to Westminster tomorrow. We are summoned to a feast for the Burgundian ambassador." She grimaced. "I wish I could decline. I am sick more with this babe than with any other, except you. You, as my firstborn, were the worst."

"I will gladly postpone my travel," Tom said, grinning. "There is nothing up north that cannot wait. Besides, it will divert me to spend a day at court. It will be my pleasure to escort you, my lady."

Elizabeth smiled, and Tom noticed how childbearing increased her beauty; her skin glowed and the more rounded figure suited her. He was, if the truth be told, tired of the monotonous arrival of half-siblings—brats mostly, but his mother's marriage to King Edward had brought more rewards than he had dared dream of, and so he tolerated the many additions to the nursery. Here was one marriage where passion played a prominent part, he thought ruefully. Edward plainly worshipped Elizabeth, when he was not out whoring with his chamberlain, Will Hastings, or indeed with Tom himself. Tom's wife, on the other hand, repulsed him with her horse teeth, scrawny thighs, and pimply breasts.

Tom held the door as Elizabeth Woodville exited and he went back to the window seat. He stared out on the city wall and fancied he could see through it to Jane's father's house on Hosier Lane. Why did she haunt him so? On many occasions since the meeting at The Swan, he had thought on the cruel words of her ditty. To be sure, he had sought and found other conquests and pleasured himself with them since then, but he could not forget the mercer's lovely daughter.

Tom, Tom the whoreson. Aye, he had deserved the crude moniker. He remembered watching the tear run down her cheek, and he had been so awed by Jane's fortitude, he had not been able to stop himself reaching out and wiping it away with his thumb. As in the scene in the churchyard, he had felt something stir in his chest that disturbed him.

What a churl he had been. "Jane, I am truly sorry. If I were someone else, I would give you my heart and my hand, but I cannot," was what he had told her. Why he had hesitated to tell her more, he knew not. Why had he not revealed his identity? Would she have given in to the marquess of Dorset, son of the queen and stepson of King Edward the Fourth? Nay, it would have frightened her off, he was convinced, despite her infatuation for him.

But all Jane knew was that he was married. What did it matter? If he had played her slow game of courtly love, would she have capitulated? As far as he was concerned, his marriage contract was simply that—a contract that bound two families together and would perhaps yield children to inherit the joined wealth. He had never denied his lusts, he admitted; one took one's pleasures where one could when one was forced into a union for the sake of family, wealth, and power. His first wife had been indisputably contracted to him for her pedigree, Anne Holland having been the only child of the duke of Exeter and his wife, who in her turn was daughter of Richard, duke of York and Cecily Neville. Betrothed when they were both eleven, Anne Holland had died in childbirth five years ago along with their child, just as fifteen-year-old Tom's sensual nature was awakening. After that, his mother, the queen, had chided him almost weekly about his dalliances with mostly unsuitable ladies.

And finally, last year, Elizabeth had contracted a second marriage for Tom; this time the motive was money. Fourteen-year-old Cicely Bonvile, baroness of Harington, was the wealthiest heiress in the country, with extensive land holdings in Devon and Warwickshire. Her mother, Katherine, was a Neville, and, following Baron Harington's death, she had married the king's chamberlain and best friend, Will Hastings. Young Thomas Grey had gained not only a stepfather in King Edward, but a stepfather-in-law in Will, the two most powerful men in England.

Tom smacked the casement shut. He refused to think he was pining for a woman just because she did not give in to him. And just today, he had been informed that Jane Lambert was to be married to a respectable mercer. She would be lost to him now, Tom was certain. Cramming his velvet bonnet on his head, he strode toward the door and told himself he would move on with his life.

Back in Hosier Lane, Jane was still contemplating what life would hold for her. She shivered, partly from anticipation and partly from anxiety, and pulling a shawl around her shoulders, she put Tom Grey's guilty face from her mind and forced herself to think about the man who would call her his wife in a very few hours.

She did not know whether to laugh or cry when she thought back to William Shore's clumsy wooing of her.

"Dear Lord, protect my way forward and let William be warmer as a husband than he has been as a suitor," she prayed fervently, but then unwittingly found herself smiling at one memory. She and her betrothed had walked to St. Mary-le-Bow side by side behind John and Amy when the banns were being read. Jane was certain that, from behind, the towering William and her own diminutive figure must have looked like father and daughter, and she had had a hard time suppressing her mirth. She had written a poem later in the day, and it was one of a very few of Jane's verses that had not amused Amy.

> *A couple walking arm in arm*
> *'Tis custom'ry to see,*
> *Yet when Jane and Will are side by side*
> *Her arm begirds his knee.*

After supper, Bella had made Jane repeat it in the privacy of their chamber and had collapsed in laughter onto the feather mattress.

Thanks be to the Virgin that her mother had not denounced her to John, she thought now, but the poem had mirrored her feelings. "God's truth but I feel ridiculous with him," Jane said aloud to London's skyline.

"What did you say, Lillibet?" Bella asked sleepily. "Who is ridiculous?"

Bella was the only one who still called her by her baptismal name of Elizabeth, and Jane was unsure whether it was done to annoy her or because when the younger girl was learning to speak, Jane was still Elizabeth, and having trouble with the word, Bella's tongue discovered the lilt of Lillibet pleased it more, and the name had stuck. It had been her mother's idea to rename her Jane, all because an ancient dragon of an Aunt Elizabeth had come to live with them, and two in the same house became confusing as well as an irritation to the older owner of the name. Amy Lambert had wanted to please the well-heeled relative, who, she had guessed correctly, might well will the Lamberts property in the country. Jane hadn't much minded and had taken the change with good humor, thus earning her mother's gratitude but still only a grudging grunt from her father. It was then, at only age six, that Jane knew her father did not care about her one way or the other.

"They say talking to yourself shows the mind is softening, but I think 'tis a sign I have no one to talk to," Jane answered her sister with a laugh, and she tugged the rumpled linen off the bed. "If you would raise your idle bones, I could talk to you."

"Lillibet, you heartless wench!" Bella cried, trying to retrieve the sheet from the floor. "I shall tell Father on you, if you are not careful."

"Not anymore, you won't," Jane retorted. "Perhaps now you will know what the back of his hand feels like when he no longer has me to bully. I shall be a married woman and out of mind, praise be to St. Monica. I can snub my nose at him all the way from Coleman Street and you will have to find someone else to tattle on, Sister." Seeing Bella's head droop, she was immediately contrite. "Forgive me, you may find me snappish today because I am a little afraid . . ." She trailed off, wanting to avoid a delicate conversation and instead begged Bella to smile. "And so, I pray, help me into this gown."

Bella did as she was told and stood back to admire her lovely sibling. Despite Jane's bossiness and lack of decorum, the girl knew she would miss her sister's companionship. As Jane tucked a lacy plastron into the top of her bodice to cover her exposed skin, Bella picked up a fine ebony comb and began to ease it through Jane's thick, gold-flecked, honey blond curls, the color enhanced with the help of lemon juice and chamomile. Try as she might, nothing would make Bella's own mouse brown tresses look more than commonplace. Frustrated again that none of her physical attributes would ever outshine her sister's, she tugged at a knot, causing Jane to cry out in protest.

"Sorry," Bella mumbled.

"Sophie promised to make me a chaplet of flowers and ribbons," Jane said. "I hope she does not forget. I ache to go a day without binding up my hair. In truth, I should marry more often." And she laughed off the misgivings she felt every time she thought of William.

The shimmering folds of her cream-and-blue gown spilled around her, reinforcing her choice of Venice silk. Knowing that his daughter would show off his merchandise to his guests at the feast, John Lambert had indulged Jane on her wedding day, and Jane, understanding the value of each and every bolt of cloth in his extensive stock, had indulged herself with the best.

She would not have been surprised had she overheard the conversation between John and Amy about her choice. Instead of applauding her taste, John had opined: "Her love of luxury may put William in Newgate for debt. You would think you have not taught that girl anything about money, my dear, judging by the way she spends it." He had patted his placid wife's small hand. "Better William's problem now than mine."

"Oh, forsooth, John." Soft-spoken Amy had used her favorite disclaimer, refusing to be roused. "God knows I have tried to teach her manners, modesty, and duty, but money is your domain."

Upstairs Bella finished combing Jane's hair and asked, "Shall I see if Sophia has called? And I will bring us back something to break our fast." She threw a silken bedrobe over her shift and left Jane standing in front of the polished brass mirror propped up against her dower chest. In its reflection Jane caught sight of the crucifix on the wall behind her and promptly moved the mirror.

Jane now looked at herself with curiosity. What was it that made men stare at her so? She recognized a pretty face when she saw one, certes, and hers was passably pretty. But the rest of her? She thought she was too small, her neck too short, and her breasts too big for her slender waist. Unbidden, Tom Grey's face was conjured, and she frowned at her reflection. She had been so sure he would be the one to show her the ways of love: that love she had read about in the writings of Chaucer and her favorite Chrétien de Troyes poem about Lancelot and Guinevere. She touched her lips, remembering yet again his kiss that day and the sensation she had had when he had tongued her mouth open. Her hands dared to take the fullness of her breasts then sweep down to the curve of her waist and over her hips. How she had longed to feel Tom's hands touch her thus; she felt certain he would know how to arouse her. She exhaled deeply.

How would William look at her naked body? she wondered. He had never seemed much interested in it fully clothed, so she had little doubt he would care if she were flat-breasted and knock-kneed. Would he even care that she had preserved her maidenhead for him? Aye, tonight she would no doubt lose her virginity, but had it been worth saving for such an indifferent man as William? According to her confessor it was, and so perhaps she had remained intact to save her immortal soul. Never one to brood for long, she cheered herself up by recalling the scene in the confessional.

Not long after the contract with William had been signed, she had made confession in her beloved St. Mary-le-Bow, and had barely listened as the priest droned on from behind the wooden grille about the sanctity of marriage and that a wife must please her husband and was expected to obey him in all things. And then he had shocked her out of her daydream by first asking if she were going to her husband a virgin. She had demanded: "Why must you know? 'Tis insulting to ask." A sharp reprimand chastised her with a threat about eternal damnation for lying, and so she admitted she was indeed a virgin. She had not needed to ask whether a man must also be chaste; she could guess the answer would be no.

Then he had asked: "Have you ever taken an animal to your bed, mistress?" Certes, she was not such a green girl from the provinces that she did not know about such unholy practices, but to hear it voiced by a priest truly shocked her into silence. The priest had had to repeat himself, and Jane had stammered an assurance that she had never even imagined such an abomination. She later found out to her disgust from Sophie that it was a routine question for women about to be married. Again she doubted it was also asked of men before they took a wife.

Sensing his parishioner was becoming discouraged, the priest said more kindly: "Mistress, take heart. You should know it is a wife's right to expect affection from her husband and to enjoy the . . . the . . . ahem . . . bedding together. You do also have the right to be a mother, so the law says."

"Thank you, Father," Jane had said, shuddering at the thought of William touching her.

She pondered this all now as she leaned toward the mirror to remove a wayward hair from her fashionably plucked forehead, and not for the first time did she tell herself that the world had been made for the benefit of men. Did it matter what women wanted? And even if a woman could express what she wanted, could she ever achieve it?

"What is it that you want of life, Jane?" she asked herself aloud. "Do you know what you want, Elizabeth Jane Lambert?" Aye, a small but clear voice inside her said: I want to find real love.

When she was a child all she remembered wanting was the love of her father, and when she did not get it, she turned to her older brother, William. He was happy to be adored by the pretty, merry little girl, so he spoiled her with ribbons and candied treats, and she learned that making a man laugh and call her his "sweet Jane" got her gifts that made up for the indifference of her parent. But then William went into the church and moved away, leaving her bereft, hurt, and no longer a child.

When she had discovered her ability to win the admiration of the equally young apprentices who passed her on the streets or stood near at mass or winked at her in The King's Head on Chepeside, she had had hopes of finding true love among them, but she had waited in vain for the much touted, blinding white flame of passion to engulf her.

But then she had kissed Tom Grey.

She stamped her foot and glowered at herself in the mirror. *May he burn in eternal hellfire. He has spoiled me for all others, and certainly for cheerless, staid William Shore.*

The rain held off long enough for the wedding to take place at St. Mary's and not spoil Jane's elegant gown during the short walk from the Lambert house. The contract and vows were exchanged at the church door before the couple and their witnesses entered the sanctuary for the mass. Jane's thick, yellow hair fell to her waist, and Sophie's lovingly made blue- and white-ribboned chaplet, festooned with daisies and mayflowers, encircled her head. She was a beautiful bride, her mother told her, and even her father nodded and smiled when his eldest daughter emerged from her chamber.

Neighbors hung banners and ribbons from windows, and several children cheered and flung flowers over the couple as they processed back to the house for the feast. Everyone knew and liked Jane for her warm smile, her ability to make them laugh, and her kindness to the children, especially when they were sickly. She brought back snippets of ribbon and lace from the shop for the girls, and made the boys balls from scrap pieces of fabric and horsehair that she sewed inside whatever material was left at the end of a bolt.

John beamed at everyone lining the street and invited them to join him and Amy at the house for wafers and wine. Jane met William's eyes as they neared the front door, and she smiled shyly. Caught off guard, William smiled back.

"Mistress Shore, may I escort you in for dinner," he said, formally. Then he added quietly, "It pleases me that I have taken you to wife, Jane. I trust you, too, are content."

William had recited his vows with as much feeling as he might have discussed the weather, but Jane had been glad that he did look at her when he said them, and she took heart that he meant to keep them. He had put a fine band of gold upon her finger, intricately ornamented with carved roses, and had put his lips on hers to seal the bargain with good grace, she thought.

"Quite content, William," she answered him, hoping that this unusual unbending might lead to an easier union as husband and wife than there had been in their courtship. She went into the house happier than when she had left it an hour earlier and sought out Sophie and her Jehan, who had been invited to share the feast. Jehan openly ogled her, infuriating Jane, and she managed to steal Sophie away from him by saying she needed her friend's help up in her chamber. Unperturbed, Jehan went in search of food.

Despite her pregnancy, Sophie was able to negotiate the narrow staircase to the top floor and followed Jane into the wide loft bedchamber.

"What now?" Jane asked in desperation, turning and grasping Sophie's hands. She could feel the calluses on the silkwoman's thumb and index finger, and Jane was glad she was a weaver and not a spinner.

"Oh, Jane," Sophie said, amused, her plain face lightened by a smile. "You vill vait in bed for Villiam to come to you and if you can, make certain you blow out all the candles." Jane was used to Sophie's endearing use of a *v* for a *w* in her speech. It was the only vestige left of her Flemish parents' heavily accented English. "'Tis not so bad in the dark."

Jane was not comforted by this, and she pulled off the chaplet, its blossoms wilting, and flung it on her dower chest. "But will he know what to do? Why, he only kissed me for the first time at the church door." Sophie picked up the chaplet and, uncomfortable with idle fingers, began to rework the garland. Jane watched her friend as she imagined her in bed with Jehan. It cannot only be a duty, she concluded, there must be something more to it or poets would not write about it nor singers sing their ballads. Once, when she had felt a youth's hardness pressing through her skirts, a surge of desire had enveloped her that had made her moan. She also knew from a young age that touching herself in her private place would send pleasurable waves through her whole body. Perhaps her friend had obeyed the church teachings about such activity and Sophie did not know.

She propped herself up on her elbow. "I suppose I cannot refuse to take him to my bed, can I?" she groused. And then she smiled. "Forgive me, Sophie, but I keep wondering how someone as tall as William will manage with someone as small as me."

Sophie laughed. "Take courage, Jane. It means you need only look at his feeble chest and you do not need to look him in the eye."

That amused Jane all the more, and the two friends fell into each other's arms laughing.

THREE

Nothing could have prepared Jane for what happened on her wedding night. Try as he might, and Jane was kind and gentle with him, William Shore was unable to fulfill his duty to her as a husband on that occasion nor in the weeks that followed. Even more puzzling to the new bride was his nonchalance about his impotence. At first she was quiet and understanding as he fumbled with her breasts and tried to become aroused. After many failed attempts, she had taken matters into her own hands and attempted to seduce him, using her natural instincts to try, in vain, to bring him to climax. She was astonished at her own talent, having had no teacher, and she found herself so ready to be taken—even by William—that she would have to pleasure herself after he fell asleep exhausted by his efforts.

It was not long before Jane's initial frustration turned into anger, for it became apparent that she had been cheated even of her right to be a mother, let alone the pleasuring the priest had promised was also her due. Her mood was not helped by the weather that summer.

July was one of the worst for rain anyone could remember, and the London streets became awash in mud, muck, and rubbish that even the highest pattens could not navigate safely. The Moor Field outside the city wall at the end of Coleman Street was flooded so badly there was no harvest of vegetables, and cows stood knee-deep in water, looking as miserable as the gloomy skies above them.

Jane was thankful her husband's lodging was above his shop, thus she did not have to step out into the mire on most days to tend to customers as she had at her father's.

And then the summer heat arrived, making Londoners irritable, and babes, young children, and old people susceptible to outbreaks of disease.

"When did the July rain start?" she asked Sophie one hot August day when the flies buzzed around the rubbish left behind after the muddy streets had dried, and the two friends sat in the shade of the only tree in the Vandersands' tiny garden. William had allowed her a rare afternoon to herself, and she had made her way to Sophie's humble house, where she found her friend using her old hand spindle so she could tend to her children with her free hand when needed. Spinning silk was tedious work, and Sophie was fortunate Jehan had obtained a wheel for his wife for her indoor work, as the distaff and spindle she had learned to use at her mother's knee was slow and awkward. While Jane amused the new baby with a length of colored ribbon and watched the two older children play with a ball, Sophie worked diligently at spinning the raw silk into thread. "I was trying to remember if it had rained on St. Swithin's Day?"

"*Ja*, it rained on the saint's day but only a gentle pit-pat," Sophie replied. "How does the saying go? You taught it to me once:

> *St. Swithin's Day, if it doth rain,*
> *For forty days it will remain.*
> *St. Swithin's Day, if thou be fair,*
> *For forty days 'twill rain no more.*"

"We should set no store by it, Sophie, for it has not been forty days yet, and look at the sky now. 'Tis so hot, the blue in it has all dried up."

Sophie eyed her friend, who seemed somewhat serious this afternoon. She noted the gown Jane was wearing was very handsome for everyday wear, but she had long since given up chiding Jane for her extravagance. "You seem far away, *lieveling*," she said. "Is there something the matter?"

Jane rocked the now sleeping baby in her arms, brushing the flies away. "I knew I could not hide from you, dear Sophie. Aye, there is something wrong. There is a reason why William has not wed these forty years; he is impotent." The new word in her vocabulary fell heavily from her lips. It was the first time she had actually brought herself to say it.

Sophie gasped and stopped her spinning. "That is bad, Jane. Are you sure? Mayhap he is ill. Sometimes the men are unable to . . . you know . . . ven they are ill. Jehan had a stone inside his kidney and he left me alone for a month until it came out."

"Nay, he is not ill. He is simply not interested in me—or any woman, I would guess."

"Vat vill you do?"

Jane did not know what she would do. On the one hand, she did not have to put up with William mounting her night after night, as Sophie said Jehan was wont to do, but it did not seem right to her that he did not keep his side of the marriage bargain. "He swore before God that he agreed to love and honor me in heart, body, and mind and that our solemn union was intended among other things for the procreation of children," she said, shooing a fly off little Pieter's face. "And I swore to honor those vows, too. I want to have my own babes, Sophie, otherwise why would I have agreed to marry such a dull man as William Shore."

Sophie did not like to mention that living under her father's roof, Jane had had no choice but to do her father's bidding. She clucked her tongue instead and offered, "You are right to be sure, Jane, but you have fine clothes and a household of your own at least, vich you have always vanted."

Jane nodded sulkily. "But I wanted children, too, Sophie." And she hugged the baby to her breast.

"It has been three months only, dear friend. I have no doubt you vill interest him yet. You seem to have had no trouble attracting men to you ever since ve vere young. I used to be jealous, but now I know what it is they vant, I must say I am happy they avoided me." She made a face to express her disgust of men's lusts.

Jane had to laugh. "Certes, Sophie, it cannot be so bad or there would be no more than one child born to a couple. And"—she lowered her voice for the children's sake—"why would there be so many whores?"

"*Godallemachtig!*" Sophie exclaimed, raising her eyes to heaven. "Is it not clear? They get paid to bed a man. Mayhap if Jehan paid me, I vould be more villing."

Jane's warm, low-throated laughter woke the baby, who began to fret and want freeing from his swaddling bands. "Poor little Pieter. Are you hot, sweeting?" Jane quickly unbound the soft, pink body. Liberated, Pieter exercised every limb with burbling delight. "That is better, is it not?" Jane cooed while Sophie sadly watched her friend, who so obviously wished the baby were hers.

"You have not answered me yet. Vat vill you do?"

Jane shook her head. "I suppose I can wait a few months in case, as you say, William has an ailment he has not told me about. But after that, I shall seek the help of a priest in the matter of an annulment."

Sophie drew in a breath, shocked. "Annulment? You would seek annulment? That vould cause a scandal, vould it not?"

"It might cause William some embarrassment, but not I," she said, irony evident in her voice. "I am certain no one would think it my fault. Why, even my father thinks I am too forward with men."

Sophie shook her head. "Do not say such a thing, Jane. Your father may not pay you much heed, but he cares about you."

Jane was not so sure, but she said nothing and continued tickling little Pieter's bare midriff.

Those small faults that Jane had seen in William's physique when they had first met—his gangly legs; the lank, dull hair; his nervous sniff; his nearsighted peering at people's clothes, for William never bothered looking at the people themselves—all began to magnify in her mind each time she was with him. That night was no exception.

He was picking at his supper of pickled eels, cheese, and wastel bread with one hand and holding the shop's account roll open with the other, peering at the figures in the light of a candelabra, and Jane was at liberty to study her husband from the other end of the table. A large silver saltcellar separated them, and their trenchers were set upon spotless table linen. Soon William would roll up the accounts, push away his food, and down his wine. Jane did not approve of William's indulgence with wine at supper. It was not that she did not enjoy a cup or two herself, but she resented that he said it made him sleep better. Aye, she thought, and probably dulled the senses he needed to get her with child.

"The king is already returning from France," William suddenly said, not lifting his head from the paper. "It seems there was a treaty signed ere a shot was fired."

Jane was astonished. She had witnessed the departure of King Edward at the end of May when he had ridden with his retinue through the streets to London Bridge to take boats to Greenwich. This expedition was supposed to have regained some of the territory lost during the war against France that had endured almost one hundred years and ended in 1453. The five-year-old Prince of Wales came from Ludlow to be keeper of the realm, although his mother would have him in her charge, and the Archbishop of Canterbury, as chancellor, would have England in his. It was expected that the king and a large number of the nobility would be gone for a long time, and thus Edward had taxed his subjects to their breaking point for this glorious campaign. Once again the wealthy merchants of London had joined with the great Italian banking families like the Medicis and Portinaris to lend even more to the king to pay his massive army; both John Lambert and William Shore had added to Edward's war chest. Great things were expected of the expedition, and to hear that it was all over in the space of four months struck Jane as odd, especially as there had been no news of victory or defeat.

"How can that be?" she asked. "The king was expected to join with Charles of Burgundy and beat the French. Did King Louis surrender?"

William shook his head. "Nay, wife, it would seem our soldier sovereign was bought off with a pension from Louis if Edward left without fighting. To be fair, Burgundy failed to keep his end of the bargain and offered little or no support to Edward. Without Charles, Edward's efforts might have led to an even lengthier campaign and possible defeat. But, trust me, this news will not be well received by Englishmen. An English army returning from France with its tail between its legs? 'Tis shameful, and," he grumbled, "I doubt any of us who financed the fiasco will see our money back. 'Tis a sorry affair."

Jane privately thought the lack of loss of life and limb was a praiseworthy outcome, but as she knew William would not care about anything except his money, she kept silent. She did not want to irritate him because she had a more pressing conversation to initiate. She cleared her throat and waited for him to look up at her.

"Was there something you wished to talk to me about, Jane?" William had noticed her unusually demure demeanor and had learned it often preceded a favor. He enjoyed granting those little wishes for a new gown or pair of shoes, because it made him feel powerful over her. And it seemed to help alleviate his guilt that he could not perform in bed. He had always hated his body, wishing he could have been born strong and virile, and it had unnerved him as a youth that he did not seem to share the lustiness of his fellow apprentices. He had never visited the stews or attempted to bed a tavern wench as they had, and he was teased mercilessly as a result. He had even been called a sodomite, which was abhorrent to him. William simply did not seem to have much of a sensual nature; he took physical pleasure in fingering his purse and counting his money. Jane's sensuality frightened and disgusted him, and on many occasions he caught himself wishing he had never agreed to wed her. But the union was paying handsomely through referrals from his prominent father-in-law, and he had been able to purchase his shop premises outright with Jane's dowry. In truth, business was good, he told himself.

"Aye, William, I would talk to you about us," Jane said in as forthright a tone as she dared. "I think you know what I mean. I believe we rub together well enough as people, but we do not in between the sheets." It irked Jane further that William never appreciated her wordplay or wit, and so she did not even pause to see if tonight were different. "May I know if you have some ailment that prevents us from normal intimacy, something that prevents us from having a child?"

William's face drained of color, and he clutched his napkin over his lap. "I do not believe it is your place to ask me such a thing. I am your husband and you must submit to my will. I am sorry if you are not content with me in"—he paused to weigh his words and then blurted out angrily—"satisfying your lusts, but it cannot be helped. Now let us please change the subject or I shall leave the room."

Jane pushed back her chair and stood. "Nay, William, 'tis I who shall leave the room. But not before I remind you that I will have every right to seek an annulment if you cannot fulfill your husbandly duty." Without waiting for his response, she moved to the door and was gone so quickly, William's tongue could not form any words with which to stay her.

He rose unsteadily and went to the window, his hands trembling as he opened the shutter and stared out at the roof of the Masons' Hall next door. How could he have lost control of his wife so quickly after wedding her? What was this nonsense about an annulment? He had never struck Jane, but he was moved to violence tonight. If he had a heart, William would have acknowledged that he had deprived his wife of intimacy and ultimately motherhood. But William had grown up believing the world was against him and that if he did not take care of himself first, he would be doomed to mediocrity. He believed fervently that money bought him security, and new business ventures held the only excitement in an otherwise dreary existence. He reached down to scratch a flea bite on his leg and interrupted a mouse nibbling on a morsel of cheese, causing the creature to scuttle away. He scowled. The vermin in this city were a nuisance, but one learned to live with them—a little like an annoying wife, he decided.

If the truth be told, he had already tired of the new venture: marriage and its financial rewards. He thought about his old life, his life before Jane, and wished he could have it back. But annulment? Admit publicly to failure as a man? Nay, he could not tolerate the thought of humiliation and scandal. Annulment was out of the question, but he resolved to find out more about the law in case Jane were serious about her threat. What else could he do? he wondered; all he knew was mercery. He was good at it and had no reason to risk his position in the guild. Then he remembered a conversation he had had recently with Master Caxton, a former leader of the merchant adventurers in Flanders who was now in the household of the duchess of Burgundy and a fellow member of the mercers' guild. He had intrigued William with the lucrative possibilities of joining the merchant adventurers who used their business skills abroad in Bruges or Antwerp.

"The only trouble is, Master Shore," the printer had teased the sober-faced mercer upon their meeting, "you must be celibate to be an adventurer, and I understand you have a beautiful new bride. It would be hard to give her up, would it not?"

William grimaced as he remembered the conversation, but then the germ of a plan began to form as he watched the roofs of London fade into the twilight.

Jane walked softly into the cool sanctuary of St. Olave's church in Old Jewry, a place where she had never worshipped before. She saw that one confessional was open, and she slipped inside and pulled the curtain across the door, setting a bell to tinkling and alerting the priest he had a supplicant.

"Forgive me, Father, for I have sinned," Jane recited when the cleric had blessed her from behind the grille. After confessing a few innocuous transgressions of sloth and disobedience, she shut her eyes tightly and told the good father her dilemma. "He cannot give me a child, Father," she ended, surprised to find she was near to tears. "Am I not entitled to all the gifts of marriage, including intimacy and children? I understood this from the marriage vows and from the priest in my father's parish, who said 'twas the law. I believe my husband is not able to do his duty by me."

The priest was silent for a while. It was usual for a man to complain about his wife's abstinence or failure to provide him with adequate release in bed. He had not had to counsel a woman in such a matter before, although he knew there was a law that might be applied in such a case.

"My advice to you, child, is to wait a little longer. There may be a perfectly good reason why your husband is unable to fulfill his duty to you. In the meantime, I will find out what I can to help you in this matter. You must understand, the only way out of this union is through annulment, and only bishops may grant one following a papal decree. And it may be you have to go through the courts."

Jane left the church disheartened but not defeated and almost fell over the rotting carcass of a cat. "God's teeth!" she said under her breath as she skirted the dead animal, hurried past the Prince's Wardrobe, and up into Coleman Street. "The city gets filthier every week."

William arched a skeptical brow at her when she returned to the shop and told him she had been to confession. No good lying, she thought. God would not help her if she began her quest to end her marriage with a lie. To her surprise, William smiled and nodded. Despite her decision of a moment earlier not to lie, she resolved to use the confessional excuse again—real or not.

"We shall shut the shop on the morrow, Mistress Shore," William said. He always addressed her thus in front of his apprentices. "The king is returning, and I have been summoned to be part of a small greeting committee at Tower wharf with others of our guild." He drew her aside, his boney fingers gripping her elbow, and explained, "This will not be quite the joyous reception Edward enjoyed upon his departure in June, I can assure you. London is not pleased with its lily-livered, Louis-pensioned king, and most citizens have decided to go about their daily business and ignore his grace. But I have been thinking how we can take full advantage of the nobility who will ride past your father's shop." He rubbed his hands in anticipation, reminding Jane of her father's similar greedy gesture, but then once again he surprised her with his rare smile. "I would have you sit in the window of the workroom above the shop, Jane, dressed in your finest gown—the one I had made for you after we were promised."

Then he reached behind a velvet curtain and brought out a headdress that made Jane gasp. It was a richly brocaded, steepled hennin more than two feet high, sewn over with seed pearls and a long translucent golden veil floating from its tip. "And see, I had this made for you to match the green and gold of the gown."

Jane almost snatched the gorgeous confection from his fingers, and William was pleased. Ever since his wife had confronted him with his impotence, he had deluged her with gifts. It was as well John Lambert had conversed with him over a cup of malmsey one evening and divulged Jane's extravagance and love of finery. It had been easy to buy her silence, he thought now, watching her fit the hennin by holding it fast at the fashionable rakish angle on the back of her head. She went to the polished silver mirror and stared critically at her reflection.

"You like it, Jane?" Seeing her pleased smile, William said, "Then I would have you wear it on the morrow. It might attract some noble custom," William purred behind her, fluffing out the gauzy veil so it caught the light.

He was pleased with Jane's response: "I will be there, husband. When else will I ever have the chance to wear the gown again? We do not move in such elegant company, more's the pity. How do I look, sir?"

"You shall wear it at the Lord Mayor's banquet, my dear," William replied, ignoring her last question. "All shall see that I trade in nothing but the finest materials. Soon I shall be able to set up shop at the Mercery, like your father."

Jane looked at him in the mirror and gave a sharp laugh. "Always business with you, is it not, William? Can you not for once pay your wife a compliment?"

"I wedded you, mistress. Is that not compliment enough?" he retorted, and stalked off. Ungrateful wench, he thought to himself, wishing for the hundredth time he had come to his senses and refused John Lambert's offer. But then he relented. In some ways, he reminded himself, the union had paid off.

London proved William correct. There were no banners and flowers festooning the houses and businesses along the Chepe, no fanfares or troubadours, no children skipping along beside the king's retinue, and no shouts of "God save the king." A few groups of townspeople gathered at the great conduit and the standard a little farther along Chepeside and waited for Edward to ride by, but mostly Londoners went about their daily tasks and thus informed their sovereign of their displeasure.

It was a blue September sky, the sun warming the riders as they processed slowly through the streets. King Edward was magnificent on a black warhorse that was caparisoned from flaring nostrils to twitching tail in dagged silk, embroidered all over with York's white rose and Edward's own Sunne in Splendour badge, the leather harness decorated with gleaming brasses. The king's eyes flitted over the jaded faces of his subjects, and he felt a twinge of guilt remembering these same faces from June smiling and cheering him on to glory. Damn them, he thought, he had brought back an army without limbs lost or wounds won, and with only a few dead—mostly from disease; they should be grateful. He shifted in his saddle, aware of the aching in his joints, a new and unpleasant result of contracting a tertian fever in the low-lying marshes around Calais. His physician warned him he might suffer the pains, as well as sudden chills and fever, for the rest of his life and advised the king to be more judicious in his eating habits. Edward had been astonished to hear the diagnosis, never having had a day's serious illness in his thirty-three years, and his normal affability had deserted him then as, in a rage, he had ordered the doctor from his tent.

All at once, Edward sat straight in his saddle, his melancholic ruminations interrupted by a group of young women, gawping and smiling at him on a street corner. Edward's deceptively lazy blue eyes could never pass over female figures without singling out the prettiest and imagining her in his arms, and one of them had caught his fancy. He inclined his head and winked at her, satisfied to see the maid blush and turn her head. In that moment, riding by John Lambert's shop and looking the other way, he had failed to see the beauty sitting in the window, gazing intently at one of the young nobles in his train.

Edward may not have noticed Jane Shore, but his chamberlain had.

One of several riders behind the king, Will Hastings scanned the sullen crowd and marveled at how quickly the Londoners could change their mood. He had exulted at the exuberance Edward's exodus had generated in these same citizens not five months earlier. In truth, Will could not blame them and guiltily tried to ignore the bulging saddlebags on his squire's horse, which contained treasures given him by a relieved king of France for Will's having turned Edward around and homeward. He also misliked the humor of the English soldiers who had ridden disconsolately to their homes over the downs and along the paths from Dover and Sandwich, cheated of any spoils that would have accrued to them on the battlefield. And they all need paying, he thought. God help us if they are not.

He shook off the ominous musings and raised his eyes above the crowd to the mostly empty windows on the second and third stories of the substantial merchant houses that lined the north side of the Chepe. On his left was the Mercery, a block-long arcade of shops and stalls, some with upper floors. A figure in an open window caught his eye and the face he saw made him draw in a sharp breath. Sweet nails of Christ's cross, but she is a jewel, Will told himself. He noted the richness of her gown with the shimmering hennin crowning her oval face, the creamy rounded tops of her breasts rising just above the neckline of her bodice, the graceful wave of her hand as she saluted the riders. Even the slight frown and downturn of her full mouth did not detract from Will's *coup de foudre*. Without even speaking to the lady, he was smitten. Who was she, and how had he missed her in all his and Edward's forays into London looking for pleasure? As he eased his lean frame around in the saddle so he could observe the vision, the tunic under his cloak was visible with its black bull's head crest embroidered upon it.

Swinging just below her window was the guild sign of the

Maiden's Head. Ah, he thought, certes, 'tis the Mercery. The lady must be a mercer's wife or daughter. He slowed his horse so he could read the name inscribed above the door. JOHN LAMBERT AND SON. He made a note and rode on.

Jane's heart had leaped with surprise at the sight of Tom Grey directly behind King Edward. But then she was puzzled. Why was he among those who rode so close to the king? She barely noticed Edward but her hand continued to wave at him from force of habit while her eyes took in the rich caparison of her love's courser, the ermine-trimmed cloak with jeweled, gold clasp draped over the horse's back, and ostrich feathers fluttering from a gray velvet bonnet. This was no ordinary gentleman nor a possible minor nobleman, her experience told her. Nay, this was almost certainly a royal personage, but how? Who? And suddenly her hand flew to her mouth as she grasped the truth. "Not mere Tom Grey, but Sir Thomas Grey, marquess of Dorset, the queen's son," she announced to the dust-laden air. "Sweet Jesu, but he is a dissembler. He fooled us all. 'Tis no wonder he turned me aside. Being married was only half his tale."

"Did you say something, Lillibet?" Bella said, making Jane jump. She had forgotten for a moment that her sister was in the room with her. She shook her head and left her seat for the younger woman, who leaned out of the casement, waving eagerly.

But for Jane, all the excitement of watching the procession vanished along with Tom Grey's receding figure. She forgot she was supposed to display William's wares to potential customers, and instead she removed the hennin to better negotiate the narrow staircase down to her father's empty shop. John was among the guild members gathered on the steps of St. Paul's to greet the returning king, and although it would have been impolitic for the guilds to ignore their sovereign, they hoped to make a point by assembling only a few members of each of the twelve major companies, the mercers being the highest ranking.

Jane nodded to Matthew and slipped out of the back door through the garden and made her way carefully to Sophie's house. She was grateful it had not rained for days, and hooking the train of her gown over her arm and clutching her headdress with the other, she picked her way through the detritus in the streets and alleys until she arrived in St. Sithe's Lane, unheeding of the stares her rich attire was attracting. Jehan was at his work in Cripplegate, where most of the Flemish weavers were employed, and Sophie was quietly spinning when Jane knocked.

Sophie's warm, brown eyes welcomed her friend, and shooing a dog from the room, she pulled up Jehan's chair for Jane. "Sit, sit, *lieveling*. It has been so long since I saw you. *Ja,* have no vorry, the children are sleeping and ve are alone." She cocked her head as Jane remained silent, choosing not to ask why Jane had turned up more richly dressed than ever. "Is everything vell with you?" she asked cheerily, although she knew from Jane's expression that everything was not well. "Is is the"—she crooked her little finger— "the problem the same? With Villiam, I mean."

Jane nodded. "Aye, Sophie, still the same. And he refuses to talk about it. But that is not why I have come." She arranged the many folds of silk around her on the hardened dirt floor, wishing as usual that she could transport this decent family to more luxurious accommodations. "I have just seen Tom Grey, and this time must be the last," she admitted, picking up a stray thread of silk from the floor and winding it around her finger.

"But, Jane, I thought you vould not see him again after he told you he was vedded to another. Bad man. *Slechte man,*" she repeated, the Flemish translation emphasizing her disdain. "I hope he made penance for lying so to you." She reached out and patted Jane's fidgeting fingers. "Vere did you see him? I hope he did not force himself with you?"

Jane smiled. "Nay, my good, prim Sophie, he did not. He did not even see me." Her face fell again. "He was riding in the king's train. And 'twas only then I knew how truly foolish I had been to believe we could be lovers. You see, my sweet little *flamande,* I discovered today that Master Tom Grey is King Edward's stepson—the queen's son."

Sophie's horrified expression made Jane laugh out loud, and the noise must have woken Pieter judging by the wail that emanated from the loft where all the Vandersands slept. And then the baby began to whimper and fuss, bringing the women's conversation to a close.

"Ach, dearest Jane, it is indeed the last of Thomas Grey. I am sorry for you, but soon you vill forget. You like to valk in the sunshine too much."

How wrong you are, pragmatic Sophie, Jane wanted to say, but she kissed her friend and the baby and shut the front door quietly behind her.

As Jane sauntered home, the procession long since gone, she tried to push the memory from her heart of Tom's seductive smile, passionate caresses, and gentle words. But he lingered there, reminding her constantly that the romantic love she had always yearned for had existed for her, if only for a few weeks.

Jane was fortunate, as her friend Sophie often said, that she never felt downhearted for long. And so perhaps one day, Jane mused, she would find love again with someone new, and the thought buoyed her homeward steps and took her mind off her unfulfilled life with William Shore.

FOUR

Will pulled down on his short jacket, a fashion that tended to ride up and reveal too much of his buttocks for his liking. Then he ran his fingers through his thinning brown hair before replacing his bonnet at a jauntier angle and walking into William Shore's well-stocked shop on Coleman Street. The first person he saw, helping a young woman choose bed linens, was Jane.

But faster and hungrier than a flea finding a dog, William Shore was at the new customer's elbow. He bowed low, recognizing Lord Hastings.

"Good morrow, my lord, and indeed you are right welcome in my establishment. May I help you find something?" William saw he had not held the nobleman's attention, and his eyes followed Will's gaze to Jane. At first annoyed, he surmised his bold-eyed wife instantly attracted this noble lord with her seductive smile, but then a profitable thought overtook his resentment as he more rightly assumed this prominent customer, having noticed Jane at her father's window two weeks ago, had been thus lured to her husband's shop. How right he had been to insist Jane flaunt his wares for the king's train, for it had brought no less than the king's chamberlain to his door. For once he thanked God for his attractive wife.

"Lord Hastings, I am honored." William groveled.

"Master Shore, I give you God's greeting," Will said, bringing his attention back to the awkwardly tall mercer; it was as though the man had outstripped his boyish legs before he had learned how to use them. "I am certain I have come to the right place, as I saw the lady yonder seated in a window above Master Lambert's mercery while the king rode along the Chepe. I was immediately taken with her beauty . . . I mean, beautiful . . . gown," he corrected himself. "I knew I must seek out the same cloth for Lady Hastings, and Master Lambert was kind enough to direct me here." He paused for a second, looking again at Jane and then braved the question: "Is she . . ."

"My wife, my lord? Aye, I am proud to say she is, and Mercer Lambert's daughter," he gushed, confirming Will's unhappy suspicion. "Mistress Shore!" the mercer called, an unusually disarming smile alarming Jane as she turned toward her husband's voice. "I beg you come and greet our illustrious visitor and king's chamberlain, Lord Hastings." He reached out a welcoming arm to her and drew her possessively to his side. Jane curtseyed and folded her hands demurely in front of her as William rambled on. "She is my wife of a six-month or more. My dear, this gentle lord noticed your green and golden gown while you watched the king's return from France, do you remember? It is astonishing—and flattering—that a person of your rank, Lord Hastings, who must have endured such a long and arduous journey in the service of king and country, would have noticed a piece of my cloth that day." He rubbed his hands together. "But then that Italian silk is the finest I have, and I can understand how you must have been smitten with it. Let me show it to you now with pleasure."

Will Hastings barely smothered a laugh at the mercer's delusions that the cloth and not the wearer had attracted his attention. Then he saw Jane bite her lip and lower her head to cover her embarrassment, and he knew the young woman had no such delusion. As William turned to lead the way, she looked up at the nobleman with a mixed expression of shy curiosity and frank appraisal. Bold wench, Hastings thought, loving the way one cheek dimpled when she eventually smiled. He was a man well acquainted with the art of seduction, and he only needed a few seconds with which to study her from the top of her elaborately rolled turban to the tips of her tiny crakows, peeking from under a suitably workaday gown. It would never do, Jane's father had told her, to outdress the customers, although the cut and quality of the grosgrain spoke eloquently of the good taste of the merchant. She wished William might learn that lesson; her husband's drab gowns often bore vestiges of what he had eaten, marring the cloth.

Aye, thought her admirer, she is worth a second look. She was wed, 'twas true, but that had never stopped Will Hastings in his search for his next conquest. Why, she might even please Edward, he suddenly thought. But he would overcome that obstacle later.

He would have been dismayed to know how Jane had assessed him in return. A handsome-enough man but, like William, past his prime, she thought, although she appreciated the look of admiration he had given her. Lord Hastings! she thought with a faint thrill. William, Baron Hastings was flirting with her, she was sure of it. He had purposely sought her out; that was as plain as a pikestaff. And then her agile mind grasped a titillating nugget: sweet Jesu, he was Tom's father-in-law, she thought, astonished that she had managed to attract both men. So what if I do flirt with Hastings, she told herself; it would serve Tom right. Oh, how bored she was and how ripe for love. Then she saw William scowling at her, and she put on her most formal face.

"Excuse me, my lord," she said, curtseying once more, "but I must return to my customer. I pray your lady wife enjoys my husband's silk as much as I do."

Before Will could stay her with a whispered wish for another meeting, Jane had walked off, leaving him wondering if she had surmised his interest in her or not. Reluctantly turning to follow the eager Master Shore, he did not see Jane's surreptitious backward glance; it might have cheered him.

"So fair and with a fine wit, your grace," Will enthused upon returning to Westminster Palace and finding the king in his privy chamber, having his thigh-high boots removed by Sir Walter Hungerford, one of his many squires of the body, while another preened the feathers of Edward's valuable falcon on its customary perch near the high tester bed. After receiving soft, pointed shoes in exchange for the boots, Edward dismissed both men and selecting a plump capon leg from a platter, he stuffed it into his mouth.

"Her name is Jane Shore, the daughter of a mercer, John Lambert, and wedded to a dullard of another," Will continued, describing Jane in detail. "She is as dainty as a woodland flower and yet I sense a stalwart strength in her that will not wilt unless sorely pressed. I like a woman with a will of her own, and I doubt her whippet of a husband is man enough for her."

"And you are ready to step in and supply her need," Edward teased, laughing and wiping his greasy chin. "Christ's nails, Will, you sound besotted already. I would meet this paragon."

Will chuckled. "I think not, Ned," he answered softly, using Edward's family nickname only when they were alone. "You will snatch her from me before I can properly woo and lie with her."

Edward raised an eyebrow. "That fair, eh, Will? Now my curiosity is indeed piqued. Where is this Shore's shop? Maybe I shall have to see her for myself."

"All I will tell you is that it is not in the Mercery."

Will grinned at his master's indignation. A dozen years separated them and yet they had become fast friends during Edward's nine months of exile in Flanders six years before. He had first served Edward's father, Richard of York, as a squire and had transferred his Yorkist loyalty easily to the magnificent young earl of March when Richard had been killed at Wakefield and Edward had won the day for the Yorkists at Towton. After Edward was crowned in June 1461, Will was one of the first recipients of the Order of the Garter, and from that time on, he had served Edward as chamberlain and confidant. Ten years later, Edward had honored Hastings with the command of the left flank at Barnet and of the right flank at Tewkesbury, when the Lancastrian army was finally routed. It was with Will that Edward shared thoughts politic and acts pleasurable. Will had brought to Edward's attention more than a few ladies with whom the king had enjoyed a roll in the sheets. When Edward had tired of one, he passed her on to Hastings or, of late, his stepson Dorset. It was Will who had found lovely Elizabeth Wayte, mother of two of Edward's bastards, a worthy husband, who had quietly removed the lady from court after Edward tired of her.

"Besides, Ned, did you not promise your queen you would desist from philandering while she awaits the next child?"

Edward pouted. "I thank you for reminding me. Bessie has been in a black humor of late, and I suppose I should not cause her any distress." However, the ever-watchful Will saw a gleam in his sovereign's blue eyes that told him Edward was not averse to breaking his promise. "But she will be confined soon, and while the cat's away . . ." He took another bite of meat, smacking his lips.

"You are insatiable, my liege," Will protested, but he laughed. "By my troth, if Jane Shore likes me not, I swear I will bring her to you, if I can pluck her from her husband's clutches. He seems quite proud of her."

Edward ran his fingers through his red-gold hair, still thick and glossy after thirty-three hard-lived years. Will envied the king's good looks every time he caught sight of his own reflection and noticed the sagging cheeks, flecks of gray in his hair, and middle-aged spread. Aye, he doubted Hans Memling would choose him for a model these days, but in his prime his looks had been admired, he knew, and even still, he had no trouble attracting women. He refused to believe it was his status.

"Then I wish you God speed with the lady," Edward drawled,

sprawled out on the chair; his six-foot-three-inch frame was never comfortable in any seat, as he would often complain. "You had best move swiftly with your conquest, my friend, for are you not due to return to Calais in the New Year? It would not do to have the town's captain away for too long, or Anthony Rivers will be breathing down your neck and wresting the port back for himself."

Will had been eyeing a flea hopping erratically across the cloth on the table, and he now slammed his hand down and extinguished its pesky existence. "That popinjay!" he cried at the mention of his nemesis's name. "Is he not content to have the governorship of his nephew, your heir? The man is insufferable in his ambitions. I understand he is undertaking a pilgrimage to Italy as we speak to seek holy intervention in his wife's sickness. He has already been to Compostella. If the rumors are true and he is your sister's lover, then he should go with all speed to confess his adultery to the Holy Father. It might help him with the Almighty. He pretends piety in public but in private he plays his wife false. I for one shall be glad to see him gone for a while."

"Have a care, my friend. You are speaking of my family. Anthony is the queen's favorite brother, and it would not do to annoy Elizabeth more than you do now." Edward laughed. "You are jealous, admit it. Rivers is a better jouster, better poet, and better-looking than you, my lord, and, more than mere rumor, he *is* Margaret's lover. Besides, we have all gone on pilgrimages—albeit not so far. I do not grudge him that."

Seeing Hastings glower, Edward bit his tongue, regretting he had stirred up the bitterness that had surfaced between his trusty councilor and Anthony Rivers upon the transfer of the captaincy of Calais four years before. Perhaps he had been hasty at the time in taking the honor from Anthony to give to Hastings, he mused, but Edward considered Hastings the more capable of keeping the garrison readied and loyal. Why could everyone in his immediate circle not get along, he often wondered. He was tired of playing mediator. Elizabeth disliked Will, Will disliked Tom Grey, who returned the favor, and even his brothers George and Richard were constantly quarreling. It really was very tiresome, but he was too lazy to do anything about it, if the truth be told.

Edward decided to bring the subject back to Mistress Shore. "Lambert? Was he not one of the miserly mercers who reluctantly loosed his purse strings for the French expedition? Mayhap I should pay Master Lambert a royal visit to thank him personally for his pennies and enquire after his daughter at the same time." Edward tossed back a cup of wine, wiped his mouth with the back of his hand, and watched his friend's face fall. "Nay, I am jesting, Sir Lovelorn. She is all yours. I warrant she will not do for me. I like not poppets for partners in bed." He suddenly sat up and slapped his forehead. "Christ's nails, this lady sounds like the one Tom waxed poetic about before we went to France, do you not remember? Golden hair, green eyes, and standing less than five feet. Aye, I am certain she, too, was a mercer's daughter."

Will grimaced at the mention of the marquess of Dorset, another burr under his saddle. The inclusion of Edward's young stepson—and his own stepson-in-law—in their entertainment was an embarrassing aspect of his and Ned's friendship. The boy could be his grandson, he thought angrily. And such an arrogant and unintelligent courtier, he had long ago concluded. Could Mistress Shore be the same woman? Tom must have confided in Edward, which further irritated Will, but it was the thought that Tom might have already enjoyed Jane that really infuriated him.

"I believe the lady to have better judgment than to have dallied even a moment with a libertine like Dorset," Will declared. "It cannot be the same woman."

Edward laughed again, relishing his friend's discomfort. "And you, I suppose, my dear Will, are pure as the driven snow? I am afraid that description belongs solely to my brother Richard. What is it about Tom you dislike so? Are you angry that Bess insisted

I give him to your wealthy stepdaughter? Come now, admit it."

"Aye, I admit it," Will snapped back. "I am fond of my step-daughter and to see her wastrel husband seducing others in my sight sickens me."

"William, William," Edward purred. "Cast not out the mote from thine own eye . . . or however the scripture reads. And do not tell me you think about *your* poor wife when you are in bed with a trollop?"

And I suppose you do, Will wanted to retort, but he knew how far he could push Edward before the king became the king and no longer his adventurous companion.

"Speaking of wives, I had best go and visit mine," Edward grumbled as he rose and called for a page. "I have promised Richard a game of chess after supper this evening, so no lusty sport for us. I love that brother of mine dearly, but he is not one to make merry." He smiled as he checked his appearance in the polished silver mirror. "Did you ever meet his first love, Kate Haute? Now, there was a woman who might have brightened Richard's sober-sided aspect. Bold and beautiful—like my Bessie—but sadly an unsuitable bride for a prince."

Hastings nodded, but he was thinking: also like your Bess.

"Certes, you met her," Edward said. "Richard's Neville wife is all gentleness, but lacks the spirit of her predecessor." As he strode from the room, he called back, "Shall I see you at the council meeting on the morrow?"

Will confirmed that he would be there, but his mind was on more interesting matters as he planned his strategy for the woo-ing of Jane Shore.

"We have been summoned to Lord Hastings's house, wife," William almost shouted, bursting into Jane's chamber with barely a knock. At the interruption, Jane's maidservant, Ankarette Tyler, dropped the gold necklace she was removing from her mistress's neck. Impatient to be alone with his wife, William spoke sharply to the trembling woman before shooing her from the room. Jane picked up the jewelry and shot him a disapproving look.

"Sweet Jesu, William, you have the manners of a peasant."

His cold, hard look made her cower, and for a moment she believed that William would hit her, as her father would have done, but the news her husband wanted to convey overcame any desire to chastise her, and he disregarded her retort.

"The baron wishes to see both of us upon the morrow, Jane. And he wishes you to wear the green-and-golden gown. I should not be surprised if his lady wife is present, and she is a Neville! Can you not rejoice? This could be the making of my fortune." Then William astonished Jane by capering—aye, she thought, *capering* was the word—about the room. She had not seen him so excited before, and as it seemed to her that for once his levity was not wine-induced, she had an idea.

She rose and took off her bedrobe, going to him with a smile and acknowledgment of the wonderful news. She ran her hands up his arms and ended with his face between her fingers as she stood on tiptoe, hoping to arouse him at last. "Certes, I am happy for you—happy for us both, husband." She stroked his cheek and let her breasts press up against him. Surely she would feel his passion rise and manifest itself between them. "And, my dear husband, I would be happy for our child," she hinted.

He stared down at her sensual smile and smelled the lavender water in her hair. He did indeed feel her full bosom warming his torso, with her hand perilously near his codpiece. She was waiting to be kissed, and for the first time since wedding her, he thought to his own surprise he might bed her. He had not forgotten her taunts of annulment, and in truth he wanted no part of a separation. He feared for his growing reputation. He had ambitions to rise in the guild and become a warden, like John Lambert, and even, God willing, an alderman of the city. Nay, he could not risk a scandal at this point in his promising career.

As always, once thoughts about business again crowded his head, they drew the blood from his loins back into his brain, and he pushed Jane aside. "We cannot dally in bed when we need every second of this night to prepare. I must choose my finest wares to take with us to Lord Hastings's house. You must look your best, and so I shall leave you to sleep alone."

"Then you have forfeited your chance of keeping me as your wife, William," Jane wanted to shout. Surely the dean of Arches would grant her an annulment after she told this familiar story. She turned from him, her eyes hard, and coldly wished him a good night.

William grasped her arm and swung her back to him. "Why the disdain, mistress high and mighty? Do I not afford you all the advantages of a wealthy merchant's wife? Do you not hold the keys to the household? Have you not spent my hard-earned money on your wardrobe and jewels? Have I begrudged you your craving for luxury? How dare you turn from your husband and dismiss him with a rude 'good night.' What more do you want, mistress?"

Jane shook off his hand, her eyes now the color of an angry sea. "What I want is beyond your understanding, William. To begin with, you have no capacity to love, and even that I could forgo if you could give me the real treasure that I seek. 'Tis not the fabulous gowns nor sparkling sapphires that you bribe me with. Oh, do not take me for a fool, sir; I know full well they are bribes. Nay, what I yearn for is a babe whom I can love and who will love me. My own child is what I want." She scoffed at his astonishment. "Aye, even *your* child, husband, although I would pray he would not take after his father." She knew she had provoked him too far and as he lifted his hand to hit her, she raised her own to prevent him. "Do you wish me to have the marks of your fingers on my face when you meet with Lord Hastings, Master Shore?"

William had gone white and now a faint flush colored his

cheeks as he pulled his hand from her grip. He turned on his heel, exited the room, and slammed the door behind him. Jane threw herself down on the bed, unable to stem the uncharacteristic tears that had threatened during her defiant speech. It was one she had often dreamed about making during her waking hours while carrying out her duties as mistress of the household. She never thought she would ever have the courage to speak her mind in such a blunt manner. She was at once proud of herself and yet chastised. Had she not promised at the church door to obey her husband in all things?

Her tears were quickly spent as her practical self took over. She offered a quick prayer to the Virgin's mother, St. Anne, who was known to comfort childless women and who had become Jane's favorite intercedent with God over the past few months. "I pray you let William be well received by Lord Hastings so that he may celebrate by getting me with child. I fear greatly that if he is unable to then, I shall succumb to temptation with another." She closed her eyes tightly and hoped neither St. Anne nor God could read her mind. She did not think that either deity would approve of her committing adultery with Tom Grey. But the idea excited her, and, after crossing herself for her sinful thoughts, she got up off the bed and stood in front of the polished copper mirror. She lifted her shift to reveal her ankles and then a little more of her legs and, closing her eyes, imagined her lover removing the garment completely and taking her naked body in his arms.

Aching with unfulfilled passion, she let the skirt fall, blew out the candles, and crawled alone between the sheets.

Will Hastings's residence lay a stone's throw from Paul's Wharf to the south and Baynard's Castle to the west, and once inside the small courtyard Jane admired the warm, ivy-covered brick facade with its several large leaded windows, which she would discover illuminated the solar on the second floor to great effect. From them, one could just see the river and Southwark's growing skyline of lime-washed houses standing out against a leaden sky.

The baron's steward met their small cart at the side entrance. It was a singular honor to be met by the steward himself, William explained to Jane as he began supervising his apprentices and a household page in transporting the many bolts of damasks and velvets up the stairs to the main floor. On top of the pile was the green-and-gold satin.

Jane was ushered up alone first and admired the painted room, lavishly decorated with tapestries that could only have come from the finest weavers in Brussels or Bruges. Aye, she thought, turning to contemplate one depicting a unicorn hunt, Lord Hastings had fled into exile with the king five years ago when Edward took shelter with his brother-in-law Charles of Burgundy in Bruges. Hastings must have made the most of his time there, she concluded, throwing back the veil that William made her wear whenever they were in the street. He could not abide the lecherous looks his wife invariably attracted, and Jane, amused more than irked, had acquiesced with grace.

"The workmanship is beautiful, do you not think, Mistress Shore?" The voice was so close, Jane jumped and clutched her heart. Will Hastings smiled. "Forgive me for startling you. You were expecting me, I hope?"

Jane turned back to the wall hanging, aware Hastings was watching her. "I am very fond of the hunt, my lord, though I have been unable to pursue it lately, more's the pity."

After her self-arousal the night before, Jane was hungry to be desired that morning. She saw again the frank admiration in Will Hastings's look, and it warmed her. She noticed that, despite his age, he still had all his teeth and his legs were strong and straight. What stood out, however, were his eyes. Brown and kind. Aye, she could see the intelligence behind them, but their kindness mattered more to her. She made him a small curtsey and smiled coyly up at him.

"My lord, my husband is downstairs overseeing the unloading of his cloth. But may I tell you that we are humbled by your patronage." She smoothed the folds of her soft satin skirt to draw Will's attention to it. "My husband told me to wear this, so you might examine it more closely," she said, and saw to her sudden understanding that his eyes had not left her face and were clearly uninterested in her gown. Why, it was she whom Lord Hastings had wanted to see again, not her green-and-golden gown! The king's chamberlain was interested in her, she thought, only slightly flustered. She knew of his reputation with the wenches in the city—his and his sovereign's. And only recently had she learned to her chagrin that Tom Grey was a part of this trolloping trio. She had witnessed the landlord at the Lamberts' favorite tavern in the Chepe, where the family would take their weekly Sunday dinner, gossip about the seduction of one of his serving girls by a disguised Edward. "Imagine the king in The King's Head," he had chortled to Jane's father, "and then taking a maiden's head." Jane had seethed silently as he and John had winked and enjoyed the joke at the violated servant's expense.

But Jane was no tavern wench, and the king's most trusted councilor—arguably the most powerful man in England after the king—was treating her like a lady. Far from being cowed, she was spurred on to take a risk, especially after her unhappy evening with William. She lifted her skirt an inch or two and revealed an ankle in the process. "This is what you have a liking for, is it not, my lord? 'Twould be imprudent for me to invite you to touch, as we are alone, but as soon as William arrives with the rest of the material, you will be allowed to finger it."

Will laughed. "Why, Mistress Shore, I do believe you are flirting with me." He was delighted. The meeting was going far better than he could have dreamed, and he was charmed by her saucy innuendo. Voices in the back staircase made him seize the moment, and taking her hand he pressed it to his lips. "Indeed, you are correct. This *is* what I am interested in," he assured her before swinging around to greet the panting William, who was somewhat obscured by the bolts of cloth he carried; he was followed closely by his apprentice, Wat, and the page. "Master Shore, we greet you well. Your wife was admiring my unicorn tapestry," he remarked with bland smoothness. "It seems she enjoys the chase; I shall have to take her hunting one of these days."

William's astonishment made him let go of the cloth, his mouth agape, and then he remembered to bow. "M-my lord, you d-do us a great honor, does he not, Jane?"

Jane nodded an assent as she bent down to help neaten the bolts and cover her red face.

"Nonsense, sir, it will be my pleasure to—" Hastings began.

"Ah, husband, there you are," a woman's sharp voice intruded, cutting him off, and Jane could not help noticing the guilty look that crossed the chamberlain's face as Katherine, Lady Hastings, approached them. She was the sister of Warwick, sometimes called a maker of kings, and thus cousin to King Edward, and she had her brother's haughty bearing despite her lack of inches. Her Neville blue eyes darted from Jane to William and back to Jane before resting with suspicion on her husband's face. How long before he takes this wench to his bed, she was thinking, while dutifully acknowledging the reverences of the mercer and his wife, whom Will had hastily introduced. Despite her three dozen years, she was still a striking woman, especially when she smiled, although Jane thought the pale eyes mirrored a less attractive character underneath, and she shivered suddenly, as though a shadow had fallen over the proceedings.

"My lady, I am glad you are come, albeit you have spoiled my surprise," Will bluffed. He made convincing sheep's eyes at Katherine and explained: "I asked Mercer Shore to attend me to procure a length of this satin as a gift for your birthday. As soon as I saw it, I was determined to have it. I am particularly grateful to Master Shore for allowing me to see it fully made into a gown. Are you not as delighted by it as I am?"

William, eager to have the nobleman's business, pushed Jane forward for inspection. "Turn around, wife, and let her ladyship see the damasking properly."

As Jane did as she was told, Katherine sniffed. "And what makes you think I would want the same gown as a merchant's wife, my lord," she demanded of Hastings. "And may I add that I have never favored green, and yellow is, as we all know, the color of treachery." She looked Jane up and down and purred: "Be that as it may, the gown does, however, become you, mistress." Before Hastings could open his mouth to reproach her for her rudeness, Katherine turned to the mercer and gave him a beatific smile. "But, Master Shore, if you have other silk you could show me. I can hardly disappoint my lord husband in his gift, can I?"

While Will and Jane stood by in silence, Lady Hastings spent a goodly time pawing bolt after bolt of William's merchandise, relishing her husband's prolonged discomfort. She finally settled on a sumptuous blue velvet, and relieved, Will sent for his steward to make the arrangements. Without more ado, Will escorted Katherine from the room.

"God's truth, Will, have you not the manners to keep your harlots out of our house?" she expostulated as she dropped his arm and glided away, her attendant scurrying behind her.

Will scowled and returned to the Shores, who had already measured the desired length of the chosen velvet and were gathering up the rest of the cloth. "I am happy to have satisfied Lady Hastings, and rest assured once the gown is made and seen at court, your establishment will surely benefit, Master Shore."

William bowed low, his cheeks flushed with pleasure. Jane was afraid he would try and kiss Hastings's hand and so urged him to pick up the bolts and not waste any more of the baron's time.

"My promise will not be forgotten, mistress," Hastings assured her, watching William and his apprentice struggle to the stairs with their load. "I will invite you to the hunt very soon, if that be your wish. You do ride, I suppose?"

"And well for a lady, my lord," Jane remarked. "My father did not fail my sister and me in our education, but my husband has no time for books or hunting. My father took me on a chase once, and I should like to go again." She was astonished by her forwardness already and did not dare spend any more time in conversation with him but hurried to the staircase and was gone without a backward look.

I have no doubt you would, but I wonder how much you will enjoy being caught, Jane Shore, Will asked himself, his loins responding to his imagination of the scene.

Richard, duke of Gloucester, stepped out of a shop along goldsmiths' row in the Chepe, where he had commissioned a new collar for himself fashioned with the king's favorite *souvent me souvient* ornamentation. Recognizing the White Boar badge of his two retainers, several citizens stopped to stare at the king's youngest brother and marvel how unlike they were to look at.

"Spittin' image of 'is father," one man reminded another as they moved on. "Remember York? He wasn't tall neither. And both with dark 'air and that worried look. 'Tis uncanny."

Richard lifted his hand in salute to the bows he received and shared a quick laugh with his companion, Robert Percy. They had no sooner called for their mounts to be brought forward when a small cart piled high with bolts of cloth and pulled by two strapping youths turned the corner of Bread Street, followed by a merchant—a member of the guild of mercers, judging from the color of his gown—and a diminutive, veiled woman by his side.

Momentarily distracted, Richard and his friends failed to see the group of unkempt thugs who ran across the street to swoop upon the cart. Jane saw them coming and screamed to Richard's group, "Behind you, sirs!" before she ducked into the shop doorway that the duke had recently exited. Alerted, Richard and Robert whipped out their daggers, and Gloucester's escort, believing it was their lords who were the target, pushed the two noblemen back against the shop walls and protected them with crossed halberds.

But the robbers were more interested in the bulging purse that was giving William Shore's waistline an unnatural shape. Hastings had paid him the full value of the cloth despite William's halfhearted refusals, and William had prayed he and his merchandise would make the short trip back to Coleman Street unmolested. He had been right about a disgruntled army after the French expedition, and London was rife with crime. Unemployed and starving soldiers loitered in alleys and on street corners, looking for a carelessly or even carefully secured purse, or a piece of jewelry sparkling on a cloak or a bonnet that was easy picking for a desperate man with a knife or a club.

Too late, William attempted to bury the purse among the silks and satins, and instead shouted "Stop, thief!" miserably into thin air as the three robbers made off with the prize, hared down Bread Street, and disappeared into an alley.

"My money!" he wailed, shaking his fist at his bemused apprentices. "Why did you not stop them, you good-for-nothing wastrels? I have a good mind to deduct your wages."

The two young men were picking themselves up from the dirt and looked at their master in dismay. Richard and Robert hurried over to help pick up the scattered cloth and Jane ran to William's side.

"Do not berate the lads thus, husband," she cried, standing on tiptoe to add height to the weight of her words. "They were as helpless as the rest of us—nay, they were more helpless in that they were yoked to the cart. Never fear, Jack and Wat, I shall not allow my husband to take one groat off your wages. Now tell them yourself, William!"

Rob Percy nudged Richard and grinned. "I would not want to be that woman's husband, would you, Dickon?"

Richard shook his head and eyed the husband and wife with amusement. He had noted the elegant gown and the way it draped on the woman's slender form, and he at once knew how to make amends for the mercer's loss. He knew full well it was Edward's fault that loyal English soldiers were forced into a life of crime to feed their families. He had been proud that he had been the only one of the king's entourage to have refused King Louis's pension; he had wanted to fight the French, not sign some treaty that was no more than a bribe. He did not often disagree with his oldest brother, but in this—and in the lascivious manner in which Edward chose to live—he was adamantly opposed.

"Richard of Gloucester at your service, mercer," he said in his serious way. "I am sorry for your loss, and I regret we were unable to stop the thieves. However, I am curious if you have more of your wife's satin to offer me. It would please my lady, the duchess, of that I am certain."

Richard was rewarded by openmouthed disbelief from William. The duke sensed he was also being avised by the eyes behind the veil. Jane curtseyed low when William remained mute.

"I am afraid my husband must still be in shock, your grace, or he would have thanked you profusely. I will do so in his stead, and if you would be so kind as to send your messenger to William Shore's shop on Coleman Street, I will personally see to it that you receive a length of silk to your liking."

Richard was impressed. "Am I addressing Mistress Shore?"

Jane's merry green eyes were just visible through the filmy fabric, and Richard could tell she was smiling.

"Aye, my lord duke. I am honored to meet you," she replied, "although, I wish it had been in less harrowing circumstances."

Was the woman being forward with him? he wondered. Nay, he must have been mistaken, although just to be certain, he chose to answer her in a more reserved tone; he should end the conversation and be on his way, he decided. He inclined his head enough to be polite and said simply, "God give you a better day, mistress." He turned to William, who had recovered his composure and was bowing low, and told him, "I can assure you that I shall send my squire to fetch the cloth in a day or so, Master Shore. I am a man of my word."

"Coleman Street, your grace," William called after the retreating duke. "William Shore of Coleman Street."

Richard gave a curt nod. "I heard it the first time, mercer. I am not one to forget anything I need to remember," he remarked. "What an oddly matched couple," he confided to Rob Percy as they swung up into the saddle and trotted off.

Jane looked after them, nonplussed. What had she said that had so obviously offended the duke? Ah well, she thought, as I shall probably never speak to him again, I shall not worry about it.

On the second day of November, as Elizabeth waited at the window, the rat-tat of rain beat on the leaded glass panes, blurring the dozens of boats, shouts, barges, and ferries that plied the gray Thames below her. Not that on this particular day she could care: she was too preoccupied with the all-consuming, painful toil of labor and birthing. When Anne arrived, quickly and without fuss, four hours later, the queen looked at her fifth daughter and marveled again how each child could look so different born from the same parents. Elizabeth, Mary, and Cecily were fair-haired; poor little Margaret, may she rest in peace, was so bald it had been impossible to tell if she would have been fair like her mother, red-gold like her father, or dark like her grandfather York. But there was no mistaking these chestnut glints in the wispy tresses: they reminded Elizabeth of her brother, Anthony Rivers.

Expecting the customary visit from her husband, and only partly aware of the women who had attended her moving quietly about the chamber, she drifted into the pleasant state between waking and sleeping.

Would Edward be disappointed she had given him yet another girl to marry off with a dowry? With two sons showing signs of being healthy and strong, she hoped the king would not blame her for not tripling the York succession. She smiled whenever she thought of little Ned and his towheaded two-year-old brother, Richard. She was imagining Ned's pout when he learned he had another sister and on his own birthday, too. He had so begged his mother to come out of her chamber with another boy.

Elizabeth shifted her position, wincing from the overstretched muscles and hampered by her heavy breasts, and made up her mind she would try once more for a son, but that at age thirty-eight and after nine children, she was tired of being a brood mare. But try telling Edward, she grumbled. After all these years of marriage, he still sought her bed for pleasure, not merely for duty, and called her his beautiful Bessie. So why did he seek other women to lie with? she wondered for the thousandth time. Granted, she had often refused him her bed over the years, but surely two or three intimacies a month were sufficient for their ages. It was true, she admitted, he is five years younger than I, but even so. She contemplated the large betrothal ring on her finger, thinking back to earlier times. She had been glad when the sensual Elizabeth Wayte had been married off and sent from court, together with Edward's bastards, Arthur and the girl. That mistress had flaunted herself without shame for four long years and had had none of the good breeding of her predecessor, Eleanor Talbot. That poor woman had ended up taking her vows, Elizabeth remembered, wondering now what had become of her. She smiled grimly when she recalled the unkind moniker the nun had earned: King Edward's holiest harlot.

Eleanor, however, was out of favor by the time of Elizabeth and

Edward's secret marriage in 1464; and Elizabeth still congratulated herself for winning the most eligible bachelor in Christendom. Some thanks were due her canny mother, Elizabeth acknowledged now, remembering the love potion with which Jacquetta Woodville had tempted Edward. Who knew if her mother's witchery had worked; Elizabeth tended to put the victory squarely on her own undeniable charms and Edward's insatiable lust. She had been chagrined when Edward had not wanted to shout their union to the world, but then he was young, she remembered, and under the thumb of the high and mighty earl of Warwick, the devil take his soul. She felt no remorse for the schism her marriage had created between the king and his kingmaker, who had been negotiating a foreign match for the king and was politically embarrassed by Edward's surprise admission. Elizabeth had got what she wanted—and what her mother wanted—and the Woodvilles had risen to the top.

Elizabeth ran her hand down her body, despising the havoc birthing did to it. It was no wonder Edward sought out younger, virginal women to fornicate with—aye, that was all it was, she told herself, fornication—and she chose not to berate him every time word came to her that he and Hastings had been seen out whoring in the city. She and Lady Hastings had fallen in together mostly in mutual support against their philandering husbands, despite Katherine's Neville pride—or was it prejudice—over consorting with upstart Woodvilles. And now the two men were initiating Elizabeth's eldest and most beloved son, Tom, who was also Katherine's son-in-law, into their filthy practices. As long as no other concubine was taken under their roof again, Elizabeth had once promised Edward, she would not play the injured wife. "Out of sight, out of mind," she said aloud now.

"Are you referring to me, Bessie?" Edward's voice startled her, and her eyes flew open. She smiled at him with genuine warmth as she always did when she saw him, his lovable grin chasing his faults from her mind. What was it about him that kept her loving him? She did not know. He was exasperating, he flaunted his mistresses, drank too much, certainly ate too much, and if anyone had bothered to ask her, she was ashamed that he came home from France without firing an arrow. But he had bought her a diamond as big as a robin's egg with some of the pension, which she had snatched from him without a second thought, so she had kept her mouth shut and locked the jewel away to wear after she was churched.

Elizabeth reached out her arms, and after drawing the bed curtains, Edward climbed awkwardly onto the bed, his bulk causing it to groan.

"Nay, I was thinking about the Anjou woman," she lied easily, "and how glad I shall be when she has gone back to France. It cannot be too soon, for black melancholy follows her wherever she goes."

The French consort of dead King Henry had been a fishbone in the Yorkist family's gullet for the entire bloody civil war. Thankfully, King Louis had released the ransom money for Queen Margaret, who had been living as a virtual prisoner in Yorkist England since 1471.

Edward harrumphed. "Put all thought of her from your pretty head, my love. You have just given birth and must not allow such dark thoughts to trouble you now. Queen Margaret will be gone after yuletide, I promise. Louis has paid, and the She-wolf can go home." Edward stroked his wife's silky, silver hair, which had always been so pale he could not tell if some of the strands were now white. "Have you thought more on a name for our newborn?"

"Aye, if it pleases you, my lord, I thought we might honor your oldest sister and name this child Anne. I know you have had a soft spot for Nan, and I should probably show my gratitude for her brokering the marriage between Tom and her own daughter, God rest the girl's sweet young soul. As you know, Nan and I have been carrying at the same time," Elizabeth continued, "and

I have heard she is not well. Perhaps news of my easy birth and
that we have chosen to name the babe after her might lift her
spirits. What say you?"

Edward grinned. "'Tis not like you to be so diplomatic, Bessie."
He feigned a wince of pain as his wife thumped his leg. "Anne is also
the name of my grandmother—the one whose Mortimer name led
me to wear this crown. I like it, and I believe it will delight my sister,
too. I have no doubt the news of Exeter's drowning on the voyage
home from France will cheer her greatly. Good riddance! Another
scourge gone from my life along with the She-wolf of Anjou."

"Was it truly an accident, Ned?" Elizabeth asked softly. The
violent duke of Exeter, who had been Nan's first husband and a
fanatic Lancastrian with a possible claim to the throne, had reluctantly come into the Yorkist king's circle after being Edward's
enemy all through the civil war and had been among the lords on
the French campaign. "It is not like you to be so closemouthed."

"'Tis time I left you to sleep, my dear." Edward evaded her
question and her repartee as he heaved himself off the bed. It was
between him and God whether the dangerous Exeter's unexpected
demise had been an accident or not. So vile a husband had he been
to Nan that Edward had agreed to his sister's divorce, and she
had since married her lover. "Forget about Exeter. With him and
Margaret out of the way, I will be able to reign in peace without
looking over my shoulder. Our line will be secure."

He kissed her hand and turned to talk to Katherine Hastings,
who was hovering nearby. "See that she is not disturbed again
tonight, my lady. The queen needs her rest."

Behind him, Elizabeth's mouth curved into a half smile, thinking
of Exeter's convenient exit. Well done, Ned, she crowed. Her husband had not lost his ability to manipulate events to his advantage.

Jane knocked on the door at the back of St. Mary-le-Bow church
where the dean of the Court of Arches presided. This was the third

time she had come to see him and beg to summon William to be questioned about his impotence. She bade Ankarette wait outside and walked into the untidy office of the ecclesiastical judge who could transform her life, if he would but listen to her. Her parish priest had faithfully set her upon the lawful path to annulment, and the dean was supposed to be her savior. The unkempt old man heard her name spoken in his ear by his clerk and he groaned. "Not the mercer's wife again!"

Jane had purposely dressed to show off her charms, although she was careful not to give the impression of wantonness; she had decided the more attractive she looked the more credible her plea might be. She had read for herself the words in the theologian Thomas of Chobham's manual that were still in use regarding impotence and annulment:

> There must be a physical examination of the man's genitals by
> wise matrons. Then after food and drink, the man and wife are
> to be placed together in one bed and wise women are to be
> placed around the bed for many nights. If the man's member is
> always found useless, the couple are well able to be separated.

It had struck Jane that from what she had heard about men's members, there might be many lustier lovers who would be useless in such a situation, but in William's case it would make no difference.

Jane knelt for the cleric's blessing and then stood straight as the man slumped back into his chair, his fingers blackened from ink, and his spectacles perched on the end of his bulbous nose; judging by its color, Jane could well imagine that the dean enjoyed his wine.

"Right worshipful Dean Reynking," she addressed him in the expected way, "I beg of you to summon my husband in this matter of our marriage. It has been more than six months ere we were wed, which is the lawful time for a man and wife to have lived together before the court will hear a petition for annulment, and this is my third appeal. He has failed in his duty to me and thus I am deprived of my right of motherhood."

"I am aware of your case, Mistress Shore," Reynking snapped, "and I am reviewing it. You cannot hurry the law."

"Then the law is unfair, your worship. It must be that the law is male; I cannot think that it would make a man wait as long as I have for justice." Damnation, she thought, watching the dean's face turn purple, why had she been so bold?

"How dare you question church law, mistress," he spluttered angrily. "It would seem to me that your clattering tongue is what makes your husband limp. Perhaps you deserve a spell on the cucking stool." And he began to write something on the vellum in front of him.

Not knowing if he was making a note about her or whether he had moved on to the next case, Jane made her exit before he could blink and wonder where she had gone.

Ah, Jane, she told herself, hurrying to St. Sithe's Lane and the sanctuary of Sophie's practical presence, when will you learn prudence and keep your thoughts to yourself. She had no doubt that Dean Reynking would relegate her case to the bottom of his pile after today, and she cursed her folly all along Watling Street.

Will Hastings chose a rare warm day in November to send a messenger to Coleman Street requesting the pleasure of Mistress Shore's company for a day of hawking. Jane listened to William read the formal invitation with a mixture of eagerness and trepidation. Naturally, William was included in the outing, but there was nothing he liked less than traipsing around in nature waiting for a rabbit to be impaled on a bird of prey's claws. He could see no point in the pastime, and besides, his bony arse did not fare well on the hard saddle of a trotting horse. With business to attend to today, he was offended the baron had given no advance notice, but he looked down at Jane in cold calculation. "I will allow you to go. Perhaps he will buy more from us, wife, if you are pleasant with him."

Pleasant with him? Jane was incredulous. How stupid was William, or did he truly want his wife to succumb to the renowned seducer of Westminster? One side of her wanted her husband to protect her reputation, but the other more dangerous side hoped he would not come today. The dutiful wife found herself saying, "I think you should accompany me, William, 'twould do you good to have some fresh air. The rain of late has kept us all too much inside." But the imp in her did not remind him that he might accomplish more business with Hastings if she went alone. She waited as he contemplated her words, longing for permission yet afraid for her virtue if she gained it.

William crumpled the parchment and threw it in the fireplace. "I have too much to do, my dear. You will take Ankarette with you, and I am confident Lord Hastings will have a party of ladies and gentlemen with him, so you will be one of many. He will take good care of you. Go, wife. I know how you love to ride."

The decision taken out of her hands. Jane was ecstatic, but she controlled the urge to exult. "I confess, William, that I am delighted to hunt again, and I thank you for allowing me the chance." And before he could change his mind, she ran to her chamber to change her clothes.

She was escorted to Thames Street on her jennet, while Ankarette was mounted pillion behind one of Will's young squires. The lord chamberlain himself greeted her in the courtyard of his impressive brick town house and took her up the steps to an antechamber, where others, dressed in hunting garb, enjoyed a glass of ale. Only a week ago, she had been shown the merchant's back entrance into this inn, and now she was invited in the front door. She held herself with dignity and wished she were six inches taller as Will introduced her to the two other ladies present. As she bobbed a curtsey to the gentlewomen, she was aware of every male eye upon her, which heightened her confidence.

"Mistress Shore is a freewoman of the city, Dame Stathum," Will announced to the wife of one of his retainers who gave Jane a haughty stare, while the other woman could barely suppress a titter. "Her husband, a mercer, was unable to accompany her on such short notice, but Mistress Shore kindly helped in the choosing of cloth for my dear wife recently, and this is her reward. It seems Mistress Shore has a liking for the hunt, and thus I invited her to join us."

Jane knew instantly that the two women understood exactly why Will Hastings had included her in the party, and she hoped her face did not reveal the flush of humiliation she felt as Will tried to justify her presence. It was her first experience with shame, and she suddenly wanted to bolt from the room back to Coleman Street and the safety of her merchant-class life. She did not belong here.

"Did I hear you say the wife of Mercer Shore, Will?" The agreeable, familiar voice broke into the introductions, relieving Will greatly. He, too, was regretting his impulsiveness in including Jane in such a hunting party. They should have gone alone, he thought too late, and spared Jane any embarrassment, but he had clearly misjudged the situation in his eagerness to win her.

"My lord of Gloucester, you have the acquaintance of this lady? She will be glad to have someone pleasant to converse with, I have no doubt." He ignored the two women, who were now discredited by Richard of Gloucester's acceptance of Jane. Sensing they had offended their host, they shuffled their feet and backed away as Hastings asked: "May I leave her in your capable hands while I see if the falconers are ready with our birds, Lord Richard?"

"Willingly, my lord," the king's youngest brother replied. "Mistress Shore and I met in the Chepe while she and her husband were returning from"—he thought for a second—"why, 'twas from here, I believe. Did you know they were set upon by thieves, and a purse of gold was taken?"

Will looked genuinely concerned as he listened to Richard's accounting of the robbery. "How unfortunate, mistress. I should recompense your husband somehow. I trust you were not hurt?"

Richard spoke up, amused. "I think not. She proved the cleverest of us all and, after warning Rob Percy and me of the impending attack, hid herself in a doorway. It happened so quickly and was an unlucky affair. But 'tis all too common these days."

"Indeed it is," Will agreed. "My lord, excuse me," he said, and he took his leave.

Jane swept Richard a low reverence and murmured her thanks.

"Thanks for what, mistress?"

"For rescuing me," Jane replied, giving him her most enigmatic smile. "Twice."

"I think not, mistress. I have the impression you are not someone ever in need of rescuing."

"If I may be so bold, I would disagree, my lord duke," she told him, her eyes merry. "I would venture that most females are in need of rescuing in one fashion or another."

To her chagrin, Richard did not appear amused. Mother of God, but he is a serious man, Jane thought. She wondered what his wife was like and could not help but think life with Richard of Gloucester might be a solemn business indeed.

Hearing the hunting horn signify an imminent departure, Richard chose not to comment further but offered her his arm to escort her to her mount. A most forward lady, he mused, and at once the face of his first love, Kate, and her teasing amber eyes were conjured guiltily to his mind. He felt an unexpected stab to his heart. Aye, his former mistress was also strong-willed, but how he had loved her! He had given her up upon marriage to Anne Neville, but he still had news of his two children by her from Jack, Lord Howard, whose wife had taken Kate under her wing. He had not regretted letting Kate go as, like his father, he was a man to whom duty and loyalty meant everything in life, but he still had guilty pangs each time he remembered their heartbreaking last night together. Sweet Jesu, he had thought Kate would lose her mind. But she was of common stock and unfit for a prince, he had known all along; as a royal duke he must secure his line and his line's future. Unlike Edward, he thought, as he expertly threw his leg across his horse's back and settled into the saddle. Ned had squandered an important alliance with a foreign power by marrying an English nobody—and in secret, no less. Both younger York brothers had chosen better, Richard thought grimly: he and George had married the Neville sisters, Isobel and Anne—joint heiresses of Warwick vast wealth and power.

Then there was Ned's whoring. Who knew how many bastards his brother had left up and down the realm? Edward's penchant for pretty women knew no bounds, and Richard disdained the way he took and discarded paramours. Richard had grown to accept his sister-in-law, the queen, and wondered how she endured Ned's infidelities. He was certain Edward would never have behaved thus had their father, the duke of York, survived Wakefield and become king.

Richard observed his host, Hastings, with concern as the party trotted through the gate and out into Thames Street, their horses jostling for space on the bustling street. Here was Ned's cohort and fellow philanderer, who appeared to encourage his sovereign to live life to an excess bordering on dissipation. True, Richard could not question the man's loyalty to the king any more than Richard's own, but it disgusted Richard that Edward would often hand down his discarded concubines to Will. Even more despicable was Edward's willingness to relinquish some poor young woman to that profligate Dorset. And Tom Grey was Ned's own stepson. Aye, Ned's behavior was degrading, and it astonished him that their formidable mother, Cecily, had not left her seclusion at Berkhamsted or summoned him there to upbraid her eldest son. Perhaps she did not know, Richard mused, but then dismissed the thought with a laugh. Nothing escaped Cecily's notice, he well knew.

As the horses clattered over London Bridge, its shops and houses teetering precariously three stories above the bridge on either side and people standing aside to let the royal party pass, Richard prayed his infant son, another Edward, might not inherit any of his namesake uncle's weaknesses. He smiled to himself as he cast his thoughts northward to Middleham and the serene Yorkshire dales where his dear wife and son were impatiently waiting for him. How he longed to leave the city and return home.

Once through the city and over London Bridge, the ride to Greenwich took more than an hour, and Jane exulted in the fresh scents that allowed her to forget the foul city odors of London and its growing southern borough of Southwark. She hung back from the other ladies and fell into conversation with Nicholas Knyveton, Will Hastings's burly squire, who had been instructed to see she was not neglected.

"I have never seen the palace," Jane told him, craning her neck as they crested the hill above the red-roofed building, its graceful facade untrammeled by heavy fortifications unlike the Tower. "Such a beautiful setting on the riverbank. I can understand why 'tis the queen's favorite."

"Aye, and when Duke Humphrey built it more than a half century ago, he named it Bella Court, but it has grown since then," Knyveton replied. He was warming to the spirited young woman after having his pride hurt that his master had relegated him to damsel duty, as he called it. Jane had talked to him of poetry, a passion of the squire's, and he was amused by her reenactments of some of Geoffrey Chaucer's choice characters. Her gift for mimicry was impressive, he told her, and she had laughed and then imitated Hastings's Northampton burr so perfectly, he had slapped his thigh in mirth and frightened his horse.

When the hunting party had reached the ivy-covered watch tower atop the hill, the riders dismounted to stretch their legs and take advantage of the privy that Duke Humphrey had built for the guards stationed there day and night. The ladies were given the option of using the covered cesspit first, but Jane demurred, preferring to wander a little farther away and make use of a bush. She did not often avail herself of the public privies in the city, hating the ignominious hanging of her backside over the communal plank and doing her best to avoid soiling her skirts. Squatting behind a tree or bush seemed more civilized, she thought.

She could hear the men laughing and talking as the two pack-horses were unloaded to provide the party with a canopy, cushions, and refreshments, while the falconers and grooms set up perches for the birds and allowed the horses to graze the lush grass.

Jane rearranged the skirts of the riding gown she had designed from a fine murrey Milanese fustian, chosen for not only its warmth but also its plush look of velvet, and gratefully sat down out of sight behind a clump of blackberry bushes to stretch out her stiff limbs and knead her sore back. The late-November sun was warm enough to let her shed her mantle, and removing her jaunty feathered hat, she loosed her thick braids, which had been pinned under it, and mopped her perspiring forehead and neck with a kerchief.

"That is much better," she said aloud to a squirrel that was eyeing her from a bare birch tree. "How fortunate you are, Mistress Nutkin, to live in such a beautiful place. Do not misunderstand me, my little red friend, I love the hustle and bustle of London, but there are days when I long for an hour without a ringing bell, the constant buzzing of voices, rumbling of carts, chanting clerics, and the clatter of hoofs. Listen! Here all you hear are birds and the song of the river—except today there are our loud visiting voices. I am afraid we may disturb you, dear squirrel."

She laughed at herself for talking to an animal, but then she ruminated on why she was there at all. Why had Lord Hastings invited her? She had convinced herself she had flirted only to annoy William and to prove that she was still desirable despite her husband's snub of her the night before. She was not in the least attracted to Hastings, especially as her waking dreams were filled with young Tom Grey. When she had seen Hastings at the door this morning, he had looked old, and she was dismayed then to think he might want to seduce her. Why, he must be twice her years, she suddenly thought. Aye, what had she been thinking when she agreed to come today?

"Mistress Shore, are you quite well?" the object of her thoughts asked, peering around the bush, his face full of concern. "Lettice Strathum told me you had wandered over here. I sincerely hope the ride was not too much for you." Then his face broke into a grin. "But here you recline, looking as much a part of the woodland as a nymph or a siren, and just as lovely."

Will felt the familiar rush of blood as he admired the graceful, recumbent figure, her skirts raised to her knees, revealing slender legs and delectable ankles. He had to resist pushing those petticoats up around her waist and taking her there and then.

Jane sat up, hurriedly covered her legs, and pulled her hat back on. "Sirens live in the river, my lord," she faltered, recognizing desire in his eyes. "I am quite well, thank you, and I apologize for causing you any concern."

"The only concern we may cause is by staying behind this bush any longer, Jane. I may call you Jane, may I not?" he said as he helped her to her feet and retrieved her mantle.

Jane painstakingly pulled on her gloves to hide her reddening face. "Only if I may call you Will, my lord," she countered with false bravado. "And as I never intend to call you Will, I think you know my answer. I pray you, let me be Mistress Shore."

"God's bones, Mistress Shore, you are even lovelier when you are cornered," Will answered, disappointed but undeterred. "I had the strongest notion the first time I saw you that we would become . . . friends, at least. Tell me you are not displeased with my candor."

She looked up at him then, her composure restored, and smiled. "How can I be displeased with you, Lord Hastings, when you are so kind as to bring me to such a glorious place." They were nearing the group now, and Jane noticed Richard of Gloucester assessing her with disapproving eyes. Sweet Jesu, she thought irritably, what did he think we could have been doing in those few seconds behind a thorny bush? His gaze made her hold herself more erect and she answered Hastings quietly: "I shall be honored to be your friend, my lord, and consider myself fortunate."

If she had offended him, it was not evident, for Will became the affable host again, conversing with one, slapping another on the shoulder or bending down to offer more wine to the two ladies reclining on cushions. When Jane heard Lettice Strathum inform Will that she and her friend were too comfortable to bother with hunting, Jane knew she must refuse, too: she had caused enough gossip for one day and did not want any more attention. Instead, as the men trotted along the hillside, she chose to climb to the top of the watch tower to follow their progress and admire the falcons as they swooped upon their prey on that last fine day of the year.

At one point, Will, his white horse easily discernible among the other riders, turned in his saddle and, shading his eyes, found Jane's small figure standing alone atop the tower, and he raised his hand in salute. You have a friend in me should you need one, Jane Shore, the signal seemed to say, and Jane gave him an answering wave. He had not taken her rebuff amiss, and she was grateful.

She might have been chagrined to know that Will's salute had been accompanied with a slow smile of resolve: he would see a lot more of Jane Shore than just her legs in the not too distant future.

PART TWO

1476–1478

My want was wealth, my woe was ease at will,
My robes were rich, and braver than the sun;
My fortune then was far above my skill,
My state was great, my glass did overrun,
My fatal thread so happily was spun,
That when I sat in earthly pleasures clad,
And for a time a goddess place I had.

Thomas Churchyard, "Shore's Wife," 1562

FIVE

The queen watched her son move nimbly through the intricate steps of a country dance with his young wife, Cecily,
and wondered when Tom would tell her she would soon be a
grandmother. After all, the couple had been married almost two
years. She eyed her daughter-in-law dispassionately and had to
acknowledge that fortune or no, the girl was homely.

"They make a fine pair, do they not, your grace," Katherine
Hastings remarked by her side on the dais. "I wager we will have
word of a child soon. They have spent more time in each other's
company this yuletide than since before the French fi . . . expedition." She had almost said *fiasco*, but she knew Elizabeth would not
tolerate criticism of Edward's policies, although she and Elizabeth
had bonded over the years because of their husbands' infidelities.

"I was thinking the same thing, Katherine." She held her
thumbs for the lie.

Katherine's tiny titter told Elizabeth that Lady Hastings was
pleased with the comparison, and the queen became reflective. It
was hard to know who to trust at court; who was truly a friend or
only acting a friend because she was queen. Granted, her senior
ladies-in-waiting could be counted on: Anne Bourchier was her
sister, and Elizabeth Scales her brother Anthony's dull wife. But
Katherine was a Neville and Edward's first cousin, despite being
the sister of the kingmaker and turncoat, Warwick. Her first husband, Baron Harington, had been a loyal Yorkist supporter and
indeed had lost his life in the cause at the Battle of Wakefield,

alongside Edward's father and brother. Aye, Katherine's friendship and loyalty could be counted on, especially in the matter of their husbands' excesses.

The great hall at Elizabeth's Placentia Palace of Greenwich was alive with the toe-tapping sound of recorders, lutes, viols, and tambour that accompanied the festivities on that Twelfth Night. Elizabeth noted with a satisfied eye that her court reflected the prosperity Edward's reign had finally brought to England. After a hundred years of fighting in France, England's coffers had been nigh on empty. And the costly civil war between York and Lancaster had then also drained the kingdom of men and money, before Edward had won the crown and brought a lasting peace.

That night's feast, featuring nine courses, had given strength to the dancers, and the ten tuns of wine that had been consumed made for even more raucous conversation than some of the prior events of that yuletide season, when a sober company had celebrated first the birth and then the circumcision of the Christ child. This evening would bring the winter festival to a close with its most pagan tradition of reversing for a few hours the roles of lords and servants, all presided over by the Lord of Misrule. Elizabeth hated the ritual, but this year, because of her recent confinement, her doctor, Domenico de Serigo, had forbidden her to serve her ladies on her knees, as they had to do at special occasions, so she sat back and watched the dancing. All too soon, the wretched cake would be brought out, in which some unsuspecting person would find the fateful bean and be crowned lord of the feast and of misrule.

The musicians changed their tune, and a slow estampie began. Without warning, a grotesquely masked courtier precipitated himself in front of Elizabeth and in a husky voice asked, "May I have this dance, your grace?"

Katherine let out a little squeak of alarm at the satyr. "How now, sirrah, unmask before the queen!"

But Elizabeth rose and grandly reached down her hand to

be kissed. "By all means, sir. My lord and husband seems to have deserted me."

"And you the most beautiful woman in the room, madam. He should be ashamed." The sensual mouth under the mask curved into a smile, and it was then Katherine knew him for the king.

"For shame, cousin," she chided him. "I was about to protect the queen's honor myself."

Side by side, the king and queen made their way to the middle of the hall, chuckling at Katherine's indignation. "You are incorrigible, Ned," Elizabeth chided as the company moved aside to let them take their places. Edward laughed. His sister, Margaret of Burgundy, had used exactly the same word to describe him when they had conferred together in Calais before the French campaign. "Where did you get that hideous mask?" Elizabeth asked.

"I borrowed it from Will's man Knyveton. He tells me he has had success wooing wives with it, and I wanted to see if it would work."

Elizabeth shook her head in despair as they began the dance. Truly all men were little boys at heart, she told herself. She wished her little boy-husband would grow up and out of his pleasure-seeking ways. She gripped his hand and they stepped out together to the delight of the admiring spectators. Edward tossed the mask into the throng and concentrated on the music, for he was not skilled in the art of dance. He looked around for his brother George of Clarence, known as the finest dancer at court. Ah, good, Edward noted, he was not dancing, as there he was in conversation with Will Hastings.

Edward instinctively knew to look in the farthest corner of the room for his youngest brother, Richard. He felt a twinge of annoyance as he contemplated the intentional distance between Richard and George. Edward had treated George with generosity too many times in the past six years, not the least of which occurred after George's desertion to side with Edward's one-time ally turned traitor,

Warwick. Foolish George—he had thought Warwick would make him a king, too. With the help of their sister, Margaret, and much cajoling by their mother, Duchess Cecily, George had come back into the family fold, and Edward had welcomed him unconditionally. Like Margaret and young Richard, Edward believed in the power of loyalty to family, but somehow George had been absent when that lesson was learned.

"He does not know his place, Ned," Duchess Margaret had told Edward in Calais last year. "He was spoiled as a child for his charm, and he cannot accept his place as younger son. You must give him more responsibility; show him you trust him." Aye, George had always been Meg's favorite.

He and Elizabeth had come to the end of the hall and turned to process back down, giving him full view of Richard, sharing a quiet word with Jack Howard. He had to admit that ever since Richard was a small boy and prone to many childhood illnesses, Edward had had a soft spot for this serious youngest brother. And his kindness to Richard had been rewarded by a fierce loyalty that would have made their father proud. Aye, this was the man he could count on to hold the north strong for the Crown. He did not fit in at court, Edward knew, and resolved to send the young duke back to Middleham in a few weeks. It seemed Richard missed his wife and son, and now, dear God, he was scowling at a woman whose bodice had spilled out its pink-nippled contents to the delight of the young man dancing with her.

Edward grunted. He blamed prudish Anne Neville for Richard's pious attitude toward the court. Why had Richard set his sights on Warwick's other daughter? How much easier if he had found another match, but that was past and gone. The two brothers were now warring over their wives' joint inheritance. They were heard quarreling in corridors at Westminster, shouting insults at each other in family gatherings, and embarrassingly behaving like children. As the dance came to an end and he bowed to his wife, he decided he must put a stop to the squabbling and insist the two reconcile. It was not good for the family, and it certainly was not good for the stability of his throne. He hoped the problem would go away, resenting how much time he was forced to think about such unpleasantness. It made him irritable.

And to make matters worse, he had been kept from his wife's bed for nigh on six months now and he had no substitute at present. A few conquests in the city and on his progress through Hampshire and Wiltshire had briefly sated his lusts, but he missed the familiar feel of Bess and even of his former mistress Elizabeth Wayte, until she had been removed from court when he had tired of her. He refused to think about Eleanor Butler and his betrayal of her. Nay, that little secret would stay buried forever, he prayed. Certes, he and Hastings had never talked of it again since Bruges, so he thought it safe to presume Will had forgotten it. His eyes began to wander over the ladies in the hall, looking for a tasty prospect. The uninhibited lady with the large paps, perhaps? He grinned at her, and fluttering her eyelashes and feigning modesty, she cupped her hands over her nakedness. Then he caught sight of Richard's face, and his own smile faded.

"Spare a thought for me, my lord," Elizabeth complained on their way back to the dais; she knew exactly where Edward's eyes were focused. "I have asked you three times whether you have visited baby Anne since we removed to Greenwich."

Feeling guilty, Edward turned to her. "Forgive me, Bessie, I have those two squabbling brothers on my mind at present."

"Certes you do, Ned," Elizabeth reproached, almost smelling his lust. "But pray answer my question."

Edward grinned, caught in his fib. "I have seen little Nan, in truth," he assured his wife. "I swear she smiled when she saw me. She seems healthy, God be praised." As he helped Elizabeth onto her throne, he bent near her ear before taking his seat and enjoyed the view of her cleavage. He never failed to be moved by his wife's alabaster skin, silken hair, and delicious curves. "And I would like to get you with another, now your churching is done. May I come tonight, my love?"

Elizabeth's laugh always drew notice. It was high, silvery, and depending on the reason for it, sharp or infectious. Those close to the dais smiled as they heard it, wondering what their king had said that had so amused his queen.

No one but Elizabeth knew that the laughter masked her relief that Edward had not found a new mistress while she was confined. Instead, fully confident once more of her seductive power over him, she whispered, "I shall be retiring very soon, my lord. I, too, have missed your company."

It was not a cold winter but a dreary, drizzly one, which Jane decided was more unpleasant than snow and its resulting slush. At least with snow the rooftops were white and sparkled in the sun once the clouds had dumped their heavy loads on the city. Footsteps were muffled, children laughed and played in the fluffy whiteness, and somehow neighbors were friendlier, inviting one in to imbibe hot cider or wine and sharing in chores. But this winter, every day dawned as gray as the next and it was a question of how hard it would rain today, not if it would rain. Townspeople hurried along the muddy alleys and lanes to the next shelter and did not attempt to be sociable. Shopping in the markets was a soggy business, the barrows' canopies inadequate to shield whatever vegetables had survived since harvest and were not rotten. Jane lamented that her clothes never dried out properly despite the luxury of a fireplace in three of the Shores' rooms. She could not help but think of Sophia and her family, knowing well that the rain would be dripping through the thatch into the many vessels Jehan would place strategically to catch it. If only she controlled the money that William took in with his burgeoning business: the first thing she would do is give the Vandersands the means to roof their house with slate. That being improbable, Jane had to admit the weather was good for William's business, as customers sought cloth to replace rain-shrunken gowns and mantles.

Aye, William's spirits were high that month, but Jane did not benefit. Her husband was no longer even offering her bribes to keep her peace about his inadequacy, and thus no new gowns were forthcoming. Husband and wife ate dinner together for the sake of appearances, but since the day of the hunt, Jane had resolved to stop the pretense that either had respect for the other, and they barely spoke unless it was in front of customers. They certainly did not share the same bed.

Toward the end of January, when Jane despaired of ever seeing the sun again or knowing what being happy meant, she and William were summoned to court in a gesture of Edward's gratitude to the city merchants for their part in financing the French expedition. For very different reasons, the anticipation of this event made both husband and wife courteous with each other again. William spared no expense in dressing Jane in the most luxurious satin in his warehouse and paid a vast sum to have a hundred white silk roses sewn upon its iridescent sea green sheen.

"It matches your eyes, *lieveling*," Sophie had said when she came by on the day to bring Jane a handwoven silken belt to wear for good luck. She plucked a pendant of ambergris on a delicate gold chain from her friend's jewel casket, shaking her head at the jumble of pretty gewgaws it contained. "A simple necklace is enough, I believe."

Jane twirled for Sophie, the golden veil on her headdress floating like a sunset cloud about her. Then she stopped abruptly. "I wonder if Tom Grey will be there?"

Sophie clicked her tongue in disapproval. "You must not seek him out or speak his name, Jane. He is not for you, you know this. Promise me you vill pretend to be a lady today for Villiam's sake. He is not so bad, my dear, and he secures for you a future." She looked wistful. "I can only dream of a life like yours, Jane. Do not throw it into the river, I beg of you."

She looked so serious that Jane flung her arms about the staid young woman, laughing. "You worry too much, silly Sophie. I promise not to draw attention to myself, if that will make you feel better, but I shall do it for me and not for William. You forget, I have a friend at court now," she added, her eyes twinkling. "Lord Hastings will see me and tell me what to do and say, so have no fear on my behalf."

But Will Hastings was not there, much to Jane's chagrin. She discovered soon after her arrival at the palace that he had returned to his responsibilities as captain of Calais and would be gone for several weeks.

To Jane's astonishment, William chose to open his purse and take a wherry upriver to the Westminster pier. They would arrive in style like the wealthier courtiers instead of riding through the muck in the marshy road from the city to the palace and risk being robbed. William had taken great pains with his own wardrobe, Jane observed, and she complimented him on the fox-fur trim on his mercer's dark blue robe. Jane was pleased that this year's livery color was less garish than last year's burnt umber; the hood in particular had given most mercers' skin a deathly pallor. His hair even smelled clean for once, she noted, and the excitement of the event gave his pale face some color and his eyes a sparkle.

Westminster Hall was ablaze with light, putting the White Hart insignia of the second King Richard into sharp relief along the window embrasures. Jane lifted her eyes to the massive hammer-beamed rafters high above and wondered at the carpenters' courage. William hailed a fellow mercer and Jane found herself in conversation with his clatterer of a wife, while her eyes roamed the room doing exactly what Sophie had warned her not to do: search for Tom.

A fanfare of trumpets heralded the arrival of the king and queen, and all necks stretched a few inches in order to catch a glimpse of the royal couple. Jane was so short, she saw nothing, but would have enjoyed watching Edward clap a merchant here and there on the shoulder and move among his subjects like a man rather than a king, although there was no mistaking who was the monarch in the room. However, later, as she munched on a sweetmeat, she saw the couple plainly as they mounted the canopied dais and sat side by side on outsize, high-backed thrones.

"Ah, but she is beautiful," Jane declared to her awed companion as they gazed at Elizabeth with her perfect oval face, creamy white skin, pink-tinged cherubic mouth, and large almond-shaped eyes. "She is almost too beautiful to be real."

Jane then turned her attention to the king, whose weight had caused him to lose the five years of youth he had on the queen. She had, of course, seen him riding through the city streets on several occasions, and she had always liked the way he engaged with his subjects. You could almost imagine he was one of them, she had noticed, as he would wave expansively, smile, and even shout "God's greeting to you!"

What a handsome couple, Jane remarked to herself, staring at the queen's magnificent crimson satin overdress encrusted with seed pearls, a jeweled collar about her slender neck. Edward wore a deep purple long velvet gown trimmed in ermine, the fur exclusive to royalty. A simple coronet crowned his thick golden-red hair and a heavy gold collar of his favorite double S hung about his shoulders. A lesser man would have been weighed down by it, Jane thought, but Edward was no widow's mite. He was a giant among his people, standing six foot and three inches, and he was beginning to get a girth to match.

Soon the line formed for the presentations, and conversation came to a halt as the merchants and their wives jostled for position. Jane suddenly saw her mother and father near the front of the queue but refrained from waving or calling out, which she might have done on any other occasion. It took an hour before she and William reached the dais, but not before there had been several older female casualties behind her, women overcome from standing on the stone floor in their heavy gowns for so long, and who had to be escorted out to an antechamber to sit down or out into the fresh air.

"Mercer William Shore and Mistress Shore of Coleman Street," Chamberlain Roger Ree intoned after William had given their names. Jane thought William's back would break in two so low did he bow, and she smiled to herself as she sank into her own reverence and peeked up at the king. The expression she saw on his face wiped the smile from her own. She knew only too well the look of lust.

Sweet Jesu, she said to herself, he has seen something he wants; what now?

Edward liked entertaining his subjects. He liked being king and dispensing goodwill, whereas Elizabeth had complained that she was having to spend the afternoon watching a parade of peasants faun in front of her while she pretended to enjoy it.

As he watched the wealthy men of the city show off their finery, it gave him immense satisfaction to know his reign had resulted in a new prosperity for England. After a hundred years of war with France followed by a costly civil war between his own house of York and his predecessor's house of Lancaster, the treasury was being refilled with profits from trade, not taxes for war. These merchants were reaping the rewards of his policies, he was thinking proudly, when his thoughts were instantly quelled as "Mercer William Shore and Mistress Shore of Coleman Street" rang out, and he saw perfection step in front of him.

Bones of Christ, but this must be Hastings's paragon, he thought. And that lazy stepson of his, Tom Grey's. They did not exaggerate, he noted, and he gripped his seat arms, sat up, and sucked in his belly. Immediately, Elizabeth's uncanny intuition told her to beware of this petite but buxom beauty, and she registered the name just in case.

"We are pleased to greet you, Master Shore, mistress." Edward smiled and bowed his head first to the husband—thinking to himself that Will was right, he is insignificant—and then to Jane, although his eyes had never left Jane's face. What brazenness that she was meeting his look, and he was immediately intrigued. He loathed simpering women who flattered him, hoping to win his favor. Rarely had he taken up with a milk-and-water female; his Bess had taught him to enjoy a woman of spirit, and anyone lacking it bored him.

Edward appeared transfixed, and Elizabeth, annoyed, waved the couple on.

"He spoke to us, wife!" William exclaimed when the Shores were out of royal earshot. He was as animated as his sober personality allowed. "Did you notice? We were the only ones in our group he spoke to."

Jane despaired of him and grimaced. If he had eyes in his head or one jealous bone in his sexless body, her husband might have deduced the real reason for the king's unusual interest in Mercer Shore and his wife.

Two days later, when William had been called away unexpectedly on a business venture in Kent, a messenger came to the Coleman Street house not long after terce and left a packet for Mistress Shore. He told the servant he would return at the same time the next day for an answer.

Curious, Jane used her knife to open the bulky missive, not recognizing the rose seal, and gasped as she looked inside. A pearl the size of a filbert and set in the center of a golden rose dangled from the end of a velvet ribbon that was wrapped around a piece of parchment.

I would see you again, Mistress Shore, if you will accompany
my man on the morrow. Fear not, your husband is detained
and shall not hinder you, should you choose to come.

Jane blinked several times before she believed the signature:
Edward R.

"The king," she said out loud, and Ankarette looked up from
her mending and asked if Jane had spoken. Quickly stowing the
letter and necklace back into the packet, she replied:

"Aye, I do believe I need a cup of ale, good Ankarette. When
you have fetched it for me, I would like to be alone apace before
I prepare to tend the shop."

When she was finally by herself, she sat by the window, removed
the contents of the packet again, and placed the necklace and the
letter beside her on the window seat. She stared at them both for
a long time, her mind moving as fast as a hare fleeing a hound.
She was no fool; she was certain she knew what this meant—what
Edward wanted. But was it what she wanted? Or did that matter? How could she refuse? He was the king; she was his subject.

Jane knew she should enlist God's help or at least the Virgin
Mary's, and maybe even Sophie's. But her instinct told her to make
her own decision and sort it out with God later. If the truth be told,
she was disappointed in Him after her dismissal by the dean of
the Court of Arches. God obviously did not listen to insignificant
young female supplicants, so why should she consult Him now.

She hugged herself and knelt upon the seat, opened the window to the wintery sky, and stared over the rooftops of her beloved
London. Having the city thrumming below her always gave her
strength; she could disappear in the alleys if she chose and still find
friends to shelter her should she decide to run away from the king's
advances. It comforted her to know that London would hide her.

But why run away, Jane Shore? her mischievous imp asked her.
Had she not wanted to escape from this prison of a union, this

sham of a marriage bed? Perhaps William would divorce her once
he knew she had given herself to the king. Aye, he could wring
whatever business deal he could from Edward as the price of her
freedom, could he not? She had to laugh at herself then. Imagine
William threatening the king, she thought, but she could not. From
all she had heard, Edward did not seem to care one whit for a
lady's virtue or her husband's price. She rightly assumed he would
not give a fig about cuckolding her husband. She felt a pang of
guilt thinking about her husband, but as he was absent, he would
never know, she tentatively reasoned. And if he did, would he care?
She could not say, but she imagined he might tell her to "be pleasant, wife," as he had with Hastings, hoping for royal business. But
what of her own virtue? If she were ashamed of the looks she had
received in Greenwich Park, how much more viciously the tongues
would wag if she were to become the royal mistress.

What of the queen? Did the king not care about his wife's
feelings? The Grey Mare, as she had been dubbed by Londoners
many years ago, was known to be a cold, unapproachable woman,
for all her beauty. However, Jane had to admit, she had never heard
a whiff of scandal about her, unless you counted the gossip about
how potions may have been used to win Edward. Ah, but mayhap
Queen Elizabeth was a cold fish in bed and that was why Edward,
disappointed, cast elsewhere. And now apparently she, Mistress
Jane Shore of Coleman Street, had swum unsuspecting into his net.

She groaned. What was she to do? She longed to leave dreary,
impotent William and discover what it was like to be cherished
and desired. She looked down at the necklace and lightly rubbed
the lustrous surface of the pearl with her fingertip. She did not
dare put it on lest its temptation decide for her. But the thought
shamed her; it was shameful to be bought thus, and how dare the
king think she could be!

She held the necklace against her throat and imagined facing
Edward, alone somewhere in the labyrinth of the king's apartments,

his enormous figure making her feel like a small child. Would wearing the necklace signify her consent, or would it merely signify flattery and gratitude for such a gift? If she wore it and then refused him, would she have to return it? Would he snatch it from her throat? She held the jewel to her skin, the cold gold causing her to gasp. She imagined his fingers caressing her neck, and she grew afraid of her own thoughts.

"Mistress, you are needed downstairs." Her servant's voice broke her reverie, and she hurriedly hid the necklace.

"Thank you, Ankarette. You may enter and ready me for the shop," she called, going to the large wardrobe and selecting a simple but elegant sage green gown. She was grateful for the interruption, she had to admit, and hoped the morning routine would divert her mind.

But later at the shop, where she would preside whenever William was out and now found herself reorganizing a shelf full of delicate gauzes, she was unable to occupy her mind with anything but the king's summons.

Was she so certain the king expected her to come to him on the morrow? And if he did, would the encounter be a one-time event? What if she refused? Could she send the necklace back with a polite note? What happened when one said no to a king? Could that be construed as treason? She had no idea, but she shivered, imagining how she and William might be punished. Dear God, she panicked as a bolt of silk slipped from her grasp, could he throw her in prison? Surely not, she told herself, picking up the blue cloth and examining it for dust, but she sensed that refusing the king was a good deal more serious than refusing Will Hastings.

Will's kindly face came to mind, his hand lifted in salute as it was on that day in Greenwich Park. He, too, had desired her, she knew, and she had deftly discouraged him. There had been no recriminations, and she had not heard from him anew. True, he was in Calais, but had he been intent upon catching his sea nymph, as he had called her, surely he would have written or tried again. She pondered the contrast between these two powerful men, both attempting to reel her in like some elusive grayling: Hastings's bait had been a subtle and respectful invitation to her and her husband to ride into the country with him; the king's was a costly bauble and a cryptic note delivered to her in secret. Despite his reputation with ladies, to Jane there was something in Will Hastings's aspect that was trustworthy. And his unswerving loyalty to Edward was renowned throughout the realm.

It occurred to Jane that had the lord chamberlain been in London, she might have consulted him. He would have advised her, she knew it in her heart, and the idea of sharing an intimacy with Hastings intrigued her: she had never befriended a man before. For good St. Cuthbert's sake, she reprimanded herself, why was she thinking about Hastings? Holy Mother of God, but her mind was running like a brook in springtime, her silent babbling never-ending.

"Good day to you, Mistress Shore." The man's voice so close by made Jane jump. "I beg your pardon, mistress, I did not mean to alarm you. Your journeyman told me where to find you."

In the gloom at the back of the shop, she made out the White Boar badge on his tunic and knew him for Richard of Gloucester's man. "Sir? How can I help you?"

"My lord duke asked me to give this to Master Shore or to you," he said without expression, bowing slightly and holding out a letter. "He said you might be expecting it."

Jane thanked him, unsure if she should give him a groat for his pains but decided against it. The man had a haughty air and might be offended. It appeared he did not expect a response to the letter as he turned on his heel and exited into Coleman Street. She smiled. It seemed Richard of Gloucester liked to surround himself with men as solemn as himself.

Master Shore, we greet you well. As I promised when last we met, I would like to purchase three ells of the gold-and-green damask in question and whatever trim Mistress Shore deems appropriate for my consort, her grace the duchess, who has a delicate complexion and brown eyes. I pray you, forward the invoice along with the cloth to my town house, Crosby Place in Bishopsgate, and my treasurer will see you are properly recompensed.

R. Gloucester

The order distracted her from her dilemma, and she whiled away another hour holding up lace, fur, and embroidery trims against the satin cloth before making the perfect choice.

Back in her chamber, she paced about the room. By all that is holy, she was not thinking clearly today. She knew after all the to-ing and fro-ing she had done earlier that her decision could only be made by stripping her soul bare. She must burrow down to the most important question and answer it, if she were to sleep soundly that night. Ah, but did she dare voice that question?

Jane took a deep breath and forced herself to probe the secret part of her heart, that part where morals and conscience dwelled and where she feared to linger. Was she indeed an immoral woman . . . a trollop? There, she had said it. In truth, it was not easy to define what she thought she was, and she balked at thinking herself wanton. And yet . . .

"Admit it, Jane," she said aloud. "You desire to know love with a man yet fear being dubbed a common wagtail." Aye, that was the nub of it. "'Tis the devil's work. He is tempting me, I am certain of it," she said, and she crossed herself. She wondered what her family might say. She smiled to herself as she imagined Bella's shocked face. Or, might she be envious?

Jane was indeed facing a moral test, with or without God's

probable ire. However, at that moment, she would not worry about her soul, for she was certain merely wanting to bed a man other than her husband was a grave sin, and she was guilty of that every time she imagined herself in Tom Grey's arms.

However, she reasoned, did she not love Tom with all her heart? Surely that made her desire for him better than mere lust. Besides, at the time she would have offered herself to Tom she had been free. If the king wanted her, and she said yes, it would be adultery for both of them. She slapped the post on her tester bed, sending a shower of dust from the canopy above onto the coverlet. Was she willing to sin with Tom but not with the king? Sweet Mary, Mother of God, these were heady thoughts for the young woman, who had never before been permitted to make such a life-altering decision in her twenty-three years.

And then she came to a dazzling solution thanks to a sliver of London gossip she had remembered. If she disappointed the king, he would surely reject her. He could not punish her for being inexperienced, for not knowing how to please, could he? But, and so it was said, when the king was bored with a mistress, did he not pass her on to Will Hastings or, more importantly, to his stepson, Tom Grey? She hugged herself. Aye, she would agree to give herself to Edward on the morrow, but she would lie there like a dead fish, and he would be frustrated, impatient, and throw her aside as usual. "And, as Lord Hastings is in Calais," she crowed to the woven woman holding a rose in the tapestry opposite the bed, "the marquess of Dorset, my Tom, will be the lucky man."

Much cheered by her plan, she called out to Ankarette to ready her for bed, and slipping the necklace under her pillow, she began to pull off her stockings and roll them into a ball.

It had taken her the best part of twelve hours of her allotted twenty-four to decide what to do. She had another twelve ahead of her to while away in worrying.

It peeved Jane that Edward had been so sure of himself that he had sent a litter with one of his squires of the body at the appointed hour. But as it was raining—again—she was glad not to have to ruin the hem of her carefully chosen gown in the soggy debris that littered Coleman Street that morning. Damn, she thought, she had meant to send for the gong farmer to clear out the latrine. The rats had sorted through much of the kitchen leavings in the alley, and she saw one scuttle away as she bade farewell to the apprentice Wat, giving him charge of the shop in her absence.

"I shall not be long," she told him as he stood forlornly watching her in the doorway.

"What shall I tell Master Shore when he returns?" He was half in love with his master's wife, and so Jane took advantage of his weakness to embroil the poor man in a ruse.

"That I was called to my father's house. No need to tell him about the litter and the escort, in truth." Seeing his confusion, she took pity on him and pressed his hand. "Besides, he will not be back until after I return, so do your work and stop worrying."

"As you say, mistress," he assented, looking in wonder at her hand on his. Then he turned and disappeared through the kitchen to the shop. Relieved, Jane was about to shut the sturdy oak door, when she heard Sophie's voice calling from across the street.

"God's teeth!" Jane swore under her breath, wishing to avoid her friend at this moment. John Norrys, one of Edward's squires and her escort, was becoming impatient, and Jane decided to shut the front door and stand in the rain to shorten the conversation with Sophie.

"Jane, *lieveling*," Sophie greeted her, worry creasing her wet forehead as she eyed with suspicion the vehicle and its badgeless yet imperious escort. "Vhere do you go today? Are you not to manage the shop in Villiam's absence?"

Jane could not meet her friend's honest eyes. "'Tis my father's business I am on, Sophie," she lied, hating herself. "Forgive me, but I cannot stay."

She moved toward the litter, but Sophie put out her hand to stay her and inadvertently moved Jane's heavy cloak to one side, revealing a far more elegant gown than would be necessary to visit the Mercery. "You do not tell me the truth," Sophie lamented. "Is it Master Grey?" she asked in a hoarse whisper. "Ah, Jane, I beg of you, do not go."

"Nay, certes it is not," Jane retorted with a falsely high titter. Extending her hand to the escort, she stepped into the litter. "I regret I cannot stay longer, Sophie."

As the squire mounted his horse, Sophie peered into the opening of the vehicle. "Jane Shore, you vill please tell me vhere you are going."

Jane took a deep breath and demurred. "You will not approve, dearest Sophie, but I will satisfy your curiosity as long as you do not preach morality to me. I have been summoned by the king."

Sophie gasped, stepped back, and crossed herself as the litter carriers moved off toward Lothbury Street. *"In Godsnaam,"* she said to herself. "She has gone mad."

Jane leaned back against the cushions, careful not to shift her weight too abruptly and upset the balance of the unstable vehicle. Sophie's visit had unsettled Jane. Would her friend believe it was her duty to tell William? She shook off the fear, knowing that Sophie would never betray her, as she would never betray Sophie. Ah, but Sophie would never do anything to warrant betrayal, Jane admitted; she was too good. She put her friend from her thoughts, glad of the litter's seclusion from prying eyes that might recognize her in the Chepe. Edward must be well practiced in the art of clandestine dealings, she told herself, commending his planning.

Even so, yesterday's conviction was giving way to misgivings, which Sophie's dismay had intensified, and soon the necklace felt as though it was burning a hole in her throat. She swallowed and concentrated on the activities in the street. They were passing under the Ludgate, and the escort tossed a coin to the gatekeeper, who bowed low and tested the coin between his teeth. In the Old Bailey and under the city wall, young boys were kicking around a football made from a straw-stuffed pig's bladder, and one of her porters had to avoid tripping over a wiry towhead intent on scoring a goal. "By St. Jude!" the man swore as the litter lurched and Jane clutched the handrail. "Out of my way, you clodpole."

"Says who? The king?" the boy retorted, cocking a snoot while his fellows cheered him on.

"Aye," replied the mounted escort, maneuvering his horse between the litter and the players, "in fact he does. Now hop it."

Jane smiled as the boys stood agape, and they stared curiously at the litter, trying to see who was inside. Soon she was recognizing the magnificent row of inns on her left belonging to their graces the bishops of Exeter, Bath and Wells, Chester, and Worcester along the Strand or high street of Westminster. The porters huffed over the Strand Bridge, from where she could see the spire of St. Martin's set among the fields to her right, then the vineyard and gardens of the great abbey church of St. Peter in front of them, and she knew they were at Westminster.

The little group passed through a privy gate near the river into the king's courtyard, and Jane was ushered quickly up an outside staircase to a door on the third floor of the royal lodgings and told to wait in a richly furnished chamber that had as its focus a huge tester bed, its curtains shot with threads of silvers. She stared long and hard at it. Alone, she stood in front of the cheerful fire, warming her hands and lifting the hem of her gown to dry her stockings and little leather shoes.

"I am pleased you have come, Mistress Shore." Edward's greeting startled her, and she reddened, stepping away from the hearth and sinking into a deep curtsey. "I had almost convinced myself that you would not."

Jane looked up at the magnificent figure towering over her, conceding that her earlier vision of this encounter had not been so far-fetched. He was smiling, a smile that reached his eyes. She lowered her gaze and murmured, "God's grace with you, my lord."

"Let me take your cloak, mistress. I regret I chose such a miserable day to renew our acquaintance."

Jane untied the neck cord and let Edward slip the damp, heavy mantle from her shoulders. His eyes lingered for a moment on the necklace. "I hope the gift pleases you, Jane? I had it made especially for you, and I knew pearls would become you."

Jane was now visibly shaking. Dear God, what had possessed her to come here today? She clutched the folds of her gown to steady herself and hoped her voice would not give away her trepidation. Then a snippet from Roman de la Rose eased her mind:

> Who wishes to be loved must not too dear
> Hold his own treasure, but good will acquire
> By generous gifts.

Certes, Edward understood about courtly love; she had only to play the game. Her trembling ceased.

"'Tis a beautiful necklace, your grace," she said, fingering the precious pearl, "but why do I deserve it?" She hoped she sounded like the ladies in the poem.

"Beauty always deserves the beautiful, Jane," Edward purred, drawing her onto a small settle and holding her hand. She looked down and might have laughed: it looked like a bird's foot in a bear's paw. Indeed, she felt like the poppet her brother had given her to play with when she was six. She could smell orrisroot on the king's clothes, masking the usual manly scent of horses and sweat. His touch was as light as a feather as he explored her fingers.

"Your grace, I almost did not come today," Jane said in a rush, firmly pulling away her hand. "You are aware that I am a married woman, are you not? I do not know how to behave here and"—she rose and, stepping lightly to the fireplace, tried to bluff—"and I am unsure of what you expect of me."

Edward could not be certain at that moment if he were addressing an innocent girl or a practiced paramour. He was intrigued, but Jane was disconcerted by his amused chortle; she did not think she deserved his mockery. "I see no reason for laughter, my lord," she said, sounding hurt, and unhooking the necklace, she placed it on the table. Then she stared into the king's face with bravado, although her hands were clasped as if in prayer. Again, intrigued by this innocent display, Edward patted the seat next to him. For a moment, as she lowered her eyes, he thought she would submit, but then she raised her head, and striking a courageous pose, she blustered: "If I return your gift, will you allow me to return home, or will you have me thrown in gaol for disobedience—or whatever my crime is." She stood facing him, feet planted wide apart, arms akimbo, and chin thrust forward.

This time Edward, his long legs sprawled out in front of him, threw back his head and guffawed. "How could I even think of imprisoning such a beauty? Certes, *that* would be a crime, although if the court could see you now, Jane," he teased, wiping his eyes, "they might wonder at your lack of respect for your king. Look at yourself, my dear, you have to admit you make quite a picture. Look!" He pointed to the silver mirror framed in ebony upon the wall.

His unthreatening posture and infectious laughter made Jane obey, and she smiled sheepishly back at him in the polished surface, returning her arms to her sides. She saw his face soften as their eyes met, and she remained still as he rose and walked toward her. His mouth was on hers before she could resist, and its warmth surprised her. Even more surprising was how readily she opened hers to invite his hungry tongue.

She was on her tiptoes, her neck awkwardly crooked, and so Edward lifted her up to him with one practiced motion as though she weighed nothing. His desire was rising hard and high, and he sensed that she must be feeling it, too. Not a man who enjoyed taking a woman by force, however, he pulled away slightly. "Are you ready for me, Mistress Shore?" he asked.

Jane stiffened at the use of her formal married name, but there was no doubt she was aroused. She felt his hand reach into her gown, and a exquisite sensation swept through her as his expert fingers fondled her breast. A sudden panic overcame her as she remembered her plan, her foolproof plan. She was supposed to be dully dutiful and disappoint him to save herself for Tom.

"Well, Jane, are you?" Edward breathed in her ear.

"Aye, your grace, I . . ." She faltered for a second, trying to gain control of her surrendering body and feeling helpless so far off the ground. "I think I am. But, I pray you, if you would put me down, I would say something."

Edward reluctantly did as she asked, but his fingers began unlacing the interminable ties on the back of her dress. "Whatever you have to say, Jane, I pray you be quick, for I cannot wait very long to have you."

He was only half listening, expecting a few words about adultery and morals, but he was arrested midlace by Jane's announcement. "I am not what you think. I am a virgin."

"Nonsense!" was all he could think to say, his expression incredulous, his hands stilled. He was disappointed she affected such a lie; he had expected her to bypass the tedious court game of pretense and dissembling. Aye, he had taken her for an innocent, but in courtly wiles, not sexual ones.

He stepped back, his desire obviously dampened. "You are married to William Shore, are you not? And you were old enough to have consummated that marriage, I can see," he said, more kindly now at the sight of genuine fear in her face. "Come, come, mistress, I will not harm you. But what is this falsehood about virginity? I find it impossible to believe."

Jane turned away from him, chagrined. "I swear by all that is holy, I am a virgin, your grace. I thought you should know." This was not how she had imagined the scene would unfold, but if it worked and he rejected her, then it fit her plan just as well. She was as puzzled by her own embarrassing admission as he was. "If you were expecting an experienced bedmate, I fear I will greatly disappoint you, 'tis all. I beg of you, my lord, do not be angry with me. I have told the truth. Pray, just let me go home."

His silence made her turn around to him, and far from ire, she saw genuine compassion in his eyes. "I am sorry for you, Jane, truly I am." Then he grinned. "But in truth I am sorrier for William Shore. What a fool!" This made Jane smile, and the king chuckled. "Forgive me, Jane, I am not laughing at you nor, God in his mercy, am I angry with you. Far from it; I am delighted by you. I pray you, sit here beside me and tell me how you could still be a maid." He patted the foot of the bed, and timidly Jane perched on the edge. "I promise to just listen."

She kneaded her hands in her lap until Edward covered them with one of his. Could she really talk to him about William's failing? She had only ever told Sophie, oh, and the dean of Arches, to be sure. She thought for a moment and then, inspired, she began to recite:

"A cock without a crow, like a soldier without a foe," wishing she could have found a more dignified comparison. "Or like a farmer without a hoe, or . . ."

"Yeast without the dough," Edward joined in. "My poor Jane. How, of all women, could he have resisted you?" Then he grinned again. "Perhaps William cannot be cuckolded if he is not a true husband. Does that cheer you?"

Jane did not feel at all cheered by her predicament. "I suppose, your grace." How foolish she felt. Now Edward would not want her at all, and, what was worse, would probably run to Hastings and Tom with her humiliating story. Damn her runaway tongue!

But Edward had no such thoughts. She was now even more of a treasure in his eyes than she had been when she had walked through his door. He gently took her chin between his fingers. "It seems my necklace is a paltry gift compared with the one you are about to give me, my dear. It becomes my very pleasant duty to teach you the art of lovemaking," he said, and he pushed her gently onto her back.

Jane's headdress had fallen off and now her hair spilled around her on the tapestried coverlet in a river of gold. Edward grasped a fistful of its thick softness and bent to kiss her waiting mouth. He was gentle with her, guiding her in undressing him slowly to reveal his nakedness first. He led her fingers to his erection and urged her to stroke it lightly, easing her fear of it. "All it wants is to pleasure you, sweet Jane, but only when you, too, are good and ready," he said, delighted at how quickly she was gaining confidence.

Jane was fascinated by the velvet skin she felt between her fingers and yet how hard the member had become. Whatever she was doing obviously pleased Edward. He moaned softly, then abruptly moved away.

"You are learning too fast, Jane," he told her, not wanting to frighten her with his urgency. He flipped her over on her stomach, untied the rest of her many ribbons and laces and removed her clothes with practiced ease, congratulating himself on his own sumptuary laws, which forbade the wearing of corsets by any lower than a knight's wife. Jane shivered with excitement when Edward ran his hand over her bare buttocks, and she felt the dampness between her legs with which she had only been familiar when she had pleasured herself.

"Now let us see what my necklace has purchased," Edward teased. Turning her over again, he marveled at her perfect breasts, tipped with pink and more than even his hand could hold. Jane closed her eyes as he began to play with her nipples, putting his lips to her flat belly and slowly kissing her all the way up to her waiting mouth. All her plans for lying there limp were forgotten as she moaned, "I cannot resist, my lord. I do believe I am ready."

Wincing for only a second or two, Jane finally knew why she had saved her maidenhead for this moment. What pleasure a man and a woman could give one another, she realized as Edward moved inside her and soon climaxed with a short shout of ecstasy.

Sweet Mother of God, I have pleasured the king, she thought triumphantly, feeling assured she was indeed a desirable woman, and she delighted that it had not been the chore Sophie had described. Then she felt Edward's fingers arousing her nipples again while he slipped down between her thighs. Suddenly the world exploded as if in flashes of bright light, and her hands reached for Edward's head, tousling his hair and pushing him to pleasure her again. The waves of hitherto unknown and untold bliss washed over her, and she cried out without inhibition.

"Shall I stop, Jane?" Edward lifted his head and grinned. "You were indeed ready." He rolled off her and pulled the sheet up around them both.

"For three and twenty years I have waited for this, my lord," Jane managed to utter. "Dear God, but I must be a wanton. My friend Sophie told me the act was a duty, and thus I never imagined such transports."

Edward stroked her belly. "Madam, you are no wanton, but I must tell you that you are made to be loved." He propped himself up on his elbow and was at once serious. "From the moment I first saw you, I knew I wanted you, and as I am used to having my own way, you were not to know you could not escape me. My instincts about women are rarely wrong, but I have to admit I was wrong about you. I had imagined you more willing that you were." He grinned. "However, I was right about your being a wanton, was I not?"

Jane flushed, nodding. She timidly put out her hand to touch his face and caressed his mouth with her thumb. Dear God, she thought, here she was lying and talking with the king, King Edward the Fourth of England. Surely, she must be dreaming. A guilty thought about Bella seeing her thus flitted through her mind. This was an event she would not share with her sister.

"What gave me away, your grace?"

Edward took her hand and kissed the palm. "You stared at me boldly when you were presented, as though you were taunting me, flirting with me." Jane was astonished; she had no idea her stare that day was anything but curious. "And your body offered all I could desire," Edward was saying. "I confess I had heard of you through my chamberlain, and I was curious. He was quite smitten with you from the little he told me." He did not mention he knew of her rejection of Hastings.

At the mention of Will, Jane removed her hand. "Lord Hastings is a kind man. My own father, however, was never kind."

Edward made a mental note not to reveal to his friend that Jane's regard for him was paternal and nothing more. He relaxed, relieved that Will was not a rival for Jane's affections.

"Your father was unkind?" Edward asked. "Tell me about your family, Jane."

"Occasionally he would lash out," Jane acknowledged. "He doted on my little sister, Isabel, but he found fault with everything I did and said. I suppose I was headstrong, and I disappointed him. My tongue often gets me into trouble and has frightened off suitors. Until William. And 'tis only because he is ambitious that he took me. He had avoided marriage, and now I know why."

Edward took her into his arms and played with her long hair. "Do you hate Shore?"

"Nay, my lord. I do not hate the man, but I hate the position he has put me in. I am unloved, unfulfilled, and am denied the joy of motherhood. How I long for my own babes." She teased him then, smiling. "You, on the other hand, have enough children to relinquish one or two."

"Aye, I have a quiverful already, Jane," Edward said softly. "My wife has suffered my philandering all these years, but she will not tolerate another bastard." His voice turned serious. "You understand what I am saying, do you not? I would have to send you from court."

Jane sat up with a start and swung her legs over the side of the bed, noticing the floor was a long way down. "Send me from court? Do you mean you intend to see me again?"

It was Edward's turn to smile. "Certes, I do and often. I cannot remember when I have been so at ease with a woman," he said, but did not add "except for Bess." He got up and came around to help her to the ground, holding her from him to again drink in the curves and smoothness of her body. "By God, but you are beautiful. You know you have a colt's tooth, do you not?"

Jane laughed. "A colt's tooth, your grace?"

"It means a youthful and sensual vigor. You make me feel young again." He went to the table and picked up the necklace. Aye, Jane thought watching him, he may have eaten too much and lost his famous athletic figure, but he had not lost his sexual prowess. Tenderly, Edward clasped the necklace around her throat and bent and kissed first one breast and then the other.

"Time for you to go, Mistress Shore. You should be home when your husband returns. I hope he will not be too angry that his jaunt to Kent was for naught. I found out too late the customer I had arranged for him to see has been in Bruges this past fortnight."

Jane was again enjoying touching the satiny surface of the pearl and her eyes grew wide. "You arranged for him to go away?" Why was she not surprised? "Certes, I should have known." Aye, there was much she should have known, she realized wistfully.

Edward had already pulled on his chemise and was motioning for her to dress. "Draw the curtains about the bed, Jane, and I will send a tiring woman to you. One of my esquires will be here to help me, and I would protect you from gossip." For now, he refrained from adding. He vowed to teach Jane Shore more about the art of love and life at court; she was a most apt pupil. He was also already dangerously close to falling in love.

Edward put his head out of the door and called to a page who was waiting in the corridor. "Find Sir Walter and send him to me here." Gathering up his discarded clothes, he watched as Jane slipped the fine lawn chemise over her head, concealing that luscious body. On her part, Jane wondered what the tiring woman would make of the stranger wearing a valuable necklace in the king's bed.

"Am I allowed to keep the necklace, your grace?" Jane suddenly wondered.

"Foolish girl, you did not need to ask," Edward said, impressed that she did not expect it. This was a young woman of good breeding, he mused, pleased with his choice. It did not occur to him that he was selfishly ruining yet another gentlewoman's reputation. "Norrys will escort you home, Jane, and you will hear from me ere long, I promise you." He took her in his arms and kissed her. "You have pleased your king well."

"But did I please the man?" Jane asked, feeling fearless.

Edward put her down, grinning. "Aye, him, too."

"Then I am content, for you have surely made a woman of me."

There was a knock on the door. "I regret I must leave you. Pull the bed curtains around you while I am being dressed. May God go with you until we meet next."

"So, you mean it. I am to return?"

Edward nodded happily. "Certes, you shall return, and the sooner the better. Now quick, back into bed with you." He pulled a face. "I regret I cannot join you."

All the way home, Jane heard the words "the sooner the better" repeated in her head. From her litter, she watched Londoners going about their business, and she was astonished that they did not stop and stare at her. Could they not see into her heart and know her as a royal mistress? she wondered. How different she felt, and whole. The tryst had lasted but an hour and yet her life had changed. She touched her breasts under her mantle, marveling that they had known the king's lips upon them.

She had but one regret: the man who had taken her maiden-head was not the man she believed she loved. In her mind, she had betrayed Tom with Edward, yet, oddly she did not feel guilty. Instead her head was digesting the incredible fact that three men desired her, and none was her husband. Who could blame her for succumbing to the king; had he not desired her from the first day they met?

There was no turning back, she realized with grim resignation. She was now a whore, a wagtail, a wench, whether with a king or a yeoman. Perhaps her father had been right all along, she had to admit. One thing was certain, now Jane had tasted the joy of lovemaking, she had no intention of living without it.

As she crossed behind St. Paul's, Jane forced herself to invent a plausible story for her absence should William have returned early. Would William be able to tell she was no longer the wife to whom he had bidden farewell earlier in the day? Would her face betray her? And what if it did, she suddenly thought. She could be such a silly goose! Yet she feared her husband's displeasure. Certes, she would not dare to tell him with whom she had dallied, but if William suspected she had been unfaithful, mayhap he would cast her off. For a second she rejoiced that she had solved her problem and chided herself for not thinking of it before, but then reason stepped in. Aye, and where would that put her? Out on the street, she mused ruefully, because where could she go? Her parents would disown her, Sophie had her own worries with so many mouths to feed, and the only aunt she knew who might take her in lived in Devon. Nay, she must not allow William to suspect a thing.

Turning up Coleman Street, she settled on a lie, but as it turned out, William was not home yet. Relieved, she ordered hot water be brought upstairs for her bath. When her husband did arrive, he heard her happily singing and splashing in the copper tub in her solar. William was relieved; he was in too foul a mood to seek his wife's company, and he shut himself in his closet to brood over who had sent him on a fool's errand that day.

Another man had been sent on a similar errand that morning, but Tom Grey had chosen to ignore his stepfather's request to examine a new courser somewhere in the wilds of Essex. Instead, he happened to be standing in a covered stairwell opposite the king's lodgings as Jane Shore left by the back staircase.

"God's teeth," he seethed, understanding immediately why the lady was being led quickly to the litter waiting in the courtyard and whisked out into the village of Westminster with only one knight as escort. "The king has seduced my sweet Jane." No wonder Edward had wanted him gone. Hastings must have given away Tom's interest in Mistress Shore all those months ago, and he cursed his father-in-law. How had Edward even found Jane? His surge of temper surprised him. He had been so sure that Jane loved him, but if she had given herself to that paunchy lecher, then why had she refused *him*? Because he had not entered into her fantasy of courtly love? He scowled. Come now, Jane, he thought, you cannot believe Edward will play the courtly lover for you. The only game he wants to play is hide-and-seek with his cock.

Tom slammed his fist on the balustrade, turned on his heel, and stalked back into the building.

SIX

London, March to June 1476

L ord Hastings watched the mercer William Shore walk toward
him in an antechamber of the king's lodgings at Westminster
and wished himself back in Calais.

Edward's letter had sounded urgent, and the chamberlain and
captain of Calais had reluctantly removed himself from his comfortable quarters at the castle to cross the angry channel at the end
of February. Suffering horribly from seasickness on the overlong
voyage, he had spent two days recovering at a Dover inn before
journeying to London. The road was treacherous following all the
rain, and once when his horse had stumbled so badly, Hastings
had been pitched off into the mud and had hurt his shoulder.
Edward better have a good reason to have called him back, Will
had thought, accepting Nicholas Knyveton's dry cloak and bundling
his own into a saddlebag. He grimaced now as he remembered
the scene in Edward's private closet, where he and the king often
spent time talking over the day's events.

"Certes, 'twas important, my lord," Edward had said, annoyed
that Will was not as pleased to be home as the self-centered king
thought he should be. "It has to do with the health and well-being
of your sovereign. Is that not reason enough?"

Will had bowed. "I am here to do as I am bidden, your grace.
You know full well I am your loyal councilor and friend and always
shall be. What is it you require of me?"

"Unbend, man!" Edward cajoled, never peevish for long, and was
mindful not to clap his friend upon his uninjured shoulder. "I am

sorry that you were green on board ship, but that was days ago. I have a delicate task in mind that I can trust to you alone. You are the finest diplomat I have, Will, saving perhaps Jack Howard, but he is my brother Richard's friend, not mine. You are my friend, and I count on you. Besides, you have knowledge that makes you the perfect person to bring this mission to a satisfactory conclusion."

What had drawn the two men together over the years was a love of risk, intrigue, and the pursuit of pleasure. At once, Edward's conspiratorial tone made Hastings forget his unpleasant journey. He leaned forward in his seat and waited to know what task Edward intended for him. He need not worry about Calais for a spell; Calais was in good hands, he knew—Jack Howard was his deputy, and the king had just praised the Suffolk councilor's skills. He was aware that Edward was in rare form by the slap on the back he had received, by the coin he had thrown to a page for bringing him wine, and now he was grinning from ear to ear.

"You are in good humor, I see, my friend," Will had remarked, jovially. "What have I been missing since I left London? And has it anything to do with my 'mission'?"

"Am I so transparent, Will?" Edward had laughed—a little too heartily, Hastings thought now. "I have never felt better, in truth. And I have you to thank, in part. Aye, I am coming to it, never fear. A little more than a month ago, I made the acquaintance of your paragon, Mistress Shore. Jane Shore."

The lord chamberlain had not been aware that his expression had changed, but Edward's tone told him. "I see I have touched a wound, my lord. You told me she had rejected your advance, and it so happened I received the mercers here one day and was transported by her beauty."

"Aye, I am sure you were, your grace." Hastings had tried not to think of Jane during those weeks in Calais, but there was no denying the ache he felt for the charming young merchant's wife. He had cursed his age, thinking it the reason for Jane's rejection.

Could Edward's dozen years fewer have made him more attractive? Nay, he had to admit to himself, it was more than that. Will did not have Edward's allure—not only was the blond giant handsome, easygoing, and a practiced lover, but he was the king. Nevertheless, Hastings was a man, and a man in love, and thus he had had a hard time suppressing his anger that Edward would go behind his back and snatch Jane away. He had pretended to be engrossed in scratching the proffered belly of Edward's wolfhound while he struggled to control his temper.

Might this be the time to remind Edward that his chamberlain was keeping safe the king's dirty little secret, that Edward had promised marriage to the beautiful Eleanor Butler to get her into his bed and then had conveniently forgotten the precontract, or promise of marriage, when he fell for and married Elizabeth? Edward had felt relief when poor jilted Nell had died forgotten in a nunnery, Will well remembered. And he remembered the drunken night when Edward and he were in exile in Bruges and the king had confided in his best friend. "Not even Bessie knows, Will, and you must swear by all that is holy that you will tell no one."

Will had wondered then what Elizabeth might say or do if she ever found out the precontract by law rendered her marriage to Edward bigamous and her children bastards. It would not be pretty, he had thought with grim humor. Neither man had spoken of it since, and so, in a quick slap to the hound's scrawny haunch, Will had decided then and there that Mistress Shore was not worth the loss of his king's confidence. After all, he was Edward's loyal and devoted liegeman first; he owed all he had attained to his younger master. So he put on a smile and encouraged Edward to tell of Jane's first visit. At the mention of her maidenhead, Will had reacted with surprise, and Edward had nodded and agreed: "I did not believe it either."

Poor Jane, Will thought now while pretending to read a

document and making her impotent husband wait. He could not help but wish he were the one to cuckold this pasty-faced mercer, but when it came to Edward, Hastings would not be disloyal, and he had decided he could champion Jane just as well by being her friend. The baron was a man of his word, and he would never break his unspoken promise to her on the hill at Greenwich. Thus it was for Jane's sake as much as for his sovereign's that he was standing here now with William Shore. Jane needed to be rid of the man.

Shore finally cleared this throat, and Hastings looked up, an eyebrow arched.

"You sent for me, Lord Hastings? How can I be of service?" He smiled, rubbing his hands. "A new gown perhaps?"

Hastings forebore to laugh at the man's blindness. "Master Shore, it has come to the council's notice that your wife has been seeking an"—he paused before slowly pronouncing—"annulment." Ah, that elicited a glimmer of something akin to concern, he observed. "I shall not go into the reason for it; that is between husband and wife, but I am advising that you do not challenge the petition."

Shore's mouth opened and closed twice before he asked, "How do you know of this?"

"Very little goes on in London that the council does not know," Hastings lied airily. "Having made your wife's acquaintance, I offered to expedite the process."

Shore was so taken aback by this turn of events that he merely stammered: "I see, my lord."

And now for the unsavory business of bribing him, Hastings thought, grimacing. He walked away a pace and without looking at Shore, stated: "It is my understanding that you have been looking into merchant adventuring. Am I correct?"

The mercer, perturbed by Hastings's knowledge yet intrigued by the turn in conversation, stammered, "You are, my lord."

The evident eagerness in his voice disgusted Hastings. Was the man not even going to pretend to fight for Jane?

"If I procure a place for you and fund your move to Bruges, will you grant your wife the annulment—upon the grounds originally sought?" There, he had said it, and hoped Nicholas, who was standing silently in a corner, did not lower his high opinion of his lord.

Shore's gap-toothed stare accompanied his weak "Aye, my . . . my lord." He wanted to ask why, but his thoughts were not organized.

"And if I effect this move, sir, I must have your word you will deal no more with Mistress Shore, other than returning those goods and chattels she is owed." Hastings could not believe the man did not appear to wonder why the lord chamberlain would involve himself in such a mundane business, but if he did not seek an explanation, then none would be forthcoming.

"I agree, my lord," the seemingly incurious man said as he signed the paper Hastings laid for him on the table. As he began meticulously dotting the *i*'s in his name, he suddenly hesitated and looked up. Ah, perhaps now the man would finally demand an explanation, Hastings thought. But instead, it seemed the mercer had his own condition that had nothing to do with Jane. "I must see to my business for a few more months before transferring to Flanders. I cannot go immediately; I have apprentices and journeymen to make provision for." It was only then that something else occurred to him. "Where will my wife go? Her father will not have her back, I can promise you," he said with disdain to no one in particular, "for it would not surprise me if she has lain with others, and neither he nor I would condone a wagtail abiding with us."

Hastings was not prepared for his own indignation; with uncharacteristic rashness, he struck William across the mouth. "Leave now, Master Shore, or I may rescind my offer," he menaced and was relieved when his victim, clutching his bruised face, fled from the room.

"Good riddance, you weedy, whey-faced puttock!" he barked at the closing door.

Dean Reynking gave a loud sniff and wiped his dripping, bulbous nose on his sleeve. "You have friends with influence, I perceive, Mistress Shore," he said, staring at Jane over the top of his spectacles. "I have here the papal approval for an annulment. 'Tis astonishing how quickly it was obtained—only four months; these things usually take years. It appears you are released of your marriage contract as of today, if you would but sign this paper."

Jane took the proffered quill and, smiling triumphantly, carefully inked her name: *Elizabeth Shore*, finishing with several curling loops below the final *e*. It pleased her that she had been able to flout this rheumy old priest's patriarchal prating about church law.

"God's will be done," Jane said in parting, and as she closed the door behind her, she smiled. "Or is it the king's?"

"The king?"

William Shore stared at his erstwhile wife in disbelief. Certes he had known of her attempts to seek an annulment, but as Dean Reynking had not yet summoned him to the Court of Arches to dispute the accusation of impotence, he presumed the cleric had given him the benefit of the doubt and had dismissed Jane, as any sensible man might a whining woman. It astonished him that Jane had succeeded without his testimony. However, the manner in which she had succeeded stunned him even more.

"The *king* arranged for a papal dispensation?" he spluttered. "Pray, why would he do that? Why would he care about you—a mere mercer's wife?" It annoyed him to watch Jane calmly pour herself some ale as though she had merely commented on the weather, and so he went to the window to stare out and organize his reeling thoughts.

William had not yet connected his meeting with Hastings to

the king. He had assumed Hastings had bought his silence so the
codding old man could seduce Jane, and he had seen no reason
to intervene and ruin his chance to fulfill his latest ambition to
grow prosperous with the adventurers abroad. His wife's charms
seemed fair exchange for such professional advantage. He was not
as short-sighted as Jane thought; he had sensed the chamberlain's
attraction to Jane from the moment the man had entered the shop
on Coleman Street. Had he not encouraged his wife to go on the
hunting spree, hoping thus to solicit more business at court? But
today's news that Hastings was acting on the king's behalf was
quite unexpected. Why would Edward concern himself with a
subject's unhappy marriage?

Before he could come to his own conclusion, Jane broke into
his ruminating with a throaty laugh. "Why would he care about
me? Is it not obvious?" She mocked him, enjoying herself.

Then the truth slapped him in the face and he whirled around.
"Good Christ! So that is the way of things, is it? The king would
have you as leman?" He gave an unpleasant laugh. "My wife a
king's whore?" he sneered. "Why, Mistress Shore, how you have
risen in the world." He glared at her with disgust. "God's bones,
but I am well rid of you!"

"And I you, William. You cheated me long before I cheated you,"
Jane retorted, setting down her cup with purpose. "You cheated
me out of a loving coupling, and you cheated me out of children."

William ignored her rebuke. "When exactly did you fornicate
first with our sovereign?" he spat. "And I am certain he was not
the first."

It was Jane's turn to leave fingermarks on the mercer's face as
she reached up and slapped him hard, shocking him into silence.

"Do you remember your futile journey into Kent in February?"
she asked. "Aye, I see you do. How do you think that was arranged?"

William fondled his stinging cheek and seethed inside. He had
wondered briefly at the time whether Hastings had sent him on

a fool's errand, but the man had been in Calais and so William had dismissed his suspicion. He glowered at Jane. "Wait until I tell your father," he threatened, hoping to instill some fear in this defiant woman.

Jane laughed. "My father has never cared for me, William. I was lost to him when I was but a child. And being as greedy as you, he may well see advantages to my being close to the king." She picked up her cloak and flung it about her shoulders. "I came here to tell you the truth before you heard the talk in the taverns. The king has shown me more kindness in one meeting than you have in a whole year. I bid you farewell, and God speed on your new venture. You may deliver my few belongings to The Mermaid, where I shall stay for now." She pulled off her wedding ring and placed it on the table. "Never let it be said I took anything from you."

"I should never have agreed to marry you." William scowled as he watched her glide from the room. "A pox on all women."

Events happened so quickly for Jane after that, she hardly had time to contemplate the dramatic changes in her life. Edward's ardent wooing flattered and delighted her. He kept his promise to the queen not to set up Jane in an apartment in the palace, as he had done with Elizabeth Wayte, but found her a small but well-appointed house near Hastings's residence on Thames Street.

"'Tis but a stone's throw from my mother's castle of Baynard," Edward told her after a satisfying afternoon in his bed. "You may not want to walk too close when she is in residence, which, thank the good Lord, is not often these days. You will meet her one day, Jane, and rest assured she will know who you are. Cecily Neville has her spies everywhere to keep her eye on her 'boys.' She does not approve of my way of life, which is a pity, because I believe she would like you, if the two of you could sit down for a conversation."

Jane resolved to avoid the duchess. "Your royal mother has quite a reputation, my lord. I cannot think what I would say to a duchess, let alone she who is known as Proud Cis. Why, she could have been our queen."

Edward grinned. "Aye, she never lets people forget she is queen by right, much to my queen's irritation." He rolled onto his stomach. "Mother has never quite been the same since my father and my brother Edmund were killed. Her life is now all prayer and seclusion. However, she can still reduce me, George, and Richard to puling boys when she wants to. But enough of her, we were talking of your house."

Jane kneaded the thick muscles of Edward's back, her hair caressing his shoulders, and she followed the several battle scars on his arms with her finger, trying to imagine her lover wielding his heavy sword and fending off the blows from another equally heavy weapon. How such a warrior could also be so gentle with her between the sheets she found intriguing and endearing.

"A house of my own." She savored the words. This was not a house of her father nor of a husband where she would be subservient, but one that she would run, where she could do as she pleased. She shivered with delight, and Edward rolled over, pulling her to him, thinking she was cold.

"Does that please you, my dear?" he asked, fondling her backside with his big hands. "'Tis not a very large house, but I dare not spend any more of my hard-won French pension on my mistress."

Jane laughed. "The only way you know how to win hard, your grace, is here in bed." Did she really say that? Sweet Jesu, she had dared to poke fun at the king and the failed French expedition. She held her breath.

Edward laughed so heartily he began to cough, and Jane found herself bounced off his ample belly and onto her side. She jumped off the bed and poured him some ale. "Your pardon, my lord. I regret I was disrespectful. Am I wrong to tease your grace?"

Edward downed the bitter brew and grasped her wrist. "'Tis what I love about you, Jane. You are fearless, and you treat me not

as your king but like a man. You make me laugh, and you warm
my heart as well as my bed." He flopped back onto the pillow, and
Jane crawled back beside him, pulling the bedsheet over them both.
"But I must caution you not to speak to me so playfully in front
of the queen. She does not have my sense of humor. In truth, she
does not have much sense of humor at all, and so I shall come
to you on Thames Street, where we can be ourselves and merry."

"I should like that, your grace. I should like that very much," Jane
said simply, and kissed his stubbled cheek, grateful for Edward's love.

Jane soon adapted to her new life on Thames Street, hiring
a steward, Martin, a cook, a groom, and a chamberer, who was
under Ankarette's stern direction. Ankarette slept on a pallet in
Jane's bedchamber, unless Will was there, when she shared Cook's
and Martin's room under the eaves. Jane relished having a separate bedchamber from the solar and used the money Edward had
given her to drape the tester bed with soft silks and the walls with
tapestries of mythological scenes, her favorite of which depicted
the sea nymph Galatea and her young lover, Acis. When Will
Hastings had visited to make sure she was comfortable, he found
himself curiously reluctant to ask if she had chosen it because of
his likening her to a nymph. He wondered if Jane thought on him
as the spurned old giant Cyclops, who had attempted to woo the
beautiful Galatea with music and delicate foods. He could not think
that Edward was the youthful Acis, however, and so dismissed the
analogy, unaware of Jane's secret passion for her Acis ideal, his
stepdaughter's husband.

Edward spared her from court gossip for a few months while
he spent time with her on Thames Street in between forays out
of London, once for the annual St. George's Day ceremony at
Windsor. "I cannot wait to show you off, my rose of London,"
he said one day in May, "but I shall not inflict that burden on
you until I believe you are ready." He twisted his mouth into an

amused grimace. "And when I think Elizabeth can tolerate you."

Subtlety was not one of Edward's virtues, and Jane lowered her head and pretended to concentrate on tying the neck ribbon on her shift to hide her shame. Aye, she was reminded again, she would be naught but a harlot in Elizabeth Woodville's eyes. But she was the royal mistress and must accept the consequences; she would not exchange her old life for any amount of respectability. How she looked forward to Edward's visits, responding to his ardor with an eager thirst to learn more about pleasing him and even more about her own awakening sensuality.

However, it must be said that each time Edward left her Jane did experience a few twinges of guilt before a larger, aching regret suffused her that her lover was not Tom Grey. She pondered whether he even knew of her new status, but decided that between Edward and Will, he was bound to have been informed. Would he care? That was the question that clawed at her now that she had the leisure for such thoughts.

Jane would have been gratified to know that the marquess of Dorset had undertaken to look into the matter of Mistress Shore. He had wandered into the Shore shop and pretended to look for some lace one day a few weeks after he had witnessed Jane leaving Westminster. "I was told Mistress Shore has the best eye for such things," he told William innocently. "Is she here?"

William was flustered; he detested the position in which Jane had placed him. "She is no longer my wife, my lord. I do not know where she is," William lied. He had been told to say this by Lord Hastings no matter who the speaker. Hastings had been as good as his word, and preparations were going along nicely for William's departure for the Lowlands. He had recovered from his outrage and was much more content celibate.

Despite the man's fine clothes and aristocratic air, which usually would have made William grovel for a possible sale, he wanted no reminders of his wagtail wife and hoped the courtier would leave. Bowing low, he pretended that he had another customer waiting.

Tom closed the door quietly behind him and walked down Coleman Street toward the Chepe, his mind turning over snippets of conversation he had overheard at court: the king was certainly merrier these days; Will Hastings was seen twice at an unfamiliar house on Thames Street; and he himself had been surprised when Edward had declined a bawdy evening in the city. Could the king have found himself a new mistress? And could that woman be Jane Shore? It was unlike the king to hide his paramours, which had sometimes infuriated Tom on behalf of his mother, but there had been no evidence of a new interest, just rumors. If it were true, and Jane that woman, it would mean that her profession of love for him had been but a ruse to release her from her humdrum life. But vain Tom Grey would not countenance such a ploy; had he not seen the truth in those marvelous green eyes?

Tom had been bored of late. Solving the mystery of the mistress might alleviate his ennui, he mused, kicking a mangy dog off the carcass of some unrecognizable animal. And if Jane were that woman, how amusing to win her back from the king. He relished the challenge, and grinning to himself, he set off toward Thames Street. A visit to his stepfather-in-law might provide a clue.

But Will Hastings was unusually taciturn that day, neatly evading Tom's prying questions and sending the young man away disappointed.

"Mistress Shore, what a pleasure to see you," her father's journey-man Matthew greeted her in the Lambert shop one rainy day in May. Jane smiled as the man and the other apprentices gathered around to welcome her back. She guessed the word had reached them about her divorce, but they appeared genuinely pleased to see her.

"'Tis good to see you all again," she said. "Is my father here?"

"I am here, daughter," her father's voice boomed down from the top of the staircase leading to the room where, only nine months before, she had sat in her green-and-golden dress to watch the king's procession. "What brings you back? Have you run out of money?"

Jane's smile faded along with those of the employees, who scattered at the sound of John Lambert's raised voice. She mounted the stairs and at the top came face-to-face with her scowling parent. "God's greeting to you, Father," she said pleasantly, staring her father down. How strange, she thought, for the first time I am not afraid of him. From his questions, she concluded William had not revealed her latest status. "I am here to buy stuff for two new gowns, and I would also have you recommend the best tailor. I need them a fortnight hence."

John lowered his voice to a hiss so he might not be overheard: "You want what? My recommendation for a tailor. How dare you, madam! How dare you set foot in my shop after you have shamed your mother and me with your annulment—falsely come by, so I hear."

"Then you heard wrong, sir. I was granted an annulment legally by the courts and with a papal blessing. William did not contest it. You cared not that you wedded me to an unfit husband and that I have been denied my rights as a woman and a mother. Both you and William betrayed me."

John ignored her accusations. "'Tis all over the Mercery that you have taken up with some popinjay from Westminster, selling yourself like a common whore," he said, outraged. "Is that who is paying for your gowns? If so, I do not want his sordid money. And you will get no credit here."

Strangely, his scorn and belittling failed to move Jane. She suddenly felt a rush of power in front of the man who had made her feel a failure all her life. She could not resist the sweet revenge in breaking the news herself. It would be about town soon, she had no doubt, so why not begin the delicious story here and now, from the horse's . . . nay, whore's mouth. Her tongue relished every word of her annoucement. "The popinjay from Westminster, Father, is none other than our sovereign lord King Edward himself." She smiled sweetly. "Are you certain you will not take his money?"

John fell backward onto a chair, speechless for once. Jane continued in a falsely pleasant tone as she turned to descend the stairs. "I am certain Matthew will help me with my purchases. There is no need for you to concern yourself any longer on my behalf. I pray you, tell Mother and Isabel that I am well and that I shall visit them anon."

She thought she heard her father's strangled "Aye," but she could not be sure over the loud beating of her heart. It had taken a sleepless night and an act of courage to face her father, and now she finally felt free of him.

Later, when she received her friend Will Hastings in her sunny solar, she related the story, laughing merrily over her own bravery. Will was delighted by Jane. How he enjoyed his short visits to her pleasant solar and made a point of stopping there on his way home whenever he was not needed at Westminster. He would slip in through the back garden gate in case his wife had set spies on him. Ever since Jane Shore had come into his and Edward's lives, Katherine Hastings had nagged him about her. He knew she believed Jane was his latest conquest, and there were times when he was tempted out of impatience to lie and claim Jane was indeed his mistress. He admired Katherine's Neville lineage and her intelligence, but he knew her for a spiteful witch upon occasion and had chastised her often for her coldhearted treatment of a servant. Jane Shore's kind heart was a welcome respite from his wife's sharp tongue.

"Were you listening, my lord?" Jane enquired, amused. "Your attention seems to have flown up the chimney with the cinders. Did you hear that I stood up to my father?"

He took her hand and raised it to his lips. "Aye, sweeting, I did. How old were you when you first decided to be a rebel, Jane Shore?" Then he laughed at her astonishment.

Edward sent a barge for Jane, not his royal barge, but it was as elegant a conveyance as Jane had ever traveled in. She now counted John Norrys among her admirers, as Edward's squire had continued to be a conduit between the palace and Thames Street and had grown to like the sunny disposition of his master's latest conquest. Jane always asked about his family, how his little son was faring, and complimented him on some new bonnet he was sporting. And he liked that Jane would insist on serving him ale or wine herself when he came bearing a message or to escort her to Edward. "She puts on no airs," he had confided to his fellow squire of the body, Sir Walter Hungerford, "but is always ready to laugh."

Jane settled into the cushions on the curtained vessel and watched the scores of small boats, wherries, and shouts ply the brown water of the Thames. Several washerwomen were slapping clothes against the rocks on the south bank, exchanging gossip and shouting a greeting to a boatman passing by. It was only early June, but the heat had been relentless and had sent the queen and her household down the river to her Placentia Palace of Greenwich, allowing Edward to entertain Jane for the first time at a small feast he was giving in honor of the visiting envoy from Brittany.

"I think 'tis time the court makes your acquaintance, dear Jane," Edward had decided after a night spent in her bedchamber. "By now you are hardly my best-kept secret. I want to acknowledge you, but I needed the queen to be absent, you see."

Hastings hid a smile. Nicely put, your grace, he thought.

Jane remembered now the evening at her house, when they had entertained Will Hastings as though they were a merchant and his wife. The two men had praised her cook's culinary efforts and had laughed at Ankarette's clumsy service as she attempted to control her shaking hands. Jane smiled to herself. Edward had been the very essence of kindness to Jane's maid, and after a few spills, Ankarette had settled down and even earned the king's praise and a shilling for her efforts.

When Will had made his farewells, he had kissed Jane's hand as he always did, but that night Jane noticed melancholy in the look he gave her as Edward put his arm about her waist and wished his friend a good night. Did Hastings disapprove, or, worse, did he still desire her? Jane wondered now. He had been so solicitous when she had first moved into her new house, and hardly a day had gone by that she had not received a visit or a token nosegay from him. She knew she would not be as confident about her first public appearance had it not been for his fatherly advice and courtly expertise. She hoped she was not causing the kind man pain.

The barge was passing the hospital of St. John, built out of the ruins of the Savoy Palace, which had been burned in the peasants' revolt in the previous century. Who would have believed a mercer's daughter was cushioned in the royal barge; she hardly believed it herself. She wished her sister might see her now, but thinking of Bella spoiled her mood. She did not want to be reminded of the uncomfortable visit she had recently made to Hosier Lane, when her mother and sister had sat stiffly side by side expecting a lambasting on John's return for entertaining Jane. In that ten-minute meeting, she found out her father had forbidden them to visit her on Thames Street, and her heart had hardened anew against him. She pushed the scene from her mind and concentrated on the oarsmen's blades and the evening ahead.

Soon she would be at Westminster wharf and have to make her entrance. She shivered—from excitement or fear, she could not tell—and she hoped her gown would please the king. It was of the palest of pale blue silk, cut with a square neck and high waistline. It fell in shimmering folds to the floor. She had purposely instructed the tailor to keep the bodice modest; she had no wish to flaunt her assets to the court. Covering the bare skin above the dark-blue lace trim of the bodice was Edward's gold and pearl collar. She was certain all would be aware of who she was by now and knew every eye would be critically evaluating the king's new mistress. Let them at least see that a mercer's daughter possessed good taste.

John Norrys took her hand to help her from the boat and tucked it under his arm for the short walk to the wharfside entry into the royal lodgings. "May I say that your beauty will eclipse all others tonight, Mistress Shore?" he told her as they mounted the spiral stairs.

"You may, sir, although I fear you flatter me," Jane replied, relieved. "I must confess my knees are a little unsteady, and knowing you are here to bear me up is comforting. 'Tis as well I am so small for if I faint away, I will not be much of a burden to carry off."

Norrys laughed. "You do not appear to be the sort of female that swoons, mistress."

"Just you wait, Master Norrys," Jane rejoined. "I may surprise you."

She was thankful Edward was waiting in the private antechamber where the stairs led, and she warmed to his welcoming smile. "Dear God, Mistress Shore, but you are ravishing," he told her, taking her hand to his lips as she rose from her curtsey.

"Not now, your grace," Jane told him, all too conscious of the entourage watching. She was delighted to see Will, who came forward and kissed her hand, his smile showing approval of her modesty. If Will Hastings was pleased, then she had chosen her wardrobe well, she thought happily. "Lord Hastings," she greeted him with another deep reverence.

Edward introduced her to one of his gentlemen of the chamber, Thomas Howard, Jack Howard's son, whose greeting was courteous, and then to the steward of the household, Lord Thomas Stanley, whose curt bow and pursed lips were anything but friendly. His tall, angular wife merely inclined her head, her unblinking eyes traveling up from Jane's pointed crackows to her deep blue velvet hennin with such speed, Jane wondered how Margaret Beaufort could have formed any impression of her, let alone the disdain that curled the woman's lip. Jane decided to tread warily around the Stanleys.

They were joined by Howard's wife, Elizabeth, and his stepmother, a plump little woman not much bigger than Jane, to whom Jane immediately warmed. "Lady Margaret is missing her husband, are you not, my lady?" Edward said, raising her from her reverence. "Jack Howard is one of the most trusted of my councilors, Mistress Shore. Unfortunately, he is deputizing for Lord Hastings in Calais, but you will meet him soon. Lady Margaret and Lady Elizabeth will be your companions today, and they will see that you come to no harm." He winked at Margaret, which caused her to wag a motherly finger at him. At once Jane felt comfortable; she had come to understand how Edward put everyone at their ease, noble or commoner.

"Come, now, ladies and gentlemen, let us not keep our guest of honor waiting any longer. Will, escort Mistress Shore to her place. Come, Lady Margaret, will you serve as my consort for our entrance?"

"Make way for the king!" called the usher, and at once the hall was hushed and the assembled group parted to allow the king to pass. He graciously accepted the bows made to him right and left and paused to have a word with this one and that until he reached his throne. His purple-gowned majesty, arresting stature, and charismatic presence filled the room as if someone had suddenly opened the roof and let in the sunlight. Despite their richly made garments and many jewels, the Breton delegation was cast into the shade.

Will gripped Jane's arm reassuringly, and they stepped out a few paces behind Lord and Lady Stanley and the younger Howards. Discreetly, Will led Jane up two steps to an alcove farther down the hall, furnished with three velvet-covered chairs, and begged her to take the center seat. "The Howard women will flank you, my dear Jane, and all will know you have their blessing," he reassured her. "Tonight you must watch and learn, and it may be that Edward will not speak to you, but all will know why you are here." He saw her flinch and patted her hand. "You need to hear the truth from me. I shall not dissemble; they will need to become used to you."

Momentarily forgetting her escort's conflicted feelings, Jane clung tightly to Will's hand as she took her seat. "Sweet Jesu, but I am terrified," she confessed as she faltered in her step. "Say I at least do not look like a harlot, my lord."

Will bowed gravely and took her hand to his lips. "Far from it, Mistress Shore, you outshine every lady here. You might be a duchess," he soothed, and added with a wink, "Good luck, my dear."

As Hastings made his way back to Edward's side, he overheard someone say to his neighbor, "So, she is the well-kept secret. I cannot say I blame the king." Hastings gave the man a look that would have withered a summer rose, but he marked the moment to share with Jane later.

The musicians in a facing alcove began to play softly on lutes and recorders, and Jane's spirits lifted. No one had laughed at her, no one had pointed at her, in fact most were ignoring her, and she felt brave enough to tweak the tight sleeves over her wrists, adjust her velvet bonnet, its veil floating in a cloud of white gauze down her back, and eagerly observe the proceedings.

It was then she had the odd sensation that someone was watching her, and she turned away from the scene by the throne, where Edward was clapping the ambassador on the shoulder and laughing, and she looked right into Tom Grey's eyes.

Jane could not say if her pounding heart sent the blood rushing to or from her face, but she was aware that every nerve in her body was alive to the sight of this man who had broken yet stolen her heart. Why had she not anticipated Tom's presence this day? He attended the king, so certes he was bound to be present. She gripped her fingers together and looked away. She had rehearsed what she might say to him when next they met, but now that he was coming toward her, the phrases fled her mind.

"My lord marquess, God give you a good evening," a voice at her elbow said. Jane was unaware that in those fleeting seconds Lady Howard had joined her in the alcove, and she was startled by Margaret's greeting. "Have you made the acquaintance of my new friend, Mistress Shore? Thomas Grey, marquess of Dorset." Margaret Howard made the introduction smoothly.

Jane was astonished by the generous word *friend* but so grateful, she could have kissed the plump matron. Before she lowered her eyes, she tried to send Tom a message to deny knowing her.

Tom bowed over Lady Howard's hand, murmuring, "Lady Margaret." Then he raised his eyes to Jane. "Mistress Shore and I have been acquainted for some time, have we not, mistress?"

Jane could not say if he deliberately chose to ignore her sign or truly wanted to be friendly. But if he were baiting her, she would not bite. She inclined her head, as Will had taught her a seated lady should, and furrowed her brow. "Perhaps you could remind me of the occasion, my lord. It must have been either at my father's mercery in the Chepe or when I was presented at court as a freewoman of the city earlier in the year, for I am not used to mingling with nobility and thus would have remembered meeting a marquess. But, if I am wrong, I am glad to make your acquaintance again, and this time I shall be certain to remember you." Her demure pretense infuriated Tom.

"As you wish, mistress," was his terse response. He bowed to Margaret, turned abruptly and walked toward the knot of courtiers around the king, leaving Jane chastising herself for her wayward tongue. She had not really wanted to send him away; she only wanted him to respect the delicacy of her position. She was not to know that delicacy was not in the young marquess's unimaginative repertoire.

"Oh, nicely done, Mistress Shore," Margaret Howard congratulated her young charge. "I cannot remember when I have seen vainglorious Tom Grey's flirting so nimbly deflected."

"Was he flirting with me, my lady?" Jane thought it wise to play the innocent. "I was merely answering his question." Looking over at Tom, she saw to her dismay that he was carrying a lovely young woman's hand to his lips, who simpered as he lingered over it.

"You remind me of a friend of mine." Margaret smiled. "A young woman of spirit who won the heart of the king's brother, Richard of Gloucester." Then she was serious. "A word of warning, my dear. Stay away from Dorset. He is none too bright and is his mother's darling, an unattractive combination in a man."

But Jane was too miserable to mark her words. Tom Grey's arrival had ruined her much-anticipated debut at court.

SEVEN

"The court has taken to Jane well, I believe. What do you think, Will?" Edward asked his friend two weeks later. "With Elizabeth still at Greenwich, it has been an ideal time to bring Jane out into the open." He grinned, coyly. "I do believe I am in love with her. Imagine, at my age!"

Hastings's hand faltered as he poured his king a cup of wine and placed it on the table next to the remains of a pheasant on a silver plate. They had dined in private in Edward's solar, and now Jane was waiting in Edward's bedchamber a wall thickness away. Ankarette had brushed her mistress's hair and sprinkled her silk chemise with rosewater and was hovering nervously in a corner, listening for the king's approach.

"Age has naught to do with love, your grace," Will answered, with grim confidence. "Let me in my ancient wisdom assure you of that."

Edward twirled the stem of his cup, watching the tawny contents climb the silver sides and slither back down. "Ah! Aye, my friend, I remember that delightful Mistress Rowena—I cannot recall her family name—from Leicester. I feared for your life then, for you were so smitten, it began to irk your Katherine. And, believe me, Will, you never want to irk a Neville female. My mother is proof of that." He laughed. "So, I am not in my dotage? It is possible to fall in love with another despite being devoted to Bess?"

Will nodded and allowed Edward to believe Rowena was his example. The vision of Jane lying naked in Edward's bed next door tormented him. "You can fall in love many times, Ned, but 'tis only when that love is returned that it is worth cherishing."

Edward looked at him quizzically, but as Hastings was now yawning, gathering his mantle and tugging on his boots, he decided his friend's remark did not require further discussion.

"When will you tell your wife about Jane?" Hastings suddenly asked, straightening up and confronting Edward. "Surely you will not take Mistress Shore with you to Fotheringhay for the reinterment? I would not be your councilor if I did not caution you. Duchess Cecily for one would not countenance the presence of a mistress at the solemn ceremonies for your father and brother. You must leave her behind, Ned."

Edward pouted. "I suppose you are right, Will. With the outbreak of the pox in the city, I had thought I would leave early and have time with Jane before everyone descends on Fotheringhay. But I will not be a disrespectful son. Nor will I risk offending God at this most sacred time. I have planned for this honorable reburial of my father and Edmund for a year now, and I would not want it said Edward Plantagenet dishonored their memory."

Fotheringhay, set in the marshlands of Northamptonshire, had been the York family seat since Edward's great-grandfather, Edmund of Langley, was granted the castle in the last century. It had been sixteen years since Richard of York and his son Edmund had been killed at the battle of Wakefield during the war between York and Lancaster, their heads set upon Micklegate in York. They had then been given a perfunctory burial, and, although long overdue, it was time for Edward to bring them home to rest in the family crypt at Fotheringhay church, whose extensive renovations had prevented an appropriate ceremony until now.

"You could always take Jane with you to Windsor following the ceremonies. I can arrange for some special entertainment—a joust? Players? Dancing? Cheer up, Ned, it will only be for a few weeks." The king was usually easy to distract from the boring business of kingship, but familial duty had deeper meaning for Edward, who refused to be roused this time.

Blinded by his own ambitions and comfortable in his position as chief councilor, Hastings was unable to grasp that while for years Edward had excelled on the field of battle and in the fighting for his crown, once peace came, the business of governing and improving trade was not enough to satisfy the restless young man's thirst for adventure. And, loyal to a fault, Hastings had been all too happy to turn his sovereign to the more pleasurable side of life to alleviate Edward's boredom. With so many experiences shared and with no one threatening Edward's throne since he had been reinstated seven years earlier, neither man was able to see how far they had descended into self-serving dissipation. Together, they felt invincible. In truth, Edward and his chamberlain-confidant Hastings had brought England into a more prosperous time. However, prosperity had left Edward with little to challenge him and had done nothing positive for his reputation. Thus, with Hastings by his side, he had drifted into a life of gluttony and lechery. The only subjects who were pleased with him at this stage of his reign were the merchants and their guilds, for Edward's negotiations abroad meant trade was booming with England's allies in Europe.

Will downed the rest of his wine, believing the audience was at an end, when Edward abruptly changed the subject.

"Sweet Jesu, my brothers weary me. I do not look forward to explaining to George why I named Richard chief mourner in the cortège on its journey from Pontefract," Edward said.

Will wondered if he should return to his seat, but it seemed Edward was unaware of his friend's efforts to depart. Edward picked at the carcass on the table, brooding over the conflict he had with George of Clarence.

"That brother of mine is like a canker festering in me," Edward groused. "George has betrayed me and failed our family so many times, and yet with a smile and a honeyed word, he can charm the very devil from his hell-hole—including me, it would seem."

Will chuckled and sat down. "I see we are not finished with George yet, Ned. Go on."

Edward snorted. "Meg asked me to be kind to him. Said it was not his fault and that the man had been spoiled for his charms as a boy, and as a man he floundered, not knowing his place as a second son. She thought he was too easily flattered and thus had believed that Warwick could make him king, and she told me I should be charitable because he was weak. Pah! By God, Edmund never behaved like that when he was the second son. He was the dutiful brother to me, and"—he paused, gazing unseeing into the fire—"Christ, how I loved him."

Will made a sympathetic sound, but not liking Edward's maudlin mood, he grasped the king's slumped shoulder and said: "Do not spoil your night with Jane, Ned. You can deal with George on the morrow."

Edward patted his friend's hand and rose a little unsteadily. "Aye, Will, you are right. Thank God for a friend like you. Another cup of wine and I would have dredged up all my resentments and slipped into a fit of ire or worse, of melancholy. Poor Jane would have had a hard time arousing me in a humor like that." He slapped Hastings on the back and pushed him toward the door. "Good night, good Will. Until tomorrow. No matter how I love your company, you are now no match for what awaits me in my bed."

Will bowed and descended the staircase from the royal lodgings, his steps as heavy as his heart.

"Come with me as far as Berkhampsted, Jane," Edward coaxed. "My mother will have already left for Fotheringhay and we can enjoy the luxury of her apartments and walk and hunt in the park. Then I must go to the reburial."

Jane's fingers played with the thatch of fine hair on Edward's chest as he lay on his back, hands cupped behind his head, his long body in repose after a vigorous hour of lovemaking. She was turned on her side, her head nestled under his arm, breathing in the unmistakable scent of their pleasure. She still could not quite believe she was lying with the king of England and that he was asking her to ride with him to his mother's home. And she could not believe that she had no one to answer to for her reply but herself. Although, she smiled as she was reminded, one did not truly have freedom of choice when the king commanded.

"What say you, Jane? Are you asleep?"

"I will gladly come with you, your grace, but only if you can assure me of your mother's absence, and if you promise to take me hawking. Who else will go with us?"

Edward released his arm and pulled her close. "I agree to both conditions. As for my retinue, I shall bring friends, Jane, have no fear. Will, certes, although you may have to put up with his stiff-lipped wife. Norrys, Howard and his wife, who is already known to you, and a few others. I suppose I shall have to invite my stepson, although he has been most unpleasant of late." His tone hardened. "Not sure what has flown up his arse, but if he does not behave, I shall send him up to Fotheringhay and Mother can deal with him. Ouch, do have a care, sweet Jane, those hairs are firmly planted in my chest, I assure you."

Jane released her grip, and she was silent.

Edward took her silence for concern. "Is that too many people for your comfort? We cannot be alone, you must understand. And with Katherine Hastings and Elizabeth Howard assuring propriety, we can make merry together before I have to begin the sad ceremony of reburial."

Jane bit her lip. She did not dare request that Tom be excluded. She had been so careful so far not to give Edward any indication that even as her body belonged to the king, her heart belonged to Tom. "If you are content, then I must be, too, my lord. What of your brothers? Do they not accompany you?"

Edward raised an eyebrow. "'Tis odd you should mention George and Richard. I was only speaking of them to Will before I came to you. Do you know what offense they cause me with their constant bickering?"

Jane nodded. "I heard my father tell of the arguments they laid before you in the matter of their wives' inheritance. But 'twas two years ago. I am afraid I cared not who Clarence and Gloucester were at the time, but I marveled that two royal brothers needed the king to judge their case. What caused the argument, pray?" Jane asked without thinking. Surely Edward would not discuss family matters with her. She was merely curious, and her mouth had moved faster than her brain.

Edward did not appear offended by her curiosity, however. "Before I tell you the tale, you must know that George betrayed me not once but twice while I lost and won my crown again. He was flattered by our cousin, the earl of Warwick, who had turned against me, and Warwick promised George the crown for his treasonous support." He paused while Jane digested the disturbing facts. "I forgave him, and he came back into the fold before Barnet. Will, Elizabeth, and the council wanted to charge him with treason, but he is my brother, and I could not do it."

Jane was moved by the king's sincerity and the depth of his love for this wayward brother. His loyalty to family was far greater than hers, she mused, thinking how willingly she had turned her back on her home, and not for the first time she wondered what Bella might say if she could see her now. She gently brought the subject back to the dispute between the younger brothers, and Edward continued.

"I have given them land and wealth enough to satisfy a dozen dukes, and yet still they argue over their Neville wives' inheritance. You know they married Warwick's daughters, do you not? Certes, you do. Perhaps you do not know the extent of the quarrel? Not two years later after George married Isabel Neville, Richard begged to marry the Lady Anne. I refused at first, thinking it was not prudent for two royal brothers to marry these powerful wealthy sisters—and second cousins, no less. However, when I heard how George had tried to hide Anne away so Richard could not have her, I relented. But now I rue the day I listened to my heart and not my head."

Jane was intrigued by the story. "George really hid her away? Where? And how did they find her?"

"That boy Richard is as determined as a dog to have a bitch in heat," Edward declared. Jane winced; she often did not much care for Edward's choice of words. "He went to see Anne at the Erber—the Neville—"

". . . the Neville city residence. Aye, I know, my lord, I am a Londoner," she interrupted.

"How could I forget," he said, slapping her bare buttock playfully, "but do not interrupt your king again, wench, or I will have to resort to punishment. Like tying you up and . . ."

Jane promptly put her hand over his mouth. "I can imagine the rest, your grace. Now I pray you, tell me more about the mystery of Lady Anne's whereabouts."

Edward related how Richard of Gloucester, desperate to find his prospective bride when news of Anne's disappearance came to light, had employed some spies to search the neighborhood near the Erber. As Clarence's wife's younger sister and a widow, she had been placed under his guardianship, and he had no intention of allowing his brother access to her. "One day, getting word she may have been found, Richard went himself to rescue her, and there the poor little thing was, great Warwick's daughter, plucking chickens in the kitchen of a tavern. Can you imagine the humiliation for someone of her noble Neville blood?"

Jane privately thought that everyone ought to know how to pluck a chicken. She bit back her retort and tut-tutted sympathetically instead. She did not want to keep reminding Edward of her common stock. She was enjoying her new life, not to mention that the more she was with Edward the fonder she became of him.

"Richard of Gloucester must love his wife very much," she said quietly. "He went to extraordinary lengths to win her. She is a lucky woman."

Edward's eyes were closing. It had been a long day, and he never slept more easily than after he had been pleasured. "Aye, I believe Dickon loves her. But I warrant he will never love anyone as much as he did his Kate." He yawned. Then his eyes flew open. "By Christ's nails! That is who you remind me of, Jane. Kate Haute, Dickon's first love." That amber-eyed beauty with a voice like an angel. Edward would have taken her to bed the first time he had seen her but for the respect he had for his loyal youngest brother.

Jane was curious now: this was the second time she had been compared to Richard of Gloucester's paramour. How can I meet this woman? she wondered, sleepily. Deciding she would find out more about Kate Haute soon, she snuggled down into Edward's embrace, delighting in the sensation of skin against skin as they lay together. Before slipping into sleep, she sent a prayer to St. Elizabeth to watch over them that night.

Strangely, she dreamed about Will Hastings. It was a disturbing dream of running through dark rooms searching for her friend, and then in the gloom she saw the little towheaded boy from the Old Bailey kicking a football that was covered in blood. When she looked closer, she saw it was not a ball but a head.

Edward felt Jane's distress and held her close. "'Tis naught but a bad dream, sweet Jane. Never fear, I shall always be here," he murmured in her ear, and she calmed. He was surprised by the strength of his conviction that he was speaking the truth. He would always be there for her; he knew that now. Despite his devotion to his wife, it was this diminutive, carefree, and generous girl who had reawakened his jaded heart.

The bodies of Richard, duke of York, and his son Edmund, earl of Rutland, were transported from Pontefract to Fotheringhay in an elaborate catafalque pulled by seven horses followed by a mile-long train of mourners, the chief of these being Richard, duke of Gloucester. Behind him, also dressed all in black, rode earls, barons, knights, heralds, and squires, and as far as the eye could see marched four hundred yeomen, wearing black hoods and carrying torches. Ahead of the procession, a team of bishops had been sent to prepare the sanctuary at each night's resting place. On the seventh day, the dead duke and his son, both killed at Wakefield's battle on the last day of 1460, were greeted by the king, his queen, and his mother at the church of St. Mary at Fotheringhay, where the bodies were laid to rest on the thirtieth day of July under the newly renovated nave.

On the day following the burial, Edward had seated more than fifteen hundred people at a feast, which began at noon and lasted well into the long summer evening. Close to five thousand more were accommodated in canvas pavilions in the fields and received alms from the king, but no one was counting. Edward's new prosperity was on show, and all prayed England was now well set upon a peaceful course.

"Well, my lady Mother, are you contented now?" Edward asked Duchess Cecily as they mingled with the guests. The king looked magnificent in purple with a baldric of gold thread affixed diagonally across his chest, holding jeweled brooches, fermails, and medals. A jeweled crown topped his gold-red hair. "I regret it took so long, but have I done right by my noble father and my brother?"

"My dear Edward, you do not need to seek my approbation," Cecily replied. "You are the king and I am but your subject, and a haggish, tottering one at that."

Edward's burst of laughter caused those nearest to him to wonder what Proud Cis had said to amuse her giant of a son. Despite her sixty-one years, the duchess of York had kept her fabled beauty, and only the few lines around her eyes and on her forehead hinted at the age of her still-lucent skin. But it was her eyes, the gentian blue of her native Durham wildflower, that never failed to arrest an onlooker's attention. Also in purple and trimmed in ermine, with her widow's wimple and barbette a spotless white and her ducal crown glimmering gold, the tall, slender woman might have been a queen.

"You are still the most beautiful woman at court—*when* you are at court, Mother. Do not play humble with me, I beg of you. It does not become you. Now, answer me, please. Will Father and Edmund finally rest in peace? Will *you* rest in peace? I did this for you, you know," he fawned, looking for a moment like the boy Cecily remembered when the Yorks were a complete family.

She reached up to pat his cheek. "Aye, my son, I thank you. They are at peace now, and it will not be long before I shall be as well." She smiled sweetly at him, but her voice then took on an edge. "However, there is another matter I wish to discuss with you, Edward. Shall we walk along the Nene apace?"

Edward's face fell. He knew that look, that tone of voice. He was about to be chastised, and there was nothing he could do about it. "Aye, my lady," he agreed, remembering the last time the duchess had asked to walk with him apace had been two years before when she had demanded an explanation as to why he could not effect a reconciliation between his two brothers. He checked about him for Will, hoping his friend would come to his rescue, but his chamberlain was nowhere in sight.

"I hope you said a few aves for your own soul these past two days, my boy," Cecily began as they left the castle by the postern gate, the massive keep high upon the motte at their backs. Fotheringhay had been Cecily's favorite residence during her marriage to Richard of York; it was the principal seat of the York family, built by an ancestor, Edmund of Langley, with a moat fed from the River Nene.

"It has come to my attention that your eye has wandered from your wife again. Nay, do not dissemble, Edward," she grumbled as Edward's silence and sulky mouth revealed the truth. "Your father and I were married for more than thirty years and he did not stray from my bed." She turned the large ruby betrothal ring on her finger, a habit she had acquired every time she thought of her beloved departed husband. "I sometimes ask myself what we did wrong in your upbringing." She shook her head. "At least Richard was decent enough to rid himself of his leman before he wed his Anne." She paused, remembering something. "He tells me his bastard will join his household on the morrow. While I commend his paternal responsibility, I do not approve. Did you hear of this?"

Relieved to revert from his own indiscretion to Richard's, Edward dived right in. "His son is coming to Fotheringhay? How old must he be? John is his name, I believe. Certes, I have seen Dickon's girl here from Wingfield with my sister Suffolk. Katherine is quite a beauty, you must agree, your grace. She is the image of her mother." Christ's bones, why had he brought up Kate Haute? It would only return the subject to Jane.

He was right.

"And what is the name of your latest wagtail?" Cecily snapped. "I cannot believe Jacquetta's daughter would take this lying down . . ." Cecily grimaced at her choice of words as Edward smirked, and she immediately corrected herself. ". . . suffer this behavior from you. You should put the woman from you and concentrate on the business of governing. I suppose you know the country is filled with outlaws? Why, one of my ladies was set upon just last month as she was escorted home to Lincoln. You must govern more sternly, Edward. Your father would have done so."

Edward scowled. Not that comparison again, he thought. He wanted to shout, "Aye, but my father may have begun the fight but he did not win the crown! I did. He was not perfect either, and at least I have brought peace to the kingdom and prosperity," but he said nothing and allowed her to finish. He had far too much respect for this indomitable woman to gainsay her.

Knowing she had reached her limit with him, she relented. "You are the king, and I am your loyal subject," she reiterated. "I am merely asking, as your mother, to curb your wanton ways. There, I have said my piece, now kiss me and let us return to the feast."

"Aye, Mother," Edward said meekly enough, and bent to kiss her proffered cheek. Who was he to defy Proud Cis?

EIGHT

ENGLAND, 1477

In the months that followed the reburial, Edward worked hard to live up to his mother's expectations of him. But despite holding sessions of oyer and terminer in several counties, calling a great council to request that overtures be made to Castile for a marriage between his six-year-old heir and the Infanta Isabella, and entering into negotiations with the duke of Brittany to gain custody of the exiled Henry Tudor, earl of Richmond, Edward's popularity sagged, most especially with the London wool merchants. He was unable to reverse the recent Burgundian edict against the importing of English cloth, and thus the breakdown of trade with the wealthiest market in Europe was now hurting the economy.

Edward's sister Margaret was duchess of Burgundy, but she did not appear able to persuade her husband to revoke the edict, probably owing to Duke Charles's fanatical ambition to harness as much of Europe as he could. Thus he was rarely at home, preferring to leave Margaret to rule in his place. However, the duchess was powerless to change laws, and her husband was as stubborn as he was rash.

Not unexpectedly, yet still a shock to the rulers of Europe, Charles the Bold was killed at the siege of Nancy one frozen day in early January, leaving his heir, young and vulnerable Mary of Burgundy, in the care of her stepmother, the childless Duchess Margaret. The wool merchants would now have to wait until Mary found a husband and the new duke could be approached about the edict.

In another foreign policy failure and despite an agreement,

Edward was unable to wrest his possible rival, Henry Tudor, from the duke of Brittany, and the young earl had gone into the church sanctuary, where no one could touch him.

In the matter of his mistress, however, Edward had no intention of giving her up. His mother's ire be damned, he thought as he signed the letters of protection to accompany the new merchant adventurer, William Shore, into Burgundy that yuletide. It was more important to Edward that Jane was finally free of Shore, who would not be seen in London for many years to come.

Edward was astonished at the strength of his feeling for the dainty, strong-willed woman from the merchant class. He loved her naturalness, her ignorance of courtly pretense, her wit, warmth, and her beautiful body. But he had to admit it was Jane's generosity of spirit that touched him most deeply, a rare quality in her position.

"Mercer Etwelle, I pray you be at ease and take a seat." Jane recognized her father's former apprentice and waved him toward a carved wooden chair across the room from her. "What brings you to Thames Street on this wintery morning?"

The lanky, hawk-nosed Etwelle lowered himself onto the chair, his knobby knees safely hidden by his blue gown, the color of the mercer's livery that year. He was clearly nervous, pulling at his thin beard every few seconds and clearing his throat. Jane waited for him to gather his thoughts and played with a small, but beautiful, square-cut emerald ring, Edward's gift to her upon their six-months' anniversary.

"Mistress Shore, I do not know where to begin," her visitor faltered.

"At the beginning would be a good place, sir," Jane said, smiling encouragement at him.

"I have been accused of a crime," he blurted out, "and I am innocent." Jane's smile faded as she wondered what this mild-mannered man could have done. Loading dice, forging documents, and public drunkenness were common, she knew, but none would have led him to her door.

She rose and poured the poor man a cup of ale, which he took gratefully. "As I said before, Master Etwelle, start at the beginning."

A tale of miscalculation of several bolts of velvet purchased by the king's tailor had resulted in John Etwelle's being accused of cheating the king of a few nobles, and he was due in court within a sennight.

"'Twas a misunderstanding, mistress," the mercer explained, sitting forward in his seat. "The man's script was unclear, and I thought he had written six instead of four bolts of cloth."

His sincerity touched Jane, and she believed him. "Forgive me, sir, but why are you telling me this? I know you to be an honest man; at least you were when you were apprenticed to my father. If you are wanting my advice"—but Jane could not imagine why he would—"I would say to you to tell the truth. 'Twas a simple mistake. My father will vouch for you."

Etwelle flushed. "Aye, he has already done so, mistress, but to no avail. They say I could be imprisoned, and I have a family of four to feed." Now the tugging at the beard was accompanied by an uncontrollable knee-bobbing.

"That is dreadful news," Jane cried. "'Tis too harsh a sentence if you are telling the truth. I wish I could help, but I have no influence."

"'Tis said in the Chepe that you have the king's ear," Etwelle whispered as though there were spies in Jane's house. "You could speak for me, if you so choose. And I will repay you with money or as much cloth as you could want, Mistress Jane."

The idea that she might use her position to influence the king in this manner had not occurred to her. She warmed his bed and made him laugh, but she was a mere commoner with no knowledge of politics. She stared at the anxious mercer for a few seconds and felt sorry for him. "If you swear to me that your story is true, perhaps I would speak to the king about your case. I cannot say if it will help, but I can try."

Etwelle was on his knees and kissing her hands, and although he was a man, he seemed to have wetted them with his tears. She gently pulled away and helped him to rise. "No need for such a show, Master Etwelle, and I am not Lady Jane but plain Mistress Shore. We are all equals, are we not, both proudly brought up in the mercers' company, you a freeman and I a freewoman of London. Rise up, I pray you, sir, for I am no better than you."

Etwelle was wringing his hands, a silly grin on his face. "Aye, both Londoners, mistress, and proud of it. I cannot thank you enough for receiving me," he said, and for the first time he stared about him at the sumptuous surroundings.

Jane hoped he would tell her father how well she was situated, and she leaned forward to ask him about her family. She had not seen her mother or sister since that awkward meeting when first she moved to Thames Street. "Will you tell my sister Bella that I think of her often, Master Etwelle?" The mercer nodded, eager to oblige.

"And I beg of you to stop by my shop at the Mercery and take your pick of any cloth you like," he said. "I am most grateful to you, mistress."

Jane smiled. "I have not succeeded in my task yet, sir, and besides, I will not accept your bribe. For, in truth, that is what it is." Seeing him demur, she held up her hand. "Nay, my reward will be knowing that justice has been served and your family is provided for. I will speak to the king on the morrow."

"I can see this means much to you, sweeting," Edward said when she had timidly described Master Etwelle's visit. "I confess I know nothing of it. In truth, it is a minor matter with which only my treasurer would concern himself." He stood behind her and began to unlace her bodice, impressed that she had not deferred her request until after she had pleasured him, when he might have been more inclined to grant this favor. He slid his hands around her body to cup her warm breasts, and she gave a little squeal of protest.

"My lord, I hope your heart is not as cold as your hands." She laughed, already responding to his teasing fingers. "Shall you help Mercer Etwelle or must I have his detention on my conscience? I believe 'twas an honest mistake."

Edward nuzzled her ear as she leaned back against him. "You are too kind, Jane. 'Tis one of the things I adore about you. Do not fret, I will excuse the man of his debt to me."

Jane twisted in his arms and laid her head on his chest. He always made her feel so delicate when he embraced her like this, and she inhaled his favorite scent of orrisroot, believing she had never been happier. "Thank you, my lord," she said sincerely. "You are a most generous king."

"And you a most generous mistress," he replied.

He carried her to the mauve and white bed, and for a while they shut out the dreary winter day, losing themselves in love.

Jane begged Edward to let her dress him, and so he told his squires to wait in the hall. He was glad of the opportunity to talk further about Jane's visit from the freeman.

"I have to warn you, Jane, 'tis common for those close to the king to be asked for favors. Every day the queen, Will, Thomas Howard, Dorset, Stanley are petitioned by men and women alike to speak to me on their behalf. This Master Etwelle may be the first, but he certainly will not be the last. He is no fool. He knows you from your former life, and he knows your position now. I must caution you to pick your causes carefully. There are those who will use you for political gain, and 'twould be easy enough to put yourself in danger. A smile at court can hide a false friend who will betray you ere you can spit on the floor. You must learn whom to trust. Margaret Howard might be your guide in this. You do understand, my dear?"

"I do, your grace," Jane replied, soberly. She hoped she was clever enough to know when she was being fooled, but she was learning that courtiers were more devious than her friends and acquaintances in the city. She shivered slightly, hoping she would not fall into a flatterer's trap, and determined to ask Lady Howard for help. The kind-hearted Margaret was also a good friend to Kate Haute, so Jane knew the older woman must be unconcerned about consorting with concubines.

Edward checked his appearance in her polished silver mirror and settled his black velvet bonnet on his head.

"And now I have to call another great council to debate the matter of my brother-in-law of Burgundy's demise and my sister's preposterous suggestion that young Mary marry my widowed brother Clarence. Over my rotting corpse!"

"Christ's bones, George!" Edward shouted. "How stupid do you suppose I am? Allow you to wed the Burgundy girl and you would soon chafe to assert her paltry claim to my throne. Nay, do not turn away from me. You have tried to wear my crown before, or are you too drunk to remember?"

George of Clarence's bloodshot eyes were full of hatred. The queen sat quietly gloating over her brother-in-law's discomfort. She would never forgive the man for turning against Edward in 1469. Moreover, now that her bitterest enemy, Warwick, was dead, she held Warwick's puppet Clarence responsible for the executions of her beloved father and her brother John in the ensuing civil war. Banish the measle, she wanted to tell Edward; the man was a pus-laden boil under the royal family's skin that should be lanced and drained, leaving naught but a withered scar to show he had been there.

George, in his cups, foolishly did not let the matter rest. "Meg thinks I should wed Mary, and I want to, too," he retorted. "Why do you thwart me at every turn? Have I not proved loyal these past five years? Can you not forget my youthful mistake? I swear I will not work against you if I become Burgundy's duke." George snatched up one of his gloves from the table and threw it back down as he cried, "I want to wed Mary. Why should I not?"

The room went silent as all eyes riveted on the glove. Then Edward raised his to George's handsome face, anger boiling in him now.

"Hear this, and hear it well, little brother. I do not trust you, and I never shall. Our lord father told us once if he told us a hundred times, look to your family in the hard times for they will not let you down. I am happy he is not here to see how wrong he was. I shall keep you close, George. You will not run off to some foreign part and plot against me again. Now, go back to your claret and stay out of my sight!" Edward spat, turning his back and walking to the hearth, where the crackling logs competed with the angry discourse.

George snatched up his glove and nodded to his squire, who came forward to wrap a mantle around his lord. "You have not heard the last of this. I shall go and seek our lady mother's advice. At least she will be fair." He moved to Edward's side, and when only his brother could hear, he hissed: "Have a care, Edward. I know things about which loyalty has kept me silent. Do not provoke me, brother." As he turned to the door, he made a great show of twirling his fur-lined mantle behind him and left, somewhat unsteadily, in a blur of red velvet.

Edward stared into the fire contemplating his brother's words. To what was George referring? he wondered briefly. Nay, it was George who had always been the offender, he decided and, exasperated, sloughed off the ominous remark.

Edward was busy for the next few weeks after he called a great council at Westminster, leaving Jane to her own devices. While Edward was absent, he did not forget his mistress, and soon her ornately gilded casket was overflowing with tokens of his devotion. As much as she loved all her new finery, Jane was not greedy. She had a particular fondness for the pearl necklace and her little emerald ring, but some of the larger items she found ostentatious and knew not when she might wear them in public. She was certain many of the trinkets had been chosen by one of the king's squires, John Norrys perhaps, and so as she fingered a few of the less valuable pieces, she began to plan how to sell them.

After she had come to terms with her status as a royal mistress, Jane had bargained with St. Catherine that she would do what she could for others not as fortunate as she, if the saint would intercede for her with God when the day of judgment arrived. But there was another reason for being generous. She had been surprised at her joy when Edward had indeed pardoned Master Etwelle, and the mercer and his wife had visited her with their profuse thanks. She had vowed then she would not sit idle in her comfortable Thames Street house but would do what she could to ease others' burdens. Certes, she had always looked to help her neighbors back on Hosier Lane and Cordwainer Street and never minded visiting a sick wife or a hurt child with small gifts of food, but the act of charity toward the Etwelles had been of a more serious nature with greater stakes. She began to understand her power, and it seemed even more satisfying because she was a woman. As she contemplated where to bestow a gift, she thought of the Vandersands' leaky roof. Certes, she would begin with Sophie.

It was a showery day in late April when Jane picked her way in her high wooden pattens around the puddles and muck on her way to the Jewry. She hoped one of the Italian moneylenders she had known since her childhood would give her a fair price for one of her baubles wrapped in velvet in the pouch at her waist. An hour later, with Ankarette trailing tut-tutting behind, she emerged from a doorway and into bright sunshine, the concealed pouch now heavy with coins.

As she rounded the corner into the Poultry by St. Mary Colechurch, humming *Sumer is icumen in* and exhilarated by her success, she failed to see a horse-drawn cart lumbering toward her and too close to the building. Just in time, Ankarette pulled her mistress to safety, but not before Jane's skirts and mantle were soaked in foul-smelling spray from a deep rut in the road.

"Look where you're going!" the carter yelled back over his shoulder.

Jane crossed herself twice and thanked her resourceful servant for her escape. She well knew that other than pox and the plague, accidents like these were the commonest cause of deaths in London. She leaned against the church wall, her chest heaving and her heart pounding.

"Jane, *lieveling,* vhat are you doing here?" Sophie Vandersand's motherly voice came out of nowhere, and Jane had never been so glad to see her friend, who was accompanied by two of her children. "Look at you! *In Godsnaam,* you are filthy. You must to come to our home."

Jane was soon wrapped in Sophie's wool cloak and ensconced by the smoky fire of the downstairs room, her outer garments hanging to dry among the earthenware pots and iron utensils in the large kitchen hearth. The two younger children were sitting cross-legged in front of her, gazing in awe at their mother's friend with her soft velvet bonnet and bejeweled fingers. Sophie was wringing out a cloth in hot water from the kettle over the fire before sponging Jane's cold feet, shooing Ankarette away when the servant insisted it was her job to care for her mistress.

"Look at that, Sophie," Jane said, pointing to her foot's bright green color. "When will they ever invent a dye that does not come off leather when it rains? I do so hate getting my feet wet.

Aah, that feels wonderful." She looked around the once-familiar house and felt a pang of remorse that she had not visited Sophie before now. In truth, she had been avoiding Sophie's censure and was unsure how to reestablish their friendship. She knew Sophie could not approve of what Jane had become, and now they seemed worlds apart.

"I would have come sooner, Sophie, I promise you," she began by way of an apology. "I hope you are not too disappointed in me?" She observed the prim line of Sophie's mouth and hung her head. "Aye, I can see that you are, and 'tis the reason I have not invited you to visit me. I cannot bear your disapproval. Would it help if I told you I am happier than I have ever been? Nay, I suppose not." Then her eye lighted on her pouch that had been set on the table while her clothes dried, and she reached for it. "You asked me what I was doing in the Jewry. I have been wanting to help you and Jehan for so long, and now I can," she cried happily, jingling the coins. "I was on my way here when you found me. This is for you. 'Tis for a new slate roof so your children will be safe from fire and you do not have to worry about all those leaks. I pray you, take it and make me happy."

Sophie's expression went from sober to surprised and finally back to disapproving. "I cannot take your money, Jane. It is"—she searched for the right word—"stained."

"You mean tainted," Jane corrected, coloring. "Oh, Sophie, please take it in friendship."

From the loft above where she was caring for little Pieter, Sophie's eldest daughter called down: "Take it, Mother, please. If Aunt Jane gives it in friendship, you would be unkind to say no, and besides, a slate roof would mean we won't sleep in a wet bed all winter."

"You see, Sophie, Janneke understands," Jane pleaded. "I do not need the money, but your family does." She stroked Sophie's rough hand, noting the calluses and cuts from years of working with a spindle and raw silk, her care-worn plain face already showing signs of age, and Jane's heart ached for her less fortunate friend. "I beg of you, think of them."

Sophie looked into Jane's eyes, the firelight making them more hazel than green, and saw that for all her friend was living a life neither God nor Sophie would condone, Jane's generosity and kindness had not changed. She smiled and nodded. "If it is vhat you want, Jane, I vill take it." Then she put her hand to her mouth. "But how do I tell Jehan? He may not accept."

Jane laughed. "My dear Sophie, I have learned much about men in the last year, and I will tell you that very few have scruples enough to turn down money"—she was thinking of Edward and Will's French pension—"no matter how it was earned. Here." She pressed the bag into Sophie's trembling hand, and Janneke clapped her hands with delight, which made the other children get up and dance, pulling Ankarette into the circle. Soon Jane and Sophie could not resist joining in, and it was a bemused Jehan who walked unexpectedly into the midst of the revelry and stood staring at the laughing, jigging group singing "Ring-a-ring-o-roses."

Jane had been right. The weaver was not too proud to take the gift. All smiles, he picked Jane up and swung her around with enthusiasm.

"The Vandersands thank you, Jane Shore," he said later, when Jane was ready to leave.

"*Ja, lieveling,*" Sophie agreed, embracing her friend, "from the bottom of our hearts."

On the way home to Thames Street, Jane felt light-headed from the good she had accomplished, and she waved at a surprised carter pushing his barrow home from Paul's Market. She had even sent Ankarette ahead to ready a bath. As she slowed near the house, she began humming the children's tune again merrily to herself, unaware she was being watched by a young man leaning on a tree nearby.

"This is almost the Jane Lambert I remember," he said, stepping out in front of her, halting her progress. But he did not smile. "Carefree and innocent. But you are not so innocent now, are you, Jane?"

Jane felt the air rush from her lungs and put out her hand to steady herself on the tree. Tom Grey snatched her hand instead and pressed it to his heart.

"Whose heart is broken now, Jane?" he said low. "You gave yourself to the king after refusing me on moral grounds. Where are your morals now?" And he upswept his arm to encompass her house.

Jane swiftly withdrew her hand and hoped no one was observing them. "If I recall correctly, my lord Dorset, you refused *me* first on moral grounds." Her heart was thumping, and to her chagrin his touch had revived the strong feelings for him she had tried to suppress in the past six months. But she was Edward's mistress now, and she had no wish to betray the love with which the king had honored her, so she attempted to move on with a curt "Good day, my lord marquess."

"Not so fast, Mistress Shore," Dorset said, piqued by her cool dismissal and stepping in front of her again. "I beg of you, give me five minutes of your time."

"For what, my lord? Will you lecture me on morality? Will you risk being seen accosting the king's mistress?" she added. And again she brushed past him and reached her door.

"I have never forgotten you, Jane Shore," Tom confessed, his sincerity making her hesitate. "I would hear from you that I am forgotten, so I may shut you out of my heart."

Jane almost swooned. "You must go, my lord," she whispered, "or I shall be undone." Then she pleaded with him and could not keep the sadness from her voice. "Please, Tom, go."

Just then, upon hearing voices, Jane's steward opened the door to his mistress. Before Tom could stop her, Jane disappeared inside the house, and the door was firmly shut.

Tom stood staring at the oak carvings, deciding if he should risk Edward's ire and barge in to claim her or quietly walk away. He chose the latter, Jane's parting telling him what he needed to know: Jane Shore loved him still.

Jane was relieved that Edward did not return to her bed for a week or more for it took her several days to recover from the unexpected meeting with Tom Grey. During one of her sleepless nights, she had consumed a whole jug of wine and had dozens of imaginary conversations with the young marquess. Most of the daydreams ended with Tom declaring his undying love and the two of them fleeing abroad, but then there were other daydreams where she spurned him in favor of the king.

And all night, she ruminated on love. She did love Edward for his charisma, for his generous, easygoing nature, his sense of humor, and for the way he awakened new sensations in her every time he touched her. But was that love? How she wished she could talk to Will, who made her feel safe and respected her opinions. Perhaps, in his wisdom and, according to John Norrys, his experience with women, he could advise her, but he was still in Calais.

By the time Edward did return, Jane had begun to think she had imagined the meeting with Tom, and she was as happy to lie in Edward's arms as he was to lie in hers. Not long after her visit to the moneylender, Edward asked her about one of his gifts to her, and she was forced to admit she no longer had it.

"Did someone steal from you?" Edward began angrily. "Why did you not tell me or Norrys as soon as you discovered it was missing? By the rood, I will have the thief's guts for garters!"

Jane had hung her head. "No one stole it, your grace. I . . . I . . ."

"Aye?" Edward was perplexed by Jane's discomfort. "Did you swallow it? Drop it down the garderobe chute? 'Twas but a trinket, Jane, and there will be more, have no fear. I beg of you, tell me. I shall not chastise you, I promise."

"I . . . I sold it," Jane finally admitted, lifting her head and looking him helplessly in the eye, yet ready to take her punishment.

Edward was astonished. "Sold it? Why? Do you not have everything you need here?" he asked, looking around at the rich hangings, brightly colored Turkey rugs scattered over the floor, and polished silver candlesticks and plates on the heavy oak table. "Tell me, sweetheart, do I not reward you enough for your charms?"

Jane winced at the offhand inference to her concubine status but confessed the truth. "The money paid for a new roof for my friend Sophie's house. The children had rain dripping on them in their beds," she rattled on nervously, "and I simply had to help them." She got on her knees imploring him to forgive her.

Edward stared hard at his lovely leman for a few seconds before a smile spread across his face. "You gave away my gift to help your friend? Then the jewel was worth far more than mere marks, Jane. It was worth this king's fervent admiration."

Then he had taken her to bed again. "You are a treasure, Jane Shore," he announced later. "I shall not ask again where a bauble disappeared to, although I shall hope certain of my gifts too cherished to pawn." Jane had promised and snuggled into him.

It seemed during these times, lingering behind the silk drapes on her tester bed, that Edward had not a care in the world. Clever Jane made it her business to let him believe it, telling him snippets of London gossip, sharing a joke, laughing with him like children, and loving freely as if they were mere Master and Mistress Smith of a modest house on Thames Street. It was why, Jane believed, Edward returned time and time again.

Far from carefree, Edward's world had begun to spin out of control. He had been right to worry about George of Clarence's threat in February, for word reached Westminster that George had been making mischief that month of April in his castle at Warwick.

After surprising Jane by bustling into her solar and taking stock of her elegant surroundings, Margaret Howard sank onto a chair and launched into her tale.

"If you have seen George of Clarence, Mistress Shore, you would not believe 'tis possible for him to behave in any way uncharming or cruel, unless he has been drinking. He is handsome, intelligent, with a great love of books, and he remained faithful to his duchess until her death. 'Tis said, he is generous to his servants. But there is one servant who can now never praise or vilify him again, because she is dead by his hand these five days."

Jane raised an eyebrow but remained silent to encourage the friendly Lady Howard to continue. Under the burgundy gown, Margaret's feet attempted to reach the floor, but as the chair had been specially made for six-foot-three-inch Edward, Margaret was left with legs dangling and feeling like a child. Jane swiftly fetched a footstool, and Margaret smiled her thanks.

"It seems the Duchess Isabel had a lingering death after birthing her babe, and, without warning, Clarence sent two of his minions with eighty armed men into Somerset a fortnight ago to seek out Isabel's former servant, Dame Twynho. They broke into her house and dragged her back to Warwick with no proper authority, where Clarence accused her of poisoning his wife."

Jane drew in a breath, afraid for the victim. "Did he have proof, my lady? The Duchess Isabel died half a year ago. What happened?"

"Ankarette Twynho was imprisoned, brought before the justices, and found guilty." Margaret clicked her tongue with disdain. "Not before Clarence, I would dare to wager, had the jury in his pocket. Not satisfied with condemning the Twynho woman, the duke found another servant to accuse of murdering the newborn babe as well, and both of them were hanged, as I say, five days ago." She leaned forward. "He behaved for all he was the king. 'Tis said his grace King Edward is seething."

Jane was shocked by the story, crossed herself, and sent up a prayer for Dame Twynho's soul. She was grateful to Margaret for the news, as Edward had not been to Thames Street for a sennight. "What came over the duke?" she wondered. "I can understand the man must have grieved for his wife and babe, but to wait so long to accuse and then exact such swift and terrible justice? 'Tis strange indeed."

"My lord husband believes George is a little unbalanced, Jane," Margaret said, and it warmed Jane to hear this noblewoman call her by her Christian name. It seemed Jane's assessment of Margaret had been correct, and Jack Howard's wife had gladly spent time teaching Jane the intricacies of court life. "He is so often in his cups, most ignore his complaining. He is less and less at court, and he eats and drinks there but little, putting it about he is afraid he will be poisoned by someone close to the king. Ridiculous! However, I told Jack that I believe the duke simply wants to get his big brother's attention. He is still a spoiled little boy, I fear, and pouting because he was denied marriage with Mary of Burgundy. He is convinced Edward deprived him out of spite, although there is not a man on the council who cannot see what a danger George would be as duke of Burgundy. He is blinded by hate. 'Tis a sorry state of affairs."

Jane shook her head. "I must admit, Lady Margaret, that men's minds are hard to fathom sometimes. But it would seem to me that my lord of Clarence should not test the king's patience much more. The word in the city is that his grace has been too magnanimous with this troublesome brother." She wanted to confide that Edward did not often talk about affairs of state but refrained. "I have heard also that Richard of Gloucester is in good standing with the king, but he is wise and stays away from court."

"You have the measure of Edward's goodness toward his brothers. Those Yorks will stick together like limpets on a rock when they are pressed. But it does the Crown no good to see brother warring against brother. In truth, Edward's other brother is well acquainted with my husband and me," Margaret said, smiling wistfully. "We miss him in Suffolk."

"How so, my lady?"

Margaret twinkled. "Richard was often at Stoke, our residence in Suffolk, when he and Kate Haute were . . . were, um, close," she said. "Kate was brokenhearted to have to give up her five-year-old John when Richard claimed him last summer. She is a spirited woman and swears she will never love again and thus took the widow's wimple when her wastrel husband met his end." She smiled. "Another George, and as willful and childish as Clarence."

For the next half an hour, Jane plied Margaret with questions about Kate and her liaison with Gloucester, and by the end, she had an even more burning wish to meet the woman who had so softened the heart of the dark young duke.

"If you want to know what Kate looks like, you have only to see her daughter, Katherine, who for now resides with the king's sister, Elizabeth of Suffolk. Next time you are at court, you must ask to have her pointed out to you." Margaret watched curiously as Jane rose to pour her guest another cup of ale and was struck by Jane's daintiness. She herself was perhaps only an inch higher, but there was nothing dainty about Margaret in her middle age. She liked what she saw in Jane and would report to her husband, her dear Jack, that if Edward had to have a mistress, he had chosen well. Margaret felt a kindred common sense in Jane, and as she had never particularly warmed to the queen after all these years, it would be pleasant to spend time with the king's favorite when she was in London and on duty at the palace.

For her part, Jane was elated to have finally been accepted by a another woman at Edward's court.

Jane and Margaret would have been pleased by their prediction of Edward's intolerance for mutinous behavior from George of Clarence. They were surprised, however, by the puzzling manner in which Edward counterattacked.

Not a month after Dame Twynho was hanged, Edward chose

to pursue an old case of necromancy with connections to George.

The new trial was held in London and widely talked about, unlike the provincial Twynho case. It seemed that three years before, one John Stacy, an Oxford clerk and self-proclaimed astronomer, was thought to have used his magic art to predict the death of the king and his son. In his recent confession, Stacy implicated two others, Thomas Burdett and Thomas Blake.

"You recall Burdett, my dear? He was the maggot who invited me hunting and then wished me dead for killing his precious white buck," Edward reminded Elizabeth on an evening when they were dining privately. As he demolished half a haunch of venison, Elizabeth picked delicately at a small sliver of the meat, nodding absently from time to time and shuddering at her husband's primitive table manners. Sweet Mother of God, but he ate too much, she thought again. Despite giving birth two months before to her eighth child, she had kept her trim figure and was disgusted by Edward's gluttony and obesity, although she cherished these private times with him.

"By Christ, I should have hanged him there and then," Edward said, showering venison fragments into the air with every word and causing Elizabeth to move her cup of wine to safety. "I forgave him because he was one of George's intimates."

"And what, pray, does this Burdett person have to do with the Twynho . . . murder?" Elizabeth asked silkily. She hoped her tone would remind Edward that Clarence should pay for his outrageous act. Her dislike of her brother-in-law grew daily, and she was not above passing insidious remarks to help push Clarence over the precipice. "Wishing your death and carrying it out are very different," she said. "God knows how many times I have wished you in hell, my dear husband, especially when you come to me from that whore Shore's bed." She smiled sweetly at him, and Edward scowled at her. He had no defense when it came to his infidelity, and Elizabeth knew it. "But do go on. I am agog to know how Burdett can hurt George."

Edward knew he should tell his queen that had her tongue been less spiteful, he might not have spent so much time with Jane, but it would require far too much effort on his part this late in their married life. Besides he never intentionally wished to hurt Elizabeth's feelings. So instead he wiped his mouth with his sleeve and continued Burdett's story.

"There is evidence the man and his conspirators used sorcery to predict my death, but even more damning was that Burdett was found to have spread about treasonable poems and ballads." Edward had risen and was rinsing his fingers in the marble bowl held out to him by the gentleman usher of the chamber. "Burdett is obviously attempting to rouse the people to rebellion, and the man is not intelligent or influential enough to do this alone."

Elizabeth arched a finely plucked brow. "Clarence?"

"Who else?" Edward growled, allowing his usher to remove the heavy gold collar from his neck and pull the tunic over his head. "'Tis certain Burdett is in league with Stacy and Blake, and 'twas enough to try all three. I have no doubt they will hang."

"And what of your brother?"

Edward scowled, sitting down again to have his hose-shoes removed. "I have no proof George is involved, but I hope it serves to warn him to beware of his actions, for he can no longer count on my tolerance." How he longed for the old days when he and his brothers and sisters were a closely knit family.

When the usher bowed himself from the room, Elizabeth motioned to her lady-in-waiting to begin her undressing process. "I am so thankful those of us left in *my* family all rub along well," she said. "Our mother and father were so enamored of each other, we could not help but learn about love and loyalty from a young age."

Edward picked up his goblet. He was tired of the queen's

self-righteousness. "My dear Bess, you know very well 'twas the same with my family," he said, testily. "I know not what worm crawled into George's head to make him different. He was the best loved, I used to think. Now, I pray you, let us change the subject."

Elizabeth ignored him. "I have never liked him," she continued. "He is vain, he is never sober, and his charm is false."

Edward's patience came to an ugly end. "Enough of George, I said!" he cried, making Elizabeth's woman drop the ivory comb in her hand. "And speaking of best loved children, your description of him might fit your Tom."

Elizabeth snapped her fingers at the lady-in-waiting, who, rescuing the comb, gratefully hurried out.

"How dare you criticize Tom," she spat back, retreating to her side of the bed. "I would venture to say he is what you and Hastings have made him." She was scornful then. "Who knows what sort of legacy we are leaving our children through your bad example, my lord. At least I keep my body to myself. Unlike you and that Shore whore!"

The king's goblet landed, dented, on the floor by the opposite wall while Elizabeth took cover behind the bedpost. Edward strode to the door.

"Page! Wake up, boy, and fetch Sir Walter immediately." He began snatching up his clothes and jammed his hat on his head. "I shall not stay where I am insulted," he barked at his wife. "Look to yourself if you wish to understand why I seek the solace of another woman's bed. You have driven me to it."

Elizabeth's expression hardened, but she said nothing; she knew when she had pushed Edward too far. When Sir Walter Hungerford entered to serve his king, the queen and her tears were safely hidden behind the damask curtains of her lonely tester bed.

Jane found herself strangely drawn to the hanging at Tyburn.

The night before, Edward had arrived unannounced and in a

black humor. He had taken her more roughly than he had ever done before, and Jane had been fearful he might be angry with her or, even worse, he might be tiring of her. After he had had his fill and the candle was guttering, he suddenly gave a loud groan and turned into her arms.

"What is it, Edward?" Jane asked. "Is it something I have done?"

Edward had squeezed her tight and kissed her neck. "Nay, little love, it is not you." The use of his Christian name moved something in him, and for the first time he spoke to her of his troubles. He told her all about George and the unlawful way his brother had treated Dame Twynho. Jane already knew but did not interrupt, as she could see Edward had much on his mind that night. She lay still in his arms and learned of Edward's counterattack on Clarence.

"How I wish Will were here," Edward mumbled half to himself.

"What could he do, my lord?" Jane had asked. "Would he have cautioned you that revenge is bittersweet? I believe you perceive that now, or you would not feel so wretched. But if you truly believe this Burdett has committed treason against you, then I suppose he deserves to die. God rest his soul." She was feeling brave and could not stop herself from adding, "But if he is not guilty, then you have the power to pardon him, do you not?"

"Not only him, Jane. There are three of them. True, 'tis certain Stacy and Burdett are guilty, but I am not as sure about Blake," he lamented. "No matter, I cannot be seen to be weak, and I will not allow George to incite rebellion."

"No matter?" Jane repeated softly. "'Tis a man's life you are holding in your hands, my dear lord, as well as your immortal soul. Are you certain 'tis too late to change your mind?"

"Too late, sweet Jane," Edward replied. "Parliament has condemned them. I am afraid your counsel comes too late. I had hoped the queen would counsel me as you have, but she hates George so much, she can only think of his destruction. I have no doubt Will would have stayed me, but he is not here." He took in a deep breath, and Jane could sense his unease. "The men are guilty and will hang on the morrow."

Jane had gasped then. "So soon? Ah, their poor wives," she could not help herself saying, burrowing into his chest. "They are dependent upon their husbands, and the children on their fathers. Dear God, I cannot imagine losing you so abruptly. 'Twould break my heart, and"—she realized with a jolt—"I would be shunned and alone."

"Dear Jane, you are too soft-hearted for this world," Edward chided. "But I promise you, if aught happens to me, Will Hastings will take care of you."

Jane had shivered from cold or fear, she was not sure, but she reached down and pulled the bedcover up to her chin and had tried to sleep.

This morning, she walked slowly with Ankarette. London was emptying in a steady flow of men, women, and children eager for an excuse to take time from their everyday travails and witness someone else's misfortune. It was not Jane's first hanging; her father had taken the family to one or two over the years, but it was the first time Jane had felt a connection to the victims. She had donned her drabbest gown, left her jewels at home, and with her head covered by a simple green hood, she mingled with the crowd, Ankarette elbowing away from her mistress anyone remotely suspicious.

They crossed Smithfield marketplace and bought, from a stack piled on a vendor's head, two hot pigeon pies to eat on the way. Well-to-do merchants, spindly-legged apprentices, rotund red-cloaked clerics, and high-hatted young gentlemen mingled with prostitutes, fishmongers, gong farmers, and ferrymen as they made their way under the Newgate, along High Holborn to the place called Tyburn, set in a field large enough to hold a multitude. The word was passed that John Stacy and Thomas Burdett had been held in the Tower overnight and were on their way, and the crowd's excitement grew. "'Tis said the third man, Blake, was pardoned this morning," called out a fellow in Lincoln green, telling all he was an archer. "The bishop of Norwich spoke for him to the king."

A buxom woman selling nosegays of violets remarked: "The king is merciful for once. I wonder what came over him? Too much wine, I'll wager. Or too much of a good thing in bed!"

Roars of laughter accompanied this, and Jane hurried on, pulling her hood down to conceal her face, as many Londoners might recognize Mistress Shore of Coleman Street.

Despite her maudlin mission today, Jane's heart rejoiced that perhaps Edward had heard her plea for pardon the night before and let one man go.

Jane and Ankarette arrived in front of the gallows in time to see the cart carrying the prisoners rumble up the hill to the scaffold. A band of musicians heralded their arrival with pipes and tabors, and a cheer erupted from the waiting spectators. Those following the cart pushed and shoved their way onto the field, and screams were heard as a few people were trampled beneath their feet. Jane wished she had brought Martin, her steward, as she became aware how small and vulnerable she was in this multitude. But resourceful Ankarette had found an empty tun on their walk, and now she made Jane step up on it for a safer vantage point. Jane was amused by her servant's fearless defense of her mistress's safety and resolved to reward her later with a trinket of her choosing from a peddler.

Within a short time, the burly guards had dragged the two bound men from the cart, both white with terror, and prodded them up the steps of the scaffold. Two nooses hung loosely swinging in the wind, and as if to sanction the gruesome event, a crow took up its perch on the gibbet, occasionally adding its crass caw to the crowd's clamoring. After reading a litany of their crimes, the stouter of the two men took a tentative step forward, and the spectators quieted, respecting his wish to be heard for the last time.

"As God is my witness," he cried in an indignant voice, "I am innocent of any treachery against his grace the king."

"They all say that," shouted someone from the middle of the crowd and waited for a laugh. Instead his neighbors shushed him loudly as Burdett continued.

"I told the truth to the judges in Parliament and I reject their verdict and this unjust punishment. I wish it to be known that I go to my Maker protesting my innocence, and may God have mercy on my soul." He turned back to John Stacy, who was trembling so vigorously that people at the back of the crowd remarked upon it. Stacy's nervousness caused him to start grinning and giggling, but taking it as a sign of disrespect, the hangman wasted no time in fastening the heavy rope around the man's neck. Another guard pushed Burdett back under the second noose, frightening the crow that flapped its wings and, in a final ignominy, loosed its dropping directly onto Stacy's bared head. The crowd gave way to relieved titters after having expressed misgivings about the legitimacy of the men's fate.

As the priest began the ritual *"Indulgentiam, absolutionem et remissionem peccatorum nostorum . . ."* hoods were placed over the men's faces and with a sharp nod from the captain standing off to the side, the floorboards beneath the men's feet were snapped open, and with a great cheer from the audience, the two men fell toward the earth, their twitching bodies dancing freely in the air.

A woman's wail rose, heartrending, above the now-hushed throng, and Jane, much moved, swayed unsteadily on her precarious perch.

"Take me home, Ankarette," she begged, putting her hand out to be supported by her maid. "I should not have come. 'Tis a cruel world we live in, in truth."

All the way back to Thames Street, her feminine intuition kept telling her that Stacy's and Burdett's end might well mark the beginning of Edward's undoing.

NINE

Edward took Jane to Windsor with him the following week, although he knew Elizabeth was already in residence. He had not forgiven his wife for her sanctimonious behavior, and so he had no compunction about breaking his promise not to flaunt another mistress under her nose. However, he was taking his time getting to Windsor. He might have been irked to know that some of his gentlemen thought he was cowed by his beautiful but arrogant queen and might be purposely delaying the reunion. If they could have asked, however, Edward would have told them he merely wanted to share some of his favorite haunts along the Thames with Mistress Shore.

The royal party floated on the sumptuously furnished barge as far as Shene Palace, a favorite residence of both Margaret of Anjou and then her bitter enemy Duchess Cecily, where Edward and Jane had lingered for two days, hunting in the extensive park, before abandoning the water and riding on to Hampton. There they had feasted in his cozy hunting lodge and continued to the riverside town of Staines, over the old Roman bridge, following the river road, and on to Windsor.

"You are well liked, Jane, so have no fear," Edward said, allaying Jane's worries about her presence on this journey. "No one will dare shun you for fear of angering me, so be at ease and enjoy yourself. A word of warning, though," he added softly, "keep out of Elizabeth's way. She is likely to scratch out your eyes." Jane paled, and Edward laughed. "Windsor is big enough to avoid a meeting, sweetheart. Indeed, 'tis my favorite residence, and"—he pointed to the massive round keep rising above the fields in the distance—"there it is."

Jane was awed by the size of the castle on a mound overlooking a bend in the river, its imposing crenelated bailey wall incorporating more than a dozen sturdy square towers and enclosing the many buildings in its inner wards. It had been built by William the Conqueror to secure the western approach to London and was the most important of several fortifications built then to encircle and defend the capital.

"I could not have imagined such splendor," she said. "I believe I shall feel safe from marauders there. 'Tis a giant of a castle for a giant of a man."

Edward laughed happily. "Always one for an apt phrase, sweeting." He admired again her perfect nose in profile and her shell pink complexion, its color heightened after the ride in the late May sunshine. "I know the place suits me well, and I pray you will be comfortable. On the morrow I shall show you the work on my new chapel dedicated to St. George."

Jane nodded bravely. Although she did not look forward to the first night in this strange, forbidding place all alone, surrounded by prejudiced noblewomen, she would not let the king see her unease.

Closely followed by a few of his intimate courtiers and their wives, Edward led the way through the gatehouse and into the inner courtyard, where grooms were waiting to help the party dismount. Taking Jane's hand, Edward reassured her that he would come on the morrow and show her the rest of the castle.

"But for now, my dear, I must attend the queen. Lady Howard will be near to make sure you are comfortable. Norrys!" he called to his squire. "See Mistress Shore to her lodgings, I beg of you."

Jane felt very small and not a little afraid standing in the vast courtyard under the massive keep, watching her protector stride away. She searched the many windows of the royal lodgings, wondering if Queen Elizabeth were observing the scene, and she could not remember when she had felt so vulnerable.

June was in full bloom at Windsor and Jane had become accustomed to the castle routine, walking in the grounds, or keeping to her allotted, sunny chamber reading, weaving on her lap loom, or attempting to learn the lute, and waiting for Edward's summons. She accompanied him to the hunt once and attended several public feasts, seated far from him and the queen. He had shown her the progress on the magnificent chapel he had commissioned, its soaring nave nearing completion, and Jane had marveled at the number of brave masons who appeared suspended from nothing as they chipped away at the pillars to create the filigree decorations.

One day she had walked across the short bridge to the hamlet of Eton and seen the beginnings of the school that Edward's rival, King Henry VI, had begun before his death. Jane was impressed with the Gothic beginnings of the building and much taken with the idea of a school where the boys would lodge, but Edward had sniffed and told her King Louis's pension money was better spent on his chapel at Windsor.

Now it was midsummer's eve, the time of witches and fairies, and she was looking forward to the feasting and merrymaking. Considered a pagan festival, it was one Jane thoroughly enjoyed, although this was to be her first celebrated outside London. The bonfires had been stacked high in the wide lower bailey and in the fields across the river, and Jane could not resist wandering down to the water's edge to pick flowers to put under her pillow. It was said the ritual would ensure that dreams of love would come true.

She had Ankarette dress her in her lightest gown, for the weather had turned hot and a few of her favorite bodices were stained. In palest mauve, the square-cut gown was modest but exposed enough of her chest to invite a breeze to cool her skin. She wore a simple coif so there was nothing draped about her neck, and she decided she could endure the heat and enjoy putting her feet in the river.

She had gathered campion, yellow flag iris, heady meadow-sweet, and ragged robin and was bending over a clump of blue forget-me-nots when a small dog bounded up to her and began to lick her hand.

"Good day to you, sweet pup," Jane said, delighted by the intrusion, and petted the fluffy white bundle of energy. "What is your name, pray?"

"Ficelle! Ficelle, *viens ici,* you bad dog," a woman's voice came from over the bank. "Katherine, where did she go, did you see?"

The French immediately alerted Jane to the presence of a gently born lady, and picking up the wiggling Ficelle in her arms, she called, "I have the dog, madam. I will bring her to you."

She climbed back up the riverbank and came face-to-face with Queen Elizabeth and her lady-in-waiting, Katherine Hastings. "Oh!" was all Jane could think to say before sinking into a deep reverence. "She is not hurt, your grace. See." And keeping her head bent, she thrust the dog up at Elizabeth.

"I thank you, mistress," Elizabeth said pleasantly, cuddling Ficelle to her, but then Jane raised her face and the queen saw who she was. "You!" she snapped. "Katherine, do you see who it is. My husband's latest harlot."

Jane was miserable with confusion. Should she fall on her knees? Should she stand still, run away, or should she defend herself? Such an encounter had been her worst nightmare, and it was almost as bad as she had imagined it could be. "Aye, I . . . I am Mis . . . stress Shore," she stammered, but before she could stop herself she added the customary, "if it please you."

A high-pitched laugh like the shattering of fine glass made Jane cringe. It was not a kind nor a merry laugh but one intended to discomfit and insult. "If it please me? If it please me?" Elizabeth shrilled. "Nay, madam, it does not please me. And yet my husband chooses to flaunt you in front of me. Beware, Jane Shore, for the day will come when he will tire of you, and you will be discarded, believe me." She bent down to hiss in Jane's face: "He will forget you as he has all the others."

Jane sank back on her heels as Elizabeth put down the dog, turned around, and stalked away.

"I knew you were trouble the first time I set eyes on you, Jane Shore," Katherine Hastings added, sneering. "You have broken my dear lady's heart, and I hope one day you will pay for your wantonness. You should not have looked above my husband, my girl, for the queen is a far more formidable foe than I could ever be." Then she hurried after the queen, calling to Ficelle to follow them.

Jane's flowers discarded around her, she fell onto the mossy bank and, feeling humiliated and ashamed, she wept.

Later, after Ankarette had pampered Jane in a cooling bath perfumed with rose petals, Jane lay for an hour on the lumpy mattress, which was the best the castle could provide for a person not of noble blood, and relived the nightmare. Now, feeling brave, she conjured all manner of cleverly worded retorts that she might have parried with the queen. One of the scenarios even had her slapping Elizabeth and throwing the flowers at her. She had to laugh then, and her good humor restored, it was not long before she could look forward to the festivities that would last well into the summer's eve. The court was used to seeing Edward dancing with her and even fondling her now, although he was mindful not to when the queen was present. Jane wondered if Edward would ask for her to come to him tonight. She hoped so, because now that she had discarded her flowers, she did not want to risk dreaming about Tom Grey without them under her pillow.

Tom Grey. What was wrong with her that she could not forget him? It had not helped that he had reawakened her yearning with his unexpected presence at her house those weeks ago. Why had he come? Had he wanted to humiliate her? Or was it . . . nay, she did not dare to think he truly loved her. She frowned. He had not been among the retainers Edward had brought with him to Windsor, but Ankarette had discovered that he had gone to his residence in Devon, where his wife was in confinement. He was to be a father, she thought sadly, wishing it were she who was carrying his child and not the young, wealthy Cicely Bonvile.

Thinking of children, Jane wondered why, after being with Edward for well over a year, she had not yet quickened. True, she had learned the court ladies' trick of inserting a sponge soaked in vinegar to avoid conception, but she had also heard it was not foolproof. Perhaps her barrenness was just as well, she mused, as Edward had warned her that Elizabeth would not tolerate another bastard.

Ankarette began dressing Jane's hair an hour later, threading the thick braids that coiled around her head with pearls and tiny white sprigs of meadowsweet, creating a veritable crown. She stepped back to admire her handiwork, never missing a syllable of gossip that she could impart to her mistress. The two women were wont to discuss the happenings in the city during the ritual of dressing, but Jane had learned from Margaret Howard to listen more and talk less to a servant. Ankarette was keenly aware of her mistress's moods, but she was not often privy to the reasons for them.

Today Jane heard about an affair one of the queen's ladies was having with a handsome young squire in Edward's household, how a wise woman had helped another young girl rid herself of an unwanted babe, and that Ankarette herself had indignantly denied having been involved in the mystery of a missing ring.

"But mistress," Ankarette ran on eagerly, "all the talk today is of your meeting with the queen. I have been peppered with questions, but I never said a word, I swear."

Jane groaned. "And now I must face the court and their gossip. Perhaps I should feign a headache," she mused. But then, her curiosity aroused, she asked, "What are the clatterers saying, Ankarette?"

"That the queen will not leave her chambers until you are gone from Windsor," Ankarette blurted out. "She will not appear at the feast until you are on the road back to London."

"God's teeth!" Jane cried, turning on her servant. "Why did you not tell me this first." She began tearing the decorations from her head, making Ankarette chase the pearls all across the room, and ordered the poor woman to pack up their belongings. "I will not be made a fool of, and I will not have the king humiliated by my presence. Now find me Master Norrys at once, so I can make arrangements for a horse and an escort."

Ankarette stopped what she was doing, and putting her hands on her hips, she eyed her mistress. "Which would you like me to do first, mistress? Fetch the squire or pack? I cannot do both at the same time."

Jane raised her arm, as if to slap the insolent servant, but as quickly let it drop, realizing it was not Ankarette's fault. It was hers. She took a deep breath and spoke more gently: "I will gather our things if you would fetch John Norrys. But do not try my patience today, Ankarette Tyler, or I shall have to look for someone new to serve me."

Ankarette did not need a second bidding.

With Ankarette riding pillion on their sturdy but slow rouncy, and two men at arms to guard her, Jane found the journey back to London interminably slow. She had written Edward a hasty, apologetic note that John Norrys assured her he would put into the king's hands as soon as her party was away from Windsor. John had heard of the earlier encounter on the riverbank and thought Jane had every reason to disappear; he had seen the queen lose her temper with Edward once before and had wished himself a league hence.

On the third day, as Jane and her escort were passing the road to the hunting lodge where, on the outward journey, Edward had entertained his mistress in merry fashion, they heard horses galloping from behind. The escort drew their short swords and herded the rouncy off the road and out of harm's way as the party of more than a dozen riders came around the bend. The noise and speed of the riders made Jane's horse whinny and caper, but Jane kept the reins tight.

"The king!" one of her men shouted to the other, and both put up their swords.

Jane's heart leaped in her breast. As in the romances of old, she imagined Edward had come to claim her and carry her back to Windsor. She pushed a wayward strand of hair back under her traveling bonnet and sat serenely on the quieted horse.

Reclaiming Jane was the furthest thing from Edward's mind, and he brought his mount up sharply when he saw her, his face grim. "Why, Mistress Shore, I am happy to see you but fear I cannot linger. A matter of urgency takes me back to Westminster. However, I will walk on with you apace and explain," he said, taking her rein and pulling her mount closer. Ankarette dismounted respectfully and walked behind while the king spoke to his mistress.

"What is it, my lord? Is there ill news from France?"

"Nay, Jane, France is not the problem. But my brother Clarence is," he told her, a sadness mixed with the anger in his expression. "There is no end to his folly. I wanted to believe 'tis all simply foolishness, but this time he has really gone too far. Unheeding my warning in the execution of his familiars, he has once again overreached and now barged into a council meeting without my permission."

Jane quietly observed him, his powerful jaw set, his brow lowered over his eyes, and she shivered. This was not the Edward who laughed and made sweet love to her. She was in the presence of an angry sovereign.

"It was bad enough he chose to invade my council, bad enough that he railed at my councilors for executing 'innocent men,' but he chose that scurrilous preacher, Goddard, to read Burdett's statement from the scaffold to the council, the same scoundrel who had denounced me as king at Paul's Cross in '70 in favor of Henry."

Jane nodded. "Aye, I was there," she remembered. Then she was moved to ask: "But what makes your brother's latest actions worse than the previous ones, your grace?"

"My dear Jane, he has acted as though he is king. He has undermined me by accusing my council of hanging innocent men. And what did he think he was doing when he hanged the Twynho woman? He had no right to drag her across the country, try her, and execute her on trumped-up charges. He is behaving for all he wears the crown." His voice was rising and Jane could see he was wanting to gallop off. "By Christ's nails, he has gone too far. I shall have to deal with him once and for all. I have recalled Will from Calais; I have need of his counsel." He reached over and patted her hand. "Farewell, mistress, and"—his mouth twisted into a wry grin—"for what 'tis worth, I cannot blame you for leaving as you did." He had been sorry to hear of Jane's unfortunate encounter with the queen, but Jane's rapid departure had relieved him of an unpleasant scene with Elizabeth. He had not relished possibly having to mediate between his wife and his mistress. He blamed his wife's spiteful nature, never recognizing that he was the cause of the conflict. "I shall not stay away from Thames Street long, I promise, for I shall need you to restore my humor."

He raised his hand to his retainers and motioned them to follow him at a gallop. They left Ankarette rubbing dust out of her eyes and mouth and Jane wondering what would become of Clarence.

By the time she made her weary way to Thames Street, George of Clarence was imprisoned in the Tower and Edward was entertaining the French ambassadors with the help of Will Hastings, who had returned from Calais in haste. It seemed the hapless duke had been doomed to his incarceration for a very long time. Edward had learned from King Louis's mouthpieces that a story was circulating in Europe, said to have originated from George, that Edward was a bastard and that if he, George, had married Mary of Burgundy, he would have overthrown his brother. This mounting treason was all too much for Edward to forgive, and by the beginning of 1478, Parliament was pressing Edward for a death sentence.

But before Edward would countenance fratricide and risk his immortal soul in that most heinous of crimes, he chose to organize a wedding.

The bride and groom sat on outsize cushions bolstering their bridal thrones and took in the pageantry that unfolded before them throughout the day's celebrations. Edward's second son, Richard, duke of York, was four years old and his bride, Anne Mowbray, heiress to the great fortune of the dukes of Norfolk, was six, and thus neither could be blamed for not comprehending the meaning of the solemn oaths they had to swear in front of the exclusive congregation at St. Stephen's Chapel inside Westminster Palace.

As she was fatherless, Anne was escorted to the altar by John, earl of Lincoln, and Anthony, Lord Rivers, and the choir burst forth with a "Te Deum" that lifted Edward's spirits. As he waited for his betrothed, little Richard of York stared about him at the magnificent, colorful, and gold-leafed murals interspersed with azure carpets emblazoned with fleurs-de-lys that hung along the walls. The boy was equally well supported by his parents, his brother and sisters, and his regal but devoted grandmother, Duchess Cecily.

"We do have the papal dispensation, do we not, Edward?" Cecily had asked her son the day before. "Pointless going forward if we have not."

Edward winced at his mother's lack of confidence in him, but he did not wish to argue with her at this time of intense tension in the York family. Cecily had already made several pleas for George in the past few months, but they had fallen on deaf ears for once.

"Certes, we do, my lady Mother," he answered with forced politeness. "What a foolish question. You must know we have been requesting this for two years, not to mention all the bargaining I had to do with Norfolk's widow."

"I wonder you can remember anything at the moment, my son, with your brother languishing in the Tower. Could you not have allowed him a day of freedom for this occasion at least?"

"Nay, I could not," Edward snapped. "It astonishes me that you still side with the son who accuses you of birthing a bastard. It would seem your own words have come back to haunt you, Mother."

Cecily gave a derisive laugh. "Aye, 'tis the truth. I wonder at the petty things people choose to remember. My flippant remark all those years ago was spoken out of anger and disappointment at your marriage to Elizabeth, if you recall. It never occurred to me anyone would take it as the truth." She touched his arm. "I hope at least you know I never strayed from your father in thirty years. You are Richard Plantagenet's son, and I will swear to it on his grave." Then she tried again. "However, George is also my son, and I must not abandon him. Please look on him mercifully, Edward. 'Tis all I ask. I fear some of this conflict is my fault. We did spoil him."

"Enough of George, Mother," Edward warned her, but he could not help admiring her steadfast defense of the black sheep. "He is not worthy of your tears."

Cecily turned away. She knew when to hold her peace, but she would not give up on George, she promised herself. She would try again with Edward after the festivities.

Her youngest son, Richard of Gloucester, was given the honor of dispensing gold and silver coins to the spectators following the wedding mass, and then he and his royal cousin, Henry of Buckingham, escorted the earnest young bride back to the king's hall for the feast.

Being of average height, Richard had difficulty finding his petite wife in the throng, and he thought he had never seen so many
people in one room at one time. He was dismayed at the din, which
he considered disrespectful at such a solemn occasion, yet another
sign of Edward's uncensored court. His brother must have spent
a fortune on the event, Richard surmised and assumed that it was
probably taken from Edward's new daughter-in-law's coffers, not
surprising, since young Richard was now given the dukedom of
Norfolk to add to that of York. So much responsibility for such a
little boy, Richard thought, glad his own son, Edward, was safely
ensconced with loving nursemaids far away at Middleham.

Richard would attend the opening of Parliament in a few days
and then he and Anne would disappear north to their haven in
the dales. He did not feel at home at court anymore, and he had
no interest in taking part in the jousts that had been organized for
the Londoners in honor of the marriage. Richard took his skills
with weapons seriously; but they were supposed to be wielded in
times of war, not in times of peace. He disdained using them for
entertainment, even though he was one of the best swordsmen
in the country. Nay, he would leave tilting for sport to Rivers,
Courtenay, and Oxford.

Richard spotted Edward towering above a group of extravagantly
clothed nobles, slapping Jack Howard on the back and laughing
at something Lady Margaret had said. He smiled. They were his
good friends, and seeing them again forced his mind back to fond
memories of Tendring Hall in Suffolk, where he used to meet his
sweet Kate in secret, thanks to the discretion of the Howards.
Dear Kate, he thought wistfully, she had awakened a passion in
him he had never dreamed possible, and he cherished the love he
knew she still bore him. But duty had taken him away, and he
counted himself fortunate to have found another love in a more
suitable bride. He put thoughts of Kate aside, and as he resumed
his search for Anne, he was dismayed to see a couple kissing in

a window embrasure and that the man's prick was thickly visible in his lover's hand. The outraged Richard could not stop himself from commanding them bluntly to desist, and unsurprisingly the man's arousal instantly wilted.

Once Richard found Anne, they went arm in arm toward Richard's cousin Harry Buckingham and his wife, another Woodville woman. Raised voices caught Richard's attention to his left, and he frowned. His brother's chamberlain and the queen's eldest son were quarreling again. When Richard had challenged Edward on the conflict between Hastings and Dorset, Edward had shaken his head in despair. "I have been told, although neither will tell me who she is, that both men have their eye on the same woman. 'Tis not the first time," Edward confided. "One in his dotage and the other barely out of swaddling bands fighting over a woman is amusing, is it not?"

But Richard Plantagenet did not find it amusing, as his teasing older brother knew he would not.

The trial of George, duke of Clarence, commenced two days after the wedding festivities. It became a war of words in public between the king and his renegade brother, and all knew who would win in the end.

"'Tis a pity women are not allowed to speak, let alone be present," Edward conceded to Jane when, after a harrowing day at Westminster, he took a chance she might be at home. "If the judges could have but heard the words written to me by my sister Margaret, begging for clemency, and see my noble mother on her knees in front of me, wringing her hands, George might have had a chance. But no one came forward to speak in his defense, Jane, no one."

She had only spoken to George once, but she had noted his good looks and charming manners. Like Edward and his mother, George was an undeniably charismatic presence in any room, but observant Jane had also noticed that his winning smile never reached his eyes, which were wary and ever-moving. Insincere was the word that she had finally settled on him.

"What will happen to him, your grace?" Jane asked as she kneaded his knotted shoulders.

"I suppose I shall have to attaint him and take away all his titles and possessions. I expect he will disappear to France and curry favor with the spider king. Louis will be glad to have someone close to me nearby, I will wager. Aye, George will still be a danger, but an untitled danger, which is less of a magnet for powerful people." He pulled Jane around into his arms and cradled her against him. "Ah, Jane, how I wished he had been even a mite remorseful. Perhaps I might relent, but the man is obdurate, and thus my heart is hardened against him."

"No king could have forgiven him more times than you, my dear lord. You have done what you can for him, and now he must face justice. As the Bible says, we reap what we sow."

Edward was surprised. "This is a new side to Jane Shore. I do not believe I have ever heard you invoke the name of God or His scriptures before."

"Certes you have! Only ten minutes ago when I was pulling out those accursed hairpins," Jane retorted. "I seem to recall I used one of your favorite curses."

Edward laughed softly and then he let his hands wander over her bodice, and Jane felt her nipples respond as desire for him mounted.

"Have I ever told you that I love you, Jane?" he murmured into her long, glossy hair.

Jane's heart stopped. Had she heard right? Had the king declared his love for her? She turned in his arms to look into his face and had no doubt of his sincerity. She stroked his stubbled cheek and astonished herself with her own unwitting truth. "And I love you, too, my sweet lord," she replied.

"Close the God-forsaken window, will you?" George called to one of his keepers in his chilly chamber in the Garden Tower. He slammed down his cup, spilling long red rivulets over the table. "Tis February. Do you want me to die of cold before the executioner does his work?"

He put his head in his hands and stared blearily into the cup. If he closed his eyes and prayed hard enough, perhaps he would open them again and find he was really at the Erber, his dog at his feet and little Meggie and Ned playing quietly with their nurse, and that all of this was a bad dream. But then, why could he still hear the lions roaring in the Tower menagerie nearby, the guards outside his room throwing dice, and the boatmen's bells warning of the fog on the river a few feet from his prison?

And then his tears began to fall one by one, faster and faster into the claret as he sank into a deep melancholy.

How he hated Edward, his big golden brother who had somehow come back from the edge of disaster seven years before to snatch the crown from within George's reach and then had thwarted the chance for George to rule in Burgundy with Duchess Mary, who had since wedded Maximilian of Austria. Aye, he scoffed, Edward could never do anything wrong in his family's eyes even from a young age, forgetting it was Edmund—patient, gentle, murdered Edmund—who had earned that right, not Edward.

No one has ever cared for me, George thought, refusing in his misery to acknowledge his intelligent sister Margaret, who had been his best friend, his champion, and his favorite dance partner. He conveniently forgot how everyone had spoiled him for his blond curls, huge gentian eyes, and engaging smile. Only Dickon had stuck with him back then. But what happened there? George asked, wiping his nose and sniffling in derision. Dickon became earnest, dutiful Richard of Gloucester, jumping whenever and however high Edward asked him and had sided against his childhood playmate.

And his mother, his beautiful but haughty mother, Cecily. Does she love me? George asked himself. Where was she when he most needed her as he heard his death sentence pronounced? Why has she not come to visit me in this miserable prison? Aye, even his mother did not love him, he wept. He did not know that Cecily had prostrated herself in front of Edward and pleaded for her son's life. In fact, she was still on her knees in her private chapel at Baynard's, not a stone's throw from him, begging God and the blessed Virgin to spare her wayward son.

And so he wallowed in self-pity and despair, unwilling to take any blame for those treasonable crimes he had committed. Trumped-up charges, he had yelled back at his accusers during his trial. He had been stunned when Parliament had recommended death, and Edward had turned away, acquiescent, his signature all that remained to carry out the pronouncement.

He slurped the rest of his wine, which tasted bitter now, and he refilled his cup from the big butt of malmsey Edward had sent over for him after the king had answered George's entreaty to visit him in prison. He had never seen Edward so unmoved, and despite George's efforts to first cajole and then threaten his brother with eternal damnation, Edward had left him with no hope of freedom.

George huddled closer to the fire, trying not to think of his imminent execution. Would he show courage? Would Edward watch? He doubted his faithless brother would even drag himself away from his whore to witness his death. This made George weep further, and thus he did not hear the key in the door and visitors enter until the cleric among them spoke.

"I would hear your confession, my lord," Father Lessey said, dismayed by the slovenly figure swaying on the stool. George turned to his mother's chaplain in astonishment, the man coming into and out of focus at an alarming rate.

"Confession, Father? Now, at night, and"—he hiccoughed—"in my cups?" He wiped his runny nose on the back of his hand.

"Aye, your grace. Now. I beg of you."

George was suddenly aware of the others in the room, two burly men he had not seen before, and behind him in the doorway his usual guards. He stood up, but his legs gave way, and he would have fallen had the priest not steadied him. "What is this intrusion, sirrahs? Who are you?" he slurred, feeling the walls close in around him.

Lessey eased the drugged George to his knees and began to recite a prayer for the dead. George tried in vain to control his movements and his voice, but he ended up slipping to the ground. "Oh God, have mercy on me," he cried, and even the guards pitied the fallen duke.

Dragging the wailing, pathetic man to the large wine barrel, the two thugs pinned George's arms behind him and, as he pleaded for his life, forced his head under the deep red liquid while he tried to make his legs fight desperately to keep him upright or to kick his assailants.

"The poison should have done its work," Father Lessey cried to the guards. "Did you administer the poison?" The guards, fixated on the drowning, assented. Lessey tried pleading with the captors, but he saw they were intent on their duty. Whoever had given them their orders had obviously given them free rein to end George's life as expediently as possible. The priest was sickened by it. He fell on his knees chanting as loudly as he could to cover the hideous noise of the victim's futile efforts to survive.

When Lessey had learned that his mistress, the duchess, had won the king's permission for a private, more humane death, he had been told poison would be administered in the duke's all-too-familiar wine. But he had not anticipated this horrible drowning when he had acquiesced to seeing the duke shriven. He could not believe Edward had ordered such a degrading execution, but it was out of his hands now. Somewhere along the way he had learned that drowning was a peaceful way to die under normal circumstances, but this had turned into a horrifying end to a life, even if Lessey believed the duke deserved to pay for his crimes.

The flailing and the terrible splashing ceased after an interminable minute when the chaplain heard one of the men say, "'Tis done. He be dead, all right." Lessey crossed himself and sent up a miserere for Clarence's soul, wondering what tale would be spread concerning the manner of the hapless duke's death; he and the others had been sworn to secrecy, and Lessey was not about to jeopardize his position in Cecily's employ. All he would say was that he had been present at the execution.

Edward received the news with an eerie calm. He sat slumped on the canopied throne in his audience chamber at Westminster, flanked by the queen, his brother Richard, and his chamberlain. The king stared at the opposite wall. No one dared move for several minutes.

Richard was wondering if Edward had planned such cruel irony—George drowned in his favorite claret? Surely not. Richard looked sideways at Hastings to ascertain the man's complicity, but for once Will appeared to be as dismayed as he was. Richard could not tell if Edward had ordered this atrocity or not. Like Father Lessey, Richard had believed poison would be administered as George's merciful escape from the axe.

"Can this be true, Ned?" Richard broke the silence. He had come to dislike George more and more, but he had not wished such an ignominious death upon his brother.

Elizabeth was nervously picking at the fur on the long tippet of her sleeve, and Richard looked suspiciously at her. "You knew, did you not, Elizabeth?"

The queen turned away, unable to look at him. "Edward had been jesting," she mewled. "He was drunk, and he was joking. Someone must have heard him say that George deserved to be drowned in his own wine." She rose and then knelt beside Edward, taking his hand. "You did not mean it, did you? Did you? Oh, Ned, what will you tell your mother?"

Suddenly, the king lifted his head and gave a great cry. "God have mercy! I have killed my brother and, by this heinous act, I have condemned both of us to the torments of hell."

Richard went white, and Will Hastings fell on his knees in front of his king and wept with him.

When Duchess Cecily heard the news at Baynard's the next day, she sat rigid on the carved high-back chair that had been her husband's favorite. The silence in the solar was broken only by the skittering of sleet on the windowpanes. Her ladies, shocked by the tale, watched her anxiously, but this proud and stoic woman had weathered many a tragedy in her sixty-three years, and she sensed her son's hideous death would not be the last.

"Sir Henry," she commanded her seneschal with her usual control, "make ready for our return to Berkhamsted. I am no longer needed at this court. And ladies"—she rose and led the way—"we must pray for the duke of Clarence's soul." She did not add, "and my other son, Edward's," although she was thinking it was he who was in need of salvation and not George, for since the time of Cain and Abel, fratricide was surely one of the most grievous of all mortal sins.

As Cecily fell on her knees in Baynard's tiny chapel, she looked up at the likeness of her special protector, the Holy Mother Mary, and exclaimed: "May God have mercy on my son, because I shall not."

PART THREE

1482–1483

What steps of strife belong to high estate?
The climbing up is doubtful to endure,
The seat itself doth purchase privy hate,
And honours fame is fickle and unsure.

Thomas Churchyard, "Shore's Wife," 1562

TEN

Edward's subjects would call it his golden age; Edward was forty, and England was prospering. For the first time in a century, a monarch had no debts and money to spare. Yet, in the autumn of '82, Edward's foreign policy floundered, due in part to the unexpected demise of the young duchess of Burgundy in a riding accident. Hated by her Flemish subjects, Mary's husband, Archduke Maximilian of Austria, was unable to muster enough support from the burghers to stop France encroaching on Burgundian territory. He appealed to his brother-in-law in England for troops, but Edward, expending his forces in defending the north against a Scottish invasion, was unable to help. Who could blame the young archduke from negotiating a peace with Burgundy's longtime enemy, Louis of France?

At home, Edward had other worries, not the least of which was the escalating feud between his faithful chamberlain, Will Hastings, and the queen's family, notably her brother, Anthony Rivers, and her son, Thomas of Dorset. Over the summer months of that year, Rivers and Hastings exchanged slanders that resulted in a hanging of one of Hastings's men in Calais, who confessed he had been put up to spreading a rumor that Lord Rivers was plotting to sell Calais to the French.

"He named you, Will," Edward snapped, when the two men were left alone after a council meeting. "John Edwards accused you in front of me and Parliament. He said you threatened him with the rack if he did not do your bidding." Breathing hard, he sank back in his chair, as if the angry words had winded him.

"He lied!" Will cried, although he could see Edward did not believe him. He went on the defensive. "Rivers started the slanders last summer, saying I was plotting to sell Calais. Of all the despicable, implausible lies to lay at my door! But I would not put that past a Woodville."

"Have a care, Will," Edward warned softly. "That is my wife's family you are accusing. Do not provoke me into choosing."

Will felt a cold chill grip his heart. He had never before doubted Edward's good opinion and favor. By Christ, Will thought, Ned was so much under Elizabeth's yoke, he was now siding with that popinjay Rivers. He did not think Edward cared much for his handsome brother-in-law, but when it came to a choice between family and friend . . .

"My queen is justifiably offended, my lord," Edward was saying. "Can it be that you are still jealous of Rivers after all these years? Why, I renewed your captaincy of Calais only recently, and now you are willing to risk your position with this constant feuding?"

Will hung his head. It was true, he did resent the brilliant courtier, Rivers, who had been given the supremely flattering position of governor of the Prince of Wales. Not that Will would have wanted to be nursemaid to a boy of twelve at Ludlow in the wilds of Shropshire, but it was a high honor indeed to be responsible for the heir to the throne. He did not dare mention, however, that he hated Thomas of Dorset even more than he hated Rivers, especially as the young puppy had managed to insinuate himself into Jane's favor.

"I fear you must have that man's death on your conscience for the rest of your life, Will." Edward sighed heavily, as he did every time he thought of his dead brother. "Just as I have Clarence's."

And King Henry's and a thousand others, Will almost said, but restrained himself.

Lost in their own thoughts, the two men sat, staring absently at the exquisite murals on the walls of the Painted Chamber. Edward wished he had not brought up George's name; it only conjured dark thoughts of how his own life had been changed by the event. How even further into dissipation he had sunk, and without his mother to guide him—aye, even she had forsaken him—he felt his salvation was a lost cause. Elizabeth's interest in him had waned, and she spent most of her time at Greenwich or at her town house of Ormond's Inn. The warrior Edward wanted to regain the amazing exhilaration of those first few years of his reign, but the overweight Edward did not have the energy for action.

He forced his mind back to the problem at hand. It annoyed him that his trusted chamberlain would embroil himself in this feud with Rivers; Calais was too important to toy with. It was the gateway for English trade with Europe. Edward could not afford to lose Calais; the English would never forgive him, and these years of peace and prosperity would have been achieved for naught.

"Now, Lord Hastings, what of Maximilian and Louis? Should we invade France again?" Edward steepled his fingers together and looked over them at Will. "We should not jeopardize the two marriage contracts we have pending for Ned and my little Anne with Burgundy and Brittany, not to mention that young Elizabeth is promised to the dauphin. I have my mind and heart set on these alliances. And I foresee a problem with our pension if Maximilian of Burgundy and Francis of Brittany come to an agreement with France."

Will was relieved. Edward had moved on from accusations and was seeking his counsel again.

"I fear for the future of Burgundy if we do nothing to support her," Will replied. "And you will disappoint your sister. Her diplomatic mission two years ago was a success, and we would not want to let her down. Does she, too, beg for your help on behalf of Maximilian?"

Edward nodded. "You cannot keep Margaret quiet for long, Will, surely you know that. However, I cannot see how we can send them troops when I have none to send. Richard will not be back from Scotland in time. I am counting on you, Will, to delay Maximilian, or it could mean the end of our pension."

Hastings nodded. "I will return to Calais and see if I can deter him from plunging into any kind of treaty with France, but remember, if it happens, I did warn you." He snorted. "I would not trust Louis as far as I can see his warty bulbous nose!"

They both laughed, and Will's laughter was the louder for his being relieved. Edward seemed mollified for the moment and diverted by more serious diplomatic problems. How fragile, he thought, were the ties that bound kings and councilors.

"My lord Hastings," Jane cried, going to him with her arms outstretched. Will felt warmed by her welcome. He took her hands and kissed both tenderly, smiling down at her happy face. "It has been an age since I have seen you. Where have you been?"

"Spending too much time on a bouncing caravel being buffeted by unkind waves," Will told her, holding his stomach and pretending to heave. "I should like to take you to see Calais. You would enjoy it. 'Tis a pleasant town with a lively market. But enough of my life, what is new in yours, Jane?"

Jane dimpled and pointed out a large arras hanging on the wall over a long oak table. "The king spoils me, does he not? Speaking of the sea, it tells another part of the Galatea story." She then fetched a book wrapped in dark blue velvet and gave it to Will. "This comes from Master Caxton's printing shop at Westminster. Is it not beautiful? And see, 'tis another version of the same story translated from Ovid. I was overcome when I received it." She stroked the soft cover. "It would seem his grace sees himself as

Arcis and me as Galatea." She pointed to the tapestry. "Here 'Arcis' is giving me quantities of delectable dishes. I confess it helps me sharpen my appetite, as I often eat alone."

"Are you unhappy, my dear?" Will asked, leafing through the exquisite book. He could not imagine how Jane whiled away her days, wondering when she would be called to the king's chambers or if he would come to hers. She, of course, ran her little household, her books kept her company, and her little lap loom kept her fingers busy, but he wondered why women were not bored most of the time. Granted, Jane was often seen at banquets and on feast days at court, where she could be heard in badinage with Edward's jester Jehan LeSage. Indeed, many of her quips were quoted and laughed over again later by courtiers. Aye, Jane was no longer a newcomer. She had soared in everyone's estimation as her positive influence on the king's humor became evident. Not everyone, Will corrected himself: the queen and her adherents were the exceptions. Jane's generosity to those who had asked her to petition the king on their behalf was now legendary at court. She had earned the respect even of those who considered themselves far above her. She came to court frequently, and Edward sometimes danced with her, but only after the queen had retired. Elizabeth remained intolerant of the woman her husband now described as his merriest and favorite mistress.

Aye, Will thought now, she looked content, blooming even, and he again admired her for her refreshing optimism and her quick wit. He settled himself in a chair by the fire, noticing she had had boughs of evergreens and holly brought into the house for yuletide. Both their scent and Jane's were intoxicating to him.

"The king tells me you have become quite adept at petitioning him on behalf of the citizenry. 'Tis easy to understand how the king cannot refuse you, Jane. You know I find you irresistible, too." His tone was playful, and he winked at her, but every word was true, and he wished she could see how much he loved her. If she were mine, he thought, she would never eat alone. But he was a man in his early fifties now, and he had given up believing he would ever live out this fantasy with Jane. He would continue to keep her safe for his sovereign and be contented with that.

Jane laughed. "Are you flirting with me, my lord? While I find it flattering, you must know I have my hands tied." She clapped her hand over her mouth, but above it, her eyes sparkled mischievously. "Oh dear, I have given away one of Edward's secrets," she said, and they both enjoyed the joke.

"Is there aught that you want?" Will was at once serious. "Is there anything I can do for you?"

"Be my friend, Will Hastings. Even later when I am cast aside." Jane's expression registered concern. "The king is not as hale as he used to be. 'Tis the tertian fever he contracted in France, he says. He comes to me for respite from his worries and his wife, but"—she searched for the right, tactful words—"he is not so . . . so lusty as he was." In truth, Edward had not been intimate with her for close to six months, claiming he no longer had the appetite, although he continually assured her of his devotion. Jane feared he had tired of her after seven years—the longest he had kept a mistress—and dreaded hearing he had taken up with someone new. She had done her best to arouse him, but he often fell asleep during their intimacy.

Will frowned. Edward ill? Aye, maybe he was, Will suddenly thought, remembering the king's lassitude at their last meeting. The Edward of old would have shouted at him, stamped about, and thrown things; last week he had remained seated, just raising his voice more in exasperation than ire. He had seemed too tired to contemplate disloyalty from me, too.

Will gave Jane a reassuring smile. "I shall always be here for you, never fear. You may count on me. But I would not worry, for Edward is as strong as a horse."

They looked at each other with mutual understanding, and for a few moments only the crackle, sizzle, and spitting of the logs in the hearth broke the silence. Both were thinking the unthinkable: what if something happened to Edward? For, in different ways, both were dependent upon him.

Tom Grey was annoyed to see Hastings exit the house on Thames Street later that day. He had determined when he awoke that morning to attempt another meeting with the elusive Mistress Shore. It had been eight years since he had kissed Jane in the garden of St. Paul's, but she had remained an unconquered daydream of his ever since, if for no other reason than that she had wounded his pride.

Over the years, Tom had seen Jane at court and watched her blossom into a self-assured woman, no longer ashamed of her status. He had even danced with her, despite the subsequent grilling from his wife, when she deigned to come to court. Marchioness Cicely was pregnant again, and as she hated Tom near her during those months, he had spent more time at court. Since Jane had entered Edward's life, the king had curtailed his philandering, and thus Tom could not even count on benefiting from his stepfather's leavings. As for his wenching forays into the city with Will, those, too, had ceased as the two men's dislike for each other had grown.

Tom had been present at an intimate supper with Edward and Elizabeth the night before and had witnessed a quarrel that involved "the stunted Shore whore," as Tom's mother was fond of calling her. Edward had been in his cups as usual and had lazily ignored the insult, and Tom, sensing that perhaps Edward was tired of his concubine, thought he saw an opportunity.

And now he had come to act upon it. He adjusted his hat, a sapphire glinting in its velvety folds, and knocked on Jane's door.

Jane did not greet Tom with outstretched arms; she did not even know why she had allowed him to cross the threshold. What possible excuse for his presence could she give Edward, if the king chose to appear unexpectedly? To maintain decorum and avoid a confrontation with the king or any other callers, Jane had told Ankarette to remain in the room with her, and the servant busied herself pouring ale for the new guest and stoking the fire. As Ankarette had been hired after Jane's dismissal of Tom, she was unaware of his significance but immediately noticed her mistress's unease. A handsome, noble young man, Ankarette had thought as she ushered Tom into the solar, and clearly a better match for her mistress than the portly old baron who had just left, or even the aging king.

"Mistress Shore, God's good greeting," Tom said, standing casually several feet away and fingering the jeweled collar draped around his broad shoulders. He was impressed by the luxury of his surroundings and recognized just how highly the king regarded his mistress. "I was on an errand at the wardrobe and thought I would pay my respects. I trust I do not intrude?"

He looked at Ankarette, hoping the busy woman would leave them, but Jane dropped him a curtsey and did not invite him to sit.

"My lord marquess, did you have some news for me?" Jane hoped her voice did not betray her weak knees. She longed to sink into her cushioned chair, but she dared not. "Your children, they are well? I hear from your father-in-law that they are bonny." She knew she must keep the conversation light or she would have to ask him to leave. She motioned to Ankarette to give Tom a cup of ale. "I pray you take some refreshment before you return to . . . the palace is it?"

"I am at Ormond's Inn with my mother. 'Tis but a stone's throw from here." Tom studied the elegant Venetian glass hanap in his hand and smiled. "You have come a long way from Hosier Lane, Jane. I like to think I played some part in your success."

Ankarette's ears pricked up. How did he know where her mistress was from? And he had called her by her Christian name. It was deliciously mysterious, and she longed to hear more.

"It seems to me you abandoned me to my fate all those years

ago, my lord. And so, aye, I have enjoyed a richer life since then, but I believe it is I alone who deserves the credit for my success. I think the king, your stepfather, would agree."

"Why so unkind, Jane?" Tom put his drink on the mantel and moved closer. "Can we not be friends again?"

Jane stepped back from him, but her heel caught in her hem and she would have fallen had Tom not caught her to him. She felt his arms about her, his breath on her cheek, and she wilted. "Kiss me, Tom," she whispered, "and then go, I beg of you."

Ankarette, now thoroughly confused, hesitated for a moment more then slipped from the room.

It was the most lavish of all yuletides, and even Edward remarked upon the extravagance.

Elizabeth scoffed at him when he came to find her in her bedchamber on the morning after the Feast of the Circumcision. "You have only yourself to blame, my lord," she told him from the warmth of her downy bed, a coverlet of squirrel fur cozily tucked around her. Lady Bourchier, her sister and lady-in-waiting, curtseyed to Edward and withdrew. "Other than to justify your own squandering of English taxes, to what do I owe this rare visit?"

A fleeting expression of annoyance crossed Edward's fleshy face at the insinuation they were no longer intimate. Since May of the previous year, when they had grieved for the loss of their beloved fourteen-year-old daughter, Mary, Edward had been absent from Elizabeth's bed. Elizabeth knew that in some way Edward blamed her for Mary's sudden death from a fever that had occurred while he was at Windsor and she and the children at Greenwich. Edward had adored the frail, pale-eyed beauty with her almost white hair, telling Elizabeth she was the child that most resembled her lovely mother.

"I was not complaining, Bessie. England prospers under me, so why should I not indulge myself and my household? You do not spare yourself," Edward said, eyeing the lavish new bed curtains and fur coverlet with amusement. "But I pray you, forbid me such extravagance next year, or all my hard work will go the way of five hundred tuns of wine, a dozen deer, three boars, five sheep, seventeen peacocks, and I cannot tell you how many fish. Gobbled up!" He threw up his hands, as if all these comestibles had vanished into thin air. He smiled. "But that is not why I came. Certes, I came to see how you are, my dear. You have been abed for two days now and no one can tell me what ails you. So I thought I would come and see for myself."

"Most considerate of you, Edward," Elizabeth said sarcastically, wondering why he had not come yesterday. "Doctor de Serigo believes I have an infection of the liver, and I must be purged every twelve hours. The yellow bile is up and thus my humors are imbalanced. 'Tis nothing serious." She did not add that the good doctor worried that a lack of sexual activity had built up the seminal humor, which could be dangerous, or that he had earnestly advised her to pleasure herself as often as she wanted, even at her ripe age of forty-five. Nay, Edward did not need such details, she told herself.

Edward knew about purging; he had done it himself often enough after feasting when his gluttony had overreached his reason. He made a sympathetic face and patted his wife's hand. "Unpleasant business, my dear, and I am sorry for you. I suppose you will miss the banquet tonight? I have promised the company jugglers, mummers, and a magician." He smiled at her, all the while planning how to fetch Jane for the festivities with Elizabeth's absence now assured. "I will come and tell you all about it tomorrow. Rest that beautiful body well, my dear. I will have prayers said for you at vespers."

Elizabeth made an effort to smile. "I am sure you will have a merrier time without me, Ned." She knew full well Jane Shore would take her place by his side, and there was naught she could do to stop it. How she still hated the woman!

"Pish!" Edward said, using his mother's favorite disclaimer as he eased himself out of the chair. He did not want Elizabeth to read the truth of her words in his eyes. But before he could open the door and escape, she fired one final taunt.

"Look to your harlot, Ned. She may be deceiving you. My son, Thomas, was seen leaving her house, I've been told. Perhaps she prefers men her own age?"

Edward's hand froze for a second on the door handle, but then he strode out without another word.

"Stay away from her," Will Hastings fumed at Tom when the young marquess had tried to beg a second dance from Jane during that night's celebration. He drew his stepson-in-law into an empty room used by the king's secretary during the day. "She belongs to the king, and you would do well to remember it, Thomas."

Earlier, Edward had pulled Will aside after mass and relayed Elizabeth's accusation. "Is it true, Will?" Edward asked with a hint of desperation that surprised his friend. "Is Jane involved with Tom Grey? I cannot bear disloyalty—especially from Jane." Sweet Jesu, Will had thought, the king really did love Jane, and he was briefly amused by the irony that the same mere merchant's daughter had ensnared not only him and Edward, but Tom as well.

"Jane has never mentioned Dorset to me in any conversation we have had, your grace," Will assured the king. "Also, as you know, I am a frequent visitor and have never seen him or any of his household in the vicinity. Could the queen have jested out of jealousy? She knows we have shared women in the past, which would have made her statement seem plausible. Tom was the obvious culprit, but I believe she was baiting you, sire."

Feeling somewhat appeased, Edward nodded. "I do not doubt Bessie is jealous, and your explanation makes sense. Even so, Will, I would ask that you watch Tom Grey closely tonight."

And so Will had done his king's bidding; with his sharp eyes, he had followed the man throughout the evening and observed with growing suspicion how Tom never took his gaze from Jane. And in turn he watched Jane. Her attention, he had to admit, never wavered from Edward, except when she was being partnered by the marquess, and even then, her eyes were on the floor. He could not see how tightly she held Tom's fingers or how her heart quickened as they stepped to the rebecs, viols, recorders, and tabors. Nay, if there was interest, it was all on Tom Grey's part, Will decided. And he could put a stop to that.

In the antechamber, Tom sneered at the portly Hastings. "Jealous, are we? Aye, I have seen how you follow Mistress Shore with lovelorn eyes. I heard she rejected you many years ago—too old for her." Then he laughed. "Who could blame her for looking to a younger man after you and the king have done with her?"

Will grabbed the impudent man's wrist and twisted it so Tom was an inch from his livid face, surprising Tom with his strength. "You lie, sirrah! Jane has only ever lain with the king, and you slander her and insult the king at your peril if you say different."

"Mayhap she has and maybe she has not, my lord Hastings. It is not for me to say." Tom, too, was seething. "Now, I pray you, stand aside so I may dance with Mistress Shore a second time. She appeared to enjoy the first."

Tom's cockiness further infuriated Will, who forced the young man onto his knees, both their backs to the door and unaware the king had entered.

"Presumptuous pup! You will not enjoy her again, I promise you!" Edward's furious voice made Will let go of his prey and Tom scramble to his feet. "You have annoyed the lady enough for one evening."

Edward looked from one belligerent man to the other and stood like a bulwark between them. "My patience is at an end with your quarreling." He was unwilling to make a scene within earshot of his courtiers, but his tone was commanding nonetheless: "Will, you should know better, and Tom, 'tis about time you went home to your wife and new child. Your neglect of them discredits you and displeases me."

Will agreed with Edward's assessment of Tom; he had heard enough at home on the subject from Katherine, who was concerned about her daughter and grandchildren.

However, ignoring the king's implied command, Tom responded with a derisive snort. "And my mother, your grace? Why are you not at her sickbed instead of lewdly cavorting with your—"

"Hold your insolent tongue!" Edward interrupted. "And get you gone before I take a horsewhip to you. You are no longer welcome here!"

Will held his breath. Even as the queen's son, Tom had gone too far, and unlucky for him, his mother was not present to protect him.

Needing no further warning, he pushed past Will and fled.

Jane, too, had seen Will follow Tom into the antechamber and had held her breath as she danced to an estampie with John Norrys. When she noticed Edward's absence from his seat, she had tried in vain to find him over the press of people but prayed he had merely stepped out to the garderobe.

Jane was radiant in pearly white satin that night, a black sable collar plunging from her shoulders in a V to the gold band around the high-waisted gown at the base of her cleavage. She had attempted to augment her height with a butterfly hennin of twisted gold and white bands, its veil supported by six-inch-high invisible underwires. Edward's latest gift, a heavy gold choke necklace set with rubies, accentuated her long neck. She had been thrilled with the gift, a sign that she was still in the king's high favor.

When Edward returned to her side, she sensed the change in his humor, but she knew him well enough not to pry. His anger had somewhat abated as she thanked him again for her gift. He smiled, and offering his arm, he led her to the dance floor. Seeing

Jane smiling into his eyes, he was satisfied. 'Twas not her fault that men were so charmed by her, he decided.

On their way from the dais, and attempting to dispel his sour mood, Edward whispered, "You look like a queen tonight, my dearest."

Jane gasped at the comparison. "Do not say so, my lord. I have no wish to rival her grace, nor do I presume to rise above my station. I am your devoted mistress and loyal friend, no more."

In a happier moment, Edward might have been charmed, but now he just found himself exasperated. "Why will you not simply accept my compliment, Jane?" he said as they took their places at the head of the dancers. "'Tis no secret I adore you. Are you so independent that you have not wondered what will be your lot if I tire of you? Perhaps you should be *shoring* up wealth for that day."

Edward could instantly sense Jane's dismay at his callous remarks despite the wordplay, but for once he would not recant; Tom Grey had spoiled his pleasure and made him testy. However, Jane's hurt silence eventually pricked his conscience, making him feel churlish. Again, he admitted, her charms were not her fault, nor his adoration her design.

The flutes and lutes were wringing out the plaintive notes of a stately basse danse as all eyes remained riveted on the couple, and Jane knew she must not reveal that she was anything but merry. She forced a smile, but her thoughts were tumbling like a troupe of uncontrolled acrobats. Was Edward truly tiring of her? Dear God, she panicked, what made him say that now? True, he had not enjoyed her body for a long time, but that was through no fault of hers. Had he found someone new? It had happened to Eleanor Butler and to Elizabeth Wayte, both of whom had not lasted as long as she had. Nay, surely her friend Will would have warned her. Then she heard her little imp remind her of Tom Grey's visit, and her belly churned. Sweet Mother of God, had Edward found out? Was that why she had seen Will speak angrily to Tom earlier?

And now Tom was gone and Edward's humor had darkened. Had he been with Will and Tom?

Jane's mind and heart raced at an equally frightening pace. As she passed her partner in the dance, she raised her eyes for an instant from the floor to Edward's face and caught him watching her. His sheepish smile instantly reassured her that she was being foolish. She smiled back, genuinely this time, but apprehension still lingered.

Returning to her seat, she caught the envious looks cast her way by other ladies, scrutinizing her appearance from head to toe, hoping to find her wanting. But Jane felt secure in her outward appearance; it was her inner confidence that was failing her this night. She mulled over a conversation she had had with Margaret Howard about Alice Perrers, another royal mistress a long time ago. She had risen from poverty to be the third King Edward's concubine. "She was a greedy woman, 'tis said," Margaret had told Jane. "More than jewels, she wanted, and was given, property and power. In all, the king gave her fifty manors or more, and as he sank into his dotage, she seized the reins of government. But when Edward died, she lost everything, was tried for corruption, and banished."

Jane looked at the inquisitive faces now and wondered if people were comparing her to this scheming Perrers woman?

"Why will you not ask for more reward for your loyalty to me?" Edward jogged her from her reverie. "You have the right, in truth. I have spent seven happy years knowing you." Then he leaned in and kissed her full on the mouth before adding, "And loving you."

Jane felt sufficiently mollified to lighten the mood. If he were tiring of her, would he be so affectionate in public? she reasoned. "Perhaps I am content enough with that knowledge, your grace. I love my house, and you keep me looking regal, even if I am not." She saw a sparkle return to her lover's eyes, and she guessed whatever had irked him earlier was receding. Watching Jester LeSage end an impressive juggling display and sit back down at Edward's feet, she suddenly clapped her hands. "How like you this silly ditty that has just occurred to me, your grace?" and she began to recite, slowly, as she sought the appropriate rhymes:

> *"Mistress Shore, the king's whore,*
> *Took great pride in the clothes she wore.*
> *But once in bed*
> *With her handsome Ned,*
> *She cared not a fig for them anymore."*

Edward slapped his knee and gave a shout of laughter. The musicians faltered in their rhythm and the dancers briefly hesitated, but Edward waved them on, still laughing. Jane suddenly wished Bella could see her now. She had always enjoyed her verses, Jane recalled, again missing her sister.

"How do you do that so quickly, my little poet?" Edward was saying. "Put your mind at rest, sweetheart. I could never tire of you." He patted her hand. "I think I should get my scribe to write your verses down. So much more interesting to read for posterity than dry doings at court."

Jane pretended horror. "I would not want good Englishmen reading them down the centuries. What would they think of me?"

Edward was still wiping his eyes when Jane took this moment of good humor to return to his earlier question to her.

"I confess it has crossed my mind that you might tire of me, sire." She put up her hand to muffle her next remark. "Never fear, Will Hastings has promised to look after me."

"Has he, by God," Edward replied. "'Twill have to be over my dead body, Mistress Shore." And he winked at her.

They both laughed. The king was happy again, his subjects could see. Without the queen and with Jane Shore at Edward's side, they felt at liberty to enjoy themselves freely. Couples began flirting and even kissing in corners, hands seeking forbidden flesh, and laughter growing more raucous as the wine flowed like the Thames in flood.

"I fear my brother Richard would not approve," Edward grumbled, pointing out a pretty woman occupying the lap of a young man whose hand had disappeared up her skirt. "He is as boringly prating as a priest. But loyal. 'Tis one thing you can say about Richard: he is loyal."

Jane began to improvise again, a laugh in her voice.

> *"At Edward's court,*
> *We dine and sport,*
> *All the livelong day.*
> *But one dull duke*
> *With scowl'd rebuke*
> *Would take our sport away."*

The jester was not amused that Jane's clever verse was upstaging his capering. She was too clever for words, although he had to admit she was always the first to compliment him on a witty turn of phrase or a jest. He was redoubling his efforts to entertain his king as Edward's bevy of lovely daughters took their places on the dance floor for a carol. The musicians had just struck the first notes when there was a flurry of activity at the entrance to the hall.

"Make way for Lord Howard!" an usher shouted above the din.

The music died and a hush fell on the courtiers as Jack Howard, his stocky legs well hidden beneath the long gown he favored, marched confidently toward the dais and fell on one knee in front of his king, hat in hand. His gray-streaked hair was matted to his head, his leather riding boots sodden.

"Sire, God give you a good evening. I am come in haste from Calais. May I request a private audience." The long ends of Howard's gray mustache drooped dishearteningly; there was no good-humored smile from the councilor tonight. Will Hastings joined his deputy, looking grim; he could almost guess Jack's bad news.

Edward rose with surprising agility for his corpulence, and giving Jack Howard a nod, he motioned to the musicians to continue and for his chamberlain, his chancellor, and his steward to follow him.

"Wait for me in my chambers," he told Jane. "I shall have need of you tonight."

"Aye, your grace," Jane answered him, dismayed by the tension that had again gripped Edward's face. She, too, rose and curtseyed as Edward made his way into the same antechamber she had seen Will and Tom enter not an hour before. Without Edward, she knew her place at the festivities was awkward, and she had no wish to flaunt herself alone as royal concubine in front of Edward's young daughters. She must go.

"Do you need an escort, mistress?" As though he had read her mind, John Norrys was at her elbow, his voice all kindness. "Would you like me to see you to his grace's apartments?"

Her relieved smile gave him his answer, and he gave her his arm.

Even the music could not drown out the bellow from behind the heavy wooden door of the antechamber. Fifteen-year-old Elizabeth of York, recognizing her father's fury, called her sisters to her and led them from the hall to the princesses' private apartments. A sweet-natured girl, she hated hearing her beloved father shout.

In the stuffy antechamber, Edward's face had turned a shade of murrey to match his velvet cote. His fist thundered down on the desk, making the quills and ink pots jump.

"That villainous boil-snouted barnacle!" he spluttered. "May he grow warts all over his member and may bats fly up his arse. A treaty you say, Jack? Signed in Arras these two weeks past? The spider king has tricked us again, by God's nails. Louis has used our truce to sign with Maximilian. And I thought Burgundy was our ally. Shame on the archduke, and shame on my sister. Margaret must have known."

He sat down hard, his oversize frame causing the chair to wobble dangerously, and he put his head in his hands. "Why am I the last to know?"

"I warned you, your grace. I warned you in the autumn when I came back from Calais," Will Hastings gently reminded him. "If you remember, I advised you to send help to Burgundy, but your brother had our troops busy in Scotland."

Edward raised his livid face to his chamberlain, and Will flinched at the king's fierce ire. "Gloucester is the only one I can count on these days," he said. "At least he has won Berwick back for us. What have you done, Hastings, except to worry me with rumors about the sale of Calais to the French and weak excuses about your innocence. You should have prevented this treaty."

Will paled. He understood at once that he was to be the scapegoat. Edward needed to blame someone for the failure of his own foreign policy. He shivered and went on one knee. "Sire, I swear on the cross of St. George that those accusations against me were false," he cried, determined to defend himself. "I am your true liegeman and all here will vouch for me. Jack? Rotherham? Stanley?" He looked at each in turn and all nodded their assurance. None could find fault with their comrade's loyalty. "I have kept you informed at every turn, your grace, and when you called for me to return home, I left the ablest man as deputy. I would trust Jack Howard with my life, and certainly the defense of Calais. I swear I have done all I could do to preserve Calais and naught but your bidding, sire. My loyalty is yours till the grave."

Edward studied his friend's distraught face for a second before signaling Will to stand. "Aye, you are my loyal subject, my lord, I know that." Then he turned back to Jack Howard, leaving Will bewildered. Had he been forgiven?

Edward asked Jack: "And the pledge to wed my daughter to the dauphin? Will Louis uphold that, do you suppose?"

Howard knew the answer would enrage Edward further, but he

was not a man to dissemble. "The dauphin is pledged to Maximilian's daughter, and the girl is being readied to go to the French court despite being only three."

Again the king's fist thumped on the desk. "Young Margaret of Burgundy was contracted to Ned. She would be queen of England one day. And what do you have to say to that, Lord Hastings? Aye, you are loyal, but you have lost me my alliance. Where is a lawyer? Find me a lawyer! We shall soon see about breaking contracts."

Grateful to escape, Will quit the room, and his eye fell on the enigmatic face of one of his own retainers, William Catesby, who was leaning alone on a pillar, watching the dancing in the main hall. "Catesby," he called, beckoning to him. Simulating washing his white, womanly hands, Catesby eagerly hurried to his lord. "Come with me, William, the king has need of you."

In his uneasiness, Will did not catch the gleam of ambition in the lawyer's eye as he turned the door handle. Will had never before borne the brunt of Edward's anger, and it had unnerved him.

It seemed to Jane that during that long cold January, Edward's zest for life began to flag. He laughed rarely, and the humiliation that Louis of France had visited on the English king gripped Edward in a form of melancholy. He summoned a Parliament to discuss the Treaty of Arras and its implications for England, most importantly the broken marriage contracts.

Edward still called for Jane at Westminster, and for a few hours she was able to amuse him and make him feel loved. In between her trysts with the king, she and Will discussed the change in their lord and tried to ignore their fear for his health.

Then one day in early February, Will burst unannounced into her solar, with Ankarette complaining in his wake. He shut the door unceremoniously in her face.

"I am to go to the Tower!" he cried after Jane had leaped up to greet him. "Indefinitely."

Aghast, Jane's questions tumbled forth. "The Tower? Why, Will? You mean . . . you mean as a prisoner? Nay, you must be mistaken, my dear friend. Edward is sending you to prison? What have you done wrong?"

Will slumped into his favorite settle, and Jane's new pup, a gift from Edward, tried unsuccessfully to scramble into his lap. Staring into the fire, Will absently fondled the dog's ears, and the animal curled up at his feet.

"Is there aught I can do for you? Plead with Edward? When must you go, my lord?" Jane wondered why he had come to her. Looking out of the upstairs window, she could see the guards stationed below in the street; John Norrys was also waiting.

"I am on my way there, Jane," Will replied, flatly. "I was given leave to stop by my house, alert my household, and gather a few necessaries. John Norrys, God bless him, allowed me to see you for a few minutes as well."

Jane turned back, her hands nervously playing with her braided belt. "The king must have accused you of something, Will. What was it?"

"The king seems convinced that I had made plans to sell out Calais to the French. Lies, all lies," he insisted, "spread by Rivers. God's wounds, that man has much to answer for. 'Tis he who should be taken to the Tower, not I." He shifted his weight. "But I know Edward after all these years. He needs someone to blame for not working harder to keep France and Burgundy apart, and I am to be that man. We all saw this treaty coming, and I warned him of it many times, but in his lassitude, Edward failed to act. Believe me, the Rivers feud is not the reason." He ran his hands through his thinning hair and down over his face in a gesture of helplessness. "'Tis more than I can bear after having always been so loyal."

"He will come to his senses," Jane reassured him. After all this time, she now understood how frail the ties were that bound loyalties at court. One day you were in a lord's good graces and the next you were ostracized or worse, imprisoned and executed. She had learned to keep to herself and to trust only a few at court; her friend Margaret Howard had guided her well over the years. That the king's chief councilor could not be safe frightened her; how soon before Edward turned on her? She shook off her fear, knowing she must try and cheer her friend. "He is angry and humiliated. It will not last, I am certain. How long must you remain in the Tower?"

Will was glum. "I do not know. And to add to the ignominy, the king has removed me as master of the mint, a position I have held throughout his reign. 'Twas the first step. Then he ordered me to the Tower at his pleasure, I know not for how long. But Edward needs me," he grumbled, "so 'twill be resolved, I have no doubt. But I am much mortified."

Jane knelt beside him and laid her head on his knee. For once, Will had no other desire for her than to stroke her head and accept her sympathy.

"Would you like me to talk to Edward on your behalf, Will?"

"I must forbid it, my dear Jane. Edward must not know we spoke today; I would not forgive myself if he turned his fury on you." He rose, gentling her to her feet. "Nay, I shall bid my wife a fast farewell; she will be distraught for herself, but no doubt she will blame me for warring so long with the Woodvilles. I can hear her now: 'You have brought this on yourself, husband. Your wenching nights with Edward have led poor Elizabeth to despise you.' As well, the queen must have succeeded in exonerating her brother, Rivers, and pointing the finger at me. Katherine is right, and she has the queen's ear. Her grace has no love for me, and she certainly has no love for you either, Jane. You must have a care while I am . . . indisposed."

"I am not afraid, Will. Elizabeth would not dare do me harm while Edward is still king, for all he has changed in a very short time. Take care of yourself and do not fret one whit about me." She put her arm through his and led him toward the door. "Go now, lest adultery with the king's whore be added to your list of crimes," she said, trying to tease a smile from him. She thrust Edward's book into his hands. "To while away the hours. What else shall I bring you when I visit you? Marchpane? Capon pie? A custard?"

At the door, Jane turned to him, masking any anxiety she felt for his predicament. Her whole body exuded warmth and friendship, and he wanted to succumb to its comforting embrace. Instead he bowed over her hand, kissed it gently, lifted the latch, and left. He would have to settle for the sweet memory of her to warm the cold cell at the Tower.

Jane ran to the window and looked down on the guards in the royal colors. She watched as they marched on either side of the king's disgraced and disconsolate chamberlain, and she felt her stomach contract. John Norrys chose to look up at that moment, and she put her finger to her lips. He nodded, and she knew she could count on him to keep the meeting a secret.

Curious onlookers were pointing at Will, who bravely held up his head as they processed along Thames Street. Jane could not help begging St. Elizabeth to protect her from ever having to endure such fearful public shame. If the king could turn against his greatest friend and most loyal servant, then what could she expect should she lose his love?

ELEVEN

Richard of Gloucester sat his horse as though one born in the saddle, and he preferred to ride from Westminster to the Tower that chilly but bright morning in February instead of taking the royal barge. As constable of England, Richard was responsible for overseeing the royal armies, and during this rare visit to London from his stronghold in the north, he was on his way to inspect the Tower garrison. A few cheers greeted him at the Ludgate when his White Boar badge was recognized, although his was an unfamiliar face to most Londoners. Richard preferred the company of the more rough-and-ready northern folk and considered the south a hotbed of vainglorious and soft-bellied men who lied and schemed their way into favor with the king. It was not that Londoners mistrusted the king's brother, who, along with the popular Hastings, all acknowledged him as Edward's most loyal subject; it was just that they did not know him. And Richard was content to keep it that way.

As he rode along the main thoroughfares of London, Richard observed ample examples of how Edward's reign had brought wealth to the city. If his brother's foreign policies had not impressed Richard of late, he had no quarrel with how Edward governed his own subjects.

His small retinue rode over the two moat bridges, and the horses skittered along the cobblestoned outer ward and under the portcullised Garden Tower gate that led to the inner ward. Grooms ran to greet the duke and his men, and Richard swung off his mount to the ground, grimacing as his vulnerable spine resisted. He bore the constant aching without complaint, however. His destination was the White Tower, but all at once he was stayed by the sight of two women exiting the covered stairway from the Garden Tower. He searched his memory, wishing he had Edward's gift for remembering the most obscure names and faces, as he was certain he had seen one of the women before.

"Tell me, lad," he spoke quietly to a groom, "do you know who the lady in blue is?"

"Aye, my lord duke," the young man replied, a smile lighting his round, wind-chapped face. "She be one of us. We call her the Rose of London on account of the many kind favors she has done for us Londoners." He leaned in to Richard conspiratorially. "Besides she be the king's mistress, Jane Shore."

Two scenes sprang to his mind: one in the Chepe when a veiled, spirited mercer's wife warned him of danger from behind; and the other upon a pleasant day of hunting at Greenwich. Certes, he knew Edward had kept a mistress named Jane for many years, and perhaps, Richard thought, his brother had several others hidden in houses about the city, but he had not connected that woman with the quick-witted wife of the lanky, flustered mercer who had been robbed.

As he raised his eyes from the groom, Richard examined the object of Edward's illicit affection, doubtless one of the causes of Edward's depraved court. At exactly the same time, Jane turned her head and saw Richard. She dropped a curtsey and would have hurried away, but the duke reached her before she could take Sophie's arm and disappear under the gateway.

"*Mistress* Shore, is it not?" Richard's rhetorical question was purposely blunt. "What brings you to the Tower? Do you have family who are garrisoned here, or does your husband have a customer here he has sent you to service?"

His tone was offensive, and Jane was shaken by his crass insinuations. She arched an eyebrow and answered with icy civility: "God's good greeting to you, too, my lord Gloucester. I am surprised you remember my name after all these years." Sophie gasped at Jane's gall and then dropped a curtsey. This was the closest the silkwoman had been to royalty. Jane brought Sophie forward. "And this is my friend Mistress Vandersand of Sithe's Lane."

Richard, realizing he had foregone his usual unflagging good manners, acknowledged Sophie with a curt nod before rounding on Jane again. "I would ask you once more, what is your business here, madam? And this time, do not dissemble."

Incensed at this interrogation, Jane nevertheless forced a smile. "Your pardon, your grace. If you had asked me civilly, I would have told you straight that I was visiting Lord Hastings, who is lodged here for a short time at the king's pleasure."

"Another of your customers, mistress?" Richard brazenly asked, his smile as forced as hers. But the thoughts behind the mask were ugly. He had no doubt this strumpet frequented the lord chamberlain's bed as well as the king's and that she held both men in thrall. Would he could put a stop to it, he thought. "I presume I am right?"

Jane ignored this insult. "He is a friend," she declared and, astonished at her own daring, lied, "I came with the king's permission."

"I wager you did," he scoffed. "You will not be forced to visit Lord Hastings here much longer. Aye, it would seem he is to be released within days. My brother, for all his faults, is merciful."

Jane's face lit up. "My lord Hastings will be released?" she exclaimed, and then to Sophie, she added, "Do your hear, Sophie, my plea for him did not fall on deaf ears." She was glad she had ignored Will's directive.

But poor Sophie was wishing herself a mile away in the safety of her small house and pulled in vain at Jane's skirt.

"*Your* plea, Jane Shore?" Richard was saying. "Nay, 'twas I who intervened with the king. We cannot afford to lose the affinity so

loyal a baron, albeit one so dissolute." He refrained from com-
menting on his brother's deterioration and thought that perhaps
Edward was not thinking clearly or making wise decisions. Upon
seeing Edward after this lengthy absence, Richard had wondered
if he ought not stay in London and monitor his brother's ability
to govern. The snit with Hastings was worrisome; clearly the man
had done his duty in warning Edward of the possible treaty, and
Richard considered Hastings a good councilor, if not the most
moral of men in pursuing his pleasures.

Richard fiddled with the dagger hilt on his belt, weighing
his next words. He did not know why he was irritated by the
woman's presence; she had every right to visit a prisoner, if she
had permission, but he was inclined to think Mistress Shore and
Hastings had somehow contributed to his brother's debauchery.
Aye, he would speak his mind, he decided, and defend his beloved oldest brother.

"Hear this, and hear it well, Mistress Shore. It is lewdness and
impiety that has brought Edward to the unhealthy state I find him
in, and I blame those, such as yourself, who have encouraged him
in his corruption."

Jane gasped at his frankness, but before she could think of a
retort, he nodded, wished her adieu, and marched purposefully toward the White Tower. Jane stared after him. When he had smiled,
Jane had seen that the duke was darkly handsome, but his words
were harsh, and instinct told her to beware of him.

Sophie was already halfway back to the gatehouse by the time
an irate Jane followed her.

"I saw your whore today, brother. She claimed she had your blessing to visit Will Hastings."

Richard took off his velvet gloves and played with his signet
ring, all the while fixing his eyes on his brother's pudgy face. He

could hardly recognize the stalwart warrior of his youth in this bloated carcass of a man. His devotion to Edward had never wavered until now, and coming face-to-face with the Shore woman had hardened his heart as he rode back to Westminster.

"Come now, Richard, you do the lady a disservice. She is no whore. Jane is every whit the lady your Kate was and more. At least my mistress is educated and the daughter of an alderman."

For a second Edward saw Richard's face soften, and he pounced on the chance to tease his solemn sibling. "Ah, I see you have not forgotten that you, too, knew love with an unsuitable bedfellow. You should be flattered that I saw much of Kate Haute in Jane Shore. Face it, Dickon, you will always love that bold beauty, despite your devotion to Anne. Believe me, I understand. I am in love with Jane but am also devoted to Elizabeth." He tilted his head, amused at Richard's discomfort. "Come, come, you are not good at pretense. Admit it, sir, you have not forgotten."

Richard poured himself some ale and began pacing the room while Edward watched with amusement. Finally, Richard relented.

"How can I forget the mother of my two bastards? They are as dear to me as my legitimate son." He grinned ruefully. "In truth, there are days when I yearn to see Kate again, but I made a vow to Anne that I would stay away from Kate, and by God, I have kept that promise." He could not let the matter drop without pointing out that, unlike Edward, he had never betrayed his marriage bed with another woman. "I admire Elizabeth for her steadfastness, even if I cannot like her as your queen."

Edward laughed. "I have missed your candor, little brother. It may surprise you to know that Elizabeth thinks highly of you. And it may surprise you to know we still love each other. Whatever else she may be—ambitious, haughty, scheming—her loyalty to me has never wavered, despite my . . . my transgressions."

Richard snickered. "A dainty word for so many mortal sins." His tone became one of concern. "Are you well, Ned? You have an unhealthy mien. You are not even forty years old, but you move more like a sixty-year-old. I watch you consume twice as much as anyone at the high table, drink three times as much, and then purge yourself so you can eat more. Have a care for your heir, brother. You need to live long enough to see him to manhood before he becomes king. How old is he now, twelve?"

Edward looked at his brother quizzically. "Why, Dickon, would you see me in my grave already? Do you, too, have an itch to wear the crown? *Je m'excuse*," he apologized, seeing the shock on Richard's face. "I am but jesting. Although, by Christ's nails, you know how to drive the point home. Aye, I lack the same vigor I had when I became king, but with you fighting my battles for me in the north, and with England at peace, I have no more need for my soldiering skills. I am grateful for your concern, and I will try and curb my many appetites, but do not tell me to give up Jane. She is the joy of my life, and I believe she loves me, too."

Richard thought Edward too selfish to know real love, but he nodded gravely and changed the subject. "Tell me about my nieces, Ned. They are among the most beautiful girls I have laid eyes on, after my own Katherine, certainly." For the next hour, the two brothers conversed amicably about their children's virtues, which led to tales of their own childhood, which had been at once warm and loving yet fraught with danger.

All was well on that cold February day, but not two weeks later, Richard spurred his horse north and home to Anne, taking with him his brother's deepest gratitude for his handling of the Scottish campaign. Richard of Gloucester and his descendants were given permanent wardenship of the west marches, between Scotland and England, as well as of Carlisle and its castle and many other crown possessions in the north. As long as Edward remained king, Gloucester, as his loyal brother and Lord of the North, would keep the border safe. The monumental grant was no less than he richly deserved, Richard thought, when he had listened to Parliament consent to Edward's request. He would do better than Edward in ruling the unpredictable north country.

March brought more cold days, and Londoners hurried from one place to another muffled in warm cloaks against the biting wind.

One plump figure in black velvet, her hood lined with squirrel fur, approached with hesitant steps the house on Thames Street. She tapped the knocker lightly and stepped back. She did not have long to wait, for the door swung open and a balding man with a cherubic face greeted her and, upon hearing her name, invited her in.

"Mistress Lambert," the steward announced, ushering Amy into the warm solar, then disappearing with her cloak.

"Mother!" Jane jumped to her feet and ran to embrace her parent. "How glad I am to see you."

Amy held her daughter's hands, searching Jane's face for any sign of falseness. Seeing none, Amy smiled, reassuring Jane that her mother was happy to see her, too.

"How I have missed you," Jane cried, drawing Amy toward her own chair by the fire. Then she noticed the circles under her mother's once-luminous eyes and the worry lines carved deep in her face, and she knew something was wrong.

"Is it Father? Is he dead?" she asked, surprised that the thought of her father's demise gave her an unexpected stab of regret.

"Nay, Jane. He is as well and as stubborn as ever. 'Tis Bella," she said sorrowfully. "You knew she married Goldsmith Allen?" Seeing Jane nod, she continued: "She gave birth to a puling babe a few days ago—her third—and she is very weak and we fear for her life. She has asked for you, and I could not in good conscience refuse, if that is her wish."

"Me?" Jane said incredulously. "Why? She has not tried to see me nor has she answered any of my notes since . . . since . . ." She broke off. They both remembered the last time they all had sat together. "I should like to know my nieces," Jane said sadly. "And now she calls for me?"

Amy nodded, her conscience pricking. "You are her sister, and like me, she still loves you. We know all about the good you have done for people. Please believe that I am proud when I hear the stories." Her tone turned anxious. "But you must understand your sister and I were denied communication with you by your father. You know what he is like, Jane. We dared not gainsay him. In fact, he would beat me if he knew I had come here today. He has disowned you, as certes you know." She stared at her hands, worrying a broken fingernail, and Jane felt sorry for her. How relieved she was that she had not tolerated a similar life of servitude married to William.

"Is Bella's life truly in danger?" Jane whispered. "Shall I come with you now, Mother?"

Amy nodded, a tear running down her face. She wiped it away and tried to smile. "Ah, Jane, 'tis good to see you looking so well and not like a . . ." She bit her tongue. How could she say that she had expected Jane would resemble the well-worn whores that roamed the streets of Southwark. In truth, to Amy her wayward daughter looked lovelier than ever.

Jane came to her rescue. "I understand, Mother. Let us talk no more about it. Now take me to Bella."

She did not tell Amy that after she had heard about Bella's marriage, she had twice walked past the Allens' large establishment in Friday Street, with its polished leaded windows displaying the goldsmith's workmanship, hoping to encounter her sister, but she had failed.

"Ankarette!" Jane called through the open door. "We are going out. Pray fetch our cloaks."

Like old times, mother and daughter walked arm in arm along Thames Street, past Will Hastings's impressive town house, up onto Lambert Hill, skirting St. Paul's to get to the Chepe, and arriving at the Allens' house on Friday Street in the space of ten minutes. Gerald Allen was busy with a customer when Amy preceded Jane and Ankarette into the shop, but he nodded to Amy and jerked his head in the direction of the stairs; having never seen Jane up close, he did not recognize her and assumed she was an acquaintance of his wife's.

Once in the Allens' spacious bedchamber, the canopied tester bed a massive presence in the room, Jane wrinkled her nose. "What is that smell, Mother?"

Amy put her finger to her lips. "Brace yourself, my dear. 'Tis the childbed fever. 'Twas the same when my sister passed away. The doctor told me; 'tis unmistakable."

Jane covered her mouth to stifle a gasp of revulsion and hurried to the bed. Her sister lay like a frozen stick under the snowy sheet, her skin reminding Jane of the pale gray of dawn on an inclement morning. On the other side of the bed, a doctor was readying a fleem to bleed Bella, but when he saw Amy, he bowed and, shaking his head in helplessness, retired.

Jane gently lowered herself onto the bed and took Bella's hot, dry hand. She was surprised how warm the sick woman felt, considering her pallor. "Can you hear me, sister?" she asked. "'Tis I, Jane, come to make you well again."

The eyes on the patient fluttered open then, and the semblance of a smile flitted across her face. Bella reached out for Jane. "Lillibet, my babe is dead. They told me. 'Tis God's will."

"May she rest in peace," Jane prayed. "I am so sorry, Bella."

Bella began to whimper. "Oh, Lillibet, is it really you? I did not dare to hope you would come." An urgency seemed to overcome her. "I am so sorry I forsook you all these years. Can you ever forgive me?"

Jane patted her hand. "Nay, Bella, 'tis I who must ask forgiveness. I cannot pretend I was sad to leave my life on Coleman Street, and I certainly was not sorry to leave Father, but I have always missed you, little sister. I should have tried harder to see you and your children." She stroked the gaunt cheek and wiped away Bella's tears. "Do not cry, my dear. You will soon be well, and I promise I will come every day until you are strong."

Bella's smile widened, and she tried to lift herself from her pillow. "You will? What if Father finds out?"

Jane eased her back down, shushing her gently. "Listen to me, sweeting. You are Master Allen's wife now and out of Father's hands. He cannot hurt either of us anymore."

"Oh, Lillibet, how I have missed you. 'Tis only that . . ."

"I know, my dear," Jane said, stroking her cheek. "I know what people think, but I am still the same person you knew when we were girls, and I love you still."

Overwhelmed by her sister's kindness, more tears filled Bella's eyes. Easily tired, the ailing young woman soon slept. Jane gentled her hand from her sister's grasp and quietly left the room.

It would be the first of three more visits to Friday Street, where Jane sat with Bella and reminisced about their childhood together. Some of Jane's retellings briefly cheered the invalid, but all could see the young woman was failing and would not survive.

"Tell me about the king, Lillibet," she rasped on the third day. Why was her throat so sore? She had also broken out in a rash, and the doctor had told the family that it would not be long now. "Is he kind to you?"

And so Jane shared with her dying sister the secrets of her new life and how King Edward of England had shown her the joys of love between a man and a woman. "I cannot deny I have enjoyed being treated like a queen, but you must not think it comes without hardship. I fear God may have forsaken me—as well as my family." She leaned forward then, not wanting to sound maudlin. "But, I have another secret, Bella," she continued eagerly, not knowing if Isabel could hear her or not, "and I need to tell someone . . ." There was no response from the still figure in the bed, and so Jane held her peace.

Then Isabel's eyelids fluttered and she smiled when she recognized Jane was still there. "God be with you, Lillibet. I know you now for a good woman." Then she began to look wildly about her. "My children! Where are my children?"

Gerald Allen was by his wife's side in two strides. "My dear, you know they are with your mother. Now you must rest." He looked at Jane gratefully. "Your sister will come again tomorrow."

Jane kissed Bella's clammy forehead and prayed that tomorrow would not be too late. Her secret would have to wait. Quietly slipping out onto the street, she came face-to-face with her father, on his way to pay his last respects to his favorite daughter.

"You!" he cried, his fists balling. "What are you doing here? Who told you Isabel was ailing?"

"'Tis pleasant to see you, too, Father," Jane said without flinching. "'Tis common knowledge that the wife of such a distinguished goldsmith as Master Allen is on her deathbed." She would not betray her mother, she determined. "I came to reconcile with Bella and, with her husband's blessing, this is my fourth visit. Good day, sir." And she hurried past him.

"Wanton!" John Lambert called after her. "Harlot!"

But Jane walked on.

Bella died three days later, and when the news reached Thames Street Jane took to her bed, seeing no one except for Ankarette. How Jane now bitterly regretted the estrangement from her sister. Bella represented the carefree times in Jane's life on Hosier Lane. The girl had never asked to be her father's favorite, Jane realized now too late; she had simply been a more placid and biddable child who rarely caused her father to raise his voice. And Bella had worshipped her beautiful sister, Jane remembered guiltily. Ah, Jane, how bittersweet, she thought; your reunion came too late.

The only person who understood this part of Jane's life was Sophie, and it was to the Vandersands' greatly improved house that

Jane eventually found her way. The motherly Sophie held her friend for many minutes as Jane cried and then described Bella's bravery.

"I could not have taken my fate so calmly," Jane admitted, sadly. "I would have fought to get out of bed and defy death. Certes, I am glad 'twas not I suffering so, but I found myself begging God that I could take her place so she could live to see her children grow up. I have no children, and, indeed, I have no one I can call my own, so why was I not taken instead?" And her tears began again.

"Hush, *lieveling*," Sophie soothed. "It was God's vill. He needed Bella for some reason, but you are brave, Jane. You fought your way out of a life you hated, and look at you. You live like a lady and you are generous beyond vords with your new fortune. Aye, Bella was a good mother, but you are good, too. All of London knows Jane Shore; only a few know of Isabel Allen."

Jane stood and paced the new wooden floor that her money had provided. "Aye," she scoffed. "They know me for a harlot!"

Sophie jumped up and shook Jane. "Some, *ja*, but most know you for your good heart. The doctor you sent to tend the butcher's children with the pox; the mercer you saved from prison; the beggar you gave a cloak to. Londoners know these tales, Jane. And you will never be alone as long as Jehan and I are alive." She smiled. "Did I tell you that Janneke vants to be a king's mistress, just like you? She adores you."

That made Jane smile, too, and she kissed her friend's rosy cheek. "My thanks, Sophie. I feel a little better. Now, where is Janneke? I have brought her something for her beautiful hair." She drew a length of velvet ribbon from the pouch at her waist. "She must be attracting attention by now."

Sophie dimpled. "There is a cordwainer's son who manages to pass by the house no matter what direction he is supposed to go. He is a nice boy, but Jehan has been talking to a fellow *flamand* about his oldest boy for Janneke."

"Oh, Sophie, take warning from me. If Janneke and this boy love each other, do not force her on the *flamand*."

This was spoken with such heartrending sincerity that Sophie frowned. "Vat is it you are not telling me, *lieveling*? Are you not happy now?"

Jane hesitated but then blurted out the secret she had wanted to tell Bella. "I am still in love with Tom Grey, and I will not be happy until we are together. There, I said it!"

Sophie clicked her tongue. "It is my opinion you set too much importance on love, Jane. Men are not vat brings happiness to a woman." She tousled Pieter's blond curls, and he turned big blue eyes to his mother. "This is the love that is important, and I pray daily that you vill be blessed soon."

Jane embraced her friend, and after an hour of pleasant conversation, took her leave. On the way home she found herself noticing every little boy and girl playing in their gardens or on the street. She would be thirty years old in a few months and had not yet conceived. How she still yearned for a child of her own.

TWELVE

Will had been forgiven and was once again Edward's trusty and well-beloved councilor. In fact the two men were celebrating Easter at Windsor in each other's company and had taken Jane with them, leaving the queen and her daughters to be transported by boat to Greenwich for the holiest of feast days.

"Elizabeth has always preferred her Placentia Palace, but I am happiest at Windsor," Edward had told Jane when they climbed aboard the royal barge, its pennants and standard lifting limply in an almost windless day. "The air is more bracing, and the hunting better."

It took them two days to be conveyed between the banks bursting with early flowers: yellow primroses, pink butterbur, tiny white daisies in among the dandelions, and the purple faces of violets. Edward's jester was silent for once but for his soft strumming on a mandora that seemed to echo the plangent rippling of the water from the oars. Jane thought she had never been happier as she nestled in the crook of Edward's broad arm and listened to him discuss politics with Will opposite them.

Windsor welcomed its lord home with a hunt and a Good Friday feast featuring many dishes to tempt Edward, who hated fish. How glad he was, he said later, to have Lent finally over. A haunch of venison dominated his plate following the Easter mass. Later, he invited Jane and Will to inspect the new additions to St. George's Chapel.

"So you wish to spend eternity with me here, my friend,

instead of lying in your own new chapel at Ashby with your wife," Edward asked as the trio stopped at the shrine of John Schorn at the southeast corner of St. George's, each lighting a candle to the renowned healer. "Do you think I will need counseling in heaven?"

Will laughed. "Katherine has already commissioned her tomb at Ashby, and I was not to be a part of it, it seems. She may rest in peace there without my grousing at her forever," he said. He turned to face Edward. "In all seriousness, sire, 'twould be a supreme honor to lie near you. We have experienced so much together, I cannot imagine enjoying all heaven has to offer without you."

"Have you forgiven me for sending you to the Tower, Will?" Edward was quizzical. "Someone had to pay for Arras. Surely you knew your life was not in danger."

Will swallowed. Should he pretend he knew all along, or should he tell the truth, that he had spent a week of sleepless nights wondering when his butt of malmsey might appear? "I hoped you still needed me, my lord. I had to be patient. It was just a matter of time." He brought the subject back to the tomb. "Have you forgiven me enough to grant my wish, Ned?"

It was Edward's turn to laugh. "Thy will be done, my lord," he promised.

The burnished oak of the newly completed quire next drew their attention, and Jane exclaimed over the amusing misericords tucked under the seats and admired William Berkeley's exquisite woodcarving in the paneled stalls above, upon which the knights of the garter crests and shields were fixed. Several large earthenware pots drew Jane's attention, and Edward explained they would be placed under the floor of each stall to improve the acoustics.

When they reached the northeast corner, Edward paused and pointed at a winding stair to a chantry above them. "This is where my tomb will be one day, Will. Does that suit you?"

Jane suddenly felt cold, and she linked her arms through theirs. "My dear lords, let us go back out into the sunshine. All this talk of death and tombs is distressing." She almost dragged them back to the door.

Will whispered to the surprised Edward that Jane must still be grieving her sister's death, and Edward looked appropriately chastised.

Once away from the tombs, Jane's natural gaiety returned, and looking from one man to the other, she said, "My lords, I want to take you across the river to Eton and show you *my* project. Did our sovereign tell you I persuaded him to spare some money to finish the school?"

Edward looked across at Will over Jane's turbaned head and winked. "Mistress Shore thinks more of reading and writing than of saying her prayers. If heaven will not have her, at least she will be among the erudite in purgatory, do you not agree?"

A priest hurrying up the steps to the entrance was shocked to hear loud laughter from within the chapel's sacred space.

The voyage back to Westminster was aided by the downstream current, and as the barge was approaching the palace quay, cheers erupted from the shore. As Edward waved back to his loyal subjects, all of a sudden the figures went out of focus and he could not move his face.

Sitting in front of him, Jane noticed his unnatural, frozen stare and anxiously enquired: "Your grace, is anything wrong?"

She was about to repeat the question when Edward suddenly clutched his chest and began to shake violently, slipping into the bottom of the boat. Jane jumped up and cried out to Will for help. She threw off Edward's hat and set about loosening his high-necked shirt. Will climbed clumsily through the oarsmen from the front of the barge, where he had been talking with the master, and saw with mounting panic that the king was in the midst of a seizure.

"Hurry!" he cried back to the master of oars. "The king is unwell."

Jane was almost thrown off her feet when the barge bumped

the wooden wharf with unaccustomed speed. John Norrys and two other squires leaped from the deck and corralled three burly boatmen to help lift the king's now-inert body from the vessel.

"My lord, can you hear me?" Jane asked in Edward's ear. "Squeeze my hand if you can."

It was not much, but she felt the pressure on her fingers and told Will, "He is alive, praise be to God."

The hulking figure of the king was hoisted onto the shoulders of half a dozen men who had run to help, and they staggered with their load toward the watergate entry of the palace. By now, people were hanging from windows to see what had happened, and once inside Will barked orders to ready the king's bed and to send for the physicians. Within a very few minutes, organized chaos reigned in the corridors of Westminster as gentlemen ushers ran to do Will's bidding, others closed the windows and shutters to keep out the cold air and possible evil spirits, and a messenger was sent to speed the queen's return.

No one looked askance as Jane supervised Edward's unrobing and, once he was between the sheets, sat by his bed massaging his hand. It seemed to her that an eternity had passed since she first noticed his paralysis, but in fact no more than thirty minutes had gone by. She was aware of others in the room, and she supposed Lord Stanley, as king's steward, was hovering with Will, but she concentrated all her attention on Edward, murmuring tender words and begging him to wake.

"I can hear you, Jane." Edward's rasped words sent Jane to her knees, praising God. "Why am I here?"

Will came to the other side of the bed, his face showing a mix of relief and worry. "Sire, you were unwell for a short time, but, thanks be to God, I see you are yourself again."

Edward tried to lift himself off the pillow but fell back when the dizziness would not pass. He looked first at Jane and then at Will, and although he heard them clearly, they appeared as through an old horn window, and he blinked several times to try and clear his vision.

Doctor de Serigo scurried into the room, bloodletting tools clutched to his chest, and tut-tutted his way to displace Will, giving Jane a venomous stare. This was the queen's physician, and he was well aware of who this interloper was. He had arrived ahead of the queen's party and was the first physician the usher had stumbled upon. De Serigo was not surprised God had struck down the immoral king, who thought nothing of humiliating the doctor's good mistress with this harlot.

"*Deve andare!* You go, you understand," he ordered Jane, making shooing signs with his hands. "The queen she come soon."

"She stays!" Edward's voice came loud although slightly slurred, but his intent had been clear. "Now get on with your work, signor."

The swarthy doctor scowled but did as he was told, swiftly lancing a vein in Edward's tree of an arm. Edward turned his face away and tried to focus on Jane. In truth, the fuzziness was disconcerting, but other than a headache and tiredness, he was feeling better. He wished the pain in his ulcerous foot would diminish, but he was used to that now. Only the doctor and one groom of the chamber had seen his blackened toes recently, as he had insisted on removing his hose only after the rest of his gentlemen had left the room. The doctor had diagnosed gout, and Edward was embarrassed to be afflicted so young.

When the doctor had finished fleeming, and a goodly amount of royal blood had been caught, he gave Edward an infusion laced with mandrake to induce sleep. Edward then asked that the bed curtains be drawn so he could be alone with Jane.

"My dear Edward," she said, allowing herself to speak to him as a man, a man she had feared lost. "'Tis a miracle you have recovered so quickly. We all feared for your life." Her heart sang as he smiled and stroked her hand. "I would have never forgiven you if I had not been able to tell you once more that I love you, or how happy you have made me these past eight years."

Edward was moved to tears, which did not help his vision, and he said sleepily, "Then I am pleased I cheated death so I could hear your words, dearest Galatea." He paused, his breathing slowing with the emetic. "It pains me that had God chosen to take me today I would have left you destitute. But here . . ." He took off his favorite sapphire ring, the stone as large as a robin's egg and as brilliant as a jay's wing, and pressed it into her hand. "Keep this until you have need of what it will fetch, Jane." His humor restored, he smiled. "But if you do aught to displease me, then I shall ask for its return. So do not sell it yet," he teased. "You are a good woman, Jane Shore, and I want you to have this."

Jane stared at the jewel aghast. "I cannot . . . nay, I will not accept such a valuable gem, Edward. The queen will notice. She will say I stole it."

Edward shushed her. "Elizabeth has always hated this ring. She calls it my little ostentation. I shall tell her it fell off in the river on the way to Windsor."

"But, my dear lord, that will not work. You are a terrible liar," Jane exclaimed, laughing, then she teased, "I shall take this because I dare not deny a man so stricken . . ."

"I am not dead yet," Edward told her, although his vision was still blurred and his tongue did not seem to work. "Come, kiss me, Jane, and lie with me. To the devil with the queen."

And although fully clothed, Jane slid beside the king in the soft tester bed and kissed him tenderly on his waiting mouth. "Ah, sweetheart, you will never know a greater love than mine," Edward assured her, removing her simple cap and letting her golden hair tumble around him.

The next day, Edward's headache became a raging storm in his brain, and he complained of pains in his leg that kept him in bed. Although the king was only in his fortieth year, he seemed to know he was dying. His doctors had declared Edward had been stricken with apoplexy, for which there was no cure.

"Hastings, send for Catesby," Edward commanded after he had struggled to the garderobe and back. "I shall write a new codicil to my will just in case I do not rise from this prison of a bed. You trust him, do you not?"

Will nodded, helping his king back under the covers. "Aye, he is of my affinity and so I must. One cannot fault a man for being ambitious. Although why you believe you are expecting the Grim Reaper, I cannot fathom," he said, cheerily, hiding his underlying fear. Edward's resignation to his fate was plain. Making matters worse, the physicians were huddled in the corridor, shaking their heads, examining the king's urine and consulting the stars. Will's faith in Edward's astonishing strength was faltering as he watched his friend and sovereign sink lower on the pillow. The speech impediment was getting worse, Will thought, although he still understood Edward. "You have a chill, 'tis all. We should not have spent so much time on the river in such cool weather."

Edward smiled. "Always the loyal companion, Will, telling me what you think I need to hear. In truth, for once I want you to listen to me and not argue. Promise me that." He saw Will put his hand over his heart and was satisfied. "Elizabeth will not be pleased when she discovers she is no longer an executor. But I have always known which way the wind has blown with the nobility as far as Elizabeth is concerned, and although I have tried to raise the gentry to places of trust on my council, there will be those of nobler blood than hers who will wish that she and her Woodville relatives fade from power. Including you, Will. Nay, do not deny it. I know not whom you despise more—Elizabeth's son or her brother, Rivers. You would not rest easy if they held the power, would you?" Will could not hide the truth of Edward's statement from his face, and Edward nodded. "So you see, I believe Elizabeth is less at risk if she is not made executrix."

Will saw the wisdom of this but doubted Elizabeth would. He signaled his agreement. "'Tis imperative you appoint someone to protect the crown for young Ned," he warned, "or there will be trouble."

"I am ill, not stupid," Edward teased his chamberlain. "Gloucester shall be protector, and I doubt any will gainsay my choice. In fact, I will die peacefully knowing I have left England in Richard's good hands. Will you pledge your support?"

Will bowed his head. "I will, sire. And I will be as loyal a counselor to him as I have been to you. Together we would steer England right should aught happen to her captain." He paced to the window and back to the bed, obviously wanting to say something more.

Edward cocked an eyebrow. "Well, my lord? What else?"

Will pulled a stool up to the bed head and made sure no one was within earshot. "I need to know if anyone else knows your secret, Ned? Anyone else at all? Your brother? The queen?"

Edward bit his lip. "Sweet Jesu, I have tried to forget that nasty little complication."

Nasty little complication? Will was taken aback by Edward's cavalier description of an event that could sever his line to the throne. If the precontract with Eleanor Butler were ever brought to light, Edward's children would be declared bastards, and a bastard could not inherit the crown. Will realized what a precarious position he had been put in with this knowledge, and he shivered. "If it comes to light after . . . well, later, it will devastate the lives of Elizabeth and your children. Have you thought on that possibility? 'Tis why you must tell me who else knows? Well, sire?"

Edward held out a heavy gold cross to Will that his chaplain had given him. "Swear upon this cross that you will take this secret to your grave, and uphold my son Ned's claim to the throne.

God's teeth, after all these years, who will believe Elizabeth is not my true wife, and my children legitimate heirs of Plantagenet blood." Will swore and kissed the cross.

Edward eased his inflamed leg into a more comfortable position and thought for a moment. "Aye, there is someone else who knows," he finally admitted. "The only other is the priest who heard me plight my troth to Eleanor Butler all those years ago—Stillington, bishop of Bath and Wells."

Will let out a whistle of surprise. "That graybeard? And he has held his tongue all these years? I am impressed."

"Aye, praise God. It seems he takes an oath of fealty to his king seriously. And he has been paid royally for his silence, if you remember. I made him chancellor for a good many years before ill health incapacitated him. And now I employ him as an ambassador, as you know, so the man has done well in exchange for keeping my small secret."

Not so small a secret, in fact, Edward thought guiltily, after Will had left to find Catesby. It was then he resolved to call for Stillington and tell the old man that he was not the only one to know about the plight-troth: Will Hastings had been sworn to secrecy as well.

It would be night soon, when all of Edward's bad dreams would come alive in the shadows of the firelit room. Damn Will, he thought as he listened to the chamberers stoking the fire, taking away the half-finished platters of food and closing the shutters against the darkening sky. His chamberlain had kicked alive the embers of George's execution with his question about the plight-troth and the bishop who had witnessed it.

It was time for Edward to face his demons, if he was to meet his Maker so soon.

What Edward had not told Will was that Robert Stillington had also been in peril of his life in February of '78 when George's pathetic note had been put in Edward's hands. It had slipped Edward's mind back then that as one of George's confessors Stillington may have revealed the secret. And now Edward began to piece together that long-ago scene when he had received George's missive:

Gracious king, beloved brother and companion of my youth,
have mercy on me in this cold place. I beseech you to come
and see how ill I am kept at the Tower. But if you come, be
prepared to grant me a pardon for I have information that is
of the utmost importance pertaining to you that you may not
wish to be made public as long as you are king.

Edward recalled he had been puzzled at first, but then he remembered the rumor George had circulated about Edward's bastardy: that their mother—their noble, upstanding mother—had taken to bed in Rouen an archer named Blaybourne when her husband, the duke of York, was campaigning at Pontoise. George must be desperate to resurrect such gossip, Edward remembered thinking then, and he had crumpled the parchment and launched it at the flames in the hearth.

The scene faded as Edward pondered that rumor about his mother, and fighting the sleeping draught de Serigo had given him, he redoubled his efforts to remember what happened next back in that fateful February of '78. His heart constricted, as it did every time he thought about his brother's death. He was certain that of all the sins he had committed, this one would keep him in purgatory the longest—if not in hell. Even more than violating his plight-troth with Eleanor, committing adultery a hundred times, condoning the violent death after Tewkesbury of Edouard, Prince of Wales, slaughtering countless thousands of Englishmen in the name of the house of York, or ordering the quiet death of King Henry to secure his throne, this sin against his brother would be the hardest for God to forgive.

In his anguish over his brother's treason, Edward had visited George one night by barge from Westminster and been taken quietly to the Garden Tower. Edward was disgusted to find George slumped over the table, his chemise stained with wine, snoring in a plate of cold fish and boiled vegetables. A rat had joined him on the table and was feasting on the leftovers.

"My lord of Clarence," the Constable Dudley had said, shaking George awake. "His grace the king is here."

"Leave us, my lord," Edward remembered commanding Dudley as he proceeded to pull George to his feet and hold him upright. George had struggled to give his brother the silly smile of a drunkard. "Why, Ned, how nishe to she you," he slurred, hiccoughing loudly.

Edward had shaken his brother then and given him a quick slap on either cheek, which had caused George to yelp but get control of his swaying body. Edward seized the earthenware bowl of water left for George's ablutions and flung it over the astonished drunkard's head.

"Christ and hishaints, whassthat for?"

"I will give you five minutes, George, no more," Edward snapped. "Now sit down and tell me to what secret you were referring in your letter. Five minutes."

Edward frowned now, recalling George's glee that he had succeeded in goading his brother into visiting. George had then revealed that he had known about Eleanor Butler for a few years. "Bishop Stillington blurted your secret to me. He was angry when you removed him from the chancellorship and considered taking revenge. What do you think of that, big brother?" And George had jabbed his finger into Edward's chest. "But, if you pardon me, I swear neither he nor I will divulge the truth to a living soul."

Edward caught George's hand in an iron grip. "'Tis a lie!" he had snarled. "And you had best forget it, George. Your life depends upon it."

George had paled, Edward recalled, hating himself again for lying to his already condemned brother. But the information had signed the death warrant for the hapless duke, Edward now admitted, and following the execution, Edward had placed Robert Stillington in the Tower until the cleric had renewed his pledge of secrecy on pain of death. With Eleanor dead, there was no one else but Stillington who had witnessed the event, and besides, who would believe the old coot, Edward had reassured himself.

Thinking of the old man now, the king breathed deeply. The bishop had given him not a moment's worry since he was freed from the Tower later that year, and had in fact distinguished himself in several diplomatic missions for his king, for which Edward had rewarded him. Nay, Edward felt sure the old man was his loyal subject and the secret of the beautiful Eleanor was safe with him.

But it was a worse sin the contrite king grieved over as he willed the poppy juice to take effect and erase his guilty memories.

It was George's death that caused Edward to fear the hellfires most. Duchess Cecily had used the word *fratricide,* and ever since that fateful day Edward had kept hearing it reverberating around his brain each time he had gone on his knees to his confessor. The only salve to his sorry soul was promising George to make provisions for a bastard, which Edward had accomplished by sending the boy to their sister Margaret in Burgundy. But even that was a lie, Edward thought sadly now, knowing full well it was he who had really sired the boy and then tricked George into believing the bastard was his. Was there no end to his sinning, the dying king asked himself as, mercifully, the potion finally quietened his mind and allowed him sleep.

"Bessie, my beloved wife and consort, I beg of you be diligent in your duty to our children, and especially to young Ned. He will be well protected by Richard until he is of age in only another four years . . ." Edward's voice trailed off as he grimaced in pain.

Elizabeth applied a damp cloth soaked in witch hazel to the king's temples and tried to soothe him.

"You know I will not shirk my duty, my lord. I gave you ten children, did I not? And I put up with your mistresses," she could not resist reminding him. "I believe I have done more than my fair share of duty. But my dear Edward, why did you not name me and my brother as regents? After all, you have entrusted Ned's guardianship to Anthony at Ludlow all this time."

Edward's patience was ebbing. "You are not of royal blood, my dear," he emphasized. "Richard is." He was too weary to remind her that she and her family were still not popular with his subjects and would never be acceptable as regents. "Richard is a father; he will know how to care for Ned and Dickon. And he is my brother and thus closest to the throne after my sons."

On the other side of the bed, Tom Grey raised an eyebrow at his mother, as if to say "too close for comfort," but Elizabeth was listening to Edward's request that she leave him to his councilors "for just a little while, my dear. Go, I pray, and fetch Dickon so I may give him a father's blessing. It pains me that I cannot bless Ned and teach him what he needs to know. I pray you, Bess, give him my love."

Elizabeth nodded, much moved. Doctor de Serigo and the other physicians had advised her that Edward was near the end. It was pointless to send for the Prince of Wales now; there was no hope that the king would see his heir again.

It seemed half of Westminster was gathered in the stuffy chamber awaiting, like circling carrion crows. Temporal and spiritual lords like Hastings, Stanley, Howard father and son, and Rotherham, Morton, Russell, and Stillington had all served Edward through his twenty-two-year reign and hoped to be rewarded at the last.

All at once the king struggled to sit up, a fanatical light in his eye and grim determination on his face.

"If I am to die, I will see you, my lord Dorset, and you, my lord Hastings, forgive your differences and reconcile in front of these witnesses. Draw near and swear friendship," he ordered the two astonished subjects. "Now!"

For a brief moment, Will was tempted to refuse, especially as his young popinjay stepson-in-law's reticence was equally evident. But then he looked back at Edward, who had made such a monumental effort to effect this extraordinary reconciliation, and, despite his pride, Will walked toward the marquess, his hand outstretched.

"With all my heart, I will strive to become your friend," Will asserted, his eyes never leaving his adversary's face.

As though his arm were lead, Tom Grey raised it level with Will's, and they grasped wrists in a reluctant show of camaraderie. Edward nodded. "'Tis well done and all I ask before I leave this earth. England cannot afford such dissensions, my lords. It makes us weak and vulnerable." He gestured to the others clustered by the door. "All of you, take one another's hands. Swear you will uphold my kingdom and support my son and my brother's regency when I am gone."

When the men had complied, Will edged Tom from the bed and bent to kiss Edward's clammy forehead. "My heart and my sword are yours always, sire. My gratitude for your friendship may never be fully expressed, but all will know it by my loyalty to your sons." When Will saw his sovereign's tears, he turned away, stifling his own sadness. "Adieu, sweet king," he whispered.

"God be with you, too, faithful servant," Edward replied, unabashed.

Will composed himself and returned to his place next to Jack Howard. "Did I appear sincere with Dorset?"

"Aye, my lord," Howard replied, but Will noticed the long mustache twitch, as if the mouth were trying hard not to smile.

"Are you for Gloucester as protector?" Will asked, and was cheered to see the vigorous nod from his colleague. "Then I can call on your support if I need it? In case the family"—and he jerked his head in Elizabeth's direction—"tries to take the reins instead."

Howard raised his eyebrows. "Do you think they might? Against the king's express instructions? But aye, you can count on me, Will."

Satisfied with the reconciliation, Edward fell back onto the pillow, demanding another potion from the hovering physicians. "And then I shall rest. You may leave me, my lords."

Within a few minutes, the nine-year-old duke of York was led into the room by Thomas Howard. Dickon ran to his beloved father's bedside and hopped up onto the bed.

"They say you are not well, my lord Father. Does it hurt?"

Edward forced a grin and patted the boy's golden head. "Certes, it does not," he assured his son. "We shall have some sport in a very few days." Then he looked grave. "But if something should happen and I am not here, I want you to promise to look after your mother and your sisters, do you understand?" When Dickon nodded, his blue eyes anxious and wide, Edward took his hand. "And Ned will be king one day, and you must learn to be a loyal brother, just as my brother Richard is loyal to me. We have talked about family loyalty before, remember?"

"Aye, Father," Dickon answered.

Edward made an effort to sound more cheerful. "You are old enough to know that no one lives forever, are you not? When that day comes for me, I want you to know that you and Ned will be looked after by Uncle Richard. Promise you will obey him. He will be kind to you. He will be in charge until Ned is old enough to govern."

Dickon leaned forward and confided: "Can I tell you a secret, Father? I am glad Ned is going to be king and not me. I would rather go fishing or play kick-ball."

For the first time in days, Edward laughed, which caused a bout of congested coughing. Dickon watched full of anxiety until Edward was able to reassure his son. "It sounds worse than it is, my son. Now kneel and receive my blessing."

Later, when the prince had left the room, Edward asked Elizabeth to draw the bed curtains around them for privacy.

"My dear, I have a boon to ask of you," he said softly. "Many years ago, I sired a daughter on a woman who lived not far from Grafton." He felt Elizabeth stiffen. "The lady died and the child was left with the nuns at Delapré. I have supported the convent all these years in payment for my sin, but I would ask that you fetch Grace and let her know her half-sisters. 'Tis much to ask, I know, but will you do that for me, Bess? Maybe God will forgive my sin if I acknowledge the girl. I have seen to my other bastards, and I would not leave this one abandoned. I know I have no right to ask, but will you grant me this one last favor, love of my life?"

His declaration cracked Elizabeth's hard heart. "I will find her, Ned, never fear. I will care for her as you wish."

"I thank you," he said simply. "Now I pray you forgive me my infidelities, and I shall rest more easily. I never stopped loving you, Bessie. Not ever."

"I forgive you, Edward," Elizabeth said, deep emotion shaking her voice. Taking his head between her hands, she gently kissed his parched lips. "Oh, my dear husband, how I shall miss you. With all of my heart I shall miss you."

Edward watched her unaccustomed tears, which caused his own to well. His breathing became shallower when he suddenly clutched Elizabeth's sleeve. Words were difficult now, but he tried, and mouthed, "Forgive . . . me . . . Nell . . . Nell . . ."

Elizabeth suppressed a sharp retort. Why was he speaking his former harlot's name? He must be confused, but she was understandably hurt. Instead, as kindly as she could, she asked, "Why should Eleanor forgive you?"

But Edward was too weak to explain what had happened with Eleanor Butler all those years ago. Aye, best left a secret, he decided wearily.

Well into the dark morning hours of Wednesday, Edward confessed his sins, repenting sincerely for them. The sun was halfway
to noon when he received the last sacrament from Archbishop
Rotherham, while Elizabeth knelt with nine-year-old Dickon
and their daughters around the bed. From across the room, Will
watched, stricken, as Edward the Fourth's tumultuous forty-year
life came to a premature end.

An hour later the bells in the more than one hundred churches
in the city tolled the news to the shocked populace, and a messenger was dispatched to Middleham to take the news to Richard.
Knowing how long it would take for the duke to be informed
and journey to London, the council saw no reason for urgency in
informing him. However, the business of embalming and burying
the king must necessarily be done in a timely manner and, thus
regrettably, without Richard.

Since leaving the king the week before, Jane had taken to reading Edward's book of Ovid's *Metamorphoses* every day to comfort
herself. She knew protocol must keep her away from the palace
now. That day, she was reading the tragic story of Orpheus and
Eurydice, when she heard the first bell toll the death knell for the
king. Knowing at once its significance, she dropped the book and
fell to her knees to pray for the swift winging to heaven of her
loving protector's soul.

Later that night, the first wave of grief past, Jane could not help
wondering what would become of her now. The rosary beads put
aside, her mind was a jumble of fleeting thoughts and images of
her lover, of how much she would miss him, and of herself, of how
she would survive without him. Might her father take her back?
Nay, a futile idea. Might she, as a freewoman of London, be able
to own a business? She did not know. She knew she could always

make a wage in one of the busy silkwomen shops in Soper Lane, but the prospect was unappealing. Tom Grey's face interrupted her practical thoughts then, and she caught her breath. Might he come to her now and make her his mistress? She hardly dared to hope, but the thought felt unseemly at this solemn moment of the king's passing, and she suppressed it.

In the end, Jane determined to ask Will Hastings to help her, and, after asking God to welcome Edward to His side, she turned into the pillow and gave way to mourning the loss of the man who had given her all but his name for eight wonderful years.

THIRTEEN

The queen had barely donned her mourning gown and seen her husband laid out in state at St. Stephen's chapel when she acted.

Calling her brothers Lionel and Edward and her two adult sons to her apartments, Elizabeth began by dictating a letter to her oldest sibling, Anthony, Earl Rivers, at Ludlow, commanding him to bring the new king, twelve-year-old Edward, swiftly to London. Rivers had been supervising the late king's heir on the Welsh Marches for several years, it being a tradition that the Prince of Wales be brought up in his own household from an early age. The journey from Ludlow would take several days after the messenger arrived, so young Edward would be too late for the funeral, Elizabeth knew. Those arrangements were already in place, and as was the custom after a few days of lying in state, the king's body would be buried without delay. Elizabeth began dictating.

"Right well, beloved brother and guardian of my son, his grace, the new king of England, we greet you well from Westminster. As you may imagine, grief for my husband and lord's passing is still lying heavy upon me. And yet, I am determined to secure the right to protect my son, the king, and be named regent by the council alongside you who has best known and loved your nephew these ten years as his governor. However, it has come to our attention that there are those who would name Richard of Gloucester as protector—"

"'Those who would name'?" Tom interjected. "We were all there when the late king demanded it. Have a care, Mother."

"What are you asking of Anthony?" Sir Edward Woodville asked, stroking his long aquiline nose between his finger and thumb. "I agree with Tom here, be cautious."

"God's bones, let me finish!" Elizabeth snapped. She waved an arm at her secretary. "Continue writing, Master Gunthorpe. Now where was I?"

The queen urged Rivers to come to London with young Edward without delay and to bring a large force to deter any possible opposition to her regency.

"Should we not ask the council's advice on this?" Sir Edward tried again, awed by his sister's ability to put aside her grief and begin strategizing. "Whatever you are planning, Sister, will be of no use if you do not have support from the council."

"Ned is correct," Lionel chimed in. "You must consult the council."

Elizabeth grimaced as she looked from handsome Sir Edward to dour Lionel, the latter raised to the bishopric of Salisbury only last year thanks to her efforts. There were times when she wished she had been born a man. "Very well then, which one of you will speak for me?" she said. Seeing Lionel nod, she added, "We must convince the council that Gloucester is dangerous, and that I should be regent. Without a leader, we have the chance to bend the councilors to our bidding. Whatever the outcome of your meeting, I will send this letter to Anthony with or without their permission. We must get Ned to London as quickly as possible or we shall lose control of him." She lowered her voice so her ladies across the room could not overhear. "I have no doubt Richard of Gloucester will take charge of the council and push us away. If we lose Ned, we Woodvilles are finished."

Tom stepped forward, determination on his face. "I am constable of the Tower and thus have armaments and a garrison at my command. Not to mention guardianship of the treasury. Let me go with Lionel to the council and remind them of that. 'Twill strengthen our case to set up a regency before Gloucester arrives."

Elizabeth nodded, pleased to see Tom take the initiative. "Who else will support our case, my lords? Gloucester's friends are all up north; surely we have those who will also want to see my son crowned as soon as the coronation can be arranged. We could have counted on Bourchier, but the man decided to die three days before the king, damn him."

Elizabeth's brothers were taken aback by the callous remark, seeing a new side in their sister. "I rather liked the old earl," Sir Edward told them. "Who will take the treasurer title now, I wonder?"

"'Tis of no importance," Tom interrupted. He turned back to Elizabeth. "You cannot count on Jack Howard, Mother, he is not our ally. But remember, there is such antipathy toward the clergy nowadays, the bishops will be glad to side with whomever controls the new regime. Rotherham, Morton, and Russell, not to mention Canterbury. All were loyal to my stepfather."

"And Hastings?" Lionel asked. "Where does he stand?"

"I am not sure of Will Hastings," Elizabeth mused. "He pledged to uphold Gloucester's protectorship. He knows I dislike him and you despise him. Thus he is more likely to cleave to Gloucester than support me. They respect each other, I think."

Tom disagreed. "'Tis my belief Gloucester blames Hastings for the king's profligacy. I would not wager on those two as allies."

Elizabeth rose, statuesque in her purple mourning gown, and clicked her fingers at her dog. "Come, Ficelle, we shall have to take the air, as I am excluded from the hallowed council chamber. Tom, Lionel, go now and make our case. And do not fail me."

Elizabeth was right that the councilors were lacking leadership during those first days following Edward's death. They perceived the queen's power as an extension of her son's, and readily agreed to send for the young king on the queen's orders. However, they were wary enough to refuse her request that Earl Rivers bring a veritable army with him to guard the boy. "Who does the queen fear will attack them en route?" Howard asked his son later when the council allowed Rivers two thousand men, against Howard's better judgment. "Certes, not Richard of Gloucester. He has already sworn fealty to young Edward, so we are told."

Word was sent to Richard as soon as the king had died, but there was no mention that he was to be named protector. The duke had spent many an hour closeted with his wife and chaplain, grieving. Knowing he would be too late for the funeral, Richard chose to go to nearby York to organize masses for his brother's soul, gather the northern lords to him and swear fealty to the new king. Without a sense of urgency, he made his plans for the long journey south, certain that men such as Hastings and Howard, with the rest of Edward's loyal council, would take the reins until young Ned and he could get to London. He wrote to Anthony Rivers, in charge of the young king at Ludlow, and suggested they meet on their way south so Richard could accompany his nephew into the capital. He assumed he would be named to some sort of regency, but he was unaware of Edward's deathbed wish that he be sole protector.

He had not, however, bargained on the queen's duplicity.

Much to Elizabeth's delight, the councilors, made up of many notable lords and prelates in London for Edward's obsequies, not only agreed to set up a regency council in which she and Dorset would take a part, but also, fearing that Gloucester would seize power for himself, ignored Edward's wish that his brother be sole protector. Instead they made him one of the regents. Will had voiced his opposition to the shared regency, reminding the councilors of the king's dying wish, but he had been overruled. It was clear the Woodville power remained strong.

Will addressed the queen's obvious haste. "Why not wait for Gloucester? What has she to fear from him? They both want to see young Edward crowned, and no one could be more trustworthy than Gloucester to carry out the late king's wishes. The duke will not deny her access to her son. In all my years of close confidence with the late king, I have never seen rancor between Gloucester and the queen. Is this something new?" The unspoken answer had to be that Elizabeth wanted sole power, but no one dared to denounce the queen in public, even when she was absent.

It was later, when this council acquiesced to sending the fleet to sea, with Sir Edward Woodville in charge, to defend England's ships from French piracy and to hastening a coronation for the young Edward, that Will Hastings's suspicions intensified about the Woodville motives.

Will became incensed when Dorset boasted to him and a few others, "We Woodvilles are so powerful that even without the king's uncle, we are able to make and enforce these decisions."

"Christ's bones, you are not above the rule of the council, my lord," Will snapped.

"Young Edward is the king, Lord Hastings, and, in case you have forgotten, we are his closest blood relatives. Have a care, my lord," Dorset threatened before stalking from the room.

Hastings hid his disquiet as best he could, but as soon as the councilors disbanded for the day, he lost no time in writing a private letter to Richard of Gloucester at York. Christ's nails, why had he not anticipated the queen's intent and written to Gloucester before the king died.

Most dear and gracious duke, we greet thee well. As your brother's loyal friend, I write to urge you to come to London with all haste and bring as many as you can muster with you. I fear our new sovereign's mother and kin are looking to control him. By now you will know that the king named you as protector until your nephew is of age, and you must assume your role as soon as possible.

Will then revealed the queen's plan to overturn the late king's decree that Gloucester be sole protector and become regent herself. He assured the duke of his own loyalty to his dead brother's wishes and to the new boy king.

> *As well, Dorset persuaded the council to make his uncle, Sir Edward, commander of the fleet and sent it to sea, taking a portion of the royal treasury with him "to pay the troops." Should Woodville influence on the council and the young king be so great as to exclude you and me from it, I fear for our safety, my lord, and for the good of the realm.*

Who could he send to carry the urgent message? Once again, his eye fell on his one-time squire turned lawyer, William Catesby, whom he had mentored. "Say nothing of your mission, William, but go you with all haste to find the duke of Gloucester at York and put this into no one's hands but his."

Catesby forced an unctuous smile as he tucked the heavily sealed missive into his pleated doublet and bowed. In truth, he resented being treated like a common messenger when he preferred to remain at the council meetings, to ascertain to whom he should afix his star. The last place he wanted to be at this most dramatic time was in the cold and wild of the Yorkshire hills.

Will's letter was the second of two warnings Richard had received at York during his mourning for his brother. The duke of Buckingham, the only royal cousin Richard had left, had sent a similar missive not two days before from his castle in Wales assuring Richard of his support and requesting to join his cousin on the road to London. Buckingham had been informed of Rivers's imminent departure with the new king from nearby Ludlow, and the duke, too, worried that the royal cousins would be ousted from the new king's circle by the Woodvilles if they did not take possession of the boy before he arrived in London.

"Master Catesby, I thank you heartily," Richard said affably when he had read Will's letter. "Come, take some refreshment and tell me what you know of the situation in London. You are Hastings's lawyer, are you not?"

"Aye, my lord, and I have been privileged to be noticed by the archbishop of Canterbury as well," Catesby answered, hand-washing and bowing low again in his ingratiating manner as he took the proffered cup of ale. He could see the grief for Edward plainly on the duke's face.

Richard sat down and studied the man, who was probably the same age as he. Catesby appeared humble. His face was leanly handsome and his demeanor intelligent though watchful, but the word *fox* came to Richard's mind. "I assume you have attended the council meetings. Can you give me a fair account?"

As soon as he saw the chance to be useful to the most important man in England, Catesby's interest in his mission grew, and he wished he could have broken the seal on Hastings's letter and learned the contents. He now observed Richard of Gloucester with interest as he prepared to speak. He was impressed by the splendid mourning garb, the man's calm dignity, and his plain speaking. Loyalty Binds Me was the duke's motto, Catesby remembered, and he could well imagine, from all he had heard, that loyalty truly defined this man's character.

"I can indeed relate any information you might wish to know, your grace," Catesby began. "I have an uncanny knack for remembering even the most insignificant details, down to the color of gown a councilor was wearing." Seeing Richard's wry smile, he made bold to add, "But I usually reserve those sartorial tidbits for the ladies." He was rewarded with a hint of a chortle, and his confidence rose, though he could not tell whether Richard was really amused.

Soon Richard learned all he needed to know to reinforce the

truth of Will's and Harry's messages, and he invited Catesby to ride with him to Sheriff Hutton castle, where he was lodged for the city of York's own obsequies for Edward. He then sent word back to Will, promising to arrive in the south at the end of April with only a modest number of men. He had no intention of frightening his young nephew with a show of force. He wanted the boy to know his uncle had come to protect him and the Crown, and that he had sworn an oath to do so in front of the good people of York and written the same to the queen and the council. He wondered if the boy had been told his uncle would be protector, and assumed Rivers might choose to withhold that vital piece of information. What were those Woodvilles planning? he wondered again, especially after he was not informed at Edward's death that he was supposed to be named protector. He must think and act carefully.

"I shall have need of someone with your legal mind in my protectorate, Master Catesby. Attend me when I am settled at Westminster," he said, ending the audience.

Later, Catesby rode from the well-appointed castle and congratulated himself on his good fortune. Perhaps he would no longer have to take orders from Lord Hastings, he told himself, by whom the younger man had always felt overshadowed.

"It was magnificent, my dear," Hastings said from his pillowed position on Jane's settle, her little dog curled in the crook of his arm. "Edward would have approved. We kept vigil at St. George's all night, and on that last morning Bishops York, Lincoln, and Durham said prayers for his soul. I was one of those who placed his shield, helmet, and sword in the tomb, and then my offering of cloth of gold." His face clouded for a moment as he remembered Edward's leaden coffin being lowered into the vault. "Many there wept when we, the officers of the household, made the final gesture to mark the passing of the old reign by the casting of our staves upon the coffin. 'Tis a sound I shall not soon forget, the echo of it so startling in the quiet of that beautiful chapel Edward had so lovingly created."

Jane listened enthralled, imagining then the heralds throwing in their coats of arms after the staves, donning new ones, and crying, "Long live the king!" She swallowed the lump in her throat and stared at the Galatea tapestry, still not believing she would never see Edward again.

Sensing they were slipping into moroseness, she rose and fetched more wine. "What now, my lord?" she asked. "Do we simply wait for Richard of Gloucester and then crown young Edward?"

Hastings eased himself into a sitting position as he took the delicate glass from her. "I have written to Gloucester urging him to come at once. If Edward is crowned before Richard gets here, which is what the Woodvilles appear to be planning, then I fear he and I will be in danger."

"Danger, my lord?" she echoed fearfully. "What kind of danger? I do not understand? Why would they crown the boy without Gloucester? Did Edward not name him protector?"

"It will come down to a battle for power over who governs as regent," Will explained. "'Tis my belief the queen and her adherents will stop at nothing to retain power as blood relations of the young king. Many on the council are wavering in their loyalties. Do they support the queen if she is able to secure the power and thus keep their positions, or if Gloucester's protectorate is upheld by the rest of us, will those councilors follow us or be ousted? I believe Gloucester will never allow Elizabeth to share the regency. He views her as an upstart with no royal blood, and she knows it." Will shifted his weight. "The truth of the matter is that Gloucester is less well known here in the south, and he could be in mortal danger if Elizabeth decides to take possession of the king and oust his uncle. She cannot afford to let him live to fight back." He patted the seat beside him. "I will support Richard if it should come to a fight, and thus I must tread warily now. If Gloucester goes, so do I. Do you understand?"

Jane shivered, and Will pulled her closer; her nearness and his desire to protect her were almost overwhelming.

"What will become of me?" she asked with trepidation. "I know I must look to the future, even though it frightens me. I have even thought of reverting to my former trade as a silkwoman"—she looked up at him hesitatingly—"or asking you for a loan to set up a business. I am a freewoman of the city and have rights, and I all but ran my husband's shop, you remember."

Will thought quietly for a few moments before turning to her and taking her hands.

"It happens that your concern matches mine, my dear, and now is a good time to discuss it. Has it occurred to you that you are free to be with me now, Jane, and that I could extend to you my full protection?" Before Jane could shake her head at this extraordinary generosity, Will took her face between his hands and kissed her gently. "You must know I have loved you since the first time I saw you, and that love still burns within me. Dare I hope you could love me a little, Jane?"

"Oh, my good lord, you honor me," Jane stammered, dazed. She pulled his hands to her lap and studied them while she thought. She ought not to lie, she told herself; it was not so much of a shock, although she prayed she had done nothing to encourage him once she had become Edward's concubine. She thought quickly; his offer would be the solution to the problem that had tormented her night after night since Edward's death. Hastings was wealthy enough to keep her in the house she had come to love, and although her heart was given elsewhere, Tom Grey had not attempted to even see her since Edward's death, she had to admit with chagrin.

She looked up at Will's anxious face, a face she had grown to love as a true friend's or even, she had admitted to herself once, the loving father she had never known. But he was offering her more than friendship, she knew. He wanted her in his bed, and it was not something she had even contemplated in her musings. She had thought his initial physical attraction to her had waned long ago and that he was comfortable with their friendship.

"I pray you, my lord, allow me more time for grieving. I would hold Edward's memory close for a little while longer. Besides, you must look to yourself in the next days and keep yourself safe. It will allow me a little more time to mourn and to think, my dear friend."

Will sighed. "Friend. That is the only way you think of me, is it not? I had hoped after all these years, I might have found a different place in a corner of your heart." He patted her knee and rose. "Certes, you may have a few days, Jane. If you say yes, I promise I will make you happy, if only because you will make me the happiest of men."

He flung his mantle about his shoulders and pulled the cord through the jeweled tasseau. With some urgency, he told her, "I will not force you, but I would have you think carefully about your future. I can protect you. The queen will want you gone from court, and Gloucester will turn you out of Edward's house as soon as look at you. His loyalty to Edward does not extend to you. God's bones, but he is such a sanctimonious bore!" Will's pun on Gloucester's White Boar badge was not lost on Jane, her mind delighting in such wordplay, but she put a more serious finger to her lips.

"Caution, Will, you know not who may be listening."

But Will had not finished. "In case you were worried about my wife—Katherine and I have not shared a bed these two years, and she cares not what I do now. Think favorably on my proposal, Jane, I beg of you."

Jane allowed Will to fold her in an embrace, but she could not bring herself to let him kiss her again and turned her face so his lips found her cheek. She begged his pardon: "'Tis too soon. I will give you an answer anon, I promise."

She heard the front door shut behind him and sought the sanctuary of the settle, her knees weak and unsteady. How could he still be in love with her after all these years? Strange, Will had never given her an inkling he still lusted for her. That he felt affection and friendship for her, she well knew; it matched her own feelings for him, but to take her to his bed and expect her to accept him now as a lover after she had loved the king, she could not understand. How could she have been so blind all these years to his true feelings?

Far more important, however, was that without him she might be in danger of being evicted from Thames Street and end up in a brothel—or worse, in that wretched Ludgate gaol. Will's offer looked rosier by the minute, although she fretted that her motive was self-serving. She had to admit, however guilty it made her feel, that she was disappointed, for God only knew he was not the new protector that she yearned for. Where was Tom? Why had he not come to console her or even contact her? If he still loved her, he would have to have given her a thought now. But Jane refused to listen to the imp inside her. "Selfish coward," it said, but Jane believed Tom must have a good reason.

Events at the end of April overshadowed Will's resolve to have Jane for his own. The next time he visited her, he was bursting with news and optimism.

"Elizabeth—the queen—has gone into sanctuary along with her children, including the whey-faced Dorset," Will told Jane, taking long strides about the room in his eagerness to tell his tale. "It seems Gloucester heeded my warning and has taken control of the king's person."

"My lord, you are making no sense. Why would the queen need sanctuary? Why do you not sit down and calmly tell me what has happened. You forget I am merely a forgotten mistress of the former king; no one brings me information anymore."

Will calmed himself and took up his customary seat with Jane's dog upon the settle, unlacing his tight, padded jacket and exhaling with relief. "How I detest this new fashion and long for my loose gown," he admitted. He grinned at Jane as he removed his bonnet and gave his scalp a scratch. "Much better. So, let me see, where shall I start?"

"The queen is in sanctuary," Jane helped him.

"Ah. My lord of Gloucester is a canny one, I will give him that," he began again. "After seeing that the city officers swore fealty to young Edward, he left York and proceeded south as far as Nottingham. In the meantime, Rivers with the king came south from Ludlow and agreed to meet with Gloucester at Northampton. When Gloucester arrived, Rivers had gone on to Stony Stratford farther south. This seemed in direct defiance of the protector's orders, and one can understand Gloucester's consternation. What were the Woodvilles planning? And how large was their force? The king was now more than a dozen miles closer to London and his Woodville kin, and Gloucester feared for his own safety.

"It would seem Henry of Buckingham has been in communication with his cousin Gloucester since Edward's death," Will continued. Jane looked blankly at him. "Henry Stafford, duke of Buckingham, is the only cousin of royal blood left to Richard." He chuckled. "Ned never had much time for Harry. He thought him a buffoon—a popinjay without a brain. Perhaps the duke hopes to ingratiate himself with Richard by lending his support, I know not.

"But I digress. Where was I? Ah yes, at Northampton. While the two royal cousins contemplated hurrying after Rivers, Rivers himself doubled back into Northampton. Perhaps he felt guilty for not waiting for Richard as planned. He left the king at Stony Stratford with Richard Grey and the others."

Tom's brother, Jane thought with a jolt. She nodded politely, only mildly interested in this story so far. Will, on the other hand, consumed with the tale, ran on. "Apologizing with the feeble excuse of 'no room at the inn' for both retinues in Northampton, Rivers explained how they had moved on. 'But here I am, my lord protector, and there is no plot afoot to race you to London,' he boldly stated, or some such falsehood. Then it seems Gloucester and Buckingham entertained the self-satisfied earl in style that evening, but on the morrow arrested him on suspicion of treason."

By now Jane was agog to hear more. "Treason, Will? Is not treason only against the Crown?"

"You have the measure of it, well done," Will agreed. "Richard of Gloucester, assuming he was already protector despite lack of official sanction by the council, acted as though he *represented* the Crown. I am doubtful the council will agree; they think he acted too boldly and certainly prematurely, as they had not yet bestowed the title on him. But in fairness to Richard, he was also dismayed by the army that Rivers had traveled with, and suspecting his own life might have been in danger, he felt justified in arresting Rivers and later Grey, although"—and Will frowned, scratching his head again—"why Richard needed to arrest Sir Thomas Vaughan as well is a mystery. No doubt he had his reasons."

"The old man who is chamberlain to the Prince of Wales . . . I mean the young king?" Jane asked, shocked.

Will nodded. "Doubtless, he, Grey, and Rivers are now languishing in a cell up north as far from the other members of the Woodville faction as possible. In the end, the protector sent the rest of the army back to their homes, confiscating their arms, and now has the young king safely with him."

Jane thought of handsome Anthony Woodville, Lord Rivers, shackled and thrown in a cell at a gloomy castle in the desolation she imagined the north to be, and shivered. "Poor Rivers, he must have been surprised," she remarked. "Is that why the queen sought sanctuary, to avoid a similar arrest? Do they suspect her of treason, too?"

"I doubt Richard would have a case against her, but Elizabeth was taking no chances, especially while she has her youngest son, the heir to the throne, in her charge."

Jane thought for a second as she pinched a flea off her dog's fluffy coat and crushed it between her thumb and finger. How ironic that both Edward's women were, in their own way, forced to seek sanctuary after his death: Elizabeth with God; Jane perhaps with Will.

"Aye, certes, young Dickon of York is the heir now," she replied. "I keep forgetting."

"Dorset is with her, the lily-livered weakling. He is past thirty and still hides behind his mother's skirts. Still, happily, he cannot do much from Westminster Abbey," Will said, ignorant that Jane was resisting a retort in her favorite's defense.

"And Gloucester? He is on his way here from Northampton with the king?"

"They arrive tomorrow. I am to meet the cavalcade in Hornsey Meadow and escort the king into the city with Gloucester and Buckingham. London must see that it is Gloucester and not the queen who will govern the young king. 'Twas Edward's dying wish."

"Then I should not delay you, my lord," Jane said, rising. "You must have a deal to do to prepare for the king's entry."

Will got to his feet and stayed her with his hand. "Sweetheart, have you thought more on my proposition? I lie awake at night wondering whether we shall ever be together."

For the first time, Jane saw in his anxious face the youth that might have been Hastings thirty years before, and her heart softened.

"Aye, Will," she said, shyly putting out her hand and touching his well-lined face. "I shall be honored to be your mistress, if that is what you wish."

His mouth was upon hers before she could take another breath. His kiss was hard and urgent and so unlike Edward's seductive probing kisses it almost frightened her. She was afraid he might take her there and then, and she was not ready. With the confidence of one who had loved and been loved by a king, she gently but firmly pushed him away.

"All in good time, my impatient lord," she teased, trying to gloss over her guilt at her own lack of ardor. "Never let it be said that Jane Shore kept the lord chamberlain from his duty to the king." She went to hold open the door. "I shall be waiting when you have need of me, but now is not the time."

She had never seen Will Hastings look sheepish before, and again her heart warmed to him.

He kissed her more gently as he took his leave. She stood watching from the window and smiled as she observed the jauntiness in his stride. She wondered how different life with Will would be. Aye, he was a rich and powerful noble with great influence with the council, but he did not have power enough to say if a man lived or died as Edward had, and she was glad of it.

For the first time since Edward's death, her spirits rose. Her future, as far as she could see it, was once again secured. She turned back to survey her pleasant sanctuary—hers for the time being—and thanked God for Will Hastings.

The royal procession roused Londoners from their gloom, and they were lined from Aldersgate Street outside the city gate all the way to the Bishop of London's magnificent palace at the northwest corner of St. Paul's. Those who arrived early had clambered up the steps to the top of the city wall and were hanging precariously over the rampart. No one wanted to miss the sight of the new king arriving in his capital city, for Londoners did not know him yet, the succession having happened much sooner than anyone could have predicted.

As soon as the sun rose on the fourth day of May, Richard of Gloucester swung himself up into his saddle with an ease of one who was rarely off a horse, traveling endlessly as he had from castle to castle, keeping the north safe for his brother. He looked around him as a thin mist rose from Hornsey Meadow and was instantly transported back to a morning twelve years earlier when he had commanded the vanguard in his first battle at Barnet not ten miles from this spot. He remembered the sour taste of fear in his mouth and the looseness of his bowels as he had led his troops forward up a marshy slope in a dense fog that blotted out all but the man next to him. He had held the line, and eventually his brother Edward had vanquished his one-time mentor, but by then enemy, the earl of Warwick. People then called him Kingmaker, Edward and Richard's powerful Neville cousin, who perished on that misty day in April. It seemed so long ago now, Richard mused, watching his good-looking young nephew being helped into his saddle by a squire. The Barnet memory of his magnificent brother wielding his triumphant sword, his blood-spattered banner raised in victory, caused Richard's ever-present grief to mount. By Christ and his saints, how nearly the boy resembled his father—except for his build. Edward had been a strapping youth, taller than all his contemporaries, but Ned was delicate, like his mother. The thought of Elizabeth brought him back to reality, and any sadness vanished.

"Are you ready to greet your subjects, sire?" Richard said, looking at the solemn boy-king. "I have heard all of London has turned out to welcome you. Come, let us not disappoint them."

Young Ned gave his uncle a courteous nod, but Richard saw suspicion in his face and something like fear, and he looked away. It had not been the most jovial of reunions, he admitted, Ned having hidden behind Richard Grey when Richard and Buckingham had arrived in Stony Stratford. "Where's my uncle Rivers?" the boy had demanded. "'Tis he who is supposed to take me to London, not you."

Richard had dismounted and immediately knelt before the king, swearing an oath of fealty to him, and only then had Ned left his hiding place and accepted his uncle's gesture with practiced, graceful thanks. After Richard explained why they would now be traveling together to London without Lord Rivers, the boy seemed to have settled into a resigned acceptance of the new arrangement, although he had cried when his devoted chamberlain had been arrested and taken away. "Your royal father, my brother, left me as protector, Edward," Richard had told him kindly. "You would not want to defy his command, would you?" Then he had winked. "I promise I shall not be a wicked uncle," he said, and Ned had laughed and seemed more at ease with him.

Richard now looked beyond the young king to Cousin Henry of Buckingham, who rode on Ned's other side. A robust, florid man about the same age as Richard, Harry had given Richard his allegiance without hesitation, and Richard was grateful for Harry's royal shoulder.

The king in blue velvet and the two royal dukes, appropriately clothed in black, were preceded by trumpeters and heralds, and soon the crowds began to thicken on either side of the Great North Road to London. Behind them, riding in tandem with Richard's friend Lord Lovell, Will Hastings stared at Richard's back and wondered how the Lord of the North would handle the government of the realm.

Hastings had always liked Richard of Gloucester, although now he was not sure what the qualities were that he had admired in the young, devoted duke who had remained steadfastly loyal to Edward. Aye, perhaps that was it, Will decided; Richard's loyalty matched his own. They certainly did not have much in common apart from that, Will mused, although both had misgivings about the Woodville ambitions. Richard had greeted Will warmly the night before, and Will was confident he would retain his influence at the council table under Richard's protectorate. He wondered if young Ned knew that, had his mother and kin had their way, the boy would have been riding today to his coronation, but the events at Stony Stratford had halted that precipitous ceremony. Surely Elizabeth could have guessed the council would not have sanctioned such a swift coronation. Aye, she was better off in sanctuary, he decided after hearing that the queen was ensconced at the abbey. He was pleased with his part in helping to thwart Elizabeth's plans, whatever they had been, and tried to convince himself that all was well.

Atop the swaying horse, Will soon began to daydream about being with Jane. He would have to buy her another house, he concluded, certain Gloucester would evict her from Thames Street.

Soon all private musings dissolved in the cacophony of voices raised in shouts of "God save the king!" "Long live King Edward!" "God bless the duke of Gloucester!" Will and Richard gave themselves up to basking in the Londoners' rapturous acclaim. The mayor and aldermen, arrayed all in scarlet, were the first to greet the cavalcade and make a formal welcome, followed by five hundred chosen citizens clothed in purple. The young king was bursting with pride, his handsome face pink with excitement. He waved and thanked the dignitaries as they sank to their knees and declared their allegiance.

Standing dozens deep with Ankarette on the steps of St. Paul's, Jane's first sight of the procession was of wagons full of arms and harness that Richard had confiscated from Earl Rivers as if to prove to the Londoners that the earl's motives had been self-serving. As soon as they heard the herald decry this news, the crowd booed their derision of the ousted Rivers but were cheering again soon enough at the arrival of the new king at the palace gate.

Caught up in the excitement, Jane chanted "Long live the king" along with her fellow citizens. The boy looked so much like Edward that she felt her heart miss a beat. She waved at Will, who did not see her tiny figure jammed in the melee, and she stood on tiptoe to watch the horsemen disappear through the gate and into the palace courtyard. It was then she felt someone's hand take hers and a man lean in too close.

"Do not turn round, Jane. Meet me at dusk where we had our first tryst; I must talk to you."

Before she could whisper his name, Tom Grey had disappeared.

As Jane sought the familiar seat behind the towering cathedral, her cloak wrapped tightly around her, she hoped Tom would not be late; she did not want to risk being out after curfew. All the way from Thames Street she had been at war with herself. He had come for her, she was sure, even leaving sanctuary and risking arrest, and thus her heart rejoiced. Yet he had waited a month without a word, which had hurt her pride. She determined not to be so easily seduced now.

She was rounding the back of the church when a hand reached out and grasped her. She would have screamed if she had not recognized the figure of her dreams. "I did not hope you would really come," Tom said into her sweet-smelling hair. "Why did we waste nine years, sweetheart?"

Jane felt the blood rise, and every inch of her warmed to his touch, but she was no longer the young Jane Lambert with nothing on her mind but love. She pulled away however reluctantly, saying: "Why did you wait so long, my lord? The king has been dead for a month."

Tom drew her into the shadows, irked that she had not melted into his embrace at once, but he recognized she deserved an answer. "My time has not been my own. You must have heard that I am confined to sanctuary. I wanted to see you before now, believe me, but the abbey is closely guarded. When I heard that the young king would enter the city today, I knew everyone from Westminster would be here, and I bribed a guard to let me out. I gave him my word I would be back under the cover of dark so he will go unpunished."

"You will go back?" Jane asked, incredulous. "Why, my lord?"

"Because I promised my mother, the queen." He pressed her hand to his lips. "I had to see you, my love, my sweet Jane."

She could not resist him then. He tilted her exquisite face to his and kissed her waiting mouth. Her whole body thrilled to his touch, and Jane thought she would be consumed by the mutual passion in their kiss. She arched her back instinctively, and he lifted her with ease and pinned her between him and the cold stone wall. With a practiced hand, he pulled up her skirts and skillfully aroused her. Jane gasped as one after another pleasurable wave thrilled her. Gently he lowered her to her feet, and limp, she leaned against him.

"And you, my lord? How might you be satisfied?" Jane managed to ask. "Although I fear I may prove of little use now."

"By the rood, you are irresistible," he said, pleased with what he took to be her willingness to reciprocate. "I knew from the first moment I saw you all those years ago—and each successive time we have met since—that we were meant for each other. Do not pretend you did not feel it, too. Ah, Jane, how I have hungered for you." He pushed her down on the seat and was about to untie his codpiece when the bells for vespers pealed above them, and, startling the two lovers, scores of squawking birds flapped off their lofty perches on St. Paul's spire. Jane exclaimed at this untimely interruption, stood, and smoothed her skirts. She knew the moment of passion had passed and they should part.

Hearing the curfew bell of St. Mary-le-Bow, Tom took her arm and hurried her down the hill to Thames Street. "I suspect I can find a boatman to take me back to Westminster," Tom said absently. He had come on a mission and was pondering how best to succeed when Jane came to his rescue with an innocent question.

"Why did you really risk imprisonment to come to me, Tom?" Jane asked. She was not such a fool as to believe he had done it simply to fondle her in the churchyard, and she was right.

"I may have need of you, Jane," Tom gladly responded. "You have been left alone since Edward's death, no? Then I would ask that, if the time comes when I can flee sanctuary permanently, I have a safe place to stay. I cannot attempt escape from the abbey yet; my lady mother has need of me there. I came to find a suitable hiding place nearby so I can help gather our supporters and regain possession of my brother, the king. We believe Richard of Gloucester is planning to take the crown for himself."

Jane was confused. "But Richard of Gloucester is the legal protector, Tom. He has sworn to uphold his nephew's right and see him crowned. Why would he break his oath to his brother and to his king? It does not sound like him at all."

Tom gave an exasperated snort. "To hear you talk, I must believe you have been consorting with Will Hastings. He and Gloucester are planning something, I am sure."

Jane had no intention of betraying Will's trust any further. She would instead redeem her conscience by gleaning what information she could from Tom.

"I am not sure why you and her grace, the queen, took sanctuary. You must know there is a rumor in the city that you planned to rid yourself of the duke of Gloucester. Why would you do such a thing? What do you fear from him? We all want what is best for the little king, do we not? As long as he is crowned he—"

Tom was getting impatient with all these questions; he needed to leave. "Richard of Gloucester has already imprisoned my brother and my uncle," Tom interrupted, "and the devil only knows what he would do to me, if he got the chance. His action at Stony Stratford alarmed us enough to seek sanctuary from him. Be that as it may, I am hoping you might give me shelter until I know what Gloucester will do next." He did not elaborate.

They had reached Jane's front door, and Tom turned her into his arms, needing to kiss her again. "What say you, Jane. Will you hide me? And when I escape next, we can be together."

Again Jane argued with herself. She wanted to tell him that aye, she would harbor him and that she, too, longed for him. However, even though she was still mistress of this house, she was now under

Will's protection, and Will detested Tom. She certainly could not hide Tom in the house when Hastings was her lover.

Wanting to savor the moment, Jane pushed Will from her mind. "I will find somewhere for you, never fear, but it cannot be here. When I have, I will get word to you at the abbey. You may trust me to be discreet."

Tom was puzzled. "Why not here at your house, sweetheart? No one would look for me here."

Jane stood on the front doorstep and took his face in her hands. How unkind fate was, she thought. She had dreamed of this moment through the years, and now when she and Tom might finally be free to love each other, she was again tied to another man. She must tell Tom the truth; her debt to Will was too great to betray his trust now.

"Because I am not free," she managed to utter. "Lord Hastings is my protector now."

"What!" Tom almost spat, aghast. "That old man. You are bedding that paunchy, balding—"

"Soft, Tom." Jane was stern. "I will not have Will maligned thus. At least he was immediately concerned for my welfare when Edward died. Where were you, if you profess to be so devoted?"

"Opportunist!" Tom accused his rival. "And he who was supposed to be so loyal to my stepfather must have been courting his mistress behind his back. He disgusts me."

"'Tis a lie! I was faithful to your stepfather and Will was always loyal," she cried and then stroked his bearded cheek. "Oh, Tom, do not let us quarrel. I am sorry if I disappoint you, but I must look after myself. Will offered me protection and I accepted. It does not mean I love him the way I love you."

Tom's face brightened. "So you do love me, Mistress Shore. I thought as much."

She grasped his hands and urged, "Go quickly, Tom, before

the watch finds you. I will come to Westminster when I have a plan." Before he could protest, Jane had slipped inside the house, leaving her intoxicating rosewater scent lingering in the night air and Tom staring at the closed door.

Richard of Gloucester took a bold step by sitting in the king's chair at his first council meeting a week after his arrival, but any misgivings the lords spiritual and temporal may have had with regard to the smooth transition of reigns were soon dispelled by the protector's quick grasp of affairs and commanding leadership. There was no doubt who would be regent now, especially as Elizabeth's flight into sanctuary had reinforced the council's belief that her action had been self-serving and not for the good of the country.

Will Hastings watched with relief and hope as the lords consented and formally proclaimed Richard protector and defender of the realm, to include the governance of the young king. This was to continue until Edward came of age at sixteen in four years' time. Will felt certain Richard would rule with a fair hand and was pleased when he declared that Will would retain his positions as the king's lord chamberlain and captain of Calais. He was also given back his title of master of the mint.

After the preliminaries, a discussion arose as to appropriate housing for the new king, who was still lodged at the bishop of London's residence.

"Why not at Westminster?" the new chancellor, John Russell, bishop of Lincoln, suggested.

Will immediately raised an objection: "My lord bishop, the palace is adjacent to the abbey, where the queen and her son are lodged." His implication was backed by several lords. It was then that Henry Stafford, duke of Buckingham, began to assert his authority, which, Will noted, Richard welcomed. "The only palace fit for a king is the Tower," Buckingham said, his rather booming voice halting the discussion. "It has housed English kings since the

Conqueror, and its garrison will assure the safety of the sovereign."

Richard nodded his endorsement of this idea. "Let us waste no time in removing the king to the Tower's state apartments. I thank you, my lord duke, for your wise solution."

Next the lords consulted on a new date for the coronation, and again Buckingham offered the solution, which was immediately agreed upon: the feast of St. John the Baptist.

"May I suggest, my lords," Will began, taking the floor, "that before we can plan a coronation, we must first coax the queen and, more important, the young duke of York out of sanctuary. The people would wonder why the king's mother and brother were not in attendance."

"A good point, Lord Hastings," Richard agreed and promptly appointed a committee to assure Elizabeth and her children of their safety if they left sanctuary. Richard continued, "Let me assure you, my lords, I have not nor will I ever threaten women, and so what does the queen have to fear from me? From us? Do we all not want to see her son crowned, keep the kingdom safe for him?" Richard was pleased to see the lords agreeing with him. "After all, I did not ask for this role. I am here to honor my brother's command." It was as well to remind them, Richard thought, wishing himself back in the Yorkshire dales.

"With regard to the actions of Sir Edward Woodville, I would have him and his fleet captured. He is a danger to the peaceful transition of the government, not to mention his absconding with some of the treasury." There had been some inkling of possible threats from France, but nothing had been reported as yet, Richard knew. Nay, Sir Edward's movements again spoke of a Woodville plot to take control.

Will was impressed that Richard wasted no time, and he began to enjoy himself. Even Edward had not conducted council meetings so handily. He looked about him at the familiar faces of the late Edward's faithful councilors—Rotherham, Stanley, Howard,

FitzAlan of Arundel, John Morton, bishop of Ely, and Thomas Bourchier, archbishop of Canterbury. However there were new faces that the protector had brought with him like Francis, Lord Lovell; John, earl of Lincoln; Thomas Langton; Richard Ratcliffe; Sir James Tyrell; and Sir Robert Brackenbury, all gathered to Buckingham's side of the chamber, Will noticed. Was there any significance to this separation, he wondered? And then he dismissed the thought, as the next item up for discussion merited his complete attention.

"My lords, I would request your agreement that the charge of treason be placed upon those who would have taken possession of the king and endangered my life at Stony Stratford. I speak of the queen's brother, Lord Rivers; her son Sir Richard Grey; Sir Thomas Vaughan, the Prince of Wales's chamberlain; and Sir Richard Haute, the boy's comptroller."

Murmurs of opposition to this request outnumbered those "ayes" that came from Buckingham's group.

Thomas Rotherham, archbishop of York, raised his voice. "May I respectfully point out, my lord duke, that although we appreciated your swift action to avoid a possible coup by Queen Elizabeth, her son Dorset, and Earl Rivers, you had not yet been officially named protector by the council, ergo the crime the gentlemen in question had committed was not yet treasonable."

"Pah!" Buckingham spat. "You were naive in your dealings with the queen. You foolishly gave her the Great Seal, and now you refuse my lord of Gloucester when he so obviously saved the king and foiled a plot against his own life. He deserves the council's support in this matter, lest a dangerous precedent be set about disobeying kings with impunity. From the moment King Edward's decree was made, my lord of Gloucester became protector. Are you quibbling over dates?"

While Will was grateful for the posturing duke's support, he cringed at Buckingham's disregard of council protocol by speaking out of turn.

A glimmer of a smile crossed Richard's face at his cousin's overexuberance, but he waited quietly for the archbishop's response.

"I would also respectfully suggest you stand down on this question, my lord duke, as you were of course involved in the arrest, and are perhaps too close to be impartial," Rotherham countered, standing his ground and sending Buckingham back to his spot next to Lovell. Will caught Lord Stanley's eye, and a surreptitious wink passed between them. One point to Rotherham, it said. Buckingham deserved the archbishop's diplomatic reprimand, Will thought.

"I thank you for your caution, your grace," Richard said, getting up from his seat and approaching the councilors' benches. He turned a full circle, assessing every member's willingness to support him or not. "Is this the way you all feel? Should we take a vote?"

Several men, including Will, nodded, and the closed votes were cast and counted in Rotherham's favor. It was the first time that day that Richard of Gloucester did not get his way. The prisoners would remain in captivity pending further discussion of their fate.

"Treason or no. Which way did you vote, my lord?" Richard asked of Will as the Star Chamber emptied of councilors and he, Hastings, and Buckingham were left to discuss the day's work.

Will was taken aback. A vote of that importance was secret to protect each councilor from possible recrimination. If the vote were for treason, then the traitors' lives would be at stake. It was the one point in the long day's business on which Will had not agreed with Richard. Was Richard testing him? Surely not, but he was wary all the same.

"My dear Gloucester," Will said as amiably as he could. "You know I cannot disclose my vote. Would you ask the same of my lord Buckingham here? I think not."

Richard inclined his head and smiled. "I do not have to ask him, Will. I know how he voted." He suddenly put his hand on Will's shoulder, surprising the chamberlain, who had been used to Edward's gestures of familiarity but did not expect the same from reserved Richard. "And I hope I know that you support me, too."

Will bowed. "Certes, I do, my lord duke, but I hope that permits me to disagree with you on occasion."

"I welcome discussion, my lord," Richard said smoothly, after a pause. "However, there is a personal matter that greatly concerns me,"

Will bristled, glancing at Buckingham then back at Richard, expecting Buckingham to leave.

"I have no secrets from Harry," Richard said as Buckingham grinned down at his shorter cousin. "He has proved my most loyal friend, and my friends shall be rewarded." Richard's smile faded and he paced away from Will before announcing, "'Tis a moral matter, about that woman Shore, who I am told still resides in the house Edward provided for her, living off a royal pension. I happen to know you are familiar with her and thus I would ask that you remove the harlot and confiscate her belongings. They belong to the Crown."

Will paled. He was caught in a trap, and Richard knew it. Richard admired the chamberlain who had been his brother's right-hand man, but he deplored the private life they both had shared. And Jane Shore was central to that life. He had made up his mind to clean up Edward's dissipated court and needed assurance that Hastings was willing to live by Richard's moral code.

This would be the real test of his character, Will knew in an instant. He knew, despite the protector's friendly overtures, that he was under Richard's rigid scrutiny. Ironically, Edward had lost his verve for whoring awhile ago. Jane had apparently curbed those appetites, and through her, Will, too, had come to see of late the value of a good, constant woman.

Will looked Richard in the eye, determined not to give either the protector or Buckingham the satisfaction of seeing him ill at ease. "I have to say that you are mistaken in her character, my lord, but I do not expect to convince you," he said evenly, although inside he was seething. "I will do what is right by Mistress Shore, my lord. Good night." He bowed and withdrew before he could no longer contain his fury.

An astute observer of character, Richard had not been fooled by Hastings's equanimity and wondered the degree to which the chamberlain was himself now involved with Jane Shore.

"What do you think Hastings meant by what is right for Mistress Shore?" he mused. "'Twas ambiguous."

"Ambiguous?" the oblivious Buckingham repeated. "I saw nothing but willingness to do your bidding, cousin."

A shadow passed over Richard's face. Damnation, he thought, even more convinced now that Harry was not too bright. Ah, well, at least he was dependable. A pity Hastings seemed to have all the brains.

Other business on the council kept Will from Jane for another week, until he arrived on her doorstep unable to contain his ire. He almost knocked Ankarette off her feet as she was sprinkling water over the freshly replaced aromatic rushes and herbs on the floor to keep them in place.

"Leave us," Jane advised her servant, who glared at Will as she left with her watering pot. "My dear lord, calm yourself, I pray you. You appear as angry as a disturbed nest of wasps. Should I, too, beware your sting?"

Another time Will would have laughed, but this time he ignored the barb. "Not you, Jane, but someone should, and that someone is Henry Stafford, the puffed-up, prating duke of Buckingham who has a bean for a brain. Have you wine, mistress? I need a drink."

Jane was still in her bedrobe, her breakfast half eaten, but she gentled the big man onto the settle and went to pour wine. "I thought you were pleased Richard of Gloucester had taken the reins with Buckingham, Will. Why the change of heart?"

"Duke Richard has the right to govern, Buckingham does not. And yet he has ingratiated himself with his cousin like a lapdog, and it pains me to see how such an addle-pate has blinded Richard." As Jane handed him the goblet, Will noticed for the first time that she was not fully dressed. He slid his free hand inside the opening in her robe and caressed her soft skin through the flimsy lawn chemise. "By God but you are beautiful, Jane," he told her, but Jane gracefully slipped from his grasp and regained her seat opposite him.

They had still not consummated the new arrangement because of Will's pressing duties at Westminster, but she was far too curious now to lead him on to bed. Later, she knew, purposely procrastinating, she would have to give in.

"What has Buckingham done to upset you?"

Will cradled his wine and stared at his reflection in its velvety red depths. How could he explain that it was not exactly what Buckingham had done but what Richard had done for Buckingham that had given vent not only to his anger but also to fear.

"He has usurped your place next to the Crown, has he not?" Jane said simply. "He is where you should be, is that it, Will?"

Will looked up sharply at her. How could such a delicate, lovely woman who spent most of her day shut up in her luxurious house have found exactly the right words to explain his resentment? He nodded, ashamed he was so transparent. "Am I wrong to feel slighted?" he asked, rather like a boy asking his mother.

"You are not wrong to be jealous, Will, but it demeans you to feel anger. You have the wisdom to rise above anger. There will come a time when Richard will recognize your value, I have no doubt. Did he not recently return the office of master of the mint to you? He is merely leaning on the first person who came to his aid—Buckingham. Perhaps Richard prefers a sycophant to a wise councilor by his side. But you will be the one to advise him in the end." She picked up her psaltery and began to play softly.

Will took a deep breath. Jane would not understand how very heavily Richard was depending on his numbskull cousin, to the tune of some of the greatest grants of authority in the kingdom, including chief justice and chamberlain of all of Wales, which would make him governor of those people, as well as constable, steward, and receiver of all the castles and lordships in that country to include being keeper of the royal forests. As if that were not reward enough, Richard had accorded the duke governorship of the people of Hereford, Shropshire, Wiltshire, Somerset, and Dorset and receivership of all the castles there. In other words, Hastings fumed, Buckingham was now virtually viceroy of one of the most important regions in the country. Just listing them made Will's head spin. Nothing the late king had given his faithful chamberlain and councilor over twenty years could come close to the power and wealth Buckingham had received in a matter of three weeks.

Jane's plaintive music placated Will, and watching her he wondered if he should tell her of Richard's demand. Nay, why frighten the lady, he decided. He was annoyed with himself for not telling Richard to go to hell and that, as Jane was now his mistress, he would assume her living expenses. The time had come to make that so.

"Come here, sweetheart." Will's voice brought Jane back to the present, and she found him gazing at her with such desire, she could not refuse his invitation. Arousing herself with thoughts of Tom, she used her lustful yearning to respond to Will without inhibition. She slipped her bedrobe to the floor before kneeling before him and caressing his inner thighs as he untied her chemise and lifted it from her. Jane unpinned her braid, and a cascade of gold veiled her skillful removal of his hose and codpiece.

"Ah, Jane," Will groaned as she hoisted herself onto his lap, and after eight years of waiting, he felt what it was like to finally lose himself inside this most alluring of women. "Go slowly, I beg of you. I want to remember every second of this."

Jane did as he asked, and she was surprised to achieve as satisfying a climax as ever she had had with Edward. As she felt Will's need begin to mount, she turned his face up to hers and kissed him with an ardor that came from the very place in her heart where Will had wished to be held.

"I have asked a friend to help me find a safe place to stay nearby when I escape these cheerless, drab accommodations," Tom told his mother, the queen.

"Who is this friend that you can trust with such a mission? No one is above using such information against us, if it would advance him."

"'Tis not anyone who has influence, Mother. I asked Mistress Shore."

Elizabeth stared at him in horror. "Jane Shore? Why did you seek out that harlot? I thought never to hear her name again. 'Twas she and Hastings killed poor Edward."

Tom turned away so his mother would not see the weary look on his face. Not that conversation again, he thought. He should have just ignored Elizabeth's supplication to return. He could have rewarded the guard handsomely for not raising the alarm if he had chosen liberty. Aye, he should have stayed away and stowed aboard a vessel headed for the Low Countries.

Mustering more patience, he said, "I have my reasons for trusting Jane, and do not forget she is well connected in the city, Mother. She will know where I can hide to work on our plans and meet in secret with our followers. Everyone who comes here is bound to be reported back to Gloucester. We decided this was the best idea, and I will implement it my way, if you please."

"If I were not so tired and melancholy, I would smack your impudent face," Elizabeth retorted. "I have heard the wagtail is now in my lord Hastings's bed. Has she no shame? What am I saying? A whore knowing shame is unlikely." But she was in no mood to argue. She was weary of being in such cramped quarters with the girls squabbling and Dickon getting on everyone's nerves, and although she hid it well, she was afraid of Richard of

Gloucester after he had imprisoned her other son and her brother. She could do nothing while in the abbey, and so she gave in to her handsome, devoted son. "Very well, but let us hope Mistress Shore likes you enough not to betray you, Thomas."

His back to Elizabeth, Tom grinned at the madonna on the wall and thought, if only Mother knew, feeling Jane's hands in his hair as she had writhed in pleasure at his touch. "She likes me well enough, in truth," he countered. "And I persuaded her that our desire to see Ned crowned as soon as possible and our suspicions of Gloucester's intentions give us good cause to work toward fair treatment for Ned." He mentally crossed himself for his lie. "Now where is that other young brother of mine? I promised him a game of hide-and-seek."

"He is with the girls," Elizabeth said, nodding toward the smaller of the two chambers she and her seven children shared at the abbey. Tom shared a grim monk's cell with another man not far away. As a childish shriek shattered their peace, Elizabeth groaned. "Dear God, but I hope we can all leave soon or I shall lose my sanity."

"Has Rotherham been to see you?" Tom asked suddenly. "Is he still faithful to us? I wish we could have held on to the Great Seal, but he saw the error he had made in bringing it to you too soon, and I can just imagine how humiliated he was when Richard removed the chancellorship and gave it to Russell."

Elizabeth nodded. The seal might have made a good bartering tool, she thought, and maybe they would not still be holed up, if Rotherham had not snatched it back without warning. No doubt he was groveling to Richard now. She was glad the archbishop was paying for his false step; he always did think he was the Lord's anointed.

Tom bowed and was about to leave when Elizabeth stopped him with a parting word. "Promise me you will not consort with that Shore woman once you are free, my son. She took away my husband's love, and I could not bear to lose yours to her, too," she grumbled.

Tom wrapped his arms around her, noting how thin she had become. "Never fear, Mother, you have always been first in my heart," he told her, cleverly avoiding the promise. "Always first."

Until now, he mused, imagining Jane's soft body in his arms instead. Until now.

Tom's daydreaming abruptly came to a halt when he saw the two prelates coming toward him in the cloister and recognized the new chancellor, John Russell, bishop of Lincoln, and the hairy old bishop of Bath and Wells, Robert Stillington. They all bowed solemnly, and Tom asked casually if they were at the abbey on church or state business.

"We come on behalf of the protector, my lord," Russell said, his pleasant baritone echoing among the old stone arches. "We are here to see her grace, the queen."

"Not again," Tom muttered to himself, but he smiled politely and let them pass. He was certain Richard had sent yet another mission to persuade Elizabeth to leave sanctuary. He loitered near his mother's chambers, and when he heard her lamentations he knew he was right.

"I do not believe that Richard of Gloucester will see me safely out of sanctuary," Elizabeth cried at the long-suffering priests. "If he wants me, he can come and get me. And no, I shall never let my younger son out of my sight, coronation or no coronation. The so-called protector has taken Edward's and my oldest boy, but he shall not have Dickon. Go back and tell him so, my lord bishops. If we need to, my children and I shall spend the rest of our lives in sanctuary."

Tom, never failing to be impressed by his shrewd parent, grinned. "That's the spirit, Mother. To the devil with Richard of Gloucester."

FOURTEEN

LONDON AND WESTMINSTER, JUNE 1483

A light drizzle shrouded the spire of St. Paul's from Jane's view when she started out with Ankarette on a morning in early June to see Sophie. Will had already left for Westminster to arrange yet another council meeting, and Jane knew he would be gone until late in the day. It was her chance to fulfill her promise to Tom, although she walked along Thames Street with an uncomfortable guilt gnawing at her. She ought not to be on Tom's business while under Will's protection.

Her hood sheltering her from the weather, she chose the long way to St. Sithe's Lane not only to prolong the walk but also to make use of the Chepe's paved thoroughfare and avoid the mud along Watling Street. Somehow the rain would always make the usual stench of the city gutters smell worse, and she kept her tussie-mussie close to her nose as she picked her way on her high wooden pattens through the leavings of the gong farmer's cart, rubbish, and rotting vegetables. She crossed over to the north side of the wide street to avoid passing in front of her father's shop and walked by the Maid on the Hoop brewhouse and the entrance to Mercers' Hall, housed in the hospital of St. Thomas of Acre. She held her thumbs, hoping there was no meeting of the guild there today, and she breathed a sigh of relief as she recognized no one in her path. She was in no mood for an awkward confrontation.

Ducking behind the conduit, she was about to cross back across the Chepe into Bucklersbury Lane when she was distracted by the sound of trumpets and many horses' hoofs clopping along the pavement behind her. She and Ankarette eased themselves between two women filling buckets from the conduit and stopped to watch. Ah, Jane recalled Will's words before he had left that morning, 'twas the protector's duchess and her entourage arriving from her northern castle of Middleham. She assumed from Hastings's information that it was Richard's closest friend, Sir Francis Lovell, escorting her through the streets.

With her midnight blue cloak spread over the back of her horse, Anne Neville shyly observed the citizens of London who had stopped to gawp. She lifted her hand occasionally, and when she did, people cheered. "'Tis the Kingmaker's daughter," someone cried, and more cheers followed. Richard Neville, earl of Warwick had been a popular figure in the city, and even though he had turned traitor and betrayed King Edward, the older folk with long memories were recalling his generosity to them in a happier time. The duchess of Gloucester had rarely set foot in the city since her marriage to Richard in the early 1470s, and so Londoners were curious to catch a glimpse of her. A sweet enough expression, Jane determined, but she was not striking like her second cousins, young Elizabeth, Cecily, and Catherine of York.

As the cavalcade rode by on its way to Crosby Place, an impressive town house where the duke resided in Bishopsgate, Jane noticed a youth on a small palfrey with a striking resemblance to Richard of Gloucester.

"I wonder who that is," she remarked to Ankarette. "He is too old to be Gloucester's son. Edward of Middleham is only eight."

"He is John Plantagenet, mistress, Richard of Gloucester's bastard," stated a woman standing behind her, the pride in her voice unmistakable.

Jane turned her head and looked into the most remarkable pair of amber eyes she had ever seen. "How would you know, mistress?" she asked, noting a truant tendril of chestnut hair escaping from the widow's wimple and clinging to her damp cheek. Even with the unbecoming head covering, she was beautiful.

"Because he is my son, mistress," the widow said, smiling at Jane and admiring in her turn the delicate beauty of her fellow spectator. "I am not ashamed to admit it."

Jane's mouth gaped in delighted astonishment. "Then you must be Kate Haute, if I am not mistaken. I have heard much of you, mistress, and all of it good."

Kate's low laugh made Jane smile, too. "And who knows of me, mistress, that they can say good or ill about me?"

Jane held those golden eyes in merriment for a second before confessing, "'Twas my lord of Gloucester's brother, King Edward himself. You see, you and I are much alike. I am Jane Shore. Perhaps you have heard my name before, too?"

Now it was Kate's turn to gape before she burst out laughing. "'Tis fate placed us side by side today, Mistress Shore," she said, and she cast her eyes heavenward. "God works in mysterious ways, does he not. 'Tis a pleasure to meet you. Do you have time for ale?" And she nodded across the street to the Maid on the Hoop tavern adjacent to Mercers' Hall.

Tom's request could wait a few more minutes, Jane decided. This was too wonderful an opportunity to miss. "Certes, I do, my dear Widow Haute. We have much to talk about, and if I know my fellow citizens, in their turn, they may well talk about us," she said, tucking Kate's arm in hers. "Come, Ankarette, do not dawdle, we mistresses have much to discuss."

Ankarette looked from one lovely, laughing face to another and clicked her tongue. What could be so amusing, she thought, hurrying to keep up. Once inside the tavern, Jane and Kate found a corner of a long table in the area reserved for gentry, while Ankarette settled herself on a bench with other servants and contented herself with a flagon of ale. Recognizing Jane, the landlord brought the two women a flask of wine and begged a word with Jane.

"My son still sings your praises, Mistress Shore. Your intervention with the king's victualler saved him from disgrace. He has learned his lesson and his business has increased thanks to you."

Jane smiled an acknowledgment. "'Twas nothing, Master Troughton, although I am no longer in a position to help, more's the pity." Understanding, the innkeeper nodded sympathetically and left.

Kate watched Jane's expression change to gentle concern for the man and smiled. "I now know why word of your kind heart has spread far and wide."

Jane was astonished. How would Kate Haute have heard of the small favors she had been glad to afford some of her former neighbors? She found herself blushing and hurried to deflect attention from herself.

"I would hear more of your liaison with Richard, Kate. I can see from the light in your eye that as yet you harbor some affection for him. Has he your heart still?"

Kate grinned. "As clear as a sky after rain, am I not? Aye, there is none other in my heart now or ever, unless you count my children," she admitted. "The day I had to accept we would never more be lovers was the hardest of my life, except perhaps the day I had to give up John into Richard's keeping."

Jane's eyes widened. "Richard made you give up your son? How unkind must he be."

Kate patted Jane's hand. "It was promised from the day he knew I carried his first child that he would provide for them. It was for the best, although I could not see for tears at the time. Both Katherine and John were raised in royal households, Jane. Katherine is now lady-in-waiting to Duchess Anne, and John is squire to Sir Francis Lovell. Richard loves them as much as he loves his heir, I promise you, and I see them from time to time." Would she entrust Jane with her greatest secret? Nay, she would keep her third son, named for his father, to herself. Only Margaret and Jack Howard knew the truth: that he had been raised by Kate's brother and wife in Kent as their own child. Best leave well enough alone, Kate decided; she had no idea whether she could yet trust this Mistress Shore with a secret.

"May I be frank and ask why Richard did not keep you as his mistress? Edward had no qualms about keeping me despite his married state."

Kate's face clouded at the painful memory when Richard had told her he was to marry Anne Neville and must end their affair. "My dear Jane," Kate told her new friend, "the most important ideals in life to Richard are duty and loyalty. He could never have been unfaithful to his marriage vows, and even though I know he loved me truly, he put duty to his family and his rank before any love for me. Duty led him to wed Anne, and he has been loyal to her ever since. Do I make sense?" Kate saw Jane nod slowly. "To Richard, disloyalty is the ultimate sin. That is why I have stayed away from him, why I have kept my promise to him that we should never again live in sin. All I hope is that his memory of me remains sweet."

Jane found herself blinking back tears at this heartfelt confession. She took Kate's hand. "You do me great honor to entrust these truths to me, Kate, and certes, I must admire Richard for his fortitude. I loved Edward dearly, but I now see that his younger brother may be the more honorable man."

"I promise you he is, and Jack Howard believes his overzealousness since his brother's death has all to do with this unexpected new duty being thrust upon him," Kate mused, a smile curling her generous mouth, "but I know that earnestness well. 'Tis naught but his way of understanding his new situation and establishing control. Underneath, he is still my beloved Richard."

From Will's description of events lately, Jane was not so sure that Kate would recognize her lover now.

The rain had stopped by the time Jane and Kate bade each other farewell and went their separate ways. Jane mulled over all she had gleaned from Kate as she hurried toward the Vandersands' house. She came to the conclusion her situation had been easier than Kate's, although how she envied Kate her children. If only she had borne Edward a child.

She turned into St. Pancras Lane and almost bumped into a priest exiting Benet Sherehog church. He issued a reprimand, but Jane was too engrossed in her thoughts to notice. Before she and Kate had parted, she had asked what Kate might know of Buckingham, who appeared to have so much influence on the protector.

"Naught but what Jack Howard tells us," Kate had replied. "But 'tis true, even though he is Richard's supporter, Jack has been irked by the unfair parceling of grants that Richard has made to Buckingham. But Jane, understand this, Richard has been acting independently in the north for so long, he must feel isolated from the lords at Westminster. Do not judge him harshly. Harry is his cousin, and he must feel he can trust some-one down here."

Jane pondered Kate's information, and as she arrived at her destination, she resolved to tell Will of her findings. She hoped the news might ease his resentment of Richard's rewards to Buckingham.

The Vandersands' house was now one of the grander in the lane, and Jane was pleased with the improvements. The extra money she had provided seemed to have lessened Jehan's bouts of melancholy and impatience, allowing Sophie to blossom as a mother and settle into a happier middle age. She hesitated at the door, wondering if she had the right to ask her friends to help Tom, but she knew no one else as far removed from Tom Grey and the politics at court. Besides there was nobody she trusted more than Sophie and her now-indebted husband. She lifted the iron ring and knocked, de-termined to keep her promise to Tom.

Jane loved living by the river. She liked nothing better than to linger on the wharves on a summer's day and watch the myriad of craft that plied their never-ending journeys up and down the wide waterway while exotic cargos from the larger boats were unloaded by swarthy foreign seamen. Barrels of wine from Gascony, silks from Venice, spices from warmer climes, jewels from the Baltic, and luxuries from the Levant were all brought to London to be traded for England's chief export, wool. She had often imagined dressing as a boy and boarding a vessel so that she might see these exotic places for herself.

Today she joined other passengers on a wherry at Paul's Wharf, right behind Will's town house, and, seated in the stern, she stared up at the forbidding walls of Baynard's Castle, the London residence of the York family. Jane wondered if there were a meeting at the castle that day. During a brief stop at her house earlier, Will had relayed that the council had been split into groups to meet at different locations. He found it puzzling, he had told her, because one group did not know what another was discussing. However, Richard felt more could be accomplished in a shorter time this way, and, as usual, Buckingham had agreed with him.

The tide was up, concealing the detritus visible at low tide on the riverbed. It was always possible to see a body, bloated and rotting, washed up on the quagmire and caught among the reeds. And Londoners were not supposed to throw their rubbish into the Thames, but many did, making laundresses hold their noses as they attempted to wash their linens in the murky water. But the river sparkled in the sunlight, the gardens in full bloom running down to its banks, kingfishers, herons, and coots among the reeds, and Jane was reminded that June was her favorite time of year.

The wharf at Westminster was crowded when the boatmen skillfully steered their craft to the pier, handed her out, and accepted her fare. She was alone and disguised as a yeoman's wife, having donned a plain worsted gown that Ankarette had found her and concealing her famous yellow hair under a tightly wound white cloth. Knowing the reputation for cutpurses at Westminster, she clutched the thong of the small leather bag tied to her belt and carried a basket of bread in another to offer guards, in case she were challenged at the abbey. She wended her way up the street, past Master Caxton's sign of the Red Pale printing shop, vendors hawking pies and custards with the ubiquitous pack of curs roaming nearby hungry for any leavings. At the abbey, she made a note of how many guards were posted at all the doors, standing to attention, their pikes at the ready. How would Tom ever escape from here?

To her surprise, her smile gained her access into the cloister where visitors might see those in sanctuary, and she sat in the sunshine on a stone bench while a monk went to fetch Tom. She prayed the queen would not choose this hour to walk in the garden, as Jane had no desire to meet the haughty Elizabeth again.

"Jane, my dearest," Tom said when she rose to greet him, "you do me great honor to come." He stood apart from her and did not take her hand; none must know she was not really a yeoman goodwife taking bread to the kitchen. Once certain they were alone, he asked, "Do you have news for me?"

She longed for him to reach out and touch her, but she told herself she could wait until he was free, although how she would conduct an affair while living with Will, she was not about to contemplate yet. One day at a time, she thought, as Tom walked her into a shaded corner.

"I have found a place for you, Tom. I shall not implicate my friend, but you are expected at the Pope's Head off Cornhill any day in the next week. Ask for Master Godfrey. I have paid for a sennight for you."

"You paid?" Tom was alarmed. "You did not ask Will Hastings for money, I trust?"

"Do you think I would do such a thing, my lord?" Jane shot

back, slighted. "Then you do not know me very well. I have the means, but I expect you to pay me back." She did not tell him she had taken Edward's final gift to a lombard, who had been suspicious at first of its origins. Master Isaacs had eventually agreed when she had revealed her identity, but Jane had had to take a sum far below the large jewel's worth in exchange for the usurer's silence. After giving Jehan money for Tom's room, she had hidden the rest in a box under a discarded gown at the bottom of her clothes chest.

"Forgive me, Jane. I misspoke," Tom apologized. "I have much to be grateful for." His eyes merry, he added, "I will show you how much, once I am away from here."

Jane dared to touch his arm then. "Have a care, Tom. There are a dozen guards at the front of the abbey and several at the entrance to this cloister."

At that moment, an orderly group of chanting monks filed through the cloister and into the abbey and Tom concealed Jane in his shadow. He laughed. "Expect to see me with a tonsure soon. I have already procured a habit for my escape. It will not be long, I promise. Now go, I beg of you, before my lady mother chooses to take the air. She is touchy enough already, and I fear a glimpse of you might undo her," he said, grinning apologetically.

Jane hurried away, found her escort, and exited by the garden gate. As she turned the corner to walk down the hill and past the great hall of the palace to the wharf, she did not see a man loitering across the street from the garden entry.

William Catesby noticed her, however, and puzzled, he decided Richard of Gloucester needed to know this tidbit of information. Why would Mistress Shore visit the queen in sanctuary when it was known Elizabeth Woodville despised her husband's beloved mistress?

"Lord Hastings, have you turned Jane Shore out of the king's house yet and had her goods returned to the Crown?" Richard wiped his fingers on a spotless napkin and pushed his pewter platter away. He had invited Will to dine with him and his closest advisors, Buckingham, Sir Francis Lovell, and Sir Richard Ratcliffe, at Crosby Place following another of the splintered council meetings that day. Hastings had noted idly that his group had been those lords temporal and spiritual who had been most favored by the dead king: Stanley, archbishop Rotherham of York, Bishop Morton of Ely, and himself.

Will detected no rancor in the duke's tone, only a directness Will had come to expect. He decided now was the time to admit to his friend Richard of Gloucester that Jane had become his mistress. The man might be a prude, but surely he could not forbid such a liaison. To placate Richard, he had decided to procure a different house for Jane, but what he did there was his affair alone.

"My lord duke, we have all been about council business so much these days, I have not had a moment to tell you that Mistress Shore and I"—he smiled—"well, she is now . . . let us say, under my protection." He did not much relish admitting this and especially not with Buckingham obviously enjoying his discomfort, but he believed the truth was necessary.

Richard fingered his gold signet ring and gave no sign of his annoyance. He simply said, "You disappoint me, Lord Hastings. I had hoped you had reformed. I gave you a chance to redeem yourself in the eyes of your fellow councilors, and to show me compliance. I see I was mistaken in you."

Will wanted to reach across the table and punch the amused Buckingham in the eye, but Richard had not finished. "Is this all the thanks I get for rewarding you with the mint, with the captaincy of Calais?" Now he leveled his intense gray eyes at Will. "The truth is, I need to know I can trust you, my lord."

Will held Richard's gaze. "Aye, you may, your grace. I was steadfast in my loyalty to your late brother and am now to his son, our king. I shall obey you in all things regarding the king's welfare. As for Mistress Shore, I have arranged for her to leave your brother's house and live under my protection. She deserves nothing less," he insisted. "Even though you disapprove of my private life, you will find none so loyal as I. You have my word on it." He shot a look at Buckingham. "Who says otherwise is a liar."

"I believe you were loyal to my brother, Hastings," Richard answered, "but as yet your loyalty to me is unproven. And how do we know who Mistress Shore consorts with when you are not with her? Can you trust a whore?"

"With my life," Will avowed, angrily. He could not believe Jane a threat to anyone, and Richard's insinuations were puzzling. He was, of course, unaware that Catesby had informed on Jane's visit to Westminster Abbey and that he was being watched for any sign of complicity. "What has Mistress Shore done to you that you villify her? She is no schemer like the Woodville woman, and she has never demanded anything of me nor of your brother." He hoped by mentioning the queen, the discussion might return to the problem of Elizabeth in sanctuary.

Jack Howard's eyebrows shot up. If Hastings had sent Jane as a go-between with the queen, then why had he brought up Elizabeth now? Perhaps Will was innocent after all, but as Richard was motioning for the meeting to adjourn, Jack decided it was not worth pointing out.

The evening light was failing and candles were lit as Richard's councilors filed out to make their way home before curfew.

As he exited the courtyard, Will was surprised to see a litter arrive at Crosby Place, and even in the twilight he recognized the insignia of the bishopric of Bath and Wells upon the servants' livery.

Stillington, he said to himself, at this hour? I wonder what he wants?

Will chose to ride the length of Bishopsgate almost to the river, watching idly as citizens finished their daily tasks, or packed up their wares, or pushed their carts to safety for the night. He wished a carter good night as he skirted round the heavy vehicle laden with firewood that had just crossed over the Thames from the forests of Kent. London Bridge was directly in front of him and was silhouetted dark against an orange sky as the sun set. To his left he could just see the spire of St. Paul's over the higgledy-piggledy jumble of the city roofs stretching west, and he smiled at the sight. London must surely be the most beautiful city in the world, he thought to himself, before he returned to his dilemma and the odd conversation that night. Turning into Thames Street and clopping slowly along the long winding lane, he decided he would rehouse Jane after the full council meeting on the morrow.

At the same time, clad from head to toe in dark red velvet, a heavy silver cross around his neck the only outward sign of his profession, the small bent figure was helped from the litter at the steps of Crosby Place. He mounted the staircase to the great hall on the second floor of the imposing town house and was immediately led to the duke of Gloucester's private apartment.

"Come in, my dear bishop," Richard said, extending his arm to welcome the prelate. "To what do I owe this late visit?" Bowing to the protector, Robert Stillington, bishop of Bath and Wells put out his hand, and Richard dutifully kissed the ruby ring.

The bishop requested a private audience as he eyed the other two men present. He recognized Harry Stafford, duke of Buckingham, but he had not seen the thin, sharp-featured young man next to Buckingham before. "I have an important matter to discuss with you."

Richard smiled and indicated the carved high-back chair. "I pray you, my lord bishop, sit. You may speak freely here. I have no secrets from my closest advisors, and I do not intend to begin my protectorate with concealments. What brings you?"

Richard thought briefly of sending Lawyer Catesby out; he had not known the man long enough to be assured of his loyalty, but then he decided whatever this old cleric Stillington had to impart could not be of such great importance and would itself be a good test of Catesby's trustworthiness. Richard had been pleased that the intelligent young man had agreed to serve as legal counsel, although Richard might have been dismayed that Catesby had gone behind Hastings's back to claim the post. For now Catesby was playing the trustworthy servant on both sides. Encouraged by the protector's appreciation of news about Jane Shore's visit to the queen, Catesby had also managed to plant seeds of distrust about Hastings, all in an effort to secure his own seat on Richard's council.

Had my lord of Gloucester not been so intent on discovering why Mistress Shore might join a conspiracy with the queen and deciphering if and why William Hastings might be involved, he might have questioned why Catesby had declined to sup with the group earlier that evening. The lawyer had no intention of allow-ing Hastings to see him at Crosby Hall and had returned to the room only after the other councilors' departure.

Now in the chilly chamber, Stillington was obviously flustered, refusing the chair, and chafing his hands. He drew a deep breath. "After our meeting today regarding the young king's coronation, I could no longer maintain silence. My conscience will not allow it. This matter concerns the late king, your brother, and one Eleanor Butler, who is also dead."

Richard slowly set down his cup of wine and stared at the bishop. "Edward and Eleanor Butler. You mean, the former Eleanor Talbot, the Talbot daughter who took the veil?"

Stillington nodded. "The very one, my lord. She is dead long since."

Richard groused, "Another of Edward's whores, I presume?"

Buckingham laughed. Stillington nodded again, then continued. "But she was more than that, my lord." He was aware of every pair of eyes riveted on him as he said clearly, "I witnessed a plight-troth in secret between them one evening at Greenwich in March of '63."

"A plight-troth? In '63?" Richard repeated incredulously as the implication became clear: a plight-troth or precontract was as good as a ring in the eyes of an upstanding gentleman and the law. "Why, that was a year before Edward married Elizabeth Woodville."

A collective gasp came from the other two men as they registered the information.

"Aye, my lord duke," Stillington agreed, watching Richard's face blanch. "I had to pledge an oath of silence to his grace. I have remained true to it until now," the frightened old priest lied convincingly—Clarence was long dead, he mused. "Thus his grace the king was in an unlawful marriage with the queen all these years, making their children—"

"Bastards!" Richard cried, sitting down heavily on the table edge and tipping over an empty cup. Then he looked accusingly at the bishop. "I hope you are not lying, Stillington, or I will have your head. Your lie would dishonor my brother and his family. You do realize how serious this claim is."

It was Stillington's turn to pale. "I swear on this sacred cross," he asserted, holding it up. "I witnessed the plight-troth and gave them my blessing, God help me. Why would I lie, my lord? What would I gain?"

"Sweet Jesu, what will this mean?" Richard said, his head in his hand. "The crown cannot go to a bastard."

Buckingham went down on one knee. "It means, cousin, that you are the legitimate heir to Edward and should be king."

"Preposterous! Get up, I say, get up!" Richard cried. "'Tis not the time for that. We need time to reflect on this information. Do not forget I have sworn an oath to my nephew to uphold his kingship. I am protector, nothing more. Up, up!" He raised Buckingham bodily and began to pace the room.

"Who else knows of this, my lord bishop?"

"It is my understanding that Lord Hastings was also in the king's confidence," Stillington replied softly, remembering the scene at Edward's deathbed when he had learned of Hastings's knowledge. It had been a relief to know he was not the only one harboring the king's deception, although neither man had spoken of it to the other since Edward's death.

"Hastings knows?" Buckingham cried. "That two-faced varlet! Why did he not tell us?"

Catesby took a tiny step forward. "Perhaps he is in league with the queen, your grace." His silky insinuation made Richard look up. "Perhaps he sees his power dwindling among us . . . I mean, your good councilors. Perhaps there is a plot to take the young king from your grace's protection and use him for Woodville ends. Perhaps that is why Hastings prefers to be with others of the late king's circle—Morton, Stanley, and Rotherham. Perhaps, I would suggest, that is why Mistress Shore visited the queen in sanctuary. It all points to a conspiracy—if I may be so bold as to suggest."

A nod of agreement from Buckingham followed this little speech, but still Richard said nothing. It was true that Hastings preferred the company of Edward's former advisors, but Richard had not considered a conspiracy until Catesby had suggested it. Richard stared at the floor and fiddled with his ring, his mind racing.

Buckingham could not stand the silence. "Hastings's inaction is tantamount to treason, is it not, Richard? He has threatened the rightful royal line by remaining silent. He has put your brother's guilty secret before his duty to the Crown. He should be punished."

Stillington trembled. He had hoped for some reward if Richard of Gloucester should become king. He sidled toward the door and bowed. "If you do not require me further, your grace, I should like to return to my lodging before curfew."

Richard looked up then. "You will lodge here tonight, my lord bishop. Master Catesby, I pray you take his lordship to my privy chamber and record all the details of the precontract. Leave nothing out." He waved them away. "I thank you, Bishop Stillington.

God give you a good night. I trust you will keep your peace on this," he said. Stillington nodded, kissing his cross.

As soon as they left, Richard beckoned Buckingham to the table.

"Harry, I pray I can count on your silence." Seeing Buckingham nod, he continued: "And now, I have no choice. As much as I despise the position my brother has put me in, I must in good conscience do what is right for the realm. Here is what I propose."

After the meeting, Richard called for his secretary and dictated a letter to the mayor, aldermen, and council of the city of York. He was convinced there was a conspiracy to depose him as protector and even to do away with him. The only people he trusted were his northerners; he saw shadows in every corner of the halls and chambers of these London palaces, and he knew not who was friend or foe.

"*Right trusty and well beloved,*" he began, remembering a letter he had written not ten days earlier to the council in a far less urgent tone, promising to repay a debt to York on behalf of the young king. For a month he had pondered why the queen refused to leave sanctuary, and now he knew for certain. The queen must have known about the precontract and was conspiring with Edward's associates to rid themselves of him, his heir in Middleham, Buckingham, and anyone else who might contest the throne. They were planning on crowning a bastard, and Richard would have none of it. But he could not set it right alone; he needed help. He thought carefully and continued.

> *"As you do love the weal of us, and the weal and safety of*
> *your own selves, we heartily pray you to come unto us to*
> *London in all the diligence possible after reading this, and*
> *with as many men as you can muster to aid and assist us*
> *against the queen, her blood adherents and her affinity, which*
> *have intended, and daily do intent, to murder and utterly*

destroy us and our cousin of Buckingham and the old royal blood of this realm . . ."

He paused, wondering if his language was too dramatic, but then he felt his anger rise as he thought of the conspirators meeting in secret, plotting his downfall and death, and he continued,

". . . and it is openly known by their damnable ways that they are plotting to destroy and disherit you and all other landowners in the north as well as all men of honor."*

John Kendall looked up as soon as he had caught up with Richard's tirade. "My lord, you think this conspiracy is aimed at northerners?" he asked, thinking that perhaps his master might be overreacting to what was, as far as John was concerned, only a possibility of a plot.

"Aye, John, I do," Richard snapped. "As I am Lord of the North and am the largest landowner, all who dwell upon those lands will be subject to the queen's displeasure. Now please finish in my usual way and let me sign it."

As Catesby was busy with Stillington, Richard sent for Sir Richard Ratcliffe to hand deliver the message to the mayor of York. Then he went to his own chamber to find Anne. Although he had decided not to tell her yet about the precontract, he needed her love and comfort on this night of betrayals.

Will passed by his own town house on his way from the meeting, the gates lit by torches now that dusk had settled over the city, and squinted up at the second floor. He must speak to Katherine about her extravagant use of candles, he thought, but then he began to anticipate his evening with Jane. He fingered the package in a

---

* actual text

pouch at his belt and smiled. She would be pleased with his gift, he decided.

Ankarette let him into the solar, curtseyed, and disappeared. Jane was playing her psaltery and stood when he entered. "'Tis late, my lord. I thought not to see you tonight, but I am glad you are come."

Will went to her and held her at arm's length admiring yet again her willowy figure complemented by full breasts and a face to inspire the poets. "You are just what I need tonight, my dearest girl," he said, before gently removing her jeweled headcovering and helping her hair tumble around her shoulders. "I would stay the night with you, if you will have me."

Jane reached up and kissed him, charmed that the man to whom she owed her comfortable position now would ask permission to stay. "With all my heart I will have you, Will. How was your supper with Duke Richard? What was so important that he kept you late?"

Her innocent question sent an unexpected frisson through Will. Aye, what had been on Richard's mind? The man wanted to rid Will of Jane and claimed it was a matter of loyalty. An experienced politician, Will recognized rhetoric couched in metaphor, and that Richard meant to purify Edward's court was as clear as a mountain stream, but he could not reconcile Richard's insufferable self-righteous piety when the duke himself had not eschewed a liaison for several years with a married woman of low birth that had resulted in two bastards. In his experience, Will concluded that when confronted with sudden change and its discomfort, a man often turned to piety and self-discipline in order to cope. Perhaps setting to right Will's sinful life with Jane Shore might afford Richard a sense of achievement as he struggled to accept his new responsibilities. Whatever the reason for Richard's dislike of Jane, Will believed it stemmed from what she represented and not from the lady herself. He chose, therefore, to evade Jane's question.

"Oh, we talked of this and that," he said, airily, pouring himself some wine. "Certes, his cronies were in attendance, too, so 'twas not a private supper. Nothing but the usual manly talk of horses, politics and . . ."

"Women," Jane finished, laughing. "Come and join me on the cushions, my lord, and let me remove that jacket. You look spent."

Will knew he ought to talk to her about moving her to a new house, but he hated to spoil the romantic moment. Instead he drew a gift wrapped in blue velvet from his bag and presented it to her. "I hope you will think of me every time you look on it," he said, humbly. "I had it created especially for you."

Jane unwrapped the gift and stared in wonder at the leather-bound book, her name embossed in gold on the cover. "Jane Shore's Book of Hours," she read and opened it to the frontispiece.

For those hours when I am not with you. Remember me in your prayers as I always do you, he had written in his bold hand. Jane gentled open the pages and gasped in astonishment at the magnificent illuminations painted among the prayers. "It is the most beautiful thing I have ever seen," she declared, and putting it down carefully on the table, she wrapped her arms about him and thanked him.

For the next hour, they sat side by side on the cushions, drinking in the sweet smell of lavender, hyssop, and marjoram sprinkled in among the fresh rushes on the tiled floor, and turning the pages of the exquisite book. "Master Caxton recommended the work of his associate Wynken de Worde, and thus the illuminations have that Flemish look," Will explained. "I thought you would like it more than another jewel. Edward showered you with them, and I wanted to do something different. I am so happy you like it."

"Like it?" Jane cried, not reminding him of Edward's book. "It is more beautiful than any jewel I have ever owned, and I am humbled by the gift. I suppose I should reciprocate with a token, should I not?"

Will brazenly reached inside her bodice and touched her breast.

"This is all I ask, Jane," he said huskily. "That you love and pleasure me until the day I am too old to care."

"Then my token is easily given, my lord," and she stood, slowly undressing herself for him until her scarlet chemise fell about her feet and she was completely naked.

"Dance for me, Jane," Will requested, his arousal trapped in his codpiece. "Let me see you move like the sea nymph you are."

Jane laughed and began swaying sensually to and fro, using her arms above her head as though she were indeed in the sea. She, too, was aroused by the experience and soon her nipples hardened, standing up like tiny pink shells on the satiny skin of her breasts. Will tore off the rest of his clothes and began to sway with her, his hands caressing every undulating curve until he could wait no longer. Picking her up he carried her to the bed and, laying her on the rich coverlet, proceeded to kiss every inch of her compliant body.

"Come to me, Will, my Poseidon," Jane begged him, smiling seductively. "Tonight I think my need is greater than yours."

If Ankarette heard cries of passion in the room below, she would never have admitted it to Jane; she was always content when her mistress was happy. But she grumbled mightily to be woken by a loud knocking an hour after compline, and hoping the pompous steward Martin would open the front door, she hid her head under her bedcovering and ignored it. She was thus mortified when she heard Lord Hastings's voice demand of the visitor, "Why the late call, sirrah? The watch will be alerted by all that racket." She decided then to leave well alone, go back to sleep, and pretend she had never heard a thing.

The messenger stepped into the hall, and recognizing Lord Stanley's cognizance, Will shepherded him into the empty kitchen. "Well, sir. What means this disturbance? It had better be important."

The young man bowed and apologized. "My lord Stanley sent

me to tell you that he has had a terrible dream." He stared at the floor, embarrassed by his flimsy mission.

"Christ's nails!" Will hissed. "A dream. Has the man lost his senses?" Then, aware now he was only in his shirt, Will waved him on. He wondered vaguely how the man had known to find him at Jane's.

"I shall attempt to relate the dream word for word, as Lord Stanley instructed, my lord. He was dreaming of the council meeting on the morrow when a wild boar charged into the room and gouged both your and my lord Stanley's heads with its tusks, and the blood ran down your faces to your shoulders. He said I should remind you that the protector's badge—"

"Is a white boar. I know," Hastings interrupted, shaking his head in frustration. "And I suppose your lord believes in this superstition? Pah! Well, I do not, in truth. A dream is merely a dream. Pray thank Lord Stanley for his well-meaning concern, but I am going back to bed. I give you a good night, sir."

He held open the front door and saw the messenger safely out.

Jane had lit a candle for the sconce on the bedpost and was absently braiding her hair when Will returned. "Who was that, my lord?"

"That woman Stanley had had a bad dream, 'tis all."

"Margaret Beaufort? Why would she send someone here?"

"Nay, I did not mean Stanley's wife, Jane, I was referring to that lord's womanly mind. He saw the dream as a portent. I grant you 'twas unusual"—he described it to Jane—"but fanciful."

A shiver of fear ran up Jane's spine, and she pulled the bedclothes up to her chin. "Fanciful indeed, Will. Perhaps you should not attend the meeting tomorrow?"

"Not you, too, Jane," Will teased as he got back under the covers. "Stanley has a flea up his arse about these small meetings, 'tis all. He looks for meanings behind every event, every utterance, and he is curious why Gloucester insists on these splinter meetings. I think, like Gloucester, that small groups can accomplish more, and I certainly am more comfortable with Edward's old councilors. Gloucester's cronies are mostly unknown to us. Tomorrow we will all be together to discuss young Ned's coronation. 'Twill be a merry meeting for a change." He turned on his side and cradled Jane to him. "Now this old man needs his sleep or he will not wake in time to go and prove Stanley wrong in his fears." It took Will longer than he expected to fall asleep, but he did not resent the time he had to cherish Jane's body. He felt guilty he had not brought up the topic of her removal from the house she loved, but he wanted nothing more to spoil the solace he had found holding her in his arms following the disturbing meeting at Crosby Place.

Jane, on her part, sent a prayer to St. Elizabeth to keep Will safe. She did not admit to her lover that she, too, had a woman's fear of omens and that it had occurred to her that the meeting would fall on Friday, the thirteenth.

"I am come to keep you company on the walk to the meeting," Thomas Howard greeted Will at dawn the next day after being shown into the hall. "It is a pleasant enough day for a walk, my lord."

Will clapped him on the shoulder and grinned. "And my waist could do with the exercise," he said, patting his paunch. "Forgive me, my lord, I will not keep you but a moment. I have forgotten something important." And he winked at Howard.

He went back into the solar, where Jane was seated on the cushions, playing with her little dog. She looked up when he entered.

"Did you forget something, my lord?"

Will knelt on the floor and took her face in his hands. "Aye, sweetheart. How could I go without one final kiss."

Jane was touched. "But, Will, you kissed me before you went to greet Sir Thomas. You are becoming as foolish as a spellbound young lover," she teased.

"Aye, I think I am bewitched," he teased, smiling. "Come kiss me, my little witch."

Their lips met in a gentle kiss: Will's was born of contentment after years of aching for her; Jane's of kindness and a love born of friendship.

"I love you, Will," she said, pulling away and looking up into his eyes.

Will's heart leaped, and he tightened his hold on her. "There is naught so precious as a love that is reciprocated, my dearest. I leave you mine as I take yours with me. You have made me the happiest man on earth today, my Jane."

Then he kissed her again and at once decided that now was the moment to break the news. "When I am gone, I want you to think about finding another house. This one, in truth, belongs to the Crown, and I have no right to keep you here." Seeing a fleeting disappointment cloud her expression, he laughed at her. "Do not fret, my dear. We will find one with a garden down to the river. Be of good cheer." Jane smiled, and he was satisfied. "Now, I must go. I shall be back before noon, I promise," he said as he opened the door to rejoin Howard.

"'Tis what you always say, Will Hastings," Jane teased. "I shall believe you when I see you, and not before." They shared a laugh as she gently pushed him out into the hall.

"Then I shall have the last laugh, my dear," Will said and blew her another kiss.

"Lead on, Sir Thomas," a jaunty Will told his friend. "The sooner we get there and do our business, the sooner I can return."

The two men walked and talked as the wharfs came to life along Thames Street and yawning citizens left their beds and went about their daily routines. Approaching the Tower gate from Tower Street, Will recognized a priest exiting All Hallows Church and hailed him.

"Father John, it has been an age since we last met. How do you fare?" Will asked, cheerily.

Before the cleric could elaborate on how much his hips ached these days, Howard said impatiently, "Why linger, Lord Hastings. Unless you have need of a priest for some reason." Seeing Will's puzzled frown, he laughed. "Nay, you have no need of one yet."

"Let us pray you are right," Will replied, and they all enjoyed the joke. "We shall continue this conversation anon, Father." Behind his hand, he added, "This young man is impatient to sit in a dull council meeting, and I should not detain him from it." In good spirits, Will and Thomas proceeded through the several gates and into the Tower's inner bailey.

The handsome White Tower, enlarged and beautified by Henry the Third, almost glowed in the soft rays of the rising sun as several councilors arrived at once and climbed the steps to the entry.

"God give you a good morning, Stanley," Will greeted the former king's steward. "I trust you slept better after your nightmare?"

Thomas Stanley grunted. "I hear you were unmoved, my lord. I confess in the light of day it assumed a less threatening vision, but still, I shall be wary," he vowed, seeing Buckingham watching them, "as should you."

John Morton, his piggy face pink from the exertion of so many stairs, waved to Will and waddled his way to a chair. "Good morrow, Lord Hastings, and God has given us a beautiful morning to plan the coronation, has he not?"

Thomas had moved on to greet his father and Archbishop Rotherham, and Hastings scanned the room, perplexed. Those present comprised his usual small group of Edward's stalwarts. "I thought this was to be a full meeting of the council, my lord Buckingham. Where are the others?"

Buckingham came forward and explained that Richard had changed his mind and sent Bishop Russell and the other councilors to meet at Westminster. "My lord of Gloucester will be here shortly," he promised. "Let us go in, shall we?"

After discussing a few items, Will remembered to ask John Morton about his well-known cultivation of strawberries. At that moment, they heard voices coming from the outside staircase, and conversation stopped when the protector entered with Francis Lovell on his heels.

"Good morrow, my lords," Richard said, pleasantly. "I pray, do not let me interrupt your train of thought. What were you discussing?"

Will noticed Richard was holding his left arm stiffly, as though it was compromised, but as all soldiers had old wounds that pained them from time to time, he thought nothing of it. He also knew the duke was prone to backaches. He laughed. "I am ashamed to say 'twas not state business, your grace. I was asking if Bishop Morton's famous strawberries had ripened yet."

Morton, seated between Stanley and Rotherham, nodded. "And I told them they were indeed ripe and that I should send for some for everyone after the meeting."

Richard smiled. "Very well, then. Shall we proceed with the discussion at hand: the coronation."

Will sat back and observed how quickly Richard made decisions, agreeing to this and opposing that, all the while giving thoughtful reasons for both. He would have made a good king, Will was thinking absently, when with sudden insight, he realized that Richard had every right to be king for, certes, young Ned was a bastard and ought not to wear the crown. Had he been wrong to keep silent all these weeks—or indeed years? A few beads of sweat broke on his upper lip as he pondered his vow to Edward. Nay, it was the right thing to do. He had given his word to see Ned crowned. Besides, he had no intention of sullying his dearest friend's honor by disclosing a foolish deed done in Edward's youth.

Eleanor Butler was dead, Elizabeth was queen, and Ned would be crowned and rule well with Richard and Will close by his side.

"Lord Hastings, did you hear me?" Richard's impatient voice interrupted Will's ruminations, and he turned his attention back to the protector. "Did you wish Doctor Morton to send for strawberries or not? He is willing."

"Aye, with pleasure," Will answered, noticing a change had come over Richard. If Will had been superstitious, he might have believed the duke had been able to read his thoughts. "Strawberries would be a welcome change from"—he picked up a wizened piece of fruit from the bowl on the table—"dried plums."

Without warning, Richard scraped back his chair, stood, and announced his departure. There did not seem to be any reason for the haste, but he left the room with Buckingham following closely behind, and those councilors remaining looked at each other perplexed.

"Strawberries must disagree with him," Morton said, shrugging. "Now, where were we?"

Not an hour later, the men heard the sound of running footsteps upon the White Tower staircase and Richard stalked in, his face as sour as spoiled milk. All at the council table rose as one, startled to see him again so soon. He surveyed the room, his eye lastly falling on Will.

Then Richard pointed to his left arm. "There is sorcery afoot, my lords. Look at my arm, it has no feeling. 'Tis useless."

As Richard was looking at him, Will answered good-naturedly, "I have experienced the same numbness after waking from a deep sleep, your grace. Mayhap 'tis nothing serious."

"'Tis witchery, I tell you," Richard snapped, rubbing the arm, "and I blame it on the queen and her accomplice, the harlot Jane Shore."

Will's legs felt weak, but he held on to the table and stared, horrified, at Richard. "Jane Shore is no accomplice and certainly no witch!" he averred. "Why accuse her, my lord?"

"She consorts with that sorceress, that spawn of Melusine, Elizabeth Woodville," Richard almost spat. "Do not pretend you did not send your leman with messages to the queen. The lawyer Catesby witnessed one of her visits."

Before Will could recover his astonishment, Richard thundered, "I would ask each of you, my lords, what would *you* do if you discovered a plot to destroy me, the protector of the realm and guardian of the king? A heinous conspiracy conceived by one I thought was a friend."

Will felt no fear for himself, as he was innocent of any wrongdoing, but he quickly assessed who else at the table might be guilty of betrayal. He dismissed Jack Howard and his son, Thomas; they were solidly behind Richard. He knew Morton and Stanley were closely tied through Stanley's wife, Margaret Beaufort, the Lancastrian countess of royal lineage and mother of the exiled Henry Tudor, whose ambition for her son was no secret. Morton had served Lancaster until it was expedient to change coats and follow York, and Stanley was known to be easily led. As well, Will had heard that Margaret Beaufort had been seen entering the lodgings at Westminster Abbey on more than one occasion. Perhaps these three were plotting with the queen to overthrow Richard. It was the only possibility, Will concluded.

"I am waiting," Richard barked. "What would you do?"

All were speechless for a moment, whether from fear, Will could not tell, but on his part his innocence prompted a response. "I think I speak for all present, your grace," he said, his expression grave and his voice sincere. "The cowards should be punished as all traitors must."

Richard's gloved fist hammered down on the heavy wooden table, making the goblets jump, spilling inkhorns and scattering parchments. "Then punished they will be!" he declared, glaring at Will and shouting, "Treason!"

As though prearranged, men-at-arms appeared out of nowhere,

causing chaos in the room. The lords, who were still standing, were rudely pushed aside as the soldiers rushed at Will, locking his arms behind his back. Lord Stanley was knocked to the floor, and hitting his head on the corner of the table, blood flowed from a gash to his head. Seeing Stanley bleeding reminded Will instantly of Stanley's dream. He suddenly felt cold as he watched, helpless, as the injured councilor was pulled to his feet. Across the room Morton cowered against the wall, but he, too, was apprehended, as was Archbishop Rotherham.

His skin the color of the gray stone wall behind him, Will struggled with his captors before insisting: "I am innocent of any wrongdoing, my lord duke. I swear on your brother's grave. What is it you think I have done?"

"You have betrayed me, the council, and the English people."

Will frantically tried to imagine the nature of his betrayal. Richard was a reasonable man; he would listen to the truth—to reason. "I ask again, Duke Richard, what is this betrayal? I confess that I have lately taken Jane Shore as mistress, and I swear 'tis the only thing I have done that might displease you, but that is hardly betraying anyone except my wife. Besides, have you forgotten your past—" He bit his tongue; no need to rile an already rabid dog.

Richard glared at him. "Your morals disgust me, my lord. I long ago rejected my sinful past, but your liaison with my late brother's harlot is not reason for arrest. You have betrayed England by your silence and your conspiracy." He turned to the men-at-arms. "Take these three to a cell," Richard commanded them, pointing to the two bishops and the bloody Stanley. Even in his confusion, Will noted the trio did not resist. Were they indeed guilty of conspiring? But he was not a part of it; he had to convince Richard that he was not part of any plot.

Richard spoke a few words to Thomas Howard, who bowed and retired, giving Will a sad look as he left. Will did not notice; he was confounded by the reference to Jane and the queen, and wondered if Jane, too, had been arrested. But his own danger seemed far more imminent.

Alone with Richard, Buckingham, and Jack Howard, Will felt certain he could assert his innocence and be heard. He began in a level but serious tone.

"I have never had discourse with those three lords outside council meetings, Richard. I swear. If they have done wrong, I am ignorant of what it is. I am and always have been a loyal supporter of the house of York, first serving your father and then your brother, as his closest advisor and friend. 'Twas I who wrote to you at York begging for you to come to London immediately, have you forgotten? Why would I betray you? And in what way have I done so? I deserve to know, if I am to be imprisoned for it."

Richard leaned both arms on the table. Will noted, staring, that the left one seemed just as strong as the right now. It seemed far from useless. Had that just been an excuse to accuse Jane of witchcraft; or worse, could Richard have his sights set on the crown?

The protector leveled his cool, slate eyes at Will. "You want to know what you have done?" he repeated. "You withheld from me that my nephews were bastards. Were you prepared to see an illegitimate son of my brother wear the crown, flying in the face of all the laws of this land?"

Will tasted the bile in his mouth and tried to swallow. So that was it, he thought, Edward's secret was out. But how did Richard discover it? No one else knew except . . . dear God almighty, Stillington! And then the image of the bishop of Bath and Wells's litter arriving at Crosby Place the night before rose clearly in his mind.

"I can explain, my lord," Will said, trying to control his panic. "My oath, renewed to your brother on his deathbed—"

Richard banged his fist on the table again. "I will not listen to your lies or your oaths. You have no excuse. Your loyalty now is to me as protector of the crown, not to my dead brother. I have lain awake all night pondering your reasons for keeping this terrible secret from the people of this realm, and I can only deduce that by conspiring with the queen you seek to displace me and resume your position as the king's closest advisor."

Will shook his head vigorously and tried to ease his guards' viselike grip on his arms. "Nay, Richard, you have it wrong. I have never thought to displace you, and I have never communicated with the queen in sanctuary. I swear my silence has all to do with the promise I made your brother. The secret of the precontract was safe with me—"

"Ha!" Richard cried. "You are condemned by your own admission. Away with him," he ordered, raising his left arm and pointing at the door. "Find him a priest to shrive him, but I will see him dead with his secret before noon!"

The room swam dizzily as Will fought to remain erect. "Dead, my lord? You mean to execute me? Here? Now? Without trial?" In a tremendous force of will, he threw off his guards and stood his ground. Now he regarded Richard with contempt. "You are a hypocrite, Richard of Gloucester!" he cried, red spots of anger standing out on his cheeks. "It seems you use your 'useless' arm quite well again," he could not stop from saying. "And you stand there and pontificate about morality and justice, and yet you refuse me a fair trial. Who are you to be judge and jury? Who are you to play God?" The guards were fighting with Will now, and he fell to his knees. "I have been York's staunchest supporter for all fifty-two years of my life. You at least owe me a trial." But Richard had turned toward the window and avoided Will's accusing eyes.

"Take him away, I say!" Richard barked, his fists clenched and his mouth a thin, grim line. "Find a place to punish him. I will see him no more in this life."

The guards pulled Will roughly to his feet and all but dragged him from the room to the staircase. It was so clear to Will that Richard intended to take the crown that, having nothing to lose now, he began struggling with his captors, shouting: "Remember your oath, Richard of Gloucester! You pledged to protect your nephew's right. God help you if you fail." Then he made a last desperate attempt to appeal to Buckingham and Jack Howard. "Mark my words, my lords, Gloucester seeks the crown."

The three men left in the room above stood silent, each with their own memories of the man who had all but ruled England for the past fifteen years. Only Jack Howard felt pity for the councilor and friend who had served his king loyally and with honor.

Yet no one had stepped forward to defend him.

A solitary magpie hopped upon the lawn outside the White Tower searching for grubs, but it took flight when soldiers clattered down the staircase and out into the sunshine. Will saw it and then his brave heart succumbed to tears. "One for sorrow," he quoted the old adage, wondering why his legs would not support him. His guards dragged him along the path, looking for somewhere to carry out the protector's orders.

"There, John," one of the group said, pointing to some timber stacked for building near the Beauchamp Tower. A small curious crowd of people who worked inside the Tower walls gathered, and when they recognized Will Hastings they gasped in surprise. Understanding what was about to happen, they all fell to their knees to pray for a swift passage to heaven for Lord Hastings's soul. A priest hurried from the Tower chapel of St. Peter ad Vincula, summoned to give the prisoner his last rites, which he did as Will was flung to the ground and told to remove his jacket. How ironic, Will thought with wry humor. How often had he wished himself out of this uncomfortably tight fashion, but now all he wanted was to wake from his nightmare and be happily marooned in the safe haven of Jane's sunny solar.

He could scarcely hear the priest's words for the blood rushing like an angry sea through his brain. His fingers were trembling as he unhooked the many buttons on his jacket, and he did not resist when one of the soldiers ripped it open and pulled it off him. A large timber of oak was transported by three of the men-at-arms and flung down beside the kneeling Hastings.

"God have mercy on your soul," the priest intoned, dropping oil on the head of one of England's most respected councilors. What must the man have done to earn such an unworthy death? he wondered. Even those hanged at Tyburn were allowed to be shriven quietly in private and to speak out upon the scaffold. "*In nomine padre, filii et spiritu sancti,*" he blessed the victim as a huge man carrying an axe arrived on the scene.

In that moment, Will knew there was no hope of rescue, no hope of pardon, and he would come face-to-face with his Maker in a matter of seconds. He crossed himself and prayed for God's mercy and forgiveness for his many sins. Perhaps He would be kind to the man who had never broken his king's trust, even in death. Then he looked up into the perfect blue sky for the last time before the blindfold was placed over his eyes and he could see no more. But in his mind's eye he could envision Jane, lying on the pillow as she had the night before, her hair shimmering around her and a smile of contentment on her face.

"Jane!" His anguished cry touched all who had come to watch, even the hardened soldiers hovering nearby. "I am so sorry, so heartily sorry. Forgive me, my love, and may God protect you." A moment of humor caused him a wry smile as his head was forced upon the damp wood. "I have broken my promise again, have I not," he apologized under his breath. "I shall not be home—"

The axe flashed through the air, the blade blinding in the sunshine, and cut off the final words of the man who died certain he was guilty of nothing more than faithfully loving Jane Shore and having honorably served his beloved king, Edward Plantagenet.

Not a mile away, as Will's last hour played out, Jane was poring over her new gift, smiling with delight at each brilliant illumination, colorful flowers in relief decorating their borders, and saying the devotions to herself. The book was small enough to slip into a tapestried bag she hung from her waist, and she knew she never wanted to be parted from it.

She had just turned to the page titled *Office of the Dead* with its macabre miniature of a richly clad skeleton lying on a bier in a garden of white roses, when heavy blows rained down on her front door, making her jump and Poppy bark ferociously for one so small. Hurrying to the window, she flung the casement wide and saw armed soldiers gathered below behind a grim-faced Thomas Howard. Her heart began to race; they did not look as though they were making a social call, and when the servant opened the door downstairs and the men surged in, Jane intuitively knew she was in trouble.

Pushing the book into her pouch, she ran to her wardrobe chest and removed the hidden box of coins, fumbling open the lid. Then, stripping her fingers of rings and snatching several other pieces of jewelry, she crammed them all into the box. She did not know what made her do this, but every instinct of self-preservation she had learned over the last eight years sprang into action. As she ran into the tiny garderobe and found the loose plank she had often idly thought might make a cache for valuables, she could hear the men's footsteps tramping up the stairs. She pushed the box out of sight, trod heavily on the board to press it flat, and exited the privy just as Thomas Howard flung open the door to the solar. Poppy bared her little teeth and snapped at him until Jane drew her into her arms and calmed her pet.

"Sir Thomas," she said with as much composure as she could. "What can possibly be the matter that you must break down my door to discuss? You are always welcome here."

"Jane Shore, I arrest you on suspicion of witchcraft," Thomas pronounced, and Poppy snapped at him again.

Jane clutched the dog to her and the blood left her face.

"Witchcraft, my lord? What is your proof?" Had she not been so terrified, she might have laughed. "'Tis a monstrous lie!"

"'Tis for your accusers to deliberate, madam," Thomas told her, having no idea what proof Richard of Gloucester might have against a woman who only knew how to use the gifts God had given her for pleasuring men. Thomas was certain she needed no witchcraft to accomplish that, he himself having been enchanted by her beauty and wit more than once. "You must come with me at once and leave all behind," he commanded a little more kindly, feeling awkward now that he stood face-to-face with the victim of Richard of Gloucester's accusation—unfounded, Howard had thought when told of his duty. Thus he decided to salve his conscience by allowing Ankarette to accompany Jane into custody. Surely there was no harm in it, he assured himself. He did not have the heart to add to her woes by telling her of Hastings's arrest. One calamity at a time, he decided. "You may, however, have your servant accompany you," he told her. "Come, mistress, do not make me have to remove you bodily."

"Then who will care for my dog, Sir Thomas? Nay, I shall come alone and leave Poppy with Ankarette. May I fetch a mantle? You would not wish me to die of cold in a cell before I am burned as a witch, would you?"

One of the men-at-arms sniggered, and Thomas suppressed a smile. "This is no joking matter, Jane. Aye, you may take what you need to be comfortable, but hurry, my orders are that you must be in custody by noon."

Thomas knew full well what was happening at that moment behind the high walls of the Tower, and he felt sympathy for the petite woman with the angel face once she knew of Hastings's arrest and imprisonment.

"You do know that as the former wife and daughter of guild members, I am a freewoman of the city, my lord?" Jane asked. "I have the right to say where I shall be held before a trial. I choose to stay at the Ludgate gaol, if you please." She was relieved to see Thomas nod, afraid she would not have the courage to fight him if he refused. She had visited a petitioner there once and taken his case to Edward, who had pardoned the man his minor crime. The prison was one large cell with windows overlooking St. Paul's and less dank and odoriferous than Newgate, the bigger of the two gaols on the western end of the city.

Ankarette set to weeping as soon as she was told she had to stay with Poppy. "I will not abandon you, mistress. Why can't Martin or Cook take Poppy?" she wailed, jerking her head in the direction of the kitchen.

Jane was stern. "All will be well, my loyal Ankarette. There is no need for both of us to suffer the ignominies of the Ludgate. You have done nothing wrong. In truth, neither have I," she lamented, "but the duke of Gloucester is angry with me, and I must be detained at his pleasure, it seems. You must visit me there and bring me food, you understand." She turned back to the steward and instructed him to run the little household as best he could, then she bent forward to give Poppy into Ankarette's reluctant arms and whispered, "Mistress Vandersand must know of this. Tell her what has befallen me, and if aught happens to me, she will help you."

Kissing Poppy's soft head, and folding her warmest woolen cloak over her arm, Jane nodded to Thomas, and sandwiched between two hulking men-at-arms with Thomas following, Jane emerged into the sunshine to find a crowd gathered in the street. Jane was aware of a large cart pulled up beside the house but did not give it a second thought; she was too intent on putting one foot in front of the other and reaching her prison without a stumble. Thomas noticed with satisfaction that no one gloated or jeered as the escorts marched their prisoner along Thames Street, past Baynard's and up to Ludgate Hill.

"Poor Jane," a man opined. "How quickly the wheel of fortune turns. She has done no one harm and many good."

"Aye," his neighbor replied, "and they called her the Rose of London in her youth. She will take on another scent after a few days in the Ludgate, I'll be bound." He felt sorry for her anyway.

It was as well Jane did not give her house a backward look, in spite of Ankarette's loud lamentations, because no sooner had the group gone out of earshot that those soldiers left behind began to ransack the house under the supervision of their captain and throw priceless objects from the second-story solar into the cart. Richard of Gloucester had ordered that the harlot Shore be stripped of all her possessions, claiming that they had been paid for by King Edward and thus belonged to the Crown. Never again would Jane delight in her Galatea tapestry, the books Edward had given her, her luxurious tester bed and its heavy velvet drapes, the Turkey carpets on the floor, her silver platters and Venetian glass goblets, her gorgeous gowns and jeweled headdresses, her necklaces and brooches, all, Richard had seethed when he heard of them, worth a king's ransom. It was as well Jane did not see the disaffection with which her servants were turfed out onto the street with naught but the clothes on their backs, Cook pathetically holding on to a large copper ladle.

"What will become of us," Ankarette cried to the neighbors who were dispersing and returning to their tasks, the excitement over for the day, they thought, when a horseman came galloping along the street intent upon reaching Baynard's Castle to deliver his news.

"The Lord Hastings is dead!" the rider cried to the curious onlookers. "The lord chamberlain was executed not half an hour ago. God have mercy on his soul."

Consternation broke out among the bystanders. Hastings had been well known in the city, and some ran off to the closest tavern to spread the shocking story. Jane's cook, comprehending his situation clearly, took off toward the river. He had no intention of being implicated in any wrongdoing on his mistress's part.

Ankarette took in the news, and for a second she looked the picture of calm, but suddenly without uttering a word, she fainted at the steward's feet.

"God 'elp the mistress," Martin cried, kneeling to help the fallen Ankarette. He smiled grimly to himself. "She has no one to protect her now from the lord protector. And, God's truth, if Jane Shore is finished, so are we."

Jane's little procession did not attract much attention once they turned up the narrow lane known as Athelyng Street and passed by the King's Wardrobe. When the high wall of the Dominican prior's garden gave Jane a glimpse of tall trees, she knew they would reach their destination in but a few minutes. Thomas Howard had not said another word since leaving the house, and Jane was grateful for the silence.

Although the charge of witchcraft was a serious one, Jane was certain there had been some mistake, and as soon as Will heard of it, he would defend and free her. Why would her name be linked to the queen? she puzzled. Everyone knew Elizabeth hated her. And then she thought of Tom and whether he might come to her rescue. But he was still in sanctuary and probably ignorant of her arrest. Her shoulders sagged, as though she were resigned to her incarceration, and reverted to her only hope: Will.

It was as well he was on good terms with Gloucester, she mused, and surely Will could persuade the oddly sanctimonious duke that his accusation was unfounded. Jane had known many women of the city who were rumored to be witches, and she had learned to rise above such superstition, especially when she had known one of them all her life and that the goodwife had merely been adept with plants and herbs, which she used to cure the incurable. Amy Lambert had staunchly defended her friend, and even John Lambert had vouched for the woman when he had been alderman, and the charges had been dismissed.

Aye, she had no doubt Duke Richard was disdainful of her

relations with the former king and Will, but to retaliate in such a way seemed senseless. She remembered Kate Haute's loving smile when she had attempted to explain Richard's flaws, such as his sudden anger, and Jane felt reassured that Will would talk Richard out of these charges.

By the time they turned down Bower Row, where the imposing Ludgate filled her view, Jane was feeling better. Peasants, farmers, merchants, and priests mingled with gentry and soldiers, all pressing through the narrow opening that led in and out of the city, and some of them stared at Jane, wondering how much trouble the well-dressed woman could possibly be in.

All of a sudden a rider cantered past St. Paul's and approached the gate, forcing those nearest him out of his way.

"What ho!" Thomas cried, stepping perilously into the horse's path.

The man skillfully reined in his mount, recognizing the Howard livery on Jane's escorts.

"Have a care, man! There are women and children about. What is your haste, sirrah?" Thomas shouted, sternly.

"Have you not heard, my lord?" the messenger said breathlessly, doffing his cap, his white boar badge now plain to see upon his sleeve. "The king's lord chamberlain, William Hastings, was executed for treason not fifteen minutes ago on the lord protector's orders. I am to take the news to Westminster." A gasp went up from the crowd, and then rumblings of discontent. What had the popular councilor done wrong, they asked one another, anger swelling among the citizens at the suddenness of the execution and the absence of law.

Her face white with fear, Jane whirled to face Thomas. "Sir Thomas, can this be true? Will is dead, and without a trial?" Dear God, she thought, fighting desperately to control her trembling. Please God, let the man be a braggart and a liar. How can Will be dead? It must be someone else: the king's steward perhaps, that mealymouthed Stanley married to that bony Beaufort woman. "You knew! You came to my house and you knew!" she accused Thomas, crumpling to the ground.

Thomas leaped forward and caught her to him. "How could I tell you, Jane? It was bad enough having to arrest you. I could not find the words to tell you," he cried. "Aye, I was aware Will would be accused, but I swear I did not know he would be . . . killed. Not today, and"—he held Jane's reproachful gaze—"not without trial. Please believe me." Thomas had taken his father's word that Richard of Gloucester was an honorable man. In truth, the messenger's news had shocked him, too. He wondered now what his father thought of this hasty execution; Thomas understood why Richard may have felt betrayed, but to execute a patriot of Hastings's stature without trial was ignominy.

He steadied Jane's shaking body and helped her to the entrance of the gaol, its rusted iron bars guarding the friendless gray stone edifice, green slime slipping from its crevices.

"Open in the name of his grace the duke of Gloucester, the lord protector," Thomas called to the sentry. "I am here to deliver a prisoner, Mistress Jane Shore, freewoman of this city."

Jane allowed herself to be helped up the steps and into the warden's cheerless office, where the occupant listened as Thomas described her crime.

"Why, Mistress Shore," the toothless, bald warden sneered, leering at Jane. "Never thought to see you here as an inmate. Witchery, eh? I pray you will not indulge your evil skills while you are my guest."

Jane's denial of Will's death was shielding her from grief for the moment, allowing her to state her name and address and listen humbly as Thomas negotiated with the man for a bed of straw and food for the next two days. Some money changed hands, and Jane tried to protest.

"'Tis the least I can do for you," Thomas told her as she promised to pay him back. "My stepmother has a fondness for you, and she would expect me to be kind. You know Lady Margaret."

The gaoler picked up a heavy bunch of keys, jerked his head in the direction of a door in the back of the room, and barked at Jane, "Come with me."

Jane turned her sad, sea-green eyes to her escort and thanked him for his courtesy. "If you would speak up for me, Sir Thomas, I would be forever in your debt. You must know I am innocent." Sweet Jesu, how fleeting are life and happiness, she said to herself. In truth, she felt she had only herself to blame, for she had chosen her path many years ago and had few regrets. Will's cruel death must surely have been the greatest.

She was shaking as Thomas bowed over her hand, stifling a strong urge to protect this fragile creature. He could not imagine Mistress Shore surviving in the cold, dank prison after so many years of luxury. "I am heartily sorry for you, mistress, and I shall keep you in my prayers," he murmured. "Will Hastings was a good man. Nay, he was the best of men, and my family shall grieve for him, too."

Jane nodded her thanks, and seeing the warden's back turned as he unlocked another door, she fumbled with the pouch at her belt, freed it, and pressed it into Thomas's hand. "If you loved Lord Hastings, I pray you keep this safe for me. 'Tis all I have left of him."

Thomas tucked the bag inside his tunic as the warden returned and grabbed Jane's arm. "God bless you, Jane." Thomas's words were sincere. "If it helps at all, I do believe in your innocence."

He watched her be led from the room, clutching her folded mantle to her chest, and he wondered at her courage.

FIFTEEN

All of London was abuzz over the shocking news of Hastings's death and that Edward's loyal councilors, Rotherham, Morton, and Stanley, were imprisoned in the Tower. It was then that rumors began to spread that Richard of Gloucester might have designs upon the throne. No one had seen the little king outside the Tower walls for nigh on a month, the queen was still afraid to leave sanctuary or relinquish her younger son, and it was rumored in the lanes and alleys of the city that Gloucester was removing those loyal to the old king to make way for his own circle of advisors. People did not care for change, especially after twelve peaceful years under Edward's prosperous rule, and they grumbled.

Jane spent a sleepless night in the foul-smelling gaol, the stench from two dozen dirty inmates, soiled straw, and the jakes overpowering, in fear one of her fellow inmates would try to molest her, steal her cloak or the shoes from her feet. She was horrified when she felt a rat tug at her sleeve. She dozed off a few times and dreamed first of Tom, and then the nightmare of the boy kicking Will's bloody head about in the street returned. She awoke weeping.

In the light of day, she looked about her and thought her fellow inmates did not seem as threatening. She rose stiffly from her straw pallet to use the jakes, turning her back on the others in embarrassment. The blaring of a trumpet diverted the prisoners' attention, and they crowded around the window to see who was arriving at St. Paul's. A few moments later, Jane joined them just in time to hear her own name upon the lips of the herald.

"Good citizens of London, draw near and hear this, that yesterday William, Lord Hastings was executed for treason after it was discovered he was conspiring with others, including the queen, to overthrow and kill his grace the duke of Gloucester, the lord protector, and his kinsman, Henry Stafford, duke of Buckingham, and seize his grace the king. Furthermore, 'tis well known that this same Lord Hastings led our late, lamented King Edward into debauchery and certain death, and had taken to bed the harlot Jane Shore, with whom he had lain nightly even unto the day of his death." Jane gasped and fell back, confirming her identity to the curious inmates. "This Mistress Shore was also in secret counsel with the queen," the herald went on, "and thus, for the comfort of their graces of Gloucester and Buckingham, and for the surety of our gracious king, she is now languishing in the Ludgate goal at the protector's pleasure."

Jane shrank back from her fellows, feeling dozens of pairs of eyes on her, and her shame showed rosy-red on her neck and cheeks. "'Tis a lie," she averred. "I have never had counsel with the queen. Sweet Jesu, she hates me! And I swear I never did anyone harm."

Many of the prisoners were, like Jane, of the merchant class and thus freemen of the city. Unlike the Fleet and the Clink, where the more dangerous criminals were held, their crimes were minor, and they were either awaiting a hearing or for a relative to pay their fines for debts unpaid or customers cheated. Two or more of the women were whores, and Jane hoped they would feel a kinship and stand with her. But they eyed her fine gown and mantle, creamy, pampered skin, and soft hands, all of which marked her as wealthy, and said nothing. Finally a man Jane recognized as a customer of her father's stepped forward. "Good day, Jane," he said not unkindly as he herded the others back.

"I know this woman, and apart from shaming her father all these years, she was never one to tell a lie. Let us not forget how she used her favors with the king to help some of us. You have all heard of the kindness of Jane Shore, have you not?"

Jane watched as one by one the men and women nodded and drifted back to conversations on their pallets or stools that relatives had brought in to them. She was now clearly the focus of their gossip, but there was nothing she could do about it. She approached her champion and after thanking him for defending her, she asked, "Master Davies, I trust your wife is better? I heard she was suffering from a palsy. I am heartily sorry for it. I remember her well as a cheerful, merry soul."

And with her gentle concern, she won the respect of another man. Master Davies kept her company during the interminable daylight hours in the stuffy, ill-lit cell, which allowed a grateful Jane a less fitful second night.

Then on that balmy Sunday in June, when the city was still in turmoil and many were gathered on street corners or crowded into taverns to discuss the sudden turn of events, a carter with his load passed under the Ludgate in full view of the prison window and began to shout his news to all who would listen.

"There are soldiers and dogs scouring the marshes," he cried, jerking his thumb back in the direction of Westminster. Expectant, people moved toward him and the man played to his audience. "The queen's son has escaped from the abbey. Leading 'em a merry dance, he be."

"The little boy?" a woman shouted back. "You mean the little duke? God save 'im!"

"Nay, you foolish woman!" the carter scoffed. "Not 'im! The queen's oldest. Thomas of Dorset, 'e be!"

Jane and her fellow prisoners crowded round the window, exclaiming at the carter's news, but her lack of inches meant she was easily pushed aside. She fell back and went to sit on her bed of straw. She put her hand to her cheek, hot to the touch now, as she thought of Tom hiding among rushes or at the bottom of a cart carrying him into the city. He must have chosen today because the streets were full of townspeople eager to hear more news of the lord chamberlain's death. Aye, the wharves might be deserted as all would wend their way to Paul's Cross for any announcements. 'Twas a perfect time for Tom to sneak to the Pope's Head and take up his lodging, she thought with relief.

Then she shook her head, trying to comprehend what had happened to her in the past forty-eight hours: she had bidden farewell to her dearest friend and lord unsuspecting it was an adieu; Will had then been put to death; she had been accused of witchcraft, arrested, and incarcerated; her belongings had been confiscated, she had learned from Ankarette on her visit the previous day; and she was once again alone. And just when her life might have been salvaged by Dorset's escape, she was a prisoner in this hellish prison fighting off lice, bedbugs, rats, and a lecher. She realized Tom could not help her; he was a fugitive and must lie low. A feeling of utter hopelessness now washed over her.

She lay down on her stomach, hid her head in her arms, and cried. Even through all the years, first with her father and then with her husband, William, Jane had never really despaired—until now.

Tom heard the dogs baying in the distance as he lay curled up inside an empty wine barrel among others on a shout sailing down the Thames. He should have gone upstream, he decided too late, when he witnessed the number of soldiers sent to beat down the rushes east of Westminster. He hoped they would find the cloak one of his adherents had planted by the riverside and assume he had drowned. His friend, the bribable guard, had arranged for him to be smuggled inside the barrel on board the small vessel, and as the hue and cry had begun after he was safely under way, he tried to make the best of his discomfort and await unloading at Hay Wharf at the bottom of All Hallows Lane.

Thanks to his years of philandering, he knew every rat-run between taverns and brew houses and would have no trouble evading capture. He patted the bulge tucked inside his undershirt, concealed by the monk's habit he had been given as a disguise, and smiled. Gloucester would not get some of the king's treasury back, he swore to himself. How clever his mother had been to insist they take much of it with them into sanctuary. It would come in useful for bribes, he mused, and his possible flight to Flanders if the circumstances warranted it.

As he congratulated himself on his escape, he could hear the lapping of the waves against the sides of the boat. He hoped Jane's friend was trustworthy; he would reward the man certainly for his pains, he told himself. Yearning for Jane, he was tempted to go straight to her house on Thames Street instead of to his hiding place, and her lovely face swam into his mind. Aye, she would be alone, in need of comfort now, and would gladly welcome him to her bed, he had no doubt. He was counting on taking refuge with her after hiding at the Pope's Head. His and Jane's names had never been linked, he reminded himself, so that measle Gloucester would not look for him there.

The reason for Jane's empty bed brought Tom solemnly back to Will Hastings's awful fate, and he shuddered. The queen had fallen on her knees when she was told the news, and Tom had been surprised to see his mother weep so for her husband's best friend. Her own charge of conspiracy seemed to Tom not to have affected her as much as Hastings's death. What could the man have possibly done to warrant such a swift death? he asked himself. Aye, he and Will had never rubbed together well, but Tom had admired his statesmanship and his loyalty to Edward. And occasionally, the two of them had shared a drink and a wench in good companionship, he remembered. Nay, Mother's instincts were correct, he thought. Gloucester was a dangerous man, and she was right to stay in sanctuary. The former frequent visits from Bishops Morton and Rotherham, as well as Lord Stanley and his wife, had kept Elizabeth positive that she would prevail and see Gloucester put aside. She had thus been devastated to learn of those men's arrests but had dismissed her own accusation as "unprovable."

Footsteps hurrying across the deck and loud shouting from the wharf alerted Tom that the boat was about to dock, and he braced himself for the jolt. In very short order, his conveyance was rolled off the gangplank and onto the pier and then stood in a cluster with others. When the double knock signal was given him, he pushed off the lid, climbed out, and disappeared up All Hallows Lane.

It was as well Tom had left that day, for on the morrow, Elizabeth was once again visited in sanctuary by a delegation from Richard. This time it was headed by eighty-year-old Thomas Bourchier, Archbishop of Canterbury, who bowed into the queen's presence with Jack Howard and Bishop Russell of Lincoln flanking him.

"Not again," Elizabeth protested, kissing Bourchier's ring and kneeling for his blessing. "I have not changed my mind, my lords, so I pray do not waste your time."

It was Jack Howard who responded. "The lord protector is angered by the marquess of Dorset's flight, madam. He is most anxious that you should know he does not hold it against you, and warns you he cannot look upon Dorset's action as anything but mischief-making."

"Christ's bones, but *the lord protector,*" and she mimicked Howard's words, "is taking his position far too high-handedly. My son has every right to walk the streets of London like any other loyal subject of his brother and my son, his grace King Edward. Therefore, Jack, I should say—enough of this nonsense. Why are you really here? To accuse me of witchcraft again?"

Jack Howard bowed and stepped aside for the archbishop to state his mission. He marveled again at the Woodville woman's composure and astonishing beauty. Even in her midforties, Elizabeth dazzled. Edward certainly had known how to pick his women, he thought, although Jack preferred a woman of a more cheerful disposition than Elizabeth, and his Margaret suited him well. He listened as Bourchier rambled on about how deeply disappointed the English people would be if the young king were crowned without his brother in attendance. "May I suggest strongly that you let your son, Richard, go to be with his brother. The king is lonely and asks for his brother daily. I can assure you, the protector only wants what is best for his nephews."

The three men were not prepared for the torrent of expletives that erupted from Elizabeth's weeks of confinement and frustration. Bourchier physically flinched at the venom that the queen spat at her visitors. "I do not even know if my Ned is safe and well, and Gloucester accuses me of witchcraft and would no doubt like to see me burn. Why should I release my other son to him, my lords? You tell me why."

Then she broke down and cried. "You would take away my darling boy, my sweet Dickon? When shall I see either son again?" Her bosom began to heave, and her loud lamenting embarrassed the archbishop, who kept motioning his hand up and down in a futile effort to calm her.

Jack Howard stared at the weeping woman, relieved his wife had never succumbed to wailing. Is she feigning? he wondered briefly, but when her oldest daughter, Bess, came running into the room, he assumed the hysterics were not usual. Bess was followed by the other daughters, all gathering around their mother like protective pups. Finally, the object of the discussion arrived from a different part of the lodgings and ran headlong into Jack Howard's legs, almost knocking the stocky lord over.

Jack bent down and sternly gripped the boy in an attempt to restrain him.

"What is wrong with Mama?" Dickon cried, trying to shake lose from Jack's hold. "Leave me be, sir. I am the duke of York and you must obey me."

If the scene had not been so fraught with drama, Jack Howard might have laughed. Instead he seized the moment to entice the ten-year-old boy with the prospect of joining his brother.

"How would you like to see Ned again?" Jack asked, crouching down to the boy's level and loosening his grip on Dickon's arm.

Dickon's eyes lit up. "Is he coming to see me, my lord?"

"Nay, he is not allowed here," Jack lied. "But you can go to him. He asks for you every day, your grace. He is lonely in his big apartments at the Tower. He has no one to practice with at the archery butts, no one to wrestle with, and most of all no one to share a bed with and fight off his fears in the dark. He needs you, Dickon, and you could go to him if you but ask your mother."

"Truly?" the boy answered, looking over at Elizabeth, who was now seated calmly and having her face wiped with wet linen. He ran to her and knelt at her knee. "Is it true, Mama? I can be with Ned if you say I can? Please, please let me go. I hate it here with all of these silly girls. They don't want to play kick-ball or shoot arrows, and I could do that with Ned." He focused his pleading blue eyes on her, one of his eyebrows slightly misformed and reminding her so much of his father that Elizabeth finally relented.

"Oh, take him, you wretches! You have worn me down these past weeks, my lord bishop," she addressed Russell, who had been Richard's chief envoy until today, "and I am tired. My heart will break, but it seems Gloucester does not care a damn about my heart or my family." She gathered Dickon into her arms, and the men were dismayed to see her sob once more. "When will I see you again, my dearest child? Or my beloved Ned? Life is too cruel; I do not know why I do not simply take my own life and end it all."

The two clerics gasped at the heresy, and Elizabeth gave a derisive snort. "Fear not, my lords, you will not see the end of this Grey Mare so easily. He may have dispensed with Edward's loyal Hastings, but I would not give Richard of Gloucester the satisfaction of my death as well. Tell him that, Jack Howard. Her grace the dowager queen is not finished with him yet." She gave her son one last kiss, admonishing him to be good and to give his big brother a kiss from her, and set him down. As he turned to walk toward Howard, Elizabeth suddenly swept him back into her arms. "Nay, I cannot allow it!" she cried. "He has to stay with me." But she had not counted on her son's yearning for his brother, and Elizabeth, no match for a ten-year-old's strength of will, finally gave him up. "Go now. Take him! Before I change my mind."

When the three men, Jack holding Dickon's hand, turned and walked through the arch to the cloister, Elizabeth shouted ominously: "Beware Gloucester, my lords. He plans to take the crown for himself." Then she laughed harshly and muttered softly to herself, "Although how he will justify that, God or the devil only knows."

The duke and duchess of Gloucester took little Dickon of York to the Tower, and they stood back to watch the two brothers reunite.

"Uncle Richard told me you might come, Dickon," Ned said, his face glowing. "Now I shall have someone to talk to who isn't old and boring."

"Aye, and we can have sword fights and shoot arrows and play fox and geese and pretend we are on a crusade and . . ." He stopped as Ned laughed and said: "And what, Dickon? You are still a clacking magpie, I see. Our sisters must be glad you left them behind."

Dickon snorted. "Pah! Those silly girls. Always crying and complaining. I hate them!"

"You should never say 'hate,' Dickon," Duchess Anne's quiet voice broke in. "'Tis a strong word, and you must only use it when you really mean it."

"Our lady mother uses it all the time," Dickon blurted out, and then he put his hand over his mouth. She used it when she referred to Uncle Dickon, he suddenly realized, and even a ten-year-old boy knew when he had said enough. He looked anxiously at his uncle, but Richard laughed and invited the boys to sit for some refreshment. He told them he would send his son, John, to keep them company if they wished, as he was the same age as Ned and already training to be a knight.

"But he is a bastard," Ned sniffed. "I am not sure a king should consort with a bastard."

Richard gritted his teeth and chose to ignore the ironic remark, thinking that Anthony, Lord Rivers had a lot to answer for in the arrogant education of the future king. And Anthony an upstart himself!

"John is well loved by his father here and by me, who does not have to be his mother to love him," Anne Neville suddenly said, rescuing Richard. "He is a good boy and has royal blood in his veins, just like you." Ned lowered his eyes and apologized.

Richard felt sorry for the boy. "Do you know you have another cousin? He is Edward, Aunt Anne's and my son. He had to stay behind at Middleham when Aunt Anne came to London, because he is only eight and had a cold. Your aunt misses him very much, and so she is happy to see you both today."

Ned turned his large, solemn eyes on his aunt and smiled. She was not nearly as pretty as his mother, he noted, but she had a kind face. He longed to know why his mother would not come to see him, and although he understood what sanctuary was, he did not know why she chose to remain there. Uncle Richard seemed kind enough, although Ned would never forgive him for taking away his beloved chamberlain, Sir Thomas Vaughan, at Stony Stratford. He missed his Uncle Rivers, too, but Sir Thomas was as close to a grandfather as the boy had ever known.

Dickon popped a sweetmeat into his mouth and turned his innocent eyes on Richard. "What will I wear at the coronation, my lord uncle? Will there be enough time for someone to make me a jacket? I should very much like blue. 'Tis my favorite color."

Only Ned noticed the imperceptible furrowing of Richard's

brow as Anne replied with enthusiasm, "Why, Dickon, I think blue would be a most suitable color for your gown. You have no objection, do you, Richard?"

Richard of Gloucester had prayed the coronation would not be brought up at this meeting with the little princes. He was not prone to lying, but he did so now.

"I agree with Aunt Anne, blue would be very suitable and complement your brother's white cloth of gold coronation robes."

Dear God, Richard thought, when would he be able to bring himself to tell Ned he could not now be king. He would put it off until the last, he decided. First he needed to inform the whole council of the truth. Fiddling with his signet ring, he left Anne to carry the rest of the conversation as he questioned his own conscience while pacing the richly appointed solar. Harry wanted him to be king, he knew, as did Francis Lovell. No one else knew of the precontract yet, except Catesby, but he felt sure Jack Howard and his son Thomas would support him, as would his brother-in-law Suffolk and his nephew John, earl of Lincoln.

Richard watched as Anne listened intently to the two boys as they chatted and saw that they blossomed with her gentle encouragement. Instinctively he knew she would not want the responsibility that being queen would entail, but she would dutifully follow whatever path he took.

The larger question was whether he, Richard, wished to be king? Only if it were his duty, he concluded gloomily.

"Bastard slips shall ne'er take root," preached the learned Friar Shaw the following Sunday to a multitude crowded around Paul's Cross beside the cathedral. Londoners had wondered what was afoot when they viewed the bulletins posted on church doors and the standard on the Chepe encouraging all to attend, and those who could read told others that the lord protector would be present to hear the famous orator speak. And indeed, Richard of Gloucester

had ridden in solemn procession with many lords and magnates
to listen to the mayor's brother deliver his sermon.

It soon became plain why the preacher had chosen that particular biblical text. He began by praising the late duke of York,
founder of the ruling house, and quickly brought the focus of his
speech to Richard, duke of Gloucester. He exhorted that Richard
was the only one of York's sons to have been born in England,
the only one who resembled his royal father, and of such noble
character that he was worthy of the crown.

Richard sat stoically on his horse and people watched him
curiously. One of those was Kate Haute, standing with Margaret
Howard and listening to the extraordinary sermon. Kate hoped he
knew she was there, but she dared not reveal herself. Her heart
went out to him, knowing how he hated these public occasions.
He would rather be hawking in the dales, she was ready to wager.

Richard knew what Shaw was about to reveal to the citizens,
and he judged from the lowering brows, mutterings, and stony
stares that the tenor of the crowd was not friendly. His cousin
Harry had suggested he should attend the event that Harry had
orchestrated. He had entrusted his cousin with the crux of Shaw's
sermon, but in what terms the news would be couched, only the
preacher knew. Richard had longed to stay away, but Anne had
prevailed, reminding him that when duty called, Richard would
not disobey. Thus he heard, along with his fellow Englishmen and
women, how the late King Edward had been betrothed in secret
before his marriage to Elizabeth Woodville, nulling the second
marriage and making bastards of their children. Gasps and cluck-
ing followed the news as now the spectators began to understand
where the friar's words were leading.

However, Kate was shocked when Shaw proclaimed, "It is said
even the late king was not born of his father's blood." Then the
loud voice of the preacher was drowned out by the angry protes-
tations of the crowd who defended Cecily of York's reputation

as a pious, honorable consort of the late duke of York. It was too much for some, and several people began to turn away. Kate saw Richard flinch at the damning words about his mother and give Buckingham an irate look. She guessed they were none of Richard's writing, and yet who would believe him when this event had so obviously been planned. Aye, Kate thought sadly, he could say nothing without calling the whole sermon into question as Friar Shaw continued, "And as the offspring of King Edward are illegitimate and the duke of Clarence's son attainted through his father's treason, the only true heir to York and rightful king of England must be Richard Plantagenet, duke of Gloucester, now named protector."

A stunned silence came over the crowd as every head turned to look at Richard, unsmiling upon his mount. Kate willed him to show the world the face she loved, but instead she could see his pain plainly. Buckingham tried to raise Richard's arm in the air to receive accolades at this pivotal moment, but other than a few cheers from those planted in the crowd by that duke, the citizens quietly went back to their homes to mull over this unexpected turn of events.

Richard gave Friar Shaw a salutary nod, swiveled his horse, and returned to Westminster the way he had come, along Bower Row to the Ludgate, where he looked up at the window of the gaol, unaware that Jane Shore was watching.

Elizabeth's shrieks of rage and despair rent the cloister's tranquil silence, causing monks to hesitate in their prayer and laymen to stop their labor. The young priest who had brought her the news of Edward's disinheritance ducked as a cup of ale was flung at his head. He tripped on his robe as he raced from her presence, and sprawled onto the flagstones before scrambling away. The queen had finally gone mad, he decided, congratulating himself on his escape.

Her daughters and her ladies rushed to her aid, and it was a good half an hour before Bess could calm her mother and discover the cause of her distress.

"It must be a lie!" Bess cried. "Father would not have endangered us like this. Surely a proper marriage supplants the precontract?"

Elizabeth stopped crying for a second and admitted: "We, too, were married in secret, Bess. As much as I want to shout 'tis a lie, your father was not above deceiving desirable noble ladies to get into their beds. I am proof, God damn him to hell," she said and she began to sob again. "Your father was a monster. We are undone! Do you not understand? We are destitute. His lust has reduced us to nothing. I hate him, I hate him!" she spat. "May he rot in hell!"

"Did you know about this, Mother?"

"No, I did not!" Elizabeth averred, and she beat her pillow. "I would have taken care of it long ago, had I known. Your father was a fool!" She turned onto her stomach and motioned them all away. "I want to be alone." How many other secrets had Edward kept from her? she wondered. He could have confessed it to her when he learned of Eleanor's death. They could have sorted it out, surely. Could they not have remarried and this time in public? Ah, but now it was too late. The dreadful deed was done, Edward was dead, and the whole world knew her children were bastards.

She lay weeping for most of the day, but then, experiencing a moment of brilliant clarity, she sat up. "Christ's nails," she said aloud, "Edward was not confused at all at the end. He was trying to confess the secret plight-troth to me right there on his deathbed, not ask Nell's forgiveness."

The inmates of the Ludgate had not been able to hear the speech from Paul's Cross, but their gaolers were happy to impart all the news that was racing around the city. Boredom became a thing of the past. They heard that not only had the late king's children been declared bastards, but also that the duke of Buckingham had used his oratory, on Monday, to persuade Parliament and, on Tuesday, the members of the all-important guilds gathered at the Guildhall that Richard of Gloucester should be proclaimed king of England.

Jane was not as surprised as the rest of her fellow prisoners, for if she weighed all the extraordinary events that she had heard firsthand from Will, the news of the precontract and Richard's attempt to connect her to the queen in a plot, she could see where it all would lead. The question for her was, would Richard now let her rot in gaol, as he had more lofty goals to achieve, or would he now have the authority to punish her more severely? If he were king, he might accuse her of treason, as he had done so falsely with Will. Jane knew she might face the stake, and, shivering, she stared around forlornly at her bleak surroundings and felt chilled.

At the end of the tumultuous week, when Londoners heard Richard accept the crown offered by the duke of Buckingham on behalf of a great crowd of lords and commons who had gone to Baynard's to beg him to take it, word was brought to Elizabeth that her brother Rivers, her younger Grey son, and Sir Thomas Vaughan had been executed at Pontefract Castle for treason. Her tears spent for her little boy lost, she could only fall on her knees and pray for the three men's souls.

Then she turned her focus to her own fate. Witchcraft, if it were proved, would mean burning at the stake. How she wished her mother, Jacquetta, had not been so boastful of their ancestor, Melusine. Had those potions Jacquetta had given Edward actually caused the king to fall in love and marry her? Richard had seized his opportunity to charge Elizabeth with witchcraft just as Warwick had done with her mother fifteen years before to no avail. Certainly Richard had used the well-worn story in his proclamation against Elizabeth. Pah, she thought, where was his proof? Since her mother's death, there had been no whisper of Woodville witchcraft. It was just an excuse, she decided, although why he had not leveled the charge of conspiracy and treason on her if she was supposed to have been embroiled with Hastings, she could not fathom. No matter, she thought, as either an accusation of treason or of witchcraft carried the same punishment for a woman—the stake. She shuddered and prayed fervently that none of her adherents would turn against her. They had indeed been plotting to overturn Richard's protectorate and restore her young son to the throne, which reminded the queen of her duty as a mother.

"And may God have mercy on my young sons," she begged the miniature of the Virgin and Child from whom she found comfort, and, railing at herself again for letting Dickon go, she added, "and keep them safe."

Surely, under Richard of Gloucester's care, they would come to no harm.

SIXTEEN

Despite their initial misgivings, Londoners could not resist a festive occasion, and they flocked to Westminster to catch a glimpse of the new king. They watched as Richard, clothed in purple and heralded by trumpets and tabors, walked barefoot along the red carpet from the palace to the abbey, followed by the highest magnates on his council bearing the royal regalia: the swords of state, justice, and mercy; the mace; the scepter; and at last the jeweled crown borne by the newest duke in the kingdom, John Howard, now duke of Norfolk. Henry Stafford, duke of Buckingham, had the honor of carrying Richard's train, and Margaret Beaufort, Lady Stanley, carried the queen's.

When the great bells of the ancient abbey dedicated to St. Peter signaled the new king was anointed and crowned, carillons from the hundred churches throughout the city pealed in unison. Not long afterward, Richard and Anne stepped out through the west door, their crowns glinting in the July sunshine, and a roar of "God save the king" filled the dusty, unpaved streets of Westminster. Richard waved right and left as he walked back to the palace great hall under an elaborately embroidered canopy held by the wardens of the Cinque Ports.

Elizabeth, ensconced in her sanctuary on the other side of the wall in the abbey, hid her head under a pillow and begged her daughters to sing songs as loudly as they could to drown out the joyful bells and earsplitting cheers.

As a "Te Deum" from the choir filtered through the ancient

stones at one point, she cried, "It should have been for my son. It should have been for Ned." All she could hope now was that Richard would release her boys to her, but she had not heard another word from him since she had been demoted to plain Dame Grey. And stubbornly, she refused to leave sanctuary.

At the other end of the city behind the high gray walls of the Tower, her son, who had been denied his throne and even a place at the coronation for fear of confusing the populace, sank to his knees upon hearing the bells and feared for his and his little brother's future.

A few days later, the royal household floated in a colorful flotilla of pageantry down the Thames to Greenwich to plan the route of Richard's royal progress through England, and London returned to its routine.

When Jane heard from Sophie that Richard had left Westminster, she panicked. "Sweet Jesu, what is to become of me now?" she asked her friend. "Am I to rot here in Ludgate for the rest of my days? I cannot believe it has come to this."

"Hush, *lieveling,* all vill be well," Sophie soothed. "You vill not be forgotten, you see. I have prayed to Saint Catherine for you," she added, knowing the saint especially favored spinners like herself. Sophie had a hard time not wrinkling her nose at her friend's rank odor. She could not begin to understand how Jane had borne her new circumstance so valiantly after the life of luxury she had led. All Sophie could do was bring cheerful news of the Vandersand family and gossip from the market and the Mercery.

"Your Tom has been good to Jehan, Jane. He is pleased with the Pope's Head lodging, and he has asked me about you," Sophie told the listless Jane, whose face lit up at the mention of his name. It was true, Tom had enquired about Jane's whereabouts when he had first arrived at the Pope's Head after finding the Thames Street house vacant, but he had not been by St. Sithe's Lane since.

Sophie did not think Jane needed to know all that, so she held her thumbs at the white lie.

"Do you think he will come here, Sophie?"

Sophie shook her head. "You must not hope for it, *lieveling*. He must be hidden." After a few days, it had seemed to Sophie that Richard had given up the search for the marquess, supposing he would have fled to Europe by now. But still, Tom could not afford to wander the streets. She quickly changed the subject. "Here, my dear, have some good bread from my oven," she said, and she took a loaf wrapped in a cloth from her basket and pressed it into Jane's hands. "I must go now, Jane. I come back very soon, *ja*."

As soon as Jane returned to her pallet, she began to break up the yeasty bread to share with the other prisoners. She did this anytime a visitor brought her food, and even the hardened strumpets had warmed to the king's whore. For all her fine clothes, Jane did not put on airs, big-bosomed Betty had decided, although after almost a month, Betty had teased Jane, the one-time favorite of the king looked just as bedraggled as the rest of them.

Jane lay down on her straw and nibbled at her bread although she did not feel like eating. Why had Tom not even sent a letter with Sophie? What had he thought when he learned she was in prison? He had found a way to escape sanctuary; could he not find a way to free her? She had helped him; why could he not help her? She did not dare wonder if he had used her. Thoughts of him and a reunion were the only rays of hope for her in these dismal surroundings.

Dear God, how had she sunk so low? Her sinful life must have led her here, she determined, and had more than once promised Him that she would reform once she was at liberty. But then why was she imagining lying with Tom? She had squeezed her eyes shut and was trying to pray when the warden unexpectedly appeared at the barred door to the large cell.

"Jane Shore, step up. The king's attorney is waiting to question you," the man barked, startling Jane from her trance. She rose, gave Betty the pieces of bread to parcel out, and smoothed out her soiled skirts.

"Good luck, Jane!" several inmates called after her as the door was unlocked and she slipped through to follow the warden.

Thomas Lyneham was staring out of the barred slit of a window when Jane was shoved inside a small holding room. Chestnut hair curled thickly from under the lawyer's tall felt hat, the latest fashion from Burgundy, and Jane noticed his strong shapely hands clasped behind his back before he swung round to greet her.

"You may go, sirrah," he told the warden, who was hovering behind Jane, hoping to hear the exchange. Jane stood straight and noted the lawyer's square jaw, full mouth, and warm brown eyes before she lowered her own eyes and dropped a small curtsey.

Thomas Lyneham had heard of Jane Shore when he had been a young law student at the Chancery, but moving directly into the employ of Richard of Gloucester in the north, he had never set eyes on her. Even with her unkempt hair, torn garments, and blackened fingernails, he recognized her loveliness. When his silence invited her to raise her eyes to his, he could not make up his mind if they were the color of the sea below Richard's castle of Scarborough or of a lake close to where he had grown up. He realized he was staring and quickly cleared his throat.

"My name is Thomas Lyneham and I am his grace King Richard's solicitor." His northern burr compelled Jane to pay more attention to his words, and she cocked her head to concentrate more fully. "Mistress Shore, have you been told why you are here?"

"For engaging in witchcraft with the queen, sir, although 'tis false. I have never believed in witchcraft, and I have only met the queen on one occasion many years ago," Jane said and grimaced. "It is not a pleasant memory."

Lyneham hid a smile; he could well imagine an uncomfortable meeting between the king's wife and his mistress.

"You will be pleased to hear that no one has come forward to help prove that charge, but"—he held up his hand as he saw relief on her face—"I regret to inform you that you are also accused of harlotry."

Jane was indignant. "Aye, sir, but I was unaware 'twas a crime."

Thomas was surprised; did she not comprehend the trouble she was in? There was no hint of defiance nor of fear in her voice, but more important, he saw no evidence of seductiveness in her demeanor. In fact, she was behaving as any upright freewoman might who had been gaoled merely for failure to pay her debts. True, her beauty was unmistakable, but she could not help that God-given gift. He found himself feeling sorry for the woman, although, like his master the new king, he had a sober streak in him and had been shocked by the immorality of Edward's court upon his arrival with Richard in May. Thus, he had no qualms about carrying out his duty.

"The king has graciously allowed me to deliver your sentence in private here in Ludgate. It seems you have a friend at court, mistress, who spoke kindly to the king on your behalf."

Jane was puzzled. "I was unaware I had any friends left at court, Master Lyneham." Suddenly a rhyme came to her and, without thinking, she began to recite,

> "The king's whore
> She is no more,
> For she hath fallen far.
> On silken sheets she used to lay
> But now her bed it is of hay,
> And her fate is in the stars.
> Poor, poor Mistress Shore!"

Thomas could not stop himself and let loose a throaty laugh that made Jane think of Will. She smiled despite herself. "Pay me no mind, Master Lyneham. I conjure verses to amuse myself. But

I would know who spoke for me at court, now that the two men, who, as you know, might have are dead."

His laughter died. "Do you admit your harlotry, then?"

"I cannot deny it, and I am resigned to paying the usual fine—though how, I do not know, as I am told all my goods have been confiscated." Unsure her box of treasures remained hidden, she chose not to mention it. It was her hope for the future, and she would not give it up unless she were forced to. But she also hoped she would avoid the other customary punishment: time in the stocks. She looked steadily at the lawyer. "What have I ever done to Richard of Gloucester that he hates me so, Master Lyneham? I would know, if you please."

"His grace found his brother's court to be dissolute, Mistress Shore, and believes you and his chamberlain corrupted the late king's morals and hastened his death. King Richard is convinced 'tis God's will that he cleanse the court of impiety, corruption and"—he hesitated—"and . . ."

". . . harlots like me," Jane finished, and Thomas nodded. "So I am to be his scapegoat?"

Thomas was taken aback by her quick and accurate comprehension, and he decided to end the interview; the woman's beauty and wit were unsettling. "There will be no fine, mistress. The king has decreed that you do penance for your sinful behavior upon Sunday next, when you will leave here and walk through the streets in naught but your shift, carrying a taper and be humbled in front of your fellow citizens. You will finish your penance inside Saint Paul's, where you will confess your crime to God and his bishop and beg forgiveness. Do you understand?"

He saw by her pallor that she did. "In naught but my shift, sir?" she repeated, horrified. She had not heard of such a penance for a harlot in all her years in London. She blushed as she realized how much the transparent garment would reveal. "But 'twould be as if I were naked."

Thomas was perplexed by her modesty. Surely a woman whose body was her living would not be as embarrassed as Mistress Shore appeared to be. He was intrigued. "That is the punishment, mistress, and it could be worse, for then you will be free to go. May God forgive you and help you mend your ways."

He called to the guard to open the door, gave Jane a curt bow, and left her staring at the agonized face of Christ on the crucifix opposite her. The warden had to drag her on trembling legs upstairs and throw her back down carelessly among the stinking rushes.

It was Betty who hurried forward and gently helped Jane to her feet. "Courage, mistress," she insisted when she learned of Jane's fate. "I have endured the stocks for a day. Your penance will not last but an hour and then you will be free. Think only of that. Freedom, Jane!"

Jane gave her new friend a grateful smile. "You are kind, Betty. But I fear there is no woman who is completely free in this life. 'Tis men who decide our fate."

Sophie came to see Jane the day before the penance, and bribing one of the guards, she was able to bring a bucket of water with some ash soap and help Jane wash herself before her ordeal. Master Davies and Betty held Jane's and Sophie's cloaks up to shield the two women from prying eyes, and Jane was grateful most of all to have her long, golden hair clean again.

"Do not vorry, my friend, you vill come to our house when it is over. It is arranged with Jehan," Sophie told her, combing through Jane's waist-long hair. "Ankarette is vaiting for you."

Jane was cheered by this news: she had not dared to hope that Tom might come for her. She had all but given up on help from him. "And my house on Thames Street? Is it still empty?"

Sophie nodded. "I see guards outside, but no one inside. But is nothing left, Jane. You cannot go back."

"But I must, Sophie," Jane insisted. "I have left some valuables hidden there."

Sophie rolled her eyes. "*God in hemel,* Jane, but you are a trouble. You must vorry about that later. Now, *lieveling,* I go, but I vill be there tomorrow, I promise."

All night long a light summer drizzle trickled down the city walls and dripped off roofs of the closely built dwellings into the dirt of the lanes and alleys, making even the rats think twice about raiding the rotting piles of refuse.

Jane found herself shivering, although the air was still heavy and humid in the cell. She willed herself to sleep, but none came. She listened to the snoring of her fellows, the drip, drip, drip of a leak into a bowl near her head, and the telltale scrabbling of rats' claws looking for anything to feed on. Jane pretended she was back in her downy tester bed with fine linen bedsheets caressing her body, the smell of lavender and hyssop assailing her nostrils from deep in her pillow, and she found herself crying. How could she have come to this? she asked herself for the thousandth time since descending into this hell.

She finally fell asleep, but it was not long before the cocks set up their crowing, and a welcome ray of sunlight filtered into the long dark room, wakening her. She thanked God for the fine day, which meant that at least her shift would not cling damply to her body as she walked. Then, upon gloomy reflection, she wondered if the rain might have kept gawkers in their homes. She turned on her side and forced herself to conjure happy thoughts, imagining her reunion with Tom, although she hoped he would not be in the crowd to see her so abased.

Certes, Tom was not free, she told herself; Cicely Bonvile was very much alive and the mother of Tom's children, and Jane would still be a mistress, still be an adultress, but how could God look unkindly on her after all the years of waiting for true love?

"Up! Up! You lazy sluggards," one of the guards bawled, running the keys along the bars on the door, grating on everyone's ears. "The chaplain will be here soon for matins, and then Jane Shore will do her penance." He leered at Jane as she held her mantle over her bodice and rose from the straw.

Within an hour, after the paltry breakfast of coarse bread and bad ale had been distributed and the bells of St. Paul's had rung for matins, a priest arrived and yawned through his perfunctory prayers. It was a pittance he was paid to bring the word of God to these miscreants, and he gabbled the Latin words as fast as he could so he could return to his chapter house and enjoy a full meal.

Jane knew her time had almost come. Her heart began to beat faster, and she noticed her hands were shaking. The warden appeared behind the barred door and beckoned to her. For once he spoke to her in a measured tone and allowed her a few minutes to bid farewell to her fellow inmates.

"You'll see, dearie," Betty told her, unaccustomed tears wetting her cheeks, "'twill be over sooner than a boy's prick loses its wad."

Jane forced a smile. "I shall not forget you, Betty." Then she turned to Master Davies, who had learned his case would be heard that week. "Nor your kindness, sir. I will pray for your return to your family."

She was led downstairs to the little room where she was to remove her torn, faded gown and underdress and lastly her shoes. One of the guards was to escort her down to the gate of the gaol where she would be handed over to the sheriff's men. Her clothes would await her at the cathedral, the warden told her. "God have mercy on you, Jane Shore. You have been an easy prisoner, I confess, and I pray you will mend your ways and never see the inside of this place again."

"With all my heart I wish it, too, warden." A twinge of remorse made her turn away, knowing she had every intention of sinning again, but then she found herself trembling as she heard the crowd's buzz close to the walls of the goal.

"Now give me your mantle, mistress," he demanded, holding out his hand.

The warden was only the first of hundreds lining the penitential route Jane was to walk who stared with bold admiration at the diminutive, full-breasted woman whose charms were but flimsily covered by her lawn chemise. Jane's hair flowed in a curtain of wavy gold about her shoulders and down her back as she stepped out of the gaol and onto Bower Row. A candle almost as high as she was thrust in her hands and lit, and then she was nudged into full view of the throng. In front of her walked a priest holding a silver cross and behind her two black-hooded monks intoning prayers as they went. Men-at-arms pushed the noisy crowds back as Jane made her way along the south side of the cathedral, and the sheriff's men went before the little procession crying out in the name of King Richard for all to come and witness the humiliation of this fallen woman.

"This is the harlot who seduced our good sovereign Edward and lay with his friend, the traitor Hastings, not a week after the king's death," the sheriff cried, enjoying himself. "We are commanded by the king to witness Jane Shore's penance."

As Jane gazed out over a sea of expectant faces, her belly contracted, and she felt the warm piss of fear run down her legs. Dear God, she could not do this, she told herself; dear St. Elizabeth, she begged her favorite saint, let her be swallowed up by one of the wide cart ruts London was famous for. But the rut she stepped her bare feet into was full of mud and horse dung, and she heard and felt the disgusting squelch as soon as she took another step, sinking up to her ankles. The monks were none too gentle as they helped her out and on her way. The heavy candle had slipped from her hands and the flame was extinguished, but the sheriff had planned for that eventuality and used his tinder box to relight it.

The first stone to cut Jane's foot lay no more than ten yards from the prison. She winced as it cut into her instep and she cried out in pain, but the monks pushed her along and she hobbled for a few steps. A few more yards and several bawdy slanders later, a rotten egg landed with a splat on her back, making her stumble again, and she could feel its stinking, sulphuric contents slithering down her body. Her shift was wet now, and she was shamefully aware her breasts and mound must be clearly visible through the filmy fabric.

"Nice tits, Jane!" one man shouted, jiggling his hands under his chest, and his neighbors joined in with ribald laughter.

"Aye, I'll wager the king enjoyed those rosy apples, and the treasure between your legs," cried another, and Jane felt the blood rising up her neck and into her cheeks, especially when she saw Thomas Howard with another noble on horseback at the edge of the crowd. He must be Richard's spy, Jane thought sadly, although the man's compassion showed plainly on his face. His companion's ogling, however, did not escape her, and she lowered her eyes.

Seeing Howard, whom the king had newly created earl of Surrey, reminded her of the thirteenth of June, the day he had come to fetch Will for that fateful meeting at the Tower. She suddenly halted as she realized today, too, was the thirteenth, and feeling Will's presence, she looked up to heaven and sent a silent plea to him for support this day. Had it been but a month since his death? It had felt like three. She jerked when a jab in her back from one of the monks urged her forward, and she painfully set one foot in front of the other again, gathering strength with thoughts of Will, a man she had loved as a friend, but who had had the fortitude to watch her be seduced by Edward yet show her how deeply and loyally a man could love.

The man whom Jane believed she loved the most was also witness to her disgrace. Tom Grey, now disguised as a seaman, his beard grown out, stood on the corner of Watling Street and willed Jane to look his way. He dared not cry out to her for fear of attracting the sheriff's men, but when a lout standing next to him launched a handful of mud at Jane, he could not help but wrestle the man to the ground, unwittingly drawing unwanted notice. Realizing his folly, Tom disappeared into the crowd before Jane ever knew he was there. At that point in her ordeal, she would have been cheered by his presence; nevertheless, she plodded on, convincing herself she could endure the last quarter mile.

Do not look at them, she told herself at every ribald comment and clod of filth that was slung at her. She must focus on the ground where she was treading. All her life she had skillfully avoided the dung and other animal waste that lay in wait for an unsuspecting pedestrian, but now she welcomed the warm, soft horse droppings under her lacerated feet, and sought out the glistening, steaming manure. It was kinder than the sharp, unforgiving stones.

Then a woman, her accent revealing her Flemish heritage, cried out, "Who among you is perfect? Who of you has not tried to better yourself? Who else here has been helped by Mistress Shore, who never asked anything in return? I tell you true, my family has much to thank Jane Shore for."

Sophie! Dearest Sophie, and Jane fought to hold back her tears. She looked up and found her friend's cherished, long face in the crowd, standing with Ankarette and Jehan, and they nodded and smiled their encouragement.

"The goodwife is right," cried Mercer Etwelle, who had heard of the penance and told his apprentices to come, watch, and foster respect among their neighbors in the crowd. "I would not be standing here, my family prospering, if not for Mistress Shore. How quickly we forget! Have pity on her. She is still our Rose of London."

"Our Rose of London!" a group of children took up the chant, standing near St. Paul's gate on the northeast end of the cathedral. "She's our Rose of London!"

At once the hostile crowd began to quieten, and by the time Jane had reached Pater Noster Row, even a few cheers were heard.

How many times had she walked these streets knowing it only took but a few minutes to reach anywhere within the city wall, and yet today she felt as though she had walked a hundred miles. Her feet were raw from the city's rough cobblestones, many of them made from flint, and she wondered if she would be able to finish the walk without crawling on her knees. The hot wax from the taper dripped relentlessly over her hands, scalding her skin until she could feel them no more, but she set her jaw and, putting one foot in front of the other, she willed her steps toward the west door of the massive cathedral. By this time, her beauty, courage, and humility had touched many in the crowd. She had not flinched from their derision, she had lowered her eyes and blushed, and she had shed no tears of self-pity. Aye, they were proud of their fellow Londoner and showed their respect by gradually disappearing back to their homes.

As she gratefully reached the smooth steps at the great west door, Jane looked at a small group standing in the marketplace and groaned when she recognized her mother and father. Her father had aged, she noticed, but his face held the same contempt it had always shown when Jane had disappointed him. It was then Jane's eyes showed defiance for the first time that morning. If not for his forcing her to wed William Shore, she might not have been disgracing him all these years later. She hoped he might feel guilty, but she assumed that hope was wasted. Before casting her eyes back to her feet, she was dismayed to notice her mother's tears. She did not deserve this, Jane thought bitterly, but then she saw Amy's hand lift in a gesture of secret sympathy, and she felt relief.

The church had emptied, and Jane, now enveloped in her mantle and unburdened of the candle, was left to face her judges, the priests. She was told to prostrate herself, and noticing the blood-soaked hem of her chemise, the bishop hurried the confession and prayer of the penitent so the woman's feet could be tended to. He had a tender heart, not to mention a young woman of his own who warmed his bed, and his prayer of forgiveness included one for himself.

"Go in peace, Jane Shore," he said after giving her the blessing, "and sin no more."

The monks helped Jane to her feet, then bowed to the bishop and returned to their monastery. She limped toward the door, and sat down heavily on a stone seat in the darkness of a little side chapel. She was afraid to exit the church; she had endured enough humiliation for one day. Besides, the gloom hid her tears and her shame.

It was there that Ankarette, carrying a pail of water and clean bandages, found her mistress a few minutes later. Jane had never touched her servant before, but when she saw the faithful woman's round, cheerful face, she let Ankarette fold her in a comforting embrace and rock her exhausted body and bruised soul.

Jane did not remember the first week at Sophie's house. Whether from the deprivation and filth of the prison or from the infected sores upon her feet, a fever ravaged her that caused Sophie to send for a doctor. He bled his patient then prescribed bed rest and quiet. The Vandersand children tiptoed around the loft where the family slept and spoke softly when downstairs, earning praise from their mother and smiles of approval from the faithful Ankarette, who would not leave Jane's side, along with Poppy, who, ecstatic to see her mistress again, lay curled on the bed at Jane's feet.

Toward the end of July, when the king had left on his progress, Sophie and her daughter, Janneke, dragged a wooden tub into the house and began heating water in kettles over the fire. Clothed in one of Sophie's billowing homespun dresses, Jane, even thinner after prison and sickness, crept gingerly down the wooden stepladder to an eagerly anticipated bath. Sophie put her second daughter in charge of Pieter, and rolled up her sleeves. Ankarette had picked rosemary, lavender, and rose petals to sprinkle in the warm water, and when Jane finally sank into its scented depths, she sighed with pleasure. Her arms and legs were spotted with bedbug bites, one or two festering, and the herbal water soothed them.

Sophie and Janneke had been shocked by Jane's uninhibited stripping to her bare skin, never having exposed their nakedness even for a bath, but Jane laughed at them. "Come, come, we are all women here. You both must have cleaned me, changed my linen, while I was ill," she chided them. "Surely I hold no secrets from you, now?"

Ankarette tut-tutted, Janneke grinned broadly, and Sophie tittered. "*Ja*, you have no secrets, Jane," Sophie told her. She leaned into her friend conspiratorially, "And we know which man you vant to see. Tom. You call his name many times in your fever, *lieveling*."

Jane's face fell. "I may call his name, but he has not come, has he? Does he know where I am?"

Sophie nodded. "But Jehan told him not to come vhen you are so sick, Jane. Soon you vill see him." She had been unimpressed by Tom Grey's nonchalance when told of Jane's illness, but Jehan had excused the marquess on the grounds he was concerned his hiding place might be discovered if he ventured forth too many times from the Pope's Head.

Jane forced a laughed. "A pox on him! I think I have had enough of men, Sophie." She wagged her finger at Janneke. "I hope you have learned from my mistakes, my dear. If I had listened to my father and stayed with my husband, like an obedient wife, my life would not have come to this."

"Was it very frightening, Mistress Jane? The walk I mean," Janneke ventured shyly. "I would have died if it had been me."

"Enough, daughter. Mistress Jane does not vant to talk—"

"Ah, but I do, Sophie," Jane cut her off kindly. "I will never forget it, but if I do not talk to someone about it, it will fester in me like a canker and I shall never laugh or love life again."

And for the next ten minutes, while Ankarette sponged her

hair with a mixture of lemon juice and camomile, and Janneke and Sophie gently scrubbed away the rest of the grime of Ludgate goal and the city's streets from her body, Jane described the sadness, anger, hate, and humiliation she had experienced in every agonizing step on her penitential journey. Her eyes full of love, she thanked Sophie for her daring outburst of support in the street, and she shed tears when she recalled her parents' pain and Amy's gentle gesture of sympathy. By the time she had finished, all three of the women around the tub had stopped what they were doing and were deep in reflection about what Jane had gone through.

"I made my choices, right or wrong," Jane admitted, shaking her head, "and I have lived like a queen, but none of it was worth the depths of indignity and despair I have gone through in the past few months since Edward's death. And there were nights in Ludgate when I believed the devil had gnawed at my soul."

Then seeing the compassion in their faces, she was quick to reassure her friends. "Never fear, poor, poor Mistress Shore is quite reformed." She cupped Janneke's round face in her fingers. "And I would exchange any of the years I spent wallowing in luxury for holding my own sweet child, like you, in my arms."

The midday meal was a merry one when Jehan arrived home. He grinned at Jane and nodded his approval. "You look well again, Jane. That is good."

He waited until the younger children had been sent outside to play afterward before regaling the women with the latest rumors from the weavers' hall where he worked. "A plot was foiled to rescue the two little boys from the Tower," he announced, and lowering his voice, he added: "Jane's marquess was part of it, they say. With the king far from London and the nobles and their retinues disappeared back to their homes in the country, the time was ripe to try."

Jane was quizzical. "Why would anyone want to rescue them?

They are now no longer important. Besides, why would they need rescuing from the comfortable royal apartments?"

"They say the boys were in danger," Jehan declared.

"Who says?" Jane retorted. "And in danger from whom? The king is crowned, the boys are bastards, and there is an end to it. Richard may have executed my friend Will for no good reason that I can see, but Will opposed Richard, so he was vulnerable." Jane had been surprised to learn from one of the newest inmates in Ludgate that Richard had so far not attainted Will, and in fact he had even placed Katherine Hastings and her properties under his protection. Jane believed it spoke volumes of the guilt Richard must have felt for his swift elimination of the loyal councilor.

"But as much as I hate Gloucester—I mean, the king," she continued, "I do not believe he would harm his nephews. He is too moral for that, and he loved his brother too well." She thought for a moment and then decided, "It would seem more likely that the queen and Dorset would want to use the boys to try and mount a rebellion. That is not the same as claiming they are in danger."

Jehan persisted. "The duke of Buckingham thought it was important enough to stay behind when the king left. He is often seen at the Tower with the new constable, Brackenbury. 'Tis said they foiled the plot." Then he leaned forward with more urgency. "The second rumor is"—and he savored this one with more relish—"that the boys have been . . ." And he drew his finger across his throat.

At this his audience gasped in unison, and Jane felt a frison along the backs of her arms and up her neck, as though Jehan's words had cast a shadow over her. "No one has seen them in the garden playing for nigh on a week," he said, placing his finger to his lips, as though the king had a spy hiding in the Vandersand loft. "They used to play with their bows and arrows every day. So where are they?"

Sophie snorted. "Ill. They are perhaps ill, Jehan. Our Jane vas ill for one veek. Any mother knows a child can be ill for a veek, maybe two. You should not listen to such gossip, husband," she admonished him, and Jane hid a smile.

"I am simply telling you what I have heard," Jehan replied, sulking. "Now fetch me some more ale, wife, and get on with your woman's work."

Sophie, Ankarette, and Janneke rose to do his bidding, but Jane sat quietly pondering Jehan's disturbing rumor.

Behind the sanctuary walls of Westminster, Elizabeth had also been made aware of the possibility that her sons were dead. It was her son Tom who sent her word, through a trusted messenger, regretting the failure to rescue the boys and saying that he feared they had been murdered. Elizabeth only half believed him; she had known Richard of Gloucester for a long time, and in her heart, she could not reconcile him as a murderer of children. She preferred to think he had sent them away, or that Tom had been listening to drunken gossip.

Besides, the queen had done with weeping. It was time she found another way to regain what she and Edward's other children had lost. Elizabeth had ignored Richard's emissaries asking that she leave sanctuary and saying that Richard would do right by her and her children. She did not trust the man to keep his promise, and therefore her self-enforced confinement continued.

She was now officially addressed as Dame Grey, her marriage to Edward declared null and void. Her girls could now only look forward to meager matches, and so Elizabeth, from the safety of sanctuary, was ready to negotiate with whomever she could to improve their lot. Now was the time for action, she determined, and within a few days, through her chaplain, she had had the first of several conversations with Lady Margaret Beaufort, otherwise known as Lady Stanley, mother of the exiled Henry Tudor. In Lady Margaret, Elizabeth found her match; both were ambitious women adept at political scheming. United in their disgust of Richard of

Gloucester's perceived usurpation of the crown, the two unlikely allies made a mothers' pact to support a betrothal between Margaret's
son Henry and Bess, Edward's oldest daughter.

"But I do not know this man, Tudor," Bess complained, when
her mother took her aside and explained that Bess was lucky to
be considered by a man who had a claim to the throne.

Elizabeth contained her exasperation. Bess appeared to have
inherited none of her mother's ambition and drive, and was in
danger of being as passive about political matters as her father in
his later years. "My dear daughter, I have no wish to keep reminding you that you are no longer in a position to expect much more
than a husband of the lesser nobility now that you and your sisters
are illegitimate in the eyes of the church. Henry Tudor—should
anything happen to Richard and his puling brat—could claim the
throne through his mother. She has a direct line to King Edward
the Third." Failing to mention that it was the excluded Beaufort
bastard line, she hurried on, "And if Henry is agreeable to wed you,
you have the chance of becoming queen of England." She ended
on a triumphant note, anticipating an improvement in Bess's sullen
countenance. She was disappointed.

"I will say again, Mother, I don't even know him. I want to be
happy with whomever I marry—like you and father," she persisted,
knowing her mother had no defense against that argument. "If I
am not to marry the French prince because I am a bastard, then
let me find someone I love."

"Pah! Love," Elizabeth spat. "Your father and I were lucky at
first, 'tis all. And our marriage was not all it seemed. Remember
Jane Shore?"

Bess blushed. "I hardly think this is the time to talk about Mistress
Shore. I prefer to remember the late king as my loving father." She
looked at her mother defiantly then. "He once told me that both
sets of my grandparents married with love. Was that 'luck,' too?"

"Ah, Bess, you exasperate me. Maybe I should offer Cecily to

Henry instead. Of all your sisters, she is the one who might see sense."

Bess tossed her head but demurred. "I am sorry, Mother, I will do as you say." Then a thought occurred to her. "Can a bastard be a queen? Nay, I thought not," she said, seeing her mother's doubtful expression. "Then why would Henry wed me?"

"As soon as Henry is king, he will undo Richard's declaration and make you all legitimate again, do you not see?"

"But if Henry makes your children legitimate, Mother, then what does he do with Ned? My brother would then have to be the king. It makes no sense."

Elizabeth took a deep breath. She would not give up hope that this nightmare would end, that Stillington would confess he had lied about the precontract and Ned would be restored to the throne. But in the worst case that Tom's rumor was correct, she had to prepare her daughter. "I do not know how to tell you this, but Tom believes Ned and Dickon are gone."

Bess gripped her mother's hand. "What do you mean, gone? Away? Abroad?" She watched her mother lower her eyes, and her face twisted in pain. "Are you saying my brothers are . . . are dead? How can that be? Have they been ill?"

Elizabeth shook her head, and now she felt like crying. Was that why Richard had ignored her pleas to be reunited with her boys? What other explanation was there? "What can we think but that Richard ordered their deaths," she said. "But, as much as I loathe him for disinheriting us, I cannot believe he would snuff out the light of those innocent babes. 'Tis said, however, they have not been seen for nigh on a fortnight, Bess, and even Ned's physician Doctor Argentine is forbidden entry into their apartments. It must mean they are no longer there."

Bess was aghast. "Perhaps they were secretly sent away. Uncle Richard loves Ned and Dickon. He may not like you, Mother, but he is not a murderer."

"Nay?" Elizabeth retorted. "Do not forget your stepbrother, Richard, nor your Uncle Anthony nor poor Will Hastings."

But Bess was thinking. "Then someone else must have . . ." She could not bring herself to say the painful words. She patted her mother's hand. "We must believe he has sent them somewhere safe. To our Aunt Margaret in Burgundy or up to one of his northern castles."

"Safe from what, from whom if not himself?" Elizabeth snapped. "I am the only one who wants them back, bastards or not. They would be safe here with me," she said, and finally, after having stoically borne her tribulations in the cramped confines of sanctuary for so many weeks, her face betrayed her genuine anguish. Kindhearted Bess gathered Elizabeth into her arms and rocked the frail woman as a mother might a child.

"Are you mad! Did the devil himself spawn you?" Richard shouted at his cousin, Buckingham, as the duke stared aghast at his enraged king. Richard grasped Harry's arm and almost dragged him to the garderobe, where they might not be overheard.

Harry threw off Richard's hand and felt for his dagger. He was afraid for his life. Had he not been so self-centered, he might have empathized with Hastings's fear on the day of the chamberlain's arrest and execution. He was now experiencing the full force of Richard's wrath, and it was formidable. All he knew now was that he had made a terrible mistake in believing Richard would be glad he had rid the king of his bastard nephews. He had galloped hard to Gloucester from London, asked for a private interview, and had been welcomed gladly by his king, who had clapped him on the shoulder and called him his "dear cousin." In the spirit of such a warm reception, he had simply blurted out his news. "Your grace, cousin, you need never again worry for your crown. I have taken care of the boys in the Tower. They cannot threaten you anymore. They are with God." Sweet Jesu, he had never seen a man's face change so quickly. Should he now deny it? Say he had been joking? Should he blame Brackenbury?

"Take your hand off your weapon, my lord," Richard's icy voice broke into Harry's jumbled thoughts. "Sit down," he commanded, pushing his larger cousin onto the wooden garderobe seat, "and tell me exactly what you have done."

Harry put his head in his hands and began to mumble his terrible tale. Several times Richard prodded him to speak up, confess his sin, and omit nothing. As he listened in horror, Richard's stomach contracted little by little with every odious detail, and a deep sorrow gradually fell upon him. What was he to do? He had raised his cousin up to heights that nearly touched his own. Everyone knew the two were hand-in-glove from the moment they arrived in London from Stony Stratford with young Ned. He had consulted with Harry on everything and embraced his only royal cousin as councilor.

So who would believe that Harry had acted on his own? Who would believe Richard himself had not ordered the deaths of the princes? If he accused Harry, who among those nobles who had only halfheartedly supported his taking of the crown would believe the two of them had not planned this scheme together? And then 'twould be his word against Harry's, for surely Harry would swear Richard had been complicit. He forced himself to listen to this man for whom all respect was now cascading down the garderobe chute with its customary effluence.

"The boatman rowed us out of sight of the lights at Westminster, and once on land among the trees, I promised the boys fresh horses sent from you would be waiting." Buckingham was all but sobbing now.

Richard stiffened. "So not satisfied with lying to them about the 'adventure' you were secretly taking them on, you let them believe 'twas *I* who planned it. They died believing their Uncle Richard would take them to safety in the morning. Dear God, Harry, you have consigned both our souls to hell!" he hissed. "Continue! I would hear you confess your crime, make you relive it, and for my sins—because I see you believed I would condone this heinous act—so imprint it on my mind that I shall never rest again. Now, tell me!"

"They felt no pain, I swear to you. They were sleeping peacefully and I bundled up my mantle and smothered . . ." He could not finish as the memory of first one and then the other young prince wriggling and struggling for breath overcame him, and he blubbered like a child. Richard was so sickened by this monstrous crime that he threw his cousin from the privy seat and vomited down the chute. Harry was crouched on the floor, wiping his nose on his sleeve when Richard dragged him up against the wall and rasped in his face: "What did you do with them? Did you at least give them a decent burial?"

Harry had had enough. He pushed the smaller Richard off him roughly. "I said a prayer, covered them with branches and ferns, and left them where they lay." He walked out of the confined space and pulled himself together. Why should he feel remorse for a sacrifice he believed he had made for Richard? Certes, his cousin had never voiced such a wish, but Harry was sure Richard had secretly desired it. And besides, he was a Stafford with Plantagenet blood in his veins and should not be mistreated like a lackey. His resentment mounted.

"And what reward were you hoping from the king for this little favor, my lord Buckingham?" Richard demanded, following hard on Harry's heels. "Were you not satisfied with becoming constable of England? Or with my promise of the rest of the Bohun inheritance that would make you, next to me, the wealthiest and most powerful man in the kingdom?" His voice rose with each question until his fury exploded, and hurling a goblet across the room, he shouted, "Christ's nails, I trusted you! Get out of my sight!"

Harry glowered at him for a moment, then turned on his heel and strode to the door. "Their blood is as much on your hands, coz, as mine," he hissed. "Do not deny you wished it. I was merely your instrument."

"Get out!" Richard bellowed, and Harry went, slamming the door behind him. Within a few minutes, he was galloping out of Gloucester, over the little channel to Alney Island, through the handsome gate guarding the bridge that spanned the Severn, and onto the road to Wales.

Alone, Richard slumped into a chair and stared despondently at the black and red tiles that checkered the floor. In the space of a short half hour, he had succeeded in making an enemy of his closest advisor, and more important, he was sure he had consigned his own soul to hell.

"Edward," he addressed his dead brother aloud, "your sins have come back to haunt me."

PART FOUR

1483-1484

My great mischance, my fall and heavy state,
Is such a mark, whereat each tongue doth shoot,
That my good name is pluck'd up by the root.
This wandering world bewitched me with wiles,
And won my wits, with wanton sugared joys,
In Fortune's frekes,* who trusts her when she smiles,
Shall find her false and full of fickle toys.

Thomas Churchyard, "Shore's Wife," 1562

---

* whims

SEVENTEEN

Jane ran her hands down the smooth skin of her belly to her thighs, still tingling from the sensation of Tom's body upon her, and hoped she had more than pleased her lover. She wondered he had still desired her; after all, she was now, at thirty-one, past her prime. She turned on her side and watched the sleeping Tom, marveling at his handsome profile, broad chest boasting curling chestnut hair, and strong, capable hands. Their new hiding place, to which Tom had had to move after the dismal failure of the Tower rescue had alerted the authorities to the fact he was still in the city, was a small room in the attic of a warehouse in Billingsgate.

"I am afraid I stink of fish, Jane," Tom had apologized when he had eventually made his way to St. Sithe's Lane a week ago, and Jane had not disagreed with him. She had begun to believe Tom had forgotten about her when he came knocking on the door that day and slipped inside the house wearing Lincoln green, the garb of an archer. He had taken her breath away with his bold kiss, and she almost forgave him the unexplained delay in seeking her out.

"Why have you taken so long to come?" she had asked when they were seated in the shade of the Vandersands' apple tree in the hot mid-August sun. "Jehan informed you I was here, did he not?"

Tom had avoided her eyes. "It was too dangerous," he excused himself.

Jane hoped he would ask her about her ordeal in prison and her penance, but he appeared preoccupied with winding his finger round an escaped lock of her hair. In Jane's care while Sophie was spinning inside, little Pieter was playing with a ball nearby. Jane finally could not wait. "Did you hear about my penance, Tom?"

"Hear about it? I was there, Jane. I saw you."

Jane gasped. "I did not see you. But you came?" She hung her head. "'Twas the worst day of my life," she admitted, mortified anew now she knew that Tom had seen her.

Tom leaned over and kissed her cheek. "I pray it has not spoiled you for becoming my leman after we have waited for so long, mistress?" he teased. "You will, won't you?"

Jane had been surprised by her own reaction then. She had removed his hand from her shoulder and stood up. "Come, Pieter," she called to the child. "'Tis time for your dinner."

She turned to Tom, who was scrambling to his feet. "I must think about that, Tom, if you please. You forget I confessed my sins that day and swore to reform."

Tom's face had darkened. "Are you playing with me, Jane? I do not enjoy being made a fool of. With every meeting, you have led me to believe you wanted me, and I tasted your desire in today's kiss. Do not dissemble. Not now."

If she had trusted her first instinct to turn away, Jane might not have hesitated. She could not lie; she wanted him, but her horrific penance had had its effect. Did she want to be branded a harlot again? Risk her immortal soul? "What about your wife? Does she know where you are?" she asked feebly. The marchioness was rarely at court and seemed content to stay on her country estates giving birth to Tom's children. Tom seemed to care not a jot about her.

"No one will know while I am in hiding," he had persuaded her. "And my wife does not care, as long as she can cleave to her estates. So, let us not waste the time we have."

The scene from last week faded as Jane now contemplated Tom's profile in the candlelight. It had not taken her long to succumb to his advances, and last night she had agreed to lie with him. All those years of yearning for him had led her to expect that something mystical would happen between them, that because their love was true, God would be kind. But if she were honest, it had been nothing more—or less—than lusty passion. She blamed her disappointment on the foul-smelling attic, the lack of a feather bed, and her usual grumpiness before her courses came, but Tom had groaned in ecstasy several times during the night, and so she knew she had not lost her gift for pleasing men. Then why did she feel unfulfilled? Had she changed? She closed her eyes and, to her dismay, instead of pleasurable thoughts of the night of lovemaking, the shame of her walk filled her mind, and she opened them again quickly. Was that it? she wondered. Had her penance truly changed her?

"What is it, Jane?" Tom asked, sensing movement beside him. "I beg of you, seduce me no more tonight, my lovely siren. I am spent!" He reached out and pulled her to him, and she snuggled gratefully into his embrace. Things would look rosier in the morning, she thought, blowing out the candle and finally closing her eyes.

Jane and Tom made love countless times in the next few days, rarely leaving the attic except for food and in Jane's case, a visit to Sophie. Tom was a demanding and sometimes rough lover, and Jane discovered soon after they had spent two weeks together that he had a jealous streak that manifested itself when, one day, she lingered longer than planned at the market.

It had been almost two months since her penance, and Londoners, if they did recognize her, were too preoccupied with their own lives to pay her any attention. She had hidden her hair in a simple hood with a wimple, and her borrowed oversize gown disguised her charms so that, with a basket on her arm, she resembled any other goodwife off to market. The only place she chose to avoid was her old house on Thames Street. She had heard the king had placed guards outside, as it belonged to the Crown, and as she had no desire to remind Richard again of her existence, she had put off stealing into the house to collect her box of jewels. But Tom was rapidly depleting the money he had sequestered with him from sanctuary and she would need to retrieve her valuables if he were to eat.

That day she had encountered Master Davies's wife along the way, and she spent half an hour hearing about the friendly mercer's court proceedings and release from Ludgate. Then she had seen Buxom Betty sipping a cup of ale outside a tavern in the Poultry, and the two former inmates greeted each other like long-lost friends. Jane heard from Betty the unsettling rumor that Londoners believed the princes had been murdered. Nay, Betty said she had not heard it from a witness or anyone who worked in the palace. "Cock's bones, Jane, if anyone was there, they was probably threatened with torture or worse if they said something. 'Tis a mystery all right."

Jane had nodded. "You are right, Betty. We shall probably never know."

When she arrived back in Bosse Alley, she found Tom waiting for her on the bottom step of the outside staircase. "Where have you been?" he demanded, jumping to his feet. "Did anyone follow you? Or did you find some other man's bed to warm?"

Jane froze. "How dare you accuse me?" she retorted, but then, seeing he had been drinking, and her innate generosity understanding the anxiety he had lived with for three months in hiding, she sought to mollify him. "There is none but you, Tom," she soothed him. "And no one followed me, I am sure. Now, if you will, take my basket. You must be hungry?"

When with the back of his hand he slapped her cheek, she dropped the basket in shock, scattering plums, bread, and a pie onto the dirt. But as soon as she put her fingers to her smarting face, Tom was all contrition. "I am so sorry, Jane. Forgive me, I was overcome by jealousy." He knelt down and began retrieving the fallen items, apologizing further as he went. When he stood up and faced her again, he looked so much like a small boy, she could not forbear a smile of forgiveness.

"I swear, it will never happen again," Tom promised, tenderly touching the welt on her cheek. "You know that I adore you, Jane."

Sophie saw through the cheerful facade Jane put on when she went to St. Sithe's Lane to look for Ankarette.

"Vat is wrong?" Sophie asked as she bent to pick up a fallen tassel she had just finished crafting. "You have Tom at last. Is that not vat you vanted?" She shook the silken bauble and laid it next to three identical ones that would decorate some gentleman's jacket. Sophie had been opposed to Jane's new liaison, believing it would bring Jane no good. But her soft heart wanted her friend to be happy after the heartaches of the past few months, and she had eventually given up preaching. Jehan had been surprised when Jane had left the house, and he was unhappy to know where she had gone. "Let us hope our involvement with a royal fugitive does not bring disaster on our house, wife. Could you not remind her of the perils of living in sin? Has the foolish woman forgotten so quickly?" And Sophie had recounted Jane's long history with the marquess and how Jane believed Tom was her one true love, to which Jehan had scoffed: "Love? 'Tis only for poets and troubadours." He failed to notice his wife's subsequent lapse into silence.

Jane fingered the beautiful black and gold tassels, weighing her words. She would not tell Sophie about Tom's violence; it had been simply an act of pent-up frustration, she was sure. It would not happen again and thus was not worth dwelling upon. "Aye, Tom was my heart's desire," she began, "but either he has changed or I have, Sophie. Something is missing between us—at least for me. There seems to be no love in our lovemaking, and yet I have dreamed of being with him for so long. Is there any such thing as real love, my friend? If there is, I fear I shall never know it now."

These ramblings were a little lost on Sophie, only ever having known Jehan, but she thought carefully before giving her opinion. "Perhaps 'tis a contract that he is unable to give you," she offered. "You are both living dangerously. When you are young, is no matter. It is delicious. But you are grown up now and you, Jane, know vell the consequences of this unlawful liaison. I ask you again to leave this man. He can hurt you, my dear friend, and bad."

Jane put her arms around her childhood companion and gave her a squeeze. "You are no longer 'silly Sophie,' are you? Now you have enough common sense for both of us." Aye, her own had vanished with that first exquisite night of passion with Tom. She wandered to the hearth and stirred the contents of a pipkin, inhaling the aroma of bacon and cabbage simmering over the fire. "I expect you are right about Tom, Sophie, but I cannot give him up—yet. Please try to understand, and let us change the subject."

At that moment, Ankarette arrived back from the Mercery with more silk for Sophie to work, and she exclaimed in delight at seeing her mistress.

"I am glad you are returned, Ankarette," Jane said, leaving her task. "I need both of your help in a venture that requires your secrecy."

Again? Sophie thought to herself, wondering in what Jane might embroil her next.

"Can you visit Sophie tomorrow after terce?" Tom asked Jane a few days later after a meager supper of stale bread and cheese. "I must meet with some of my mother's friends, and they do not need to know of our arrangement."

Jane nodded. "Nor does your mother," she quipped, and Tom grinned. "Is there another plot afoot?"

"Perhaps. The less you know, the safer you will be. I hear Gloucester is none too kind to those he extracts information from," he teased with dark humor.

Tom refused to acknowledge Richard as king, continuing to

use his former title, and Jane had gladly acquiesced; she had no reason to think kindly of him. They had just heard how Richard's son had been created Prince of Wales while the king was on his progress in Yorkshire. "'Twas the only place in the kingdom where Richard would feel safe to hold the investiture," Tom had remarked, bitterly. "How those clotpole northerners love him. In the meantime, my stepbrother, the true Prince of Wales, lies languishing in the Tower"—his brow furrowed—"if the poor brat is still alive," he finished.

"Aye, it seems all London thinks they are dead," Jane told him. "It puzzles me why Richard would put them to death. They are no threat to him now. Poor boys."

Tom was thoughtful for a moment as Jane cleared the remains of the food off the rickety table they had found in another empty room above the warehouse. He was more curious about his mother's cryptic message, which had been delivered earlier that day.

We are looking across the water for deliverance from the usurper surely meant Henry Tudor in Brittany, he thought. So did Mother know for certain young Ned was already dead? How he hated his confinement and lack of information other than whatever Jane could glean from gossip. He had heard the rumor from one of his co-conspirators in the failed rescue of the boys, but no one seemed to have proof. And he could well imagine that had they been murdered, any witnesses would have been threatened with torture or death if they so much as breathed a word. Nay, there were few minions these days who could not either be bought off or punished for blabbing.

How he longed to escape London, where Gloucester's spies must be everywhere. He would not risk returning to his estates, and the prospect of facing his complaining wife was unappealing. Besides, Tom was a creature of habit, and he was used to doing his imperious mother's bidding. He was not her favorite for nothing, he told himself. He still admired her strength of purpose and her wily intelligence enough to do as he was told. If his mother required him to stay in London, then in this hell-hole he would stay. It had been greatly enlivened by the presence of the beautiful and willing Jane Shore, he admitted, but he still chafed to be free and do something useful.

He bade Jane stay away the next day until at least the bells rang for sext, and watched her departure from the small door under the roof, which must have been used when a rope and pulley outside would hoist bales of hay and other merchandise into the loft. The opening served as the only source of light but meant the rain and wind penetrated the space on less summery days.

Jane hurried up St. Mary Hill Lane to Eastchepe and traversed the long street until it turned into Watling Street. Within ten minutes of leaving Tom, she was knocking on Sophie's door.

"We must do it today, Sophie," Jane said before Sophie could greet her guest. "Is Ankarette here?"

"I am, mistress." Ankarette peeked out from behind Sophie, and Sophie drew Jane into the house and shut the door. "I have been watching your old house, as you asked, and there appear to be only two guards on duty at any time. They are bored and mostly sit on their arses, scratch their loins, and pick their noses."

"Thank you, Ankarette, although we do not need so much detail," Jane said, hiding a smile. "Now, ladies, are you sure you understand the plan? Aye, then let us go."

Sophie and Ankarette left first, linking arms and gossiping, and later Jane, carrying a covered basket and taking a different route that would allow her to arrive at her old house on Thames Street several minutes after her friends. She sent a quick prayer to St. Elizabeth, although she usually made supplications to her name saint for her barrenness and not to help her break in to a house. Rounding the corner onto Thames Street, she was relieved to see Sophie and Ankarette already there fulfilling their end of the bargain. One of the guards was peeking into Ankarette's basket to see what she was offering, and straitlaced Sophie was successfully flirting with the other. Neither man saw the tiny figure slip around the back across the garden and into the house through the kitchens.

Sadly, Jane took in the bare walls of her once richly decorated solar and a gulp wedged itself uncomfortably in her throat. Nay, she must not give way to moroseness, she quickly told herself, and hurried into the garderobe. There, undisturbed after these many weeks, the loose floorboard revealed its hidden treasure, and concealing the box in her basket, she ran down the back stairs, through the garden, and into the street. Sophie saw her, and when Jane nodded and walked away, Sophie slapped the guard's encroaching hand from her thigh, called to Ankarette to hurry along, and the two women marched off, leaving their unwitting victims staring after them in bewilderment.

Jane was so pleased with herself, she forgot Tom's admonishment to stay away until sext and ran up the stairs and into the attic room waving the box and crying: "Tom, Tom, look what I—"

Three pairs of eyes swiveled to rest on her, two in wonder and the other in irritation. She recognized the two courtiers from Edward's household, and her heart sank as they recognized her with flourishing bows.

"Mistress Shore, what a pleasant surprise," the younger man said, raising an eyebrow at Tom. "I see you are not quite alone in your discomfort, my lord." The other man grinned.

"I . . . I am sorry for the intrusion, sirs," Jane faltered, backing up to the open door. "I . . . must go . . ." And she flew down the stairs and hid in a shed in the yard until the men disappeared around the corner of the building and into Bosse Alley.

A pox on them, she thought, climbing back to the garrett. Expecting a rebuke, she was pleased to see Tom seated calmly on the three-legged stool deep in thought. She pretended nothing had happened, knelt at his feet, and took his hand to her cheek.

"A groat for your musing, my love. Do you have good news?"

Tom bent and kissed her lips, his eyes merry. "Aye, Jane, I do. I cannot tell you what it is, and 'tis best you do not know, but 'tis good news indeed." He pulled her to her feet and into his arms.

Jane was relieved. "Then you do not mind those men saw me," she said. "I am truly sorry for coming home early but I could not wait to tell you what I accomplished today."

She fetched the basket and pulled out the exquisitely carved box. Pressing a concealed button underneath it, the lid clicked open, revealing the contents. "We can buy some good food now, Tom," she said proudly, knowing some of Tom's dark moods were attributable to the unaccustomed penury in which he found himself. He had begun to despair that his mother would never leave sanctuary or have a plan for him, and until today, he had thought about slinking home to his wife in Warwickshire. He might have had an uncomfortable moment or two if Cicely had been informed of his liaison with Jane, but at least he would dine off silver again, be able to bathe, and enjoy a change of clothes.

But, as always with Tom, his mother's bidding took priority.

Jane found and slipped on her favorite emerald ring, and she closed her eyes, remembering happy times with Edward.

Tom was busy counting the gold nobles, and when he replaced them, he laughed. "You never cease to astonish me, Jane. Aye, food, and then send Ankarette to fetch the best wine the master at the Pope's Head can find for us." He paused and cupping her breast in one hand and pulling off her ugly widow's hood with the other, he added meaningfully, "Only, later."

Whether it was the lifting of Tom's black humor or the knowledge they could enjoy some luxury for a while, she did not care, for their lovemaking was long and tender that afternoon, and Jane thought she was finally happy.

Her euphoria did not last a day. Arriving back the following morning from Sophie's with a basketful of succulent pies, roasted meats, and even a custard, Jane took the stairs two at a time and entered the darkened room.

It was empty.

Jane dropped the basket on the floor, flung open the small door to the yard below, and called her lover's name. She stared at the pegs where Tom's second shirt, his jacket, and his cloak should have been, and then she rummaged under the pile of straw where he kept a bag with a comb, his velvet bonnet, extra hose, and quill pen. All gone. Only then did she notice the yellowed piece of parchment, torn from his prayer book no doubt, that had fallen to the floor. She snatched it up and took it to the light.

Dearest Jane, forgive me. My mother wills that I join her brother, the bishop of Salisbury. There is much at stake and I believe you will be glad to know it is all in an effort to restore Ned to the throne. We will be together again when the goal is reached. Your company has been sweet and I will always think on you kindly.

Go with God,
Tom

Jane could hardly read the postscript for her angry tears.

Destroy this when you have read it. T

She flung herself down on the bed, the earthy smell of straw mingling with the unmistakable scent of their lovemaking, and beat the scratchy mattress with her fists.

"Damn you, Tom! I hate you!" she cried. He could have waited to explain in person, waited to say farewell. "What a coward!" Then the awful gnawing feeling in her belly returned in full force when she realized she was alone once more. "Sweet Mother of God, what shall I do now?"

She lay facedown on the coarse sheet for several minutes, her mind a morass of thoughts. Had she not expected him to leave, if she had been honest with herself? She was not such a fool as to think their time together would last forever. Was he not always at his mother's beck and call? She grimaced. Not to mention his wife's, she thought ruefully. Aye, foolish Jane, she had no hold on the marquess of Dorset, son of the former queen, husband to the richest woman in England. What had she expected? She knew he was not hers to keep, and she should have listened to Sophie. He had used her, she admitted angrily, despising herself for her romantic weakness. How blinded by love she had been once again. "Nay," she said to herself, "be honest, Jane. 'Twas lust, not love, that bound you." He was not a good man. She saw that now, and she had known better men. Much better, as she thought of good-natured, honest Edward and loyal Will.

As she calmed herself with her reasonings, she gained strength. "You will get over him," she said sternly, "eventually."

Despite her anger and disillusionment, she was comforted in the knowledge she was not destitute. Did she now not have a small fortune in nobles and jewelry that would buy her a room at a respectable inn until she could find work? She had not lost her skills as a silkwoman. Aye, she reassured herself, the money would help, and she had friends in the merchant community. She sat up, tucked her disheveled hair under her hood, and reached under her side of the straw bed for her insurance—her precious box of coins and gems.

"Sweet Jesu, no!" she screamed. It was gone.

She leaped up and began frantically to pull apart the straw. "God damn you to hell, Tom Grey!" she raged in a panic. He had taken everything. He had not been satisfied to take her body and her love, he had taken everything she owned as well. She picked up the stool and flung it at the wall; the pies, meats, and custard followed soon after. She overturned the table, and then slammed and reslammed the door, enjoying the satisfying bangs that reverberated in the empty warehouse. "Take that, and that, and that," she cried with every slam.

She had never felt so betrayed in her whole life—not even by her father or by William Shore, and she wished Tom Grey were there so she could kick him where a man hurts most. But her hurt went deeper; the man she risked everything for had not given a thought to her safety or her survival. He had left her destitute, and she would be reduced to beggary.

What was she to do now?

"But, my lord bishop, my claim to the throne is almost as good as Richard's," Buckingham reminded John Morton, bishop of Ely, as they talked in the tower chamber of Brecon Castle, where the bishop was still a prisoner. Below them, the end-of-summer shallow River Usk babbled its way past the plum-colored walls of the motte and bailey castle that had been built by the Normans three centuries earlier to keep out the hostile Welsh. In a few months, the water would become a torrent and an added barrier protecting the lords of Brecon.

Morton steepled his pudgy fingers, the ruby of his episcopal ring catching the light, and watched the more volatile Harry pace around the room. His instructions from Margaret Beaufort had been clear: persuade the angry duke of Buckingham to turn against the king and join her, the queen, and Morton himself in a rebellion to remove Richard from the throne and place Henry Tudor there, with Edward the Fourth's eldest daughter, Bess, as his queen. To that end, Morton had worked tirelessly to convince Buckingham that his way lay with the plotters, now that he and Richard were seemingly at odds.

He recalled clearly the state of high dudgeon in which the belligerent young duke had arrived at Brecon that day more than a month ago. Why Harry had wanted to come directly to him in his quarters, the bishop had not known then. Whatever had happened at Gloucester, Morton deduced it must have been a serious breach of loyalty for Richard to have turned his only royal cousin and councilor away so abruptly. That first meeting had been the first of many where Morton had little by little poisoned his prey against his king, and finally, today, he had wheedled the truth about the meeting in Gloucester from him.

"If it had not been you, it would have been someone else looking for the king's favor," Morton said, dismissing the crime. "The boys were of no account anymore." He then proceeded to reel in the dejected duke with as much nonchalance as a fisherman baiting his hook. "Besides, everyone knows Richard wanted the crown. Who will believe it was not he who ordered their deaths? We can even start the rumors," he said, trying to keep the glee from his voice. "Think no more of it, my dear Buckingham. If the disappearance becomes public, it will give our cause even more weight. Trust me, your tale is safe with me. Now are you with us or not?"

Buckingham eyed the persuasive prelate with a pout and grudging respect.

"You told me bluntly that I should fight for my claim when I first came from Gloucester," Buckingham whined. "Tudor has but a hairsbreadth of a claim to the throne. He is of Beaufort bastard descent, and my line is unsullied. Do not forget the special edict of the fourth Henry when he legitimized his half-siblings at the turn of the century: no one of the Beaufort line may inherit the throne."

"Aye, my lord, but do not forget right by conquest. Also, the Beaufort barring can easily be reversed and then Henry Tudor has a better claim than you. I do not believe the people will support you, even though, my lord duke," Morton purred, flicking a speck of lint from his black robe, "you are a most capable man, and we could not consider this plan without your support. Think, your grace, if you succeed in putting Henry upon the throne—just as you did the usurper Richard, they will begin to call you Kingmaker." He knew he had chosen his words well when he saw the look of self-importance on his victim's face. How transparent the duke was! Today, he was getting somewhere with his persuasive powers, he decided, enjoying himself, and he had the duke's confession with which to force the issue, if needed. "For her part, the countess of Richmond, Lady Stanley, has all the connections to assemble a Lancastrian force, which I do not believe you can do. Am I right?"

Morton smiled benignly at Harry, who acquiesced with a reluctant nod. "And then there is the proposed joining of Lancaster and York by the marriage of Tudor and young Elizabeth of York. The people will welcome the end of this civil strife that has eaten at the kingdom for so long. Unfortunately, your grace, you are already married." He watched the curly-haired Buckingham digest all this, his already meager respect for the fickle duke slipping by the second. "Can you now not see that Tudor is our only chance for success? Especially now that you have taken care of the possibility of an anti-Richard faction using young Ned to lead a rebellion."

Buckingham did indeed see. And so, with more flattery and promise of power in the new regime, Harry of Buckingham agreed to turn his coat and rebel against his cousin, conveniently forgetting that, in four short months, that same cousin had showered him with great rewards and the promise of power for his loyalty.

Richard needed some air.

He nodded to Francis Lovell, and the two friends ran up the stone spiral to the ramparts high above Sheriff Hutton's inner bailey. He had to escape the smoky hall and constant chatter so he could think. The familiar Yorkshire east wind off the Northern Sea carried a nip of autumn in it, making the men turn to have it at their backs as they stood on the southern side of the castle and looked out over the forest of Galtres and to the towers of York's minster in the far distance.

"What news, Richard?" Francis came straight to the point, knowing the taciturn king detested idle banter. The messenger had arrived not an hour before, his high leather boots caked in mud, and his face ruddy from his long ride, and Francis sensed the news was not good. "You looked as though you had seen a ghost back there."

Richard stopped and leaned against the battlements. "I was not expecting it so soon, Francis. Jack Howard writes there is rebellion afoot, and that I should return to London at once."

"Rebellion? By whom?" Francis demanded.

"Does it matter?" the king answered sadly. "Jack says there is talk of it in the southern counties. 'Twas our good fortune he was on his own progress to his new estates in Surrey and Sussex, where he was informed. He will no doubt deal with it should it erupt, but it seems 'tis more widespread."

Francis tried to sound unconcerned. "You have not been away long enough to warrant complaints. 'Tis those southerners, Richard; you have never trusted them."

Richard turned away toward the hills. "I wish it were as easy as that, Francis," he said somberly. "There is more to this unrest than you know." He stopped short then. Howard had intimated that people were asking about the boys in the Tower; there was a rumor afoot they had been done away with. It was a terrible secret he had kept for a few weeks now—to Richard it seemed an eternity, but he must shoulder the responsibility. He did not want to unload it onto others. Only Anne knew why Buckingham was no longer in favor, and apparently no one else questioned the duke's extended absence. Here in the north, Richard felt cushioned from the heinous events, but when he got to London, he would have to face them, he knew. At least the boys' guards only knew that Lord Buckingham had whisked the boys away, presumably to a safer place. He had paid them well to deny they had seen or heard anything. Foolish, headstrong Harry! It was now up to Richard to think of a plausible reason for their disappearance, and to deal with their mother's questions.

Returning his focus to the present, Richard sensed Francis was waiting for an explanation, but how much should he say to the man he trusted most in the world, if he trusted anyone. If the truth be told, there were only two people he knew were unconditionally loyal to him: the two women he had loved, which was odd, he had once surmised, as most men distrusted women's tongues far more than men's. After Harry's confession at Gloucester, Richard had experienced such terrible nightmares Anne could not help but gentle the truth from him. She had been kind but frightened, and he wished now he had not told her. He was afraid she was not strong enough to share such a burden, but tomorrow she would return to her preferred life at Middleham with their beloved son, and perhaps she would benefit from the change of air.

The other woman he longed to tell was Kate. He had been reminded of her a few days ago when he had knighted their son, John, on the day of little Ned's investiture. What a fine boy, he thought fondly, and Kate should be proud.

While Francis waited, he watched the bustling below him of the many carpenters, bowyers, potters, blacksmiths, laundresses, and soldiers that kept a castle running smoothly. He was used to Richard's brooding. He preferred this way of dealing with crises rather than his friend's occasional rash actions, like the Hastings beheading. But he could usually depend on the rational Richard, and he would follow him down whatever path his king might lead him. His friend's remark had left Francis wondering, but he knew better than to probe. Richard would tell him in his own good time—or not. And so he waited.

In a very few minutes, his patience was rewarded, for Richard turned to him and slapped him on the back, his chin determined and his voice strong. "Come, let us join the ladies and have ourselves a fine farewell feast, giving them no cause for concern. But on the morrow, we shall cheerfully wave Anne and Ned good-bye, and as soon as they are out of sight, we shall make haste for London."

Whatever "more" there was to this uprising, Richard had decided to keep to himself, Francis thought, leading the way back down the winding stairs. He had no misgivings about putting down any rebellion; his king was the finest soldier in the kingdom.

The spires of Lincoln Cathedral's three magnificent towers had dominated the horizon for the past twenty miles as Richard and his retinue approached the city on Ermine Street from the north.

The weak October sun was setting when, weary of his saddle, Richard dismounted at the wide steps up to the west front door of the cathedral and was greeted by a prelate in the service of its absent bishop and Richard's new chancellor, John Russell. Richard strode down the flagged floor of the nave to the choir, followed by his personal household, and the priest led them in a prayer of Thanksgiving for the king's safe entry into the city that had once been England's third largest during the previous century's prosperous wool trade.

It was getting dark when on the short walk under the Exchequer Gate across Bailgate to the castle, Richard and his entourage heard galloping hooves on the cobblestones. A sergeant-at-arms lit a flambeau and held it high as the approaching horseman slowed up the steep hill and came into the light.

Immediately recognizing the Howard white lion and azure crescent on the messenger's livery, Richard ordered that the man be brought into his presence without delay and hurried through the castle gate and into the great hall. Lord Stanley, Francis Lovell, and several esquires of the body followed him into the smaller audience chamber, where a welcome fire was taking the chill off the room.

The duke of Norfolk's man was soon kneeling at his king's feet, carefully articulating the exact words Jack Howard had made him learn by heart.

"Your servant, his grace of Norfolk greets you well, my lord king. He bids me tell you that Kent has risen and is intent on taking London in your absence. The more troubling news is that these rebels of Kent are claiming they are led by none other than his grace, the duke of Buckingham."

The man got no further, for a roar of disbelief had erupted from those in the room and Richard himself was on his feet.

"Harry?" Richard repeated hoarsely, the blood draining from his face. "Harry leads the rebels?" He turned his back on the audience, who was loudly discussing the shocking news, and he stared at the crackling logs in the hearth. "Dear Mother of God, what have I done?"

Richard slept badly. He rose before the cock crowed and called for John Kendall, his faithful secretary. After answering Jack Howard's call to action, the second letter he dictated was to Chancellor Russell, in which he graciously thanked the bishop for the kind welcome the prelate had arranged at his cathedral and city the day before, despite being indisposed at Westminster, and wished Russell a speedy recovery. Then he proceeded to reassure the chancellor that he was fully informed in the matter of the insurgency.

But, I pray you send the Great Seal to me at once; I have much to do before the rebellion can be put down.

He finished with the usual salutations and watched as Kendall put the final flourish on "written this twelfth day of October at Lincoln in the first year of our reign," before dribbling wax upon the parchment. As he pressed the royal seal into the hot liquid to make the document official, Richard suddenly snatched the quill out of the secretary's hand, dipped it in the inkwell, and handwrote a postcript:

Here, loved be God, is all well and truly determined, and for
to resist the malice of him that had best cause to be true, the
duke of Buckingham, the most . . .

He paused and looked at Kendall. "I know not what to say of
him," Richard said sadly, and Kendall was moved to see tears in
his king's eyes. Brushing them aside, Richard dipped the pen again
and nodded to himself.

. . . the most untrue creature living; whom with God's grace
we shall not be long till that we will be in those parts, and
subdue his malice. We assure there was never false traitor
better purveyed for, as this bearer shall show you.

*Ricardus R.**

John Kendall carefully folded the missives, assigned more wax
to seal them, and left the room without a word to put them personally into the hands of the waiting messenger. He closed the
door quietly behind him.

Alone in the room, Richard went to stand by the window, the
same dark thoughts running around in his head. Why had he not
immediately denounced Harry upon hearing of the unspeakable
crime the man had committed? His reasonable mind told him that
there was not anyone who would have believed the order to kill
the two boys had not come from him. With men already calling
him usurper, his fragile hold on the crown would be wrenched
from him with an accusation of murder—and of his brother's
children, no less.

But by keeping silent, he would have to bear the guilt alone and
remain in a living hell. Neither way was acceptable, he concluded

---

* actual text

as his unabashed tears spilled down his cheeks as freely as the rain upon the windowpanes.

London was on high alert. Not since King Edward had regained his throne in '71 had so many armed soldiers filled the main thoroughfares, preparing the capital for a possible attack, this time from Kentish rebels.

"We had begun to believe we were safe at last," Jehan grumbled to his wife and Jane, who was once again welcomed into the Vandersand household. The two women were busy chopping leeks, onions, and cabbages for the customary pottage that percolated over the fire, their sleeves rolled up and their aprons smeared with blood from the rabbit that had gone into the pot first. Jehan was sharpening a stave he kept handy to ward off intruders and was ready to defend his family if the need arose.

"How close are the rebels to the city?" Jane asked. "That must be why I saw Lord Howard ride by in the Chepe yesterday." She did not tell her friends that he had waved at her; she tried to avoid reminding them of her previous royal connections.

Sophie had, of course, consoled Jane after Tom's desertion. She was not surprised by his behavior but was glad to know Jane had come to see him for the bum-bailey he was. Nay, worse than that, he was a romancer, a liar, and a thief. And so Jane had taken up residency on Sithe's Lane once more, playing aunt or nursemaid to Sophie's two younger children and taking over kitchen duty from Sophie, allowing the hardworking spinner to produce more thread for sale. During her two stays, she had also taught her friend to read.

"Vhy are the men of Kent rebelling?" Sophie asked, throwing the last handful of cabbage into the pot.

Jehan shrugged. "It is in their nature," he said. "It would seem most rebellions I remember hearing about began in Kent. The drawbridge is raised on London Bridge, and all boats have been moved to the city side of the river. I heard last night in the Pope's

Head that Lord Howard's troops are already on their way to halting the rebels before they get to Southwark."

"Then ve are safe, husband, *ja*?" Sophie said. "You vill not need
your stick."

"Let us hope not," Jane agreed, and then recited:

> *"The weaver dropped his trusty weft*
> *To sharpen up his stave,*
> *We hope he never uses it*
> *For the consequence is grave."*

Even Ankarette caught the double meaning and crossed herself.

The day planned for the simultaneous strikes by the rebels was
the eighteenth of October, but those in the west and Wales were
unaware the men of Kent had not waited and had been already
thwarted in their bid to capture London.

The unrelenting rain of the past week still sheeted in drenching
torrents as Buckingham and his erstwhile prisoner and now fellow conspirator John Morton, bishop of Ely, started for Hereford,
thirty miles away. Morton looked around at the force Harry had
assembled and told himself it would have to do. It seemed the duke
did not have the sway with the Welsh he had boasted of, and the
men trudging behind their captains did not appear to be relishing a long march in abominable conditions to fight for a cause
that did not concern them. With luck, Morton thought, those
leaders in the west country and the southeast will have gathered
larger and more willing armies to join with Henry Tudor when he
landed somewhere on the south coast with his force from Brittany,
weather permitting. On the appointed day, the four arms of the
insurrection would move toward London and trap Richard coming
down from the north. Morton had prayed hard the night before
that the weeks of planning would reap the sought-after rewards.

Buckingham, however, was in fine spirits, laughing with his squires and knights as they moved toward the Severn. His unruly curls, dancing like coiled dark springs, sprayed droplets of rain around him as he turned his head this way and that. He was behaving as though he were king, Morton noted, the man's vainglory evident in every loud command, booming laugh, and dramatic gesture. Morton would rather put up with Richard as king than this buffoon, he had long ago decided, and, staring at a spot between his horse's ears, he fell back to avoid communication with the man.

The proclamation Richard published soon after leaving Lincoln condemned Buckingham and his rebels and was affixed to every church door and market cross in England. Those who read it marveled at the extraordinary news that the rebel leader was the duke of Buckingham. Richard exhorted his subjects to be ready to fight for their king, but he made clear that none of the duke's followers who resisted this treason must be harmed or taken. In the meantime, Richard began assembling a host of his own at Leicester, while Jack Howard gathered a large number of troops and stationed them at Guildford. His quick action of the previous week had allowed London's defenses to be strengthened, and by blocking the crossing at Gravesend, the Kentish rebels were unable to join those from East Anglia.

It was while bartering for a large mullet that Jane learned how close London had come to being overrun by the rebels. After Tom deserted her, she returned a little chastened to the Vandersands, and she was grateful Sophie had never resorted to saying "Did I not warn you?"

She listened as the skinny wife of the fishmonger told her husband the latest news from that wellspring of all wisdom, the Great Conduit in the Chepe, where brewers, cooks, and others who fetched fresh water for their businesses exchanged gossip and information.

"Who would've thought that high and mighty duke of Buckingham would turn traitor," the woman was saying, prompting Jane to eavesdrop. "Wants to be king I wouldn't wonder, now that them poor boys are dead and gone."

"Aw, shut yer mouth, wife," the fishmonger said. "Who sez them boys are dead? 'Ave you seen the bodies then?" And he laughed. "Aye, mistress, this mullet is a fine one. And 'cos you're so pretty, I'll give it to yer for a shilling."

"I'll give you two groats and not a penny more," Jane retorted, and the fishmonger relented and took the silver coins. "What else have you heard, goody," she asked his wife after safely stowing the fish in her basket.

"That Jack Howard saved London, mistress. Always did like 'im. My sister lives in Stepney and he gives generously in the parish," the woman confided. "He's now the duke of Norfolk, did you know?" she said, proud of her knowledge of those far above her.

Jane pretended to be surprised but was wanting more pertinent information. "Is anyone else charged in this rebellion, have you heard?"

The goodwife scratched her armpit, making Jane move a step away. "Well, wot I heard was them rebels want to put somebody called Tidder on the throne. I dunno who that is, but I don't like his name. 'E beds down in France somewhere. Why should we want a Frenchie on the throne? Can't abide 'em."

"I think they mean Henry Tudor, who is the countess of Richmond's son," Jane told her. She pulled the woman aside and asked, "Why do you think the princes are dead? Do you know someone in the Tower?"

"Nah," the fishwife said through her nose. "But 'tis said the king had them murdered." She leaned forward, her eyes as big as the mullets in Kate's basket. "Smothered them, they say, with 'is own 'ands."

"Nonsense!" Jane could not help snapping, although why she would defend Richard she did not pause to ponder. "The boys were seen playing after the king left on his progress. And he has not been back to London since. It must be he has sent them somewhere safe after that failed attempt to spirit them away from their apartments. Besides, why would the king want to murder his own nephews? They are bastards now and cannot inherit the throne."

The goodwife looked askance at Jane. "'Ere, who are yer then that yer know so much? Come to think of it, where've I seen yer afore?"

"Why, I come here to buy fish every week, mistress," Jane said airily. "I am just a Londoner like you." And she nodded good-bye and sauntered back into Fish Street Hill.

She wondered if Tom had joined the rebels, although she could not imagine why; she knew he and his mother looked on Henry Tudor as a threat not an ally. As she did not see any signs of Londoners concerned for their safety, she assumed the king was a long way from here dealing with the uprising.

Jane was correct. The rebellion fizzled when the duke of Buckingham was caught on the wrong side of the River Severn, which was in flood and all its bridges sabotaged by the king's commanders. Morton escaped first to sanctuary in his own cathedral of Ely and then to Flanders, while poor, duped Harry of Buckingham was discovered hiding in a barn a hundred miles from his disbanded army, disguised as one of his own soldiers. He was taken in chains to Salisbury, where he awaited King Richard's justice.

In the meantime, Henry Tudor, earl of Richmond, his little fleet battered by storms and unable to arrive on English shores and unify the rebels in the Southwest, returned to France, unaware the rebellion he had instigated had already collapsed.

Sophie stared at the proclamation nailed to the church door of St. Anthony's in Watling Street on her way home from the Mercery. London had ceased to be worried about an attack by rebels; King Richard's army had swiftly moved south from Coventry, and Londoners were certain Buckingham's rebellion, as it was being called, would be quickly put down.

The beginning of the document praised the pardons Richard had given the followers of the rebel leaders when they had first laid down their arms against him. But then the language of this second edict became less about treason and strangely, Sophie noted, about morality:

> *His grace, in his own person, as is well known, has addressed himself to divers parties of his realm for the equal administration of justice to every person, having confidence and trust that all oppressors and extortioners of his subjects, horrible adulterers and bawds, provoking the high indignation of displeasure of God, should be reconciled and reduced to the way of truth and virtue . . .*

Sophie shook her head in disbelief, but then something caught her eye in the next paragraph and she skipped on:

> *This not withstanding, Thomas, lately marquess of Dorset, who not fearing God nor the peril of his soul, has many and sundry maids, widows and wives damnably and without shame devoured, deflowered and defouled, holding the shameless and mischievous woman called Shore's wife in adultery**

---

* actual text

"*In Godsnaam!*" Sophie whispered. "Jane!" She peered closely at the cramped script, unsure of her new reading skills. *Ja*, there was her friend's name, accused of adultery—again. Checking that no one was watching her, she tore the paper from the door, and ran back to the house, where she found Jane playing hide-and-seek with Pieter. Jane's face was flushed from laughter as, with noisy excitement, Poppy gave away the little boy's hiding place, and Sophie opined for the hundredth time how tragic it was Jane had not had children of her own.

"Pieter, take Poppy in the garden, *alstublieft*—please, but keep her out of the midden today," Sophie told her son, who obeyed happily, her tone immediately warning Jane that something was amiss.

"What is it, Sophie?" she asked, glancing at the parchment Sophie was clutching.

Sophie thrust the proclamation at her friend and sat down heavily on the bench. When Jane came to her own name, she gasped and turned pale. "What can this mean?" she cried. "I have not seen Tom since he left in September. Who even knew we were together?"

"You mean others besides those in this house? Ach, *niet*, no one here vould betray you."

Jane nodded. "Certes, I know that. Nay, it must be one of the men who visited Tom that day I retrieved my treasure. Tom told me to stay away because he wanted no one to tell his mother or his wife he was with me. I forgot his command, and they saw me." She sank down on the bench next to Sophie and read the rest of the document, which condemned the duke of Buckingham, the bishops of Ely and Salisbury—Tom's brother, and other followers who were, according to Richard,

intending not only the destruction of the royal person of our sovereign lord and his true subjects, breaching the peace,

tranquility and common good of this realm, by abandoning
virtue and the damnable and maintaining of vices and sin,
as they have done in times past, to the great displeasure of
God and as an evil example of all Christian people.

Jane let out an unladylike whistle. "Did you read all of this, Sophie?" she asked. When Sophie shook her head, Jane read aloud the final paragraph, which told the whole world what Richard's people could expect from its king.

"Wherefore the king's highness, of his tender and loving
disposition that he has shown to the good of his realm,
and putting down and rebuking of vices, he grants that
no yeoman or commoner thus abused and blinded by these
*aforesaid traitors, adulterers and bawds . . ."**

Jane paused to contemplate the extraordinary language used by this king in his mission to purify the realm. He was obsessed with men's morals, she decided, and from reading this proclamation, it would seem Richard was more concerned with punishing adulterers and bawds than traitors. No wonder he had come looking for her.

"Go on," Sophie urged her quietly. "Is there more?"

"Oh, forgive me. Aye, there is.

"Those traitors and bawds shall not be hurt in their bodies
nor goods if they remove themselves from their false company
and meddle no further with them."†

She looked up at her friend and saw the question in Sophie's eyes. "You think I should give myself up to the authorities, confess

---

* actual text
† actual text

that I lay in adultery with Thomas Dorset, and expect Richard to pardon me again? I think not."

"But, Jane . . ." She got no further as Ankarette came huffing through the door laden with food from the market.

"Such a crowd at St. Paul's today, mistresses," she said, beaming at both of them. "But no one bargains better than Ankarette Tyler. Even one of the carters told those around me so." She began taking the food out of the baskets and remembered the scene with a proud smile. "I told him my mistress taught me," she boasted as Sophie and Jane helped stow the vegetables and bread. " 'And who might that be,' the carter asked. 'Why, Mistress Jane Shore,' I proudly announced to all who would listen."

Jane and Sophie froze midtask, and Sophie was incredulous. "Ah, Ankarette. You told everyone you were Jane's maidservant?"

Mortified, poor Ankarette whimpered, "Did I do wrong? 'Tis no secret." She looked miserably at Jane. "I am so—"

She got no further as a furious thumping on the door made Sophie drop her cabbage and Jane break two eggs she had been trying to place carefully in a pail. Ankarette went to the door and opened it a crack. "Who is it who makes such a racket?" she demanded. She was roughly pushed aside by two men-at-arms, who thrust open the door and stepped over the threshold.

"Mistress Shore?" one of them addressed Ankarette.

Ankarette tried to hide her mistress behind her larger bulk, but Jane gently pulled her aside and answered the man. "I am Jane Shore. What do you want of me?" She was astonished how calm she sounded, for her legs felt limp.

"You are to come with us to be charged on suspicion of harboring a traitor," the man replied, looking around the simple house and wondering if they had the right woman. There was nowhere to hide a fugitive, he thought. And at that moment Pieter and a neighbor's boy came charging into the house pretending to be knights with sticks for swords and followed by a barking Poppy.

"Are these your children?" the man-at-arms shouted at Jane over the din. Sophie stepped forward and claimed them as hers.

"Mistress Shore has been living with us for many veeks, sergeant," Sophie volunteered. "You may search my house, but you vill find no hiding traitors. She is innocent."

"Perhaps not at present, mistress," the man said. "But Thomas of Dorset is a foul traitor, and it is known this woman has lain in adultery with him while he plotted his treason, and thus she must come with us."

Sophie watched sadly as the two men bound Jane's hands. "May I ask how you knew vhere she vas?"

The other soldier grinned and jerked his head in Ankarette's direction. "This clatterer was prating about her bargaining skills in the market. We had been on the lookout for Mistress Shore and 'twas simple to follow this marvelous clack-dish home."

This set Ankarette to weeping, and she begged Jane to forgive her. "I have betrayed my beloved mistress," she wailed to Sophie as Jane was marched from the house between her escorts. "What will become of her? Oh, I am a wicked woman."

Sophie ran after the little group with Jane's warm cloak. "Where do you take her, sergeant?" she pleaded, giving him the garment. "She is like a sister to me."

The man saw no harm in telling the woman. The arrest had gone smoothly, and he would soon be off duty and enjoying a flagon of ale with his friends. "For what 'tis worth to you, goodwife, she is going to Ludgate gaol."

Jane stumbled and almost fell but for the strong hands that held her. "Please, God, no!" she begged, tears stinging her eyes. She did not think she could suffer through even one night in that infernal cell again. She turned to look at Sophie, who had faltered when she heard the news, her brown eyes filled with compassion.

"Pray for me, Sophie," Jane called desperately over her shoulder, although she was quite convinced that by this time God must have finally abandoned her.

Another of King Richard's prisoners was also feeling bereft of God's favor as he sat in his cell, his borrowed clothes in tatters and his body emitting an odor even the rats shunned. Harry of Buckingham was awaiting trial, and although he was miserable, he was convinced he could worm his way out of an execution. If only he could see Richard, talk to him, he thought.

He may not have enjoyed the irony that he had to face the acting constable of England, Sir Ralph Assheton, whom Richard had recently appointed to replace Buckingham, now deemed an outlaw. Harry was led in front of the commission, his head and his feet bare, and made to sit on a stool in the high-beamed town hall. After the charges were read, Harry began to unravel. He went down on his knees and confessed that he had been hoodwinked by the bishop of Ely into rebelling and revealed all he knew of the plot. In a desperate plea to save his life, he cried: "Gentlemen, I beg of you, let me see my cousin, the king. I will explain all to him. Surely I have the right to an audience?"

"The king has no wish to see you, my lord Buckingham. You have proved to be his grace's most monstrous enemy, and he is done with you," Assheton replied, lowering his brow and pointing his finger at Harry. "You will die a traitor upon the morrow. Now take him away," he commanded the guards, scorning the royal duke's tears.

Back in his cell, Harry demanded vellum and pen and scratched out a personal plea to Richard, reminding him of their friendship, of his support to put Richard upon the throne, and of the royal blood they shared. His words were heartfelt, flowery, and smudged with tears. He could not believe Richard would deny his cousin a final interview.

Whether or not Richard saw his one-time comrade's desperate

missive, Buckingham never knew. As the bells in the tallest spire
in England tolled over the marketplace, Henry Stafford, duke of
Buckingham, rebel and traitor, was led to the makeshift scaffold,
made to lay his head upon the block, and just as Will Hastings
had done not six months before, he cried out to God to have
mercy on his soul.

In his temporary lodgings at a house in the cathedral close, Richard
sat staring at the blotched parchment his cousin had sent and
listened as the bells sounded their death knell. "Christ's blood,
Harry," he said bitterly. "I could have forgiven you your rebelling,"
although he abhorred the man's double disloyalty, first to him and
then to the rebels by confessing all so readily to avert blame, "but
I can never forgive you the foul murder of my nephews."

Crumpling the letter into a ball, he threw it into the fire as
though consigning his cousin's soul equally to the flames of hell.

EIGHTEEN

"**B**ack again so soon, Mistress Shore?" the warden of Ludgate goaded his proud prisoner. "Did not learn the first time, eh? You must be getting good at this harlotry lark." He reached forward to squeeze her breast. "Might be I take a turn with you, Mistress Bawd."

Jane eyed the grimy sausage fingers pawing her and stepped back. Had her hands not been tied, she would have slapped him. "May I assume you cannot get a woman any other way?" she provoked him.

In an instant, the fondling fingers turned into a fist that slammed into her face, making Jane cry out in painful outrage. She fell to her knees, tasting blood and reeling from the injury. "That'll learn you," the gaoler rasped. He nodded to the guard. "Take her upstairs. This time she'll have to take her lumps. There is no fancy lord to buy her a bed now. Come down in the world a trifle has our king's whore."

And so Jane was half carried to the gates of the familiar cell, its foul stink taking her back to those dire days of June. The guard shoved a cup at her that would serve for both food and drink, and pushed her rudely inside, flinging her mantle on top of her.

A pair of gentle hands helped her to her feet, and a young woman of no more than sixteen gingerly touched the welt on Jane's cheek. "Bastard," she hissed. "The warden did that, did he not?"

Jane winced and nodded. "I suppose I deserved it. I insulted his manhood," she murmured, and she tried to smile at the memory, but it hurt so much, she gave a little gasp of pain. She allowed her new friend to lead her to a fresh pile of straw that she was willing to share with Jane.

"I am Anne, and I am in here until I can pay my fine." She grinned. "I cheated my neighbor out of a chicken, and she went straight to the sheriff. When my father's anger simmers down, he'll pay to get me out."

Jane was a little surprised at the girl's nonchalance; stealing used to be a hangable offense, she had once heard her father say, but that was a long time ago, and society was supposedly far more civilized now. "I am Jane Shore, and it seems I am here for hiding a fugitive." She refused to brand herself a whore or harlot. She felt her face and winced. "I suppose I shall have a black eye."

Judging from the cut of her kirtle and the fine lawn of her smock, Jane presumed the young woman came from the merchant class. Jane settled back on the straw and looked about her. This time, the inmates' genders were roughly half and half, which reassured Jane. When nighttime came, and in mid-November it came early, she curled up next to Anne, and they shared Jane's warm cloak as well as the moth-eaten blanket the prison provided.

As in her first night there in June, Jane found sleep difficult. But once the curfew had sounded and the thrum of the city subsided, she used the subsequent silent hours to assess her situation. She was puzzled. She had been accused by the sergeant-at-arms of hiding Tom, but the warden had been told to admit her for harlotry. Thinking clearly now, despite her throbbing cheek and nose, she deduced with sudden horror that had she been charged with hiding a traitor, she would be lying in a dungeon far less comfortable than this minimally guarded prison and could expect a traitor's death. As a commoner and a woman, she would be burned at the stake. She shuddered as she remembered witnessing the execution of a traitor in the Smithfield Marketplace when she was a child of ten. She was ashamed now that her most vivid memory of the occasion was of a gift of ribbons her father had uncharacteristically purchased for her from a peddler. That had been one of the few good days with John Lambert; she had been the only one of the children who had agreed to accompany their father to the event, and he had been pleased with her. She wondered how her mother could have sanctioned the outing for such a young girl, but perhaps Jane had already proven such a handful that her parents thought a taste of what could become of unruly adults might make an indelible impression. She knew she would never subject a child of hers to such a hideous scene.

Aye, but she did not have a child, did she? Jane allowed her mind to wander to thoughts of her lusty liaisons with Edward and Will when she had trusted her sponge and vinegar prevention. But, without the benefit of precautions, she and Tom had made love more in their three-week tryst than she had in all her time with Will, and yet she had remained barren. It was puzzling, and it again made her feel sad and a failure as a woman somehow. She thought of Sophie and Jehan and their brood, and she smiled. Such good friends; she did not deserve them. How glad she was she had helped them when she could. It made her feel less guilty for accepting their hospitality of late.

Before she could go back to St. Sithe's Lane, she must be prepared for what might befall her here. If one of the men who had seen her with Tom bore witness against her, then what punishment could she expect? The same as before? Please, dear Mother of Jesus, not that penance again, she begged, reliving the agonizing walk. And as her mind flew back to that horrifying hour of humility, some words began to form that finally expressed her shame. 'Twas a pity there was no one to appreciate them.

"*I had good cause this wretched man to blame,*" she began, although in her heart she did not really blame Will for her penance,

> "*Before the world I suffered open shame,*
> *Where people were as thick as is the sand,*

A penance took with taper in my hand.
Each eye did stare and look me in the face,
As I passed by the rumors on me ran,
But patience then had lent me such a grace,
My quiet looks were praised of every man."

Her eyes filled with tears as she thought lovingly of the support of her fellow Londoners. They had stood with her that day, seeing a woman who had simply offended an overly pious king but who was no guiltier of a sinful life than they were.

Would they support her again? With a sinking feeling, she somehow doubted it.

"So you, too, think they are . . . gone?" Elizabeth dared to ask, subjecting herself to the physician's expert fleeming.

She had come down with a cold the previous week, and then chills and the fever had followed. Doctor Argentine had been sent for, and he was concerned when he observed the queen dowager's pallor.

The little doctor, who had served in the former Prince of Wales's household until recently, looked dwarfed by his heavily padded jacket with its generous fox-fur trim. His close-fitting cap covered everything but his swarthy face with its beady black eyes and small button nose, reminding Elizabeth of a hedgehog. He shuffled around his patient's bed, noticing the stark difference between the paltry abbey furnishings after the magnificence of Westminster or Windsor.

"I prevailed upon Sir Robert Brackenbury to allow me to see for myself that your sons were no longer at the Tower, your grace," he told her. "He is a decent fellow and claimed he had no knowledge of their whereabouts. His story—and I believe 'tis naught but a tale he has been told to broadcast—is that the king had secretly removed them to a safe place following the failed rescue in the summer. Certes, I saw no trace of them or their guards, even in the innermost chamber, where they had been lodged the last time I saw them."

Elizabeth fluttered her free hand, agitated. "But, Doctor Argentine, we heard a rumor they were . . . dead." She faltered on the word, and Argentine was moved to see her evident anguish. "Were they well when you saw them last? Was Ned well?"

The doctor pursed his thin lips. "He complained of a pain in his jaw, but I could see naught wrong with it," he answered. "His manservant told me the lad was prone to headaches, and I left a draught with some instructions to ease them. But little Dickon was in fine form. I have not been called there lately, your grace. It is possible they have been sent away to safety."

Elizabeth watched the doctor bind up the incision after he was satisfied with the amount of blood he had let and its color. "When the king returns to London, I will request that he inform me of my boys' whereabouts," Elizabeth decided, although she was certain Richard would not attempt a meeting with her. Besides, who was she any longer to demand an audience with the king? She was grateful for the loyalty of Dr. Argentine and her two ladies. She had dismissed Dr. de Serigo many months ago, and he had returned to Italy.

She was more and more convinced that her boys had been put to death or she would never have otherwise agreed to the Beaufort woman's scheme to marry Bess to Henry of Richmond. But she needed to know for sure. Poor boys, she thought, close to tears, they were but innocents in this game of kings. She tried to comfort herself by imagining them playing fox and geese together in heaven, but it was fleeting. She had to think about the here and now. If her sons could not be kings, she would wield power again as mother of a queen. Richard may have stripped her of her title, but Elizabeth Woodville had not forgotten how to scheme. She firmly believed Richard would be overthrown if not by this rebellion, then by another, and when Henry Tudor mounted the throne, her Bess would be queen.

She suddenly thumped her free arm on the bed, startling Argentine. "Damn him!" she expostulated, and the doctor assumed she was referring to the king and hid a smile. But Elizabeth was thinking of Edward and how her husband had put her in this disastrous position. How could he have lied to her when he begged her to marry him all those years ago? she asked herself again, knowing he was already pledged to Eleanor. Had he played the same game with her? How ardently he had wooed her, cajoled her to sleep with him, and finally agreed to wed her in secret if she did. This pattern seemed to verify Stillington's revelation, she reluctantly concluded.

She sighed and turned her attention on Argentine.

"When will the king return, do you know, doctor?"

Argentine was wary; his future depended on it. He busied himself cleaning his fleeming knives and carefully covering the bowl of blood that he would inspect more thoroughly in his own closet. He needed to strike a balance between pleasing his patron, the queen, and not denouncing the new regime too loudly until it was clear what role Elizabeth would play in it.

"'Tis said the king has quickly put down the rebellion in the west country, your grace. Those executed numbered only twelve in all, including my lord Buckingham. It seems his grace was merciful, thanks be to God; it could have been many more."

Elizabeth summoned her courage to ask: "Is there word of my son, the marquess?" She prayed hard that he was not among the dozen put to death.

"Have you not been advised, your grace?" Argentine asked, surprised. "His lordship took ship for Brittany with many others to join Henry Tudor."

"Then you bring the best of tidings, doctor," Elizabeth cried, her spirits lifting. "I believe I feel better already."

Thankfully for Jane, she only had to endure two days of incarceration before she was summoned before the court. Once again, she was first led into the small chamber below the cell where she recognized the broad chest and pleasant face of Thomas Lyneham. This time she did not curtsey but met his gaze, relieved she did not look as disheveled as she had before, although a welt stood out on her cheek.

"Mistress Shore, we meet again," he began, no apparent disapproval in his tone although he frowned on seeing her injury. The Yorkshire burr was not unpleasant, Jane noticed this time. In fact it was rather appealing, given that it was spoken in a deep baritone. "Have you written any more poems?"

The question startled Jane, and she could not help but laugh. "You remembered, Master Lyneham. In a strange coincidence, it happens I composed one just last night, but sadly I lacked parchment and pen to record it for posterity. But I do not think you are here to listen to my recital of it, brilliant though cheerless it may be. Prison seems to inspire maudlin musings in me. Do you have news?"

"You may leave us, warden," Lyneham addressed the gapmouthed gaoler who appeared confounded by the exchange. "Do not bother to lock the door. I doubt I have anything to fear from Mistress Shore, except for her sharp wit." He waited until the man had left and began to pace the room, trying to tame an unaccustomed feeling of tenderness toward this prisoner. What it was about the petite woman that fascinated him, he could not rightly say, but he had thought of her often in the months following their first encounter.

Thomas Lyneham, the fourth son of eight children in a family of the northern gentry, had grown up knowing that his inheritance, if any, would be small, and he would have to live by his own wits. He had attended school and was soon better read than his teacher. Since apprenticing as a clerk of the court in York as a fifteen-year-old, he had spent the best part of his thirty-eight years diligently working his way up the legal ladder. Fortune had favored him when he came to the attention of the young duke of Gloucester at Middleham, whose legal mind had impressed him and whose trustworthiness and morality had earned him Thomas's deep respect. Sent to pass sentence on Jane Shore in June, he had been somewhat offended by Richard's command, believing he had more important cases to attend to. But as soon as he had come face-to-face with the notorious Mistress Shore, he had been strangely drawn to her.

A man with healthy appetites and a handsome appearance, he had not wanted for women whenever he had the time, but he had never formed an attachment nor had he seen the need for a wife. He enjoyed the company of his fellow lawyers and the men on the king's council who had befriended him, and his work had satisfied his intellect. He thrived upon his bachelorhood. He had risen in Richard's esteem precisely because whenever Richard needed legal advice, Thomas was to hand. His rival for the king's favor was the obsequious Catesby, a man Thomas did not trust. In fact, Lyneham's duty at Ludgate in June had felt doubly degrading because Catesby had been the one to delegate the task to him.

But when Richard had mentioned someone would have to interrogate the concubine Jane Shore in the matter of the marquess of Dorset's treason, Thomas had stepped forward and volunteered. Catesby had sniggered. "Fancy the whore, do you, Lyneham?" he had hissed out of Richard's earshot. "Well, why should you not help yourself? Everyone else has."

Thomas grimaced at the insult now as he paced back and forth. He was hoping to dispel the unsettling feelings Jane still evoked in him. Perhaps Catesby was right, perhaps he did desire her. He told himself she was a common whore, but he knew after their first meeting that this was not true. She was well born of a respected and reputable mercer and former alderman. Her mother's family were also guild members, and one of her brothers was a parish priest. And she was bright and witty; nay, this was no common strumpet.

Coming to a standstill and gazing down at her beauty, he knew she was now at his mercy, and he was uncomfortably aware of his power over her.

His task in this day's interrogation was to discern whether she had intelligence of the queen's or Dorset's plans; he had made up his mind that if Jane gave him any information, he would ask Richard to dismiss the harlotry charge. He just hoped he would not have to resort to torture. The newfangled rack was being touted as the most efficient way to extract confessions from suspects, but Thomas thought his master would balk at torturing a woman, so he prayed it would not come to that.

While she waited, Jane studied Thomas just as frankly. His pacing was methodical, and his choice of plain yet well-cut garments, his immaculately groomed head and hands, and quiet dignity told her he was a modest man with no desire to be noticed except as the king's loyal servant and competent solicitor. She decided she liked him; she was not exactly afraid, but she was wary. He had her fate in his hands, albeit ultimately to be decided by his sovereign.

"Firstly, did the warden inflict that bruise on your face?" he asked. Seeing assent in her downcast eyes, he clucked his tongue. "I shall take action only when this is over. I would not want him to take revenge."

"I am grateful, sir," Jane responded, lifting her head.

"I must ask you," the lawyer continued, as if it pained him to ask, "if it is true you have been living in sin with Thomas, marquess of Dorset."

Jane did not flinch. She did not want to lie to this man, and so she answered simply, "I would correct your tense, Master Lyneham. I *was* living with him, but not since September." Tom's face floated into her mind, and she was surprised at the vehemence with which she added under her breath: "And I swear I never shall again."

Thomas pretended he had not heard, but he was relieved to know Jane might be finished with the marquess. "Has he corresponded with you since you parted? Do you know where he went and with whom?"

Jane looked down at the wooden floor and flushed slightly. Being ignorant of the latest events in the insurgency, she had no idea where Tom was or what he was planning, but she did have one piece of intelligence that might or might not be significant: he had gone to join his uncle, the bishop of Salisbury. Part of her wanted to protect her former lover, but, like a worm eating away at a corpse, the pain he had inflicted still gnawed at her. She looked back up at Lyneham and was astonished to detect compassion in his eyes. Why should he care about her? she wondered.

"Mistress Shore, I understand your reluctance to speak, but I must remind you that you are in the king's custody, and I would strongly advise you not to lie. This is treasonous business, and you should look to your own well-being now. If you insist on concealing something, I am bound by my position as king's solicitor to turn you over to someone who will help you remember. Do I make myself clear?"

Jane paled. "You mean torture, Master Lyneham?" Was what little she knew about Tom worth being stretched upon the rack for? She hesitated and then decided she must protect herself now. Reaching into her bodice, she brought out the ragged piece of vellum on which Tom had written his farewell. "This was the last I heard of him, I swear. I found it on the table of our hiding place in Bosse Alley when he left me without a word, and"—she paused, fury choking her—"he stole every penny I had." Brushing away an angry tear, she handed the paper to the lawyer. "Now you know as much as I do, sir, I swear."

Scanning the few lines of untidy script, he was relieved and glad, not merely as a lawyer, that she had kept this piece of evidence. "I am grateful for this, madam, for not only does this prove your story, but it should also ease your conscience about betraying the man."

Jane stared glumly at the floor. "No more than he betrayed me, Master Lyneham. I kept it to protect myself, 'tis all."

Thomas nodded. "Very astute, if I may say, but you need not have worried, for it seems we know much more than you, mistress. The marquess escaped the king's army and has fled, like the traitor he is, into exile in Brittany." He was satisfied from her look of surprise that she was no longer in contact with Grey. He folded the paper carefully, and tucking it into his doublet, he found himself remarking: "If I may say, he was not worthy of you," and he walked toward the door.

His kind words reluctantly undid Jane's resolve, and she hid her face in her hands. "You must think me a milksop. I do not often cry in front of strangers. Forgive me . . ."

Dismayed, Thomas was beside her before she could finish, and gentling her hands away from her face, he assured her, "I do not think you are foolish or a milksop, Jane. I think you are a fine woman who has had an unlucky turn upon the wheel of fortune." He gave her his spotless kerchief to wipe away her tears. Patting the note in his jacket, he told her, "I will see what I can do to mollify the king. He has been merciful to the rebel traitors so far; I think I have influence enough to persuade him to extend that mercy to you. Have no fear; I shall postpone the hearing and do my best so that you may be released soon."

How could he promise all this? he asked himself. And, more important, why had he promised it? He had never let his heart interfere in his work before. But there was something about Jane Shore that made him want to protect her, and God help him, he thought he might be falling in love with her. Having had no particular opinion of the marquess of Dorset, he now felt like strangling the arrogant young coward.

Jane blew her nose and then looked guiltily at the soiled kerchief and up at its owner. "You will not want it back now," she
said with a watery smile.

"Keep it as a memento, Jane," Lyneham said, kindly. "I hope
it will convince you that not all men are varlets. Now, take heart.
I will come again as soon as the king returns to London and I
have news for you."

His gentle manner and promise of help moved Jane to reach
out and touch his arm. "I shall not forget you, Master Lyneham,
with or without the kerchief."

He could not help smiling, but then he wondered: was she
playing him? He dismissed the unkind thought, admiring how she
walked out of the room with quiet dignity and submitted to the
waiting warden's custody without a word. He reminded himself
she had probably not even noticed him as a man at all.

But Jane never missed the signs of her evident effect on men.
She did not mind climbing the stairs and returning to the cold,
dank cell, feeling delivered from the filth and her fear of the place.

Anne sidled up and said: "Odd's bodkins, Jane, what happened
down there? You look like the cat who ate the cream."

"I know not why, Anne, but I think the king's solicitor is taken
with me."

Jane's intuition had not let her down. Thomas gathered up his
papers when Jane had left the room, unable to get her out of his
mind. Had she bewitched him? He drew in a sharp breath, and
for a second he thought about the first charge Richard had laid
against the woman: witchery. But he immediately dismissed the
notion. There was nothing mystical or secretive about her; she
had not even as much as invoked a saint's name in his presence,
let alone any minion of the devil. Her charms were earthbound,
rooted in her very human sensuality, her keen intelligence, and her
lively sense of humor.

But was she purposely drawing him in? Did she hope he would ask her to be his leman when her ordeal in gaol was over? Was that her aim? Nay, he had sensed nothing but candor from her in their two meetings, and he speculated it was what he found so attractive.

As he mounted his horse and prepared to return to Westminster, he had to admit he had therefore been disappointed to learn of her illicit liaison with Dorset, and so soon after her penance. But perhaps, he defended her, she had had no other choice. For nine years she had been kept by one nobleman or another, and had Edward grown tired of her and not died when he had, Jane, like her predecessors, might have been sent away and quietly given another husband, or been wedded to the church. It had often crossed his mind that women were always dependent upon the men in their lives, and he had long ago decided he was glad to have been born a man.

He had learned of Jane's unusual annulment through the grumpy old cleric at the Court of Arches. Poor Jane! To be saddled with an impotent husband must have been difficult, especially for one whose very being spoke of a passionate nature. She must have wanted to run home to her father's loving arms, he thought sadly. He then discovered that soon after the divorce from William Shore, King Edward had set his sights on her. From all he had heard about Edward, Thomas imagined Jane would not have been able to resist, and whether by consent or no, Jane would have been foolish to refuse the king. He understood that. More difficult to understand was her immediate yielding to Lord Hastings's advances, and then to the marquess of Dorset. Where did he fit in? And where had she found the time? He had abused her kindness, Thomas thought angrily.

He brought himself up sharply and tugged a little too roughly on the reins, making his horse toss her head. What was he thinking? Was he really contemplating offering Jane Shore his protection? Did he really want to join the ranks of her lovers? He laughed out loud as he imagined the king's face when he learned his solicitor was sinning with Jane Shore. What a fool he was. He risked losing everything he had worked for all these years. And besides, what made him think she would agree? But if she did, and if he risked everything, could loving Jane Shore fulfill him more than his work?

If he believed his feisty older sister, Elizabeth, it could. Many years ago, when he had comforted her on the death of her husband, she had taken his arm as they walked by the lake and confided: "I am one of the fortunate women in this hard world. I found true love with my Rob. Happily he was eligible, and Father let me wed him. Trust me, Tommy, there is naught so fulfilling as the reciprocal love of husband and wife. It is that loss I am grieving, and because of my children, I must find a husband to care for us, but I despair of ever knowing true love again. Never wed without love, Tommy, or you will miss the greatest of God's gifts."

Thomas had not thought on that conversation in years, yet now it resonated like an oft-recited prayer. He frowned. His heart urged him to woo Jane, but his head deplored the idea. What fools love makes of us, he thought ruefully. Returning to the meeting with Jane of a few minutes before, he recalled her sea green eyes, first sparkling with humor and then with tears, her graceful carriage, and her dainty figure. And he could recall every word she had spoken and describe every gesture. He realized then without equivocation that he desired her. However, in that moment he knew it was as his wife and not as his mistress that he wanted her.

Giving himself a confident nod, he kicked his mare's flanks and cantered back to Westminster. He had made up his mind. He would wed Jane Shore, if she would have him.

The very next day, Thomas was back at Ludgate, much to the warden's surprise, and he asked the warden for a chair.

"You need to see Mistress Shore again, master lawyer? She will be honored, I'm sure," he said snidely, affecting his version of a gentleman's nasal drawl. "And shall I fetch the whore at once?"

It was all Thomas could do to stop punching the man in his good eye. "Until she is proven one, you will refer to the prisoner as Mistress Shore, do you understand? And you will respect her," he threatened. "I know of what you are capable. Now go."

A few minutes later, the sullen warden entered with Jane, who had begged Anne that morning to braid her hair and arrange it on the top of her head. She had forsaken her soiled hood, and having no headcovering made her, even at thirty-one, look like a girl again. The perfection of her head and neck thus revealed left Thomas in no doubt she was the loveliest woman he had ever seen. To cover his open admiration, he bowed over her hand, dismissing the warden with a wave.

"Sit here, Jane, if you please. I am happy to see your cheek is almost healed," Thomas began, standing behind her chair as if they were at table. Performing little tasks would help calm him, he decided. He had asked for ale and poured her a cup. "You seem surprised to see me so soon."

Jane had indeed been surprised to be summoned. The lawyer seemed nervous, she noticed, and her stomach lurched. He must have ill tidings for her, she imagined. Sweet Virgin Mary, what was to become of her now? That night she had dreamed of Will, that he had come into the cell and taken her in his arms when all of a sudden his familiar, lined face had dissolved into Master Lyneham's more youthful one. She had awakened puzzled, but perhaps it had merely presaged his visit this morning and nothing more. Believing the lawyer had bad news, Jane decided to try humor.

"Master Lyneham, it cannot be that you missed your kerchief so greatly." She hoped he saw amusement and not the wariness in her eyes, but she continued nervously in the same bantering tone, trying to calm herself. "I can assure you, I am keeping it safe. Or did you forget to say something yesterday?" She looked for any sign to verify her intuition, but as he was pacing in his usual measured way, she could not read him. "Am I to be punished, sir?" she finally found the courage to ask, her fear getting the better of her. "I beg of you tell me quickly."

Thomas stopped and swiveled back to her, and Jane saw only boyish embarrassment.

"I hope you will look on me as your champion, Jane," Thomas began softly, toying with a ring on his index finger. "And you have guessed correctly. I did forget to say something yesterday."

Jane stiffened. "Do you have another question? I assure you, I know no more about . . ."

"Nay, I am not here for that, today."

"No?"

"No." How was he to come to his point? She might laugh at him or be insulted he was not busy working for her release. He jammed the ring back on his finger and swung round to face the window. Had he lost his mind? Richard would never sanction him wedding the sinful Mistress Shore. He took a deep breath, his shoulders rising to meet his ears, and exhaled slowly.

"The reason is more personal." He saw her stiffen and hurried on. "My work requires me to thoroughly research all of my cases, and thus I know you are now alone, without means of support. I have come to propose a solution, a way out of your dilemma. I was wondering if you would consider—"

"Becoming your mistress?" Jane cried, standing, her eyes blazing and her fists clenched. "Why, you hypocrite! You have led me to believe you and your king are determined to punish me for harlotry, when you have been planning to drag me back into it as soon as I am released. 'Tis monstrous! Aye, I was a concubine, but I have my pride. Do you think I cannot survive without any of you? You are wrong. I can and I will."

Thomas was horrified. He held up his hand and tried to interject. "Nay, nay, you are mistaken, Jane. Hush, I beg of you," he said, gently urging her to sit and hear him out. God's bones, he realized, certes she would think first of that. It was what she had come to expect of life—and of men. Seeing her so distressed doubled his resolve to end her dependence on the kind of man who had selfishly used her until now.

"You are wrong, Mistress Shore. I had no intention of asking you to be my leman. But I do wish to ask you to be my wife." He was down on one knee, his face shining with his honest, earnest offer of an equality that Jane had never known with a man. "From the first day we met, I have not stopped thinking of you. I want you to share my life, become my partner, through the good times and the bad, and be together when God calls one of us to his side."

Jane was speechless. His declaration had taken her breath away, and all she could do was stare at him in disbelief. Why would this upstanding, successful man be willing to wed a fallen woman? How could he be sure of his mind and heart so soon? His proposal was so dizzying, she wondered if she had dreamed it. "Tell me I am dreaming," she finally stammered.

Thomas took her hand and kissed it. "'Tis no dream, Jane. Can you not feel the touch of my lips? In truth, I love you. The strength of my feelings took me by surprise, too," he said, smiling wryly, "but please believe me, it has been growing in my heart unawares since we met in June. Only yesterday, when I saw you again, did I know it for what it was."

Jane looked down at the hand holding hers and pondered this remarkable declaration of love. "First let me thank you for your generous proposal, Master Lyneham—"

"Thomas, my name is Thomas," he interrupted. "Call me Thomas."

"Thomas," she echoed. "You must give me time to digest this extraordinary offer. I do believe you mean your words sincerely, but to take me to wife would surely sully your name and reputation. I do not know if I can bear such responsibility. You are too generous. Let me say, I have no doubt you would make a fine husband, but not for the likes of me. Not for the infamous Mistress Shore."

"You think I have not considered everything, Jane? I have. As for your past reputation, it is simply that—the past—and I am talking about the future. I love you. I want to put the smile back in your eyes, the joy back in your step. I am serious when I say that I was smitten the first time I saw you. I do not understand it, but 'tis true. And me, a confirmed bachelor." He held her hand in both of his. "I will work every day to prove my love is true, and I dare to hope that you will grow to love me, too, because I will defend and care for you for the rest of this life."

Jane thought her heart would burst. She had waited for so many years to hear Tom Grey express such love, and yet before her stood a stranger, a man risking ridicule and rejection for love of her. Dear St. Elizabeth, she addressed her namesake, this would be no marriage of convenience or business proposition, as she had had with William Shore. Could Master Lyneham really be offering a marriage of equal partners, and if he were willing, why should she not accept him?

She placed her other hand on his and smiled at him. "You must give me time to absorb this, Thomas." He nodded happily as she raised him up and stood before him. "While I await the king's pleasure, perhaps we can find time to know each other better." And she reached up and kissed his cheek.

His lips were on hers before she could take another breath, and had she not been so caught by surprise at his passion, she might have pulled away. Instead she allowed herself the luxury of once more feeling desired.

When he released her, she seized the moment. "I have one condition, however, Thomas." She looked up earnestly at him and pleaded, "That you work to release me from this dreadful place as soon as you possibly can."

The unusual courtship of the moral lawyer and the captive concubine had begun. Jane had been allotted an hour each day to walk with Thomas around the courtyard of St. Paul's when he was able to leave his work at Westminster to visit her. Even in the cold November drizzle, the couple kept to their schedule and would huddle in their cloaks close to the cathedral wall. For those precious minutes, Jane felt freed, and she counted the hours when she would breathe the fresh air and enjoy conversing with Thomas again. In those intense and condensed sixty-minute walks, she had learned to trust him, and she found herself revealing more and more of her fears and hopes to the sympathetic Thomas. For her part, Jane had discovered he liked poetry, and she would write little verses that enchanted him.

One day, she told him her name was really Elizabeth, and he was delighted.

"I have a sister of the same name," he replied, explaining that she had lost her beloved husband early in their marriage. "She has two little boys, hellions to be honest, but she remarried and lives in York, and thus I do not have to overly suffer them," he had told her, laughing. And then he admitted it was this sister's advice he had heeded when he had come courting Jane.

"Do you not like children, then?" Jane had asked tentatively. "It has been my cross to bear that I have none of my own, although Sophie's four look upon me as a second mother."

Thomas cleared his throat. "Then I shall hope to have a daughter after witnessing what mayhem my nephews can cause."

Those close to Jane would have been astonished to see her blush at the insinuation he wanted children with her. A woman who had bedded a king, a marquess, and a lord chamberlain was surely beyond modesty, they would have said. But Jane was feeling as though she had been reborn with this man. He was not afraid to talk to her of love, and not since Will Hastings had she enjoyed this degree of friendship with a man.

After the third walk together she had returned to her prison cell and admitted to Anne she might be able to love again.

"You deserve a good man," Anne had declared, "especially after that bum-bailey Tom Grey." Jane had used worse words to describe him in her thoughts but did not wish to shock young Anne.

One day Thomas told Jane he had to seek the king's approval of the marriage. "He has honored me much, and I must do my duty by him. He should know my intention." He admitted he was risking his position, and Jane cautioned him to think carefully about angering the king.

"Look what happened to me," she reminded him, gently. "He may be moral, but he is not always kind."

But Thomas thought he knew his master, and besides he was determined to win Jane.

Richard could not resist a small smile as he dictated the letter addressed to his chancellor, the bishop of Lincoln. He wondered if Russell would see the irony but doubted the capable but insufferably dour man would be anything other than astonished.

"*Right Reverend Father in God,*" he began as John Kendall's goose quill scratched on the vellum.

> "*Signifying unto you that it has been brought to our attention that our servant and solicitor, Thomas Lyneham, marvelously blinded and abused with the former wife of William Shore, now being in the Ludgate by our commandment, has made a contract of matrimony with her, as it is said, and intends, to our marvel, to proceed to effect the same.*"

John Kendall could not help remarking, "Your grace, I see now why you were smiling. Is Thomas in his right mind? I have not seen the lady, but she has quite a reputation for beauty and—" He broke off when he saw the king's smile fade, and he bent his head to the parchment.

Richard went on more seriously.

*"We, for many causes, would be sorry that he should be so
disposed, and pray you therefore to send for him and that you
will have the goodness to exhort and stir him to the contrary.
And if you find him utterly set for to marry her and none
otherwise would be advertised, then, if it may stand with the
law of the church, we be content (the time of the marriage
being deferred to our coming next to London) that upon
sufficient assurance that her demeanor is good, you send for
her keeper and discharge him of our commandment."*

He paused, looking out of the window of the little manor
house where he was temporarily lodged in Devon. "She needs to
be housed somewhere suitable before her marriage—if Lyneham
decides he must have her. Where should I send her, John? She has
no residence, as far as I know."

"Her father was an alderman, your grace. John Lambert is an
upstanding citizen and mercers' guild member. Surely he would
take her?"

"Perfect," Richard said, beaming at his secretary.

*"And in the meantime committing her to the rule and guiding
of her father or any other suitable at your discretion."**

"My father?" Jane repeated, and Thomas was dismayed to see
the look of horror cross his betrothed's face upon his next visit to
Ludgate. "Must I?"

"But, my dear, it also means you are pardoned and free to go,"
Thomas reiterated.

He had been thoughtful after his meeting with Bishop Russell,
who had given Lyneham Richard's response. The bishop had construed

---

* actual text

Richard's letter to mean that Thomas might lose the king's favor—not to mention his position—if he chose Jane, but Thomas refused to be deterred. He had not worked for Richard all these years without recognizing the humor in his master's words of caution and disapproval. And even if Russell were right and Richard did dismiss him, he was so enamored of Jane and had so embraced the idea of marriage with her that he was prepared to sacrifice his position.

Not long after receiving Richard's letter, when Thomas sensed the softening of Jane's heart, he told her of it, and although he had hoped for Richard's goodwill, the king's answer was one he could abide by. In truth, it had been more generous than he had hoped.

He knelt beside the pensive Jane, who was trying to imagine her father's greeting. "What is wrong with returning to your home for a few weeks while we post the banns?" he asked. "It seems we do not have a choice, as there is no one else Richard would sanction." His eyes were alight with humor. "Or I could arrange for you to stay here."

They both laughed.

"Aye, you are right," Jane acknowledged. "Hosier Lane is the only logical choice. Jehan Vandersand does not quite enjoy the same respectability as my father." She had told him only the basic facts about her father and mother, that she had grown up as one of six children and that her sister had died giving birth. During one of their walks Thomas had suspected there was more to Jane's offhand comment that she was a disappointment to her father, but he had chosen not to pry. After all, they had a lifetime together to reveal their histories, he thought, although he predicted his story would be somewhat less dramatic.

"My father was furious when I left William Shore," she explained, turning her new betrothal ring on her index finger. Thomas had chosen an oval stone of green-gray jasper set in silver, and told her the stone was an ancient talisman thought to ward off evil spirits. "I could not resist it, Jane, when I recognized in the stone the color of your eyes," he told her, touching her deeply.

Jane stared down at it, still not quite believing her good fortune. "My father disowned me when I became Edward's concubine. I do not believe he has ever forgiven me, Thomas. That is why I dread going home," she confessed.

Thomas knew then what he must do.

"What can I do for you, Master Lyneham?" John Lambert was unctuous. He could see the lawyer was a gentleman. "A new gown perhaps? Something for your wife?"

Thomas smiled. "I thank you, but not today, Mercer Lambert. I wonder if we might speak privately? I have a personal matter of some importance to discuss with you." He had done his research and was not surprised by the impressive stock in the Lamberts' mercery. The man had several apprentices, he noted as he followed John up the stairs to a private room.

"A personal matter, Master Lyneham?"

Thomas decided he needed to win over Jane's father as soon as possible, so he uncharacteristically resorted to bragging. "I am his grace, King Richard's solicitor general," he began and knew from the glint in Lambert's eyes that he had chosen the right approach. "I have been put in charge of your daughter Jane's case before the court—"

"What again!" John interrupted. "The harlot is in prison again? On what charge this time, Lawyer Lyneham?" John stalked to the window and threw open the casement. How much more could a father take, he thought, anger gripping him. He could not pretend that Jane's humiliating penance had hurt his business; it had not. People had come to commiserate and had often left with an ell or two of fabric. He looked down and was dismayed to see copious mouse droppings under the window and surreptitiously scraped them out of sight with his foot as he turned to face Thomas. "Tell my daughter I will not pay her fine, whatever it is."

Thomas calmed himself. For Jane's sake, he must maintain a civil, if not pleasant, tone to his voice, but he understood now why Jane was afraid of her father. "She will be released very shortly, sir, and the charges will be dismissed. 'Twas a misunderstanding, and she has helped with our enquiries with regard to the recent rebellions."

"What a fool and an ingrate that Buckingham was," John snapped. "He deserved what was coming to him."

"Certes he did, Mercer Lambert," Thomas agreed. Now for the difficult part of the interview, he thought. Although usually implacable when defending a client or arguing a point on the king's council, he found himself perspiring. "The main reason for my visit is to discuss what happens to Mistress Shore after she leaves the Ludgate."

"She will resort to whoring again, no doubt," John interrupted with disgust. "She is good for nothing else."

Thomas had had enough. "I forbid you to use those terms when you are referring to the woman I intend to make my wife. I came here to beg your good favor in my suit, and that I shall be offering her a home and a future with me of which you should approve. I can see that I have perhaps wasted my time."

John dropped his jaw. "You would *wed* Jane? The king's solicitor would wed the royal mistress? You must be jesting with me, sir," he said scornfully, "or else my daughter has bewitched you."

"She is bewitching, Master Lambert, and I have the greatest admiration for her. She is a courageous, loyal woman and I will be honored to call her my wife. Now, do I have your good will?"

John sat down heavily in his oversize armchair and stared at the lawyer. "Well, I . . . well, I never did," he stammered. "The king's solicitor. What will Amy say? My wife, you understand." He took a deep breath and let out a low whistle, his mind grappling with this extraordinary development. "And Jane has accepted you, sir?" When he saw Lyneham's nod, he continued, "Then I certainly have no objections. No objections at all. God go with both of you." His mood lightened as he eased himself from the chair. "This is good news. Very good news," he declared, and finally showing Thomas some respect, he grasped the lawyer's arm and pumped it as if he were an old friend.

Thomas allowed himself a smile, for Jane's sake. "I am glad you will give us your blessing"—he paused for effect—"as has the king himself. In fact, his grace has commanded that before the marriage, Jane be placed under your roof, Master Lambert. I trust I may tell the king that Jane will be *safe* here." He emphasized the word and let the remark hang between them.

John was visibly flustered. "The king wishes this? You astonish me, sir. It seemed six months ago he wished for nothing but my daughter's head. Now he cares for her well-being. He is a puzzling man."

Thomas had to agree. "You have the measure of his grace, sir. He despises disloyalty and he abhors immorality, but he respects the law and acts to uphold it. He is, also, often merciful." He lowered his voice and confided, "But I would not go against his express command, Master Lambert. So will you receive Jane when she is released this week and treat her kindly?"

John was impressed with the young man. He was bold without being patronizing, and he had won over the irascible mercer with reason and respect. Aye, he would make a fair and prosperous son-in-law, he decided, with relief. As long as Jane would now be respectable and somebody else's responsibility, he could tolerate her presence again. "My wife and I will ready Jane's old room, and she will be quite safe," he promised.

King Richard returned to London on the twenty-fifth of November accompanied by an impressive array of dignitaries, who had left London to meet the victorious king at Kennington Palace on the south bank of the Thames and escort him along the mile to Southwark and over London Bridge. Londoners cheered their mayor and aldermen, all clothed in scarlet, who headed the procession of five hundred guild members and other leading men of the city in their violet gowns.

Once housed at the King's Wardrobe on Carter Lane, Richard was as good as his word in his letter to Bishop Russell. After learning that his solicitor general was still determined to have his Mistress Shore, Richard swiftly pardoned Jane.

And so, Jane went home to Hosier Lane at yuletide to a civil welcome from her father and a joyful one from her mother. Lying in her old tester bed, the familiar story of Mary Magdalene stitched into its rich tapestry curtain, and Ankarette snoring contentedly next to her, Jane thought back to the last night she had spent there. How different that wedding eve had been from the one she was looking forward to in the very near future. She hugged herself. She still could not believe her good fortune, nor could she believe that her heart, so badly trodden upon by Tom Grey, had miraculously healed and was opening to another man, who might turn out to be the best of them all. A smile curled her mouth as she remembered that familiar bursting sensation in her chest when she had first realized she was in love again.

It had happened the day she was released when Thomas came to accompany her to Hosier Lane. Once out of sight of the prying eyes of the prisoners, Jane had no sooner taken the first intoxicating breath of freedom when Thomas had suddenly pulled her into a doorway and taken her in a fierce embrace. When his mouth crushed down on hers and his tongue moved to separate her lips, Jane's body responded with its old fire. They stood locked thus for what seemed like minutes, and Jane could feel Thomas's hardness against her for the first time. She knew then, she desired him as much as he did her.

"You see," she told herself, her youthful fancies flown, "the poets were wrong. There can be true love in wedlock. Love is not only real when 'tis done in secret, and when I marry Thomas Lyneham, I shall tell anyone who will listen."

NINETEEN

J ane was touched by her mother's pleasure at her return.

"There was never a day when you were not in my thoughts," Amy said as the two women sat cozily together plying their needles. "So many questions I have for you, and three short weeks to ask them." She shooed her maidservant from the room and lowered her voice. "What was King Edward really like, Jane? Were you not afraid?"

Jane's eyes were merry at the memory. "Certes, I was afraid the first time I met him, but he was so charming and easy to talk to, I was soon emboldened to speak my mind. It seems he liked women of spirit: his mother and his queen are thus, and I can attest to the queen's frankness, Mother," she said, laughing at the memory. "Let me tell you of the time she lost her dog." Jane's ability to bring a scene to life and merrily make fun of herself had Amy laughing and regretting the years she had not had her quick-witted daughter for company.

And thus they whiled away many a happy hour during the days before the wedding, Jane learning much about her brothers, and of nieces and nephews she had never known and looked forward to meeting. One day, her mother confided her unhappiness following Isabel's death, and how, all alone in the house, she had had thoughts of taking her own life. "My children were everything to me once your father soured toward me early in our marriage. I had lost you and then Bella, and now Master Allen has another wife and the children a new mother. We see them rarely, as he is removed to Kent."

"But you did not commit that sin, Mother. You are still here and still lovely."

"Flatterer!" Amy retorted, but she was pleased. "Something happened when Bella left us," she went on pensively, "and for you 'twill be hard to believe. Your father began to look at me with more than mere tolerance. He changed, Jane. He softened, and for the first time in our marriage, he began to show me respect—and more than that, he has shown that he loves me."

Jane was astonished at her mother's honest declaration, and putting her mending down, she embraced Amy fondly. She would never now bring up those times when she had felt betrayed by Amy's weakness. Better than anyone, she now knew that every person must walk her own path in her own way and should not be judged by others.

"If you want to make me happier, my child, I would wish for a rapprochement between you and your father." When Jane tried to demur, Amy held up her hand. "I know well why you must despise him, but for my sake, can you not forgive him in your heart? He does love you in his own way, I promise you. It was just that you were always . . ."

"Defying him," Jane admitted, bitterly. "He drove me from this house with his abuse and into a wretched marriage. I was so miserable. 'Twas no wonder I could not refuse the king's advances." She softened, remembering. "Edward loved me, you know."

Amy's tone was gentle. "I understand your reluctance to forgive your father, but I shall pray for it every day, nonetheless."

That night Jane pondered her father's changed behavior, and looking back over the fortnight she had been in Hosier Lane, she admitted he seemed a quieter, more amiable man. He had not lectured her nor gloated on her fall from grace, but Jane had taken pains to disappear as much as she could when he was at home, knowing she must be a burden on him.

Aye, she had seen what harm a dour perspective on life could wreak on a person, thinking of King Richard, whose demeanor was that of a man old before his time; this was not the same carefree young duke who had captured Kate Haute's heart. His hatred of his brother's way of life had made him bitter, angry, and had hardened his heart. Was she also guilty of a hard heart when it came to her father? Was that the same heart she was offering Thomas?

"May I speak with you, Father?" Jane asked quietly, turning back instead of following her mother from the hall after supper. "It will not take long."

Amy heard the calm in Jane's voice, and assuming she was seeking advice about the marriage contract or some other business matter, she felt it was safe to leave these two volatile people alone together. Amy was glad Jane had taken the initiative and not used her as a mediator.

"As you wish, daughter." John watched Amy go and sat down again, folding his hands on the table in front of him. He had no idea what Jane wanted to say, but he had been pleased with her modesty and respectfulness since her return.

She smoothed the back of her new madder woolen gown as she settled on the bench and to reinforce her courage, Jane fiddled with the emerald ring Edward had given her, which was the only item left of her former jewels. "Before I go to be wed and leave this house anew, I would like us to be reconciled, Father." John's eyebrows shot up, but he let her finish. "I have thought hard about what I am about to say, and I pray you will consider it well."

John leaned back in his chair and moved his hands to his lap. "Go on, Jane. I am listening."

"I know I have not been the daughter you would have wished, and I acknowledge the many mistakes I have made in my life. If I have hurt and embarrassed you, then I am heartily sorry for it." Her father gave an imperceptible nod of agreement, but he said nothing. "Aye, I apologize for my mistakes, but"—she took a deep breath—"in my defense, when I was a child you showed me no particular affection and instead lavished it all upon Isabel." She observed John's discomfort now and so hurried on. "I missed your love, Father, and I know now that I misbehaved to get your attention. I do not believe I did it to spite you but to make you look my way and see a little girl who craved a father's love."

John could not help but interrupt now. "Aye," he said, getting to his feet, "you got my attention right well enough. Is that why you abandoned your husband and became a harlot?"

Jane bit back a natural retort and instead ignored the insult. "You forced me to marry William Shore, Father, and I would have done my duty and stayed with him if he had not been incapable of a loving thought or giving me children. Have pity, Father. I saw a way out and I took it. You were not disposed to help me, were you?"

"You could have taken the veil," John shot back. "Were you seeking my attention when you walked the streets half naked for all the world to see?"

Jane gripped her fingers in her lap, determined to win this battle, which would require staying measured. "Again, Father, I am truly sorry for your humiliation, yours and Mother's. But a wise man once showed me how destructive hate and anger can be, and before I marry Thomas, I have promised myself I would beg for your forgiveness, just as I forgive you now your hard-heartedness to me when I was young. Can you not see? We have both hurt each other—and my mother most of all—by our feuding. Please, Father, let us put our animosity behind us and be kind to each other for the remainder of the time God has given us." Then she went down on her knees in front of him. "I beg of you, say you forgive me, too."

Speechless, John stared down at his daughter; he had never been spoken to thus by any of his children. He saw the contrition in Jane's face, and, suddenly, struck by her resemblance to his wife, his heart softened. How glad he had been since Bella's death when he had come to understand what a jewel he had married. He had desperately tried to demonstrate his love for Amy since and compensate for the years of neglect. Had she not forgiven him? Aye, and what a pleasanter life they were leading now. Even his dealings with his customers had become more satisfying. He turned away and searched his conscience, recalling times he had rebuked Jane, slapped her, punished her—and for what? For physical gifts over which she had no control, for an inherited intelligence that had attracted him to woo Amy, and a personality that charmed where he could not. Had his behavior toward her truly led her to want to escape his authority?

He turned back. "You have spoken your piece bravely, daughter. I can see that you are changed by your experiences, and I like you better for it." He bent and raised her up. "You do not need to kneel to me, Jane"—he smiled wryly—"I am not the king. I am your father, and I am humbled that you have shown me the way to behave. I do forgive you, aye," he said, "but more than that, I am heartily sorry for having wronged you. I have heard of your good and generous spirit, and you should know that your mother and I are overjoyed to see you wed Master Lyneham. He is a fine man."

"Oh, Father," Jane cried, her tears blinked back. And for the first time in her life that she could remember, Jane went into his arms and knew a father's fond embrace.

Thinking it wise to inform his king of his intentions to wed Jane, Thomas did not wait long to meet with Richard, even if it meant putting his position as solicitor general in jeopardy, as had been implied in the king's letter. He did not wish to dishonor the trust Richard had placed in him all these years.

At the frosty meeting, Richard reeled off a list of Jane's sins, ending by reminding his solicitor, "She took her penance so lightly that she went straight to Dorset's bed not a month later. Do you truly wish her as your wife knowing all of this?"

Thomas did not hesitate in front of his king. "I do, your grace.

And I am prepared to accept the consequences. I believe Jane has a good heart and merely needs the strong, lasting love and respect of a husband to keep her from straying. I think I understand her, and I wish to care for her."

Richard relented then. "Very well, Thomas. I am right well pleased with your work these past difficult months and have always found you loyal. Thus I am disposed to keep you on my council." He held up his hand to quell the thanks Thomas was attempting to express. "But I warn you, one hint of misconduct from Mistress Shore and you will be dismissed."

"I understand fully, your grace, and I thank you." Thomas bowed low and assured his king he would work hard to deserve the royal magnanimity.

Richard had been disappointed that his beloved son Edward had not been in the cavalcade from Middleham when Anne arrived in mid-December to celebrate the yuletide season at Westminster. "He had a cold that he could not shake off," Anne told her husband. "I did not think it wise for him to travel, after the sickness he had at Pontefract in July. He has the best care in the world, Richard, and surely the bracing Yorkshire air is better for him than this damp." She wrinkled her pert nose. "It seems to seep into my bones when I am here. I am grateful for all the fireplaces. Edward spared no expense to make Westminster comfortable, I will allow him that."

Richard grinned. "Aye, we even have hot water in the conduit," he said, pointing to an decorative brass tap protruding from the wall. "You can bathe at any hour, provided they have stoked the fire under the cistern."

Again the nose-wrinkling. "'Tis not healthy to bathe in wintertime, my dear. My mother would never allow it."

"Aye, so you have told me on many occasions, Anne," Richard said patiently. He could not help but remember how Kate loved to bathe no matter the season, and he pushed out of his mind the image of her smooth, young body immersed in the scented water just before he would join her to make love. He refocused his attention on his wife, whom he loved dearly after all these years, but who, although devoted to him, did not possess Kate's passionate nature.

He watched now as Anne busied herself with her ladies, including his fifteen-year-old illegitimate daughter, Katherine, instructing them where to place her jewel chest, personal items, and her favorite Turkey carpet. He was glad she appeared to have put the deaths of his nephews from her mind, but he could not. He had hoped once he had given the order to execute Buckingham that the nightmare visions would disappear, but now Harry's fleshy face joined the boys' innocent ones to haunt and mock him. And it was a bad night when in one recurring dream Will Hastings's bloody head rolled down a hill toward him, its expression accusatory, as if to say, "Why me? What did I ever do to you, Richard of Gloucester?"

"My lord, a groat for your thoughts." Anne's voice jolted him from his reverie.

"Forgive me, my dear, I was thinking about Thomas, my solicitor," he fibbed. "Would you believe he wants to wed Jane Shore."

"How sweet," Anne replied, "but now I need your advice on which gown to wear for the Christmas banquet."

"Aye, my lord father," Katherine exclaimed, pulling him toward the collection of gowns strewn on the bed. "Which one?"

Richard allowed himself to be drawn into the decision making, and, putting his arm around his beautiful daughter, he gladly gave Anne his complete attention. Soon they chose a delicate blue and white overdress trimmed with Venetian lace, and Anne kissed him tenderly. "A man of good taste, your father," she informed Katherine kindly. "Always wed a man of good taste."

Unbeknownst to the king and queen of England, on that Christmas Day, in the great cathedral of Rennes a hundred leagues from Westminster, Henry Tudor, earl of Richmond, knelt at the altar in front of his fellow exiled compatriots and his host, the duke of Brittany, and pledged to wed Elizabeth of York should he return to his native land and win back the crown for Lancaster.

In her forlorn lodgings in Westminster sanctuary, Elizabeth Grey, as the former queen was now known, prayed she had done the right thing in facilitating the event. Would Edward have approved? She could not say, but her decision haunted her waking hours that yuletide season.

Thomas took care of all the legalities, and on one snowy January morning soon after Twelfth Night, he and Jane were married quietly with Jane's parents, Ankarette, Sophie and Jehan, and Thomas's superior and mentor, Morgan Kidwelly, in attendance. Jane's brother, Sir William Lambert, parson of the parish of St. Leonard's in Foster Lane, performed the brief ceremony outside the church door.

Jane wore a gown of palest green satin with an overdress of dark green velvet, a gift from her father. "The color of hope," she had assured Sophie as she went to be joined to Thomas, her golden hair loose about her shoulders like a maid, covered by a shimmering piece of gauze and crowned with ivy leaves. "Then your eyes are full with hope," Sophie whispered back. Even though Jane had just turned thirty-two, Sophie thought her friend had never looked more beautiful.

Thomas's hand was warm and reassuring when Jane gave him hers to receive his ring. "Wilt thou have this woman to thy wedded wife, wilt thou love her, and honor her, keep her and guard her, in sickness, as a husband should a wife, and forsaking all others on account of her, keep thee only unto her so long as ye both shall live?" Father Lambert demanded, daring Thomas to change his mind. Although he had long ago agreed to disavow his wayward sister at the behest of his father, William Lambert could never forget the childish devotion Jane had shown him, and he was glad that their father had finally forgiven her. William was now determined to see his sister happy.

"I will." Thomas's robust response mollified the priest and made Jane smile. She gave her answer just as enthusiastically and felt Thomas's fingers squeeze hers. After they spoke their vows, the ring was blessed, and considering Thomas had managed to remain a bachelor for thirty-eight years of his life, he did not flinch from firmly fitting the gold band on Jane's slender finger.

The expressions of relief on the faces of the family might have been misconstrued as signs of contentment by the few curious on-lookers witnessing the handsome couple plight their troth. John Lambert found Amy's hand and entwined his fingers in hers, which made Amy smile all the more on the happy union before them.

Thomas took Jane in his arms then and bent down to kiss her waiting lips. Her heart sang when he beamed and said, "God's greeting to you, Mistress Lyneham." She would never again be addressed as Mistress Shore and, as though reborn, she knew she could release the person she had once been as well as relinquish the many travails that name had brought her.

Thomas entered Jane's chamber clad only in his shirt, open at the throat and showing a prolific amount of chest hair. The sight caused Jane's blood to flood her lower belly and thighs in the primeval tug of desire. Although she was no longer a maid and had obviously not been averse to giving herself outside of marriage, Thomas had respected Jane's wish for celibacy throughout the betrothal period. She knew it was because she was afraid of intimacy after Tom's betrayal, but she knew she could not keep Thomas from her bed once they were married. And now, as the familiar rush readied her for his intimate touch, a seductive smile curved her lips, and she reached out her hands to him.

Gently removing the ivy crown and veil, Thomas took hand-fuls of her luxuriant hair and buried his face in it, breathing in the exotic scent of cinnamon and rosemary. Ankarette and Sophie had removed Jane's gown and underdress before, and she stood bare-foot in her spotless linen shift, the outline of her body silhouetted through it by the candles behind her. Jane let Thomas move his hands to her face and then her neck, as if he was committing to memory every satiny inch. His tenderness thrilled her, and she laid her hands on his chest and felt the muscles flex beneath her fingers. Sensing that his respect for her was making him reticent, she stepped away from him and without a word pulled loose the ribbon at her throat and let the flimsy undergarment slip off her body and to the floor.

Thomas gasped in awe. "You are even more beautiful than I imagined in my dreams," he confessed, reaching out and touching her creamy skin. Jane gave a little moan of anticipation, and seeing the telltale movement of his rising excitement under his shirt, she knew she wanted this man as passionately as he did her.

"Then step out of your dreams, Thomas, and take me to bed, I beg of you. We have waited long enough."

When they both achieved rapture at exactly the same exquisite moment, Jane experienced tears of joy in bed for the first time, and she knew, with the certainty of one who had suffered too much in her young life, that her heart had finally found its home.

A few days after the wedding, Thomas had left her at the Lamberts' when he was required, as a king's councilor, to attend Richard's first Parliament, which convened on the twenty-third of January. As he sat in a boat headed for Westminster pier and thought on his new status, he determined to prove to Richard that Jane was not the unprincipled, sinful woman the king thought she was, and he gave silent thanks for Richard's trust in him.

Thomas also prayed that, in the near future, Jane's opinion of the king might be tempered by evidence of his good governance, or fair distribution of the law. Thomas also thought Jane would be surprised by the reports that Richard had even held a festive yuletide season that might have been worthy of King Edward.

Parliament was dismissed in late February, and in mid-March the Lynehams went to look at a house for rent in the Strandway. It stood just past the bishop of Bath and Wells's impressive inn and far enough away from the crowded city to enjoy a more rural setting with a garden that ran down to the river. Jane was ecstatic.

"Are you sure we can we afford to live here?" Jane asked after running from room to room and exclaiming at the views from the second-story windows. They stood by the wide casement in the airy solar looking out over the garden to the river as a light snow fell. Jane leaned back against her husband, and he cradled her to him.

Thomas laughed. "I am on the king's council, my love, and when his grace gave me that commission to investigate a case of treason in Essex last month, I was well paid." Jane knew that Thomas had also been granted the fees associated with being named escheator for Essex and Hertfordshire, and for his services during the recent rebellion, Richard had rewarded his solicitor general a manor in Bedfordshire. "Besides I promised your father I would keep you happy, and as I have noticed you have a penchant for luxury, my love, I am keeping my promise." He chuckled mischievously as he moved one of his hands to cup her breast.

Jane slapped the hand playfully. "Be serious for a moment, Thomas," she scolded. "Then if we can afford the house, naught would make me happier than to live here."

How safe she felt, she marveled, thinking back to a year ago when Edward had begun to feel unwell and Will Hastings had been sent to the Tower for a spell. It conjured up the first—and so far only—meeting face-to-face with Edward's youngest brother, and now Richard was king. How much had transpired in one short year, she realized, including the end of her relationship with three men who had loved her and the start of one with Thomas. What fate had in store for her now, she could not begin to imagine, but she knew for certain that, barring war or the plague, Thomas Lyneham would anchor it for a long, long time, and, she hoped, forever.

Jane turned in his arms, sensing this was exactly the right moment. After all those years with Edward, the nights she shared with Will, and the lusty couplings with Tom, she had never conceived. Had God forgiven her her sins that He had waited for her to be married before quickening her womb? She and Thomas had been wed for only two months and yet she had already conceived. "I have something to tell you, Master Lyneham," she said, with a radiant smile. "God has finally looked on me kindly, my dear, and I believe we are going to have a child."

As if she were that child, Thomas lifted his wife into the air, his grin wide and his eyes shining with pride. "Thank God," he said, happily, "our prayers have been answered."

March was mild that first year of Richard's reign, and Jane was delighted to find her garden was well planted with daffodils, the flower she always associated with spring. Despite a mild dose of sickness every morning, Jane was reveling in her pregnant state. She checked each day in her polished copper mirror to see if her condition was noticeable. Ankarette laughed at her, saying, "It will grow, mistress, never fear, and then you will wish you looked thin again."

Jane was seated on a stone bench, enjoying the sunshine and listening to the birds that morning when Isabel Thomson, the nurse Thomas had hired to help when the baby arrived, hurried down the path toward her.

"His lordship, the earl of Surrey is here, mistress," Isabel announced. "I told him the master was not at home, but he wishes to see you."

Thomas Howard here? Jane thought quickly, and a tiny flicker of fear prickled up her neck. Her husband had gone to Essex on legal business for the king, and most of the lords and their retinues who had crowded the city during Parliament had returned to their estates. What could Lord Howard want with her? She had not seen him since her penance.

"Go and fetch him here," Jane ordered her servant. She was damned if she would run back to the house to greet him; he could come to her, she decided. She got up, brushed the earth from her skirts, and put up her hand to make sure her straw hat was concealing her hair. She knew she must look like a peasant in that and the plain woolen dress laced in front, but she enjoyed the freedom from formality they gave her. Besides, the Lynehams did not have many visitors other than her mother and Sophie.

She watched Thomas stride down the path, looking more like his father than ever, she thought. He and his wife had been kind to her whenever she had been at court with Edward, and she would always be grateful to them. As he approached, she smiled and went toward him.

"God's greeting to you, my lord," she said cordially. "'Tis a fine day you have chosen to visit me, or is it my husband you wish to see? He is not in the city at present."

Thomas bowed over Jane's outstretched hand. Even in her rustic garb she was still eye-catching, he thought, and she had filled out a little, which suited her, he decided. "My dear Mistress Jane. First of all, may I congratulate you on your marriage. Thomas is a good man. However, I must confess, he took the council—all except the king—by surprise when he told us. Thomas must somehow have won his grace over, for Richard took the news with equanimity. It was a pleasant diversion from the usual council business, in truth."

Jane had not been informed of the king's reaction to her marriage, only that Richard had decided to keep Thomas in his post. "Is that so. I am not out and about much anymore, preferring to enjoy my peace and quiet here, so I was unaware Thomas and I were the subject of tittle-tattle at the council." She saw his eyebrow lift and realized she might have offended the earl, but her newly married state had made her even bolder, and she hurried on. "I do hope you and your wife are keeping well. And your father, the duke, is he in good health?"

"Indeed we are all well," the earl acknowledged.

She sat down and invited Howard to join her. "What can I do for you, my lord?"

"Still as frank as ever I see, Jane," the younger Howard said, smiling. "I am not here to see your husband. In fact, I made sure he would not be at home. I am aware my duty to you might now be a little delicate, but you did put this into my keeping, do you remember?"

Jane watched, curious, as Thomas swung the pouch on his belt into his lap, undid the strings, and brought out the exquisite book of hours that Will had given her the evening before his death.

Jane's hand trembled as she took the book from him, and she ran her fingers over the embossed leather. She had not hoped to ever see the volume again. "Dear Will," she said, fighting back tears, and looked up at the compassionate face of her visitor. "He did not deserve to die."

Thomas carefully drew circles in the dirt with his foot while he weighed his words. "I may believe that, too, Jane, but promise me you did not hear it from my lips. Despite the good statutes the king has legislated in the recent Parliament, and despite the mercy he showed many of the rebels in November, Richard is troubled, and I do not think he sleeps well. My father can see no wrong in Richard, but I, and others, fear his reign may be short-lived. Henry Tudor has tried once to invade, and he is always on our minds, always hovering like a bird of prey on the other side of the Channel. 'Tis why Richard has removed the court to Nottingham. 'Tis more central for mustering an army and dealing with an invasion, wherever it may come."

Jane wrapped the book back up in its velvet protection and

placed it on the seat. "You think an invasion is inevitable, my lord Surrey? Should we be worried?"

"King Richard is the finest soldier I know, Jane. Aye, Tudor has his Lancastrian followers, but he cannot command the sort of loyalty that Richard does. Henry has spent so little time in England, and he is an unknown. Even Queen Elizabeth has come to terms with Richard as king. She must believe he has her and her daughters' welfare in his sights or she would not have left sanctuary."

Jane gasped. "She has left the abbey? Does this mean she knows her sons are safe?"

Thomas was thoughtful. "They are either safely abroad and she knows it, or they are dead and she knows it. I would wager my new manor that the king is no murderer, and that he has hidden the boys in the north somewhere. Otherwise why would Dame Grey entrust herself and her girls to him?"

"Elizabeth is a canny one, as I know well. Dorset thought they were dead," Jane mused and could have kicked herself for bringing him up. It would remind Howard that she had lain with one of the rebel leaders, and she wanted him to forget who she had been. She decided to bring the meeting to a close and jumped up from her seat. "How ill-mannered of me. May I offer you some refreshment, my lord?"

Thomas looked surprised at the abrupt close to the conversation, but upon seeing Jane's enquiring smile, he unwittingly fulfilled her goal of seeing him gone. "Nay, thank you all the same. I must return to my father's house at Stepney." He took both of Jane's hands and looked down at her. "I trust you are content now, Jane? I worried about you greatly last summer, you know."

"You are very kind. I cannot deny they were the worst three months of my life. However, may I reassure you of my happiness at present, my lord?" She confided, coyly, "You see, 'tis with great joy that I tell you I am at last with child."

"Then I must believe the child will be most fortunate in his mother," Thomas responded with a sincerity that touched Jane.

When he had taken his leave, Jane sat back down on the bench and picked up her precious gift from Will. "If you are watching from heaven, I pray you are contented for me now, dear friend. This beautiful book will remind me of you every day and remain with me always."

Richard could see the reeds clearly on the riverbed of the Cam wafting in the gentle current. Over his and Anne's head, in the delicate branches of a newly leafed-out willow, a thrush sent out its distinctive warble as if to proclaim this cloudless April day perfectly carefree. Richard thanked God for this respite among the scholarly surrounds of Cambridge, secluded as it was in the fenlands of East Anglia. He was in another world here, he thought, far from the grind of governing, and wished he could be one of the students or tutors hurrying from one temple of learning to another. He and Anne had already decided to bestow gifts upon the university in the form of endowments for the building of Queen's College and the resumption of work on the King's College chapel, begun by Edward's predecessor, Henry the Sixth. When Richard learned that Edward had neglected this worthwhile project, he was determined to have the exquisite church finished and had already released the funds from his treasury.

He sat across the river from it now, watching the masons clambering up ladders and along the precarious scaffolding as nimbly as mariners negotiating the rigging on a caravel. He could hear the tapping of metal on stone and the calls of the overseer below warning of danger or shouting commands. It fascinated him how precisely each stone fit upon the next with only a plumb line and the keen eye of the head mason. It pleased him that this building would be used for the glory of God, and his name would always be associated with it.

The tranquility of the scene helped him forget the cold response he had received from Elizabeth to his message that she could be assured her boys were safe and that he would ensure her girls were taken care of if they exited the abbey. He grimaced. It was a lie he had told her, and he had confessed it to his chaplain, albeit without revealing the truth beneath the lie. He was certain to burn in hell, but his crown was held on by so slender a thread that knowledge of Buckingham's crime would break it in an instant. He would lose his Yorkist throne to Tudor, there was no doubt; he had to remain silent.

"What are you brooding on, Richard? That is one of your serious looks," Anne said, drowsily. She had given up reading about the exploits of Sir Gawain and the Green Knight and had closed her eyes for a spell, her mind drifting home to Middleham and wishing little Ned were with them now in this peaceful place. "Can you not put governing from your mind for an hour, my love? This is a day for resting and rejoicing in God's beauty, not for pondering the next foray into France or worrying about an invasion."

Richard turned his head and smiled down at his wife, comfortably settled among her cushions. "It may surprise you to know I was only thinking about the miracle masons are working upon that chapel." He bent down and brushed her lips with his. "You look very beautiful lying there, you know. If there were not so many people walking past, I might seriously think about seducing you," he teased.

"Out here, on the grass and in broad daylight? Surely you jest, husband," Anne chided him. "Lovemaking is for the bedroom, Mother always said."

"Aye, I expect she did," he replied idly, and gazing back at the river he suddenly remembered the day when Kate had conceived their son, John, in the crystal clear waters of a river not far from here, and he had to stop himself from laughing. While he and Kate were frolicking in the river, his horse had wandered off and was rescued by a gruff peasant, who had presented it to the naked couple as they lay exhausted on the grassy bank. Richard had been mortified, but the peasant had merely complimented Richard on his lady and gone away chuckling.

With a jolt, Richard realized Anne was awaiting a response. "You are right, my lady. This is not the place for our intimacy; I should not have suggested it."

Too soon they had to resume their journey, and late April saw Richard and Anne settled in the castle built high upon a promontory at Nottingham with a commanding view of the country to the south and west. Richard gathered his closest advisors and planned a strategy for the summer months, when it was assumed Tudor would attempt another invasion. The Scots were again threatening the northern border, and the English navy was constantly under attack by marauding French ships in the Channel, no thanks to Edward's failed policies in the last months of his life.

One evening in the royal apartments in the middle bailey, after Anne's ladies had readied her for bed and Richard was bidding his daughter a good night, they heard a commotion in the courtyard. By the light of the flambeaux outside, Richard was just able to discern a rider gesticulating to the grooms and guards who had greeted him in front of the building. The king frowned but hoped his steward would see to the man's mission, for he was tired. Removing his bed robe, he joined Anne in the downy royal bed, and drew her to him. Enjoying a tender kiss in the light of the one remaining candle, Richard wished his wife pleasant dreams.

Suddenly, their solace was interrupted by a sharp rap at the door. Richard sat up and called, "Who is there?"

"'Tis I, your grace. Francis." Lovell's urgency roused Richard from the bed, and in a few strides, he was flinging wide the door, surprising the guard who stood ready to open it upon permission from the king. Richard did not recognize the young squire standing with Francis, but the muddied white boar badge and his wide, frightened eyes made Richard's stomach contract.

"Who are you, sir, and was it you I saw arriving just now? Has there been an invasion?"

"Nay, your grace," the messenger faltered.

Anne sat up abruptly. "Is something amiss?"

Observing the curiosity of the guard, Richard motioned for the messenger and Francis to enter and then slammed the door in the guard's face. The squire went on one knee, proffering Richard a letter.

"I-I am come f-from Middleham, your grace," he stammered, astonished to find himself in the king's bedchamber.

"Middleham?" Anne gasped, pulling on her bed robe and getting out of bed. "Is something wrong with my son?"

Richard ripped through the seal of the letter, read the few lines scrawled by his steward, and with a great groan, fell to his knees.

"Oh God, what have we done to deserve this?" he cried in disbelief, and he reached back for Anne, who went down on the floor with him. "My dearest wife, brace yourself. Our little Ned . . . Ned is gone. He took ill of a fever a few days ago, and nothing the physicians did could cool the heat in his blood. He is dead, Anne, our son is dead!" Taking the swooning Anne into his arms, he rocked her from side to side, tears coursing onto her limp, trembling body. He nodded to Francis, who wisely hurried the messenger from the room, closing the door quietly behind him.

The bereaved parents clung to each other, and hardened soldier as he was Richard could not have imagined such acute pain; it pierced him like a broadsword to the heart. Images of his beautiful little son filled his mind: his cheerful smile, unruly hair, blue eyes, and rather fragile arms and legs. He stroked his wife's glossy light brown hair and entreated her to be brave. Anne was staring at a point beyond him as if in a trance and her lips moved but no words emerged. Then it seemed to him that as the news sank in, so did her body, sagging like a lead weight onto his lap, her silence frightening.

"My love, I pray you look at me," he pleaded, unable to stem his own tears and turning her gently. "Let us share this grief together. I cannot bear the torment of this awful news alone. Say something, Anne, I beg of you."

His anguish roused Anne, and she brought her gaze back into focus and looked up at him pitifully. Gently, she wiped his tears with her fingers and whispered her son's name. "Ned, my little sweetheart, my little poppet, why was I not there to save you?" And then her grief came, and she buried her head in Richard's chest.

"God have mercy on his innocent soul," Richard lamented over her head, "for He has no mercy on us."

When the news reached London, church bells tolled all day and priests and townspeople alike sent up prayers for young Prince Edward's soul, so suddenly taken. But there were some who wondered if God had forsaken the new king; perhaps the rumor was true that he had done away with his nephews, and a wrathful God was seeking vengeance.

In the seclusion of their solar, Jane and Thomas mulled over the information, each with their own thoughts about the king's loss. Thomas had known the little boy during his first years with Richard at Middleham, and had admired the dedication of both parents to keeping the boy with them as much as possible. Sons and daughters of nobles were often sent from home at an early age; boys to learn Latin, French, the chivalric code, and how to become an independent man; and girls to learn how to sing, dance, read, and write, sew and run a household, and to become an accomplished marriage partner.

Queen Anne had been reluctant to let her son leave her side; she had miscarried several times, and the little boy would most likely be her only child. Richard had indulged her, mainly due to the boy's frail health; he was only nine and would grow strong and learn to be a man in time, Richard assured his wife. It had never failed to impress Thomas Lyneham that Richard devoted hours in a day to knowing both his sons: John of Gloucester, as his bastard was called, was a fine boy and beloved of his father, and perhaps because John did not have a mother to love him at Middleham, Richard gave him special attention. As soon as young Katherine had been old enough to leave her mother, she had been placed with Richard's sister, the duchess of Suffolk, and now she was lady-in-waiting to the queen. No doubt Richard would arrange a fine marriage for his beautiful daughter. But the loss of his only legitimate child and heir to the throne was different, Thomas knew, and Richard must be devastated.

Jane was lying in the crook of his arm with her own ruminations on the prince's death. Jane had no love for Richard, with good reason. He had singled her out to represent everything he had abhorred about his brother's court, and she had paid mightily. But her own penance aside, she had not found it in her heart to forgive Richard for killing Will Hastings, and for whatever had been his role in the disappearance of those two boys in the Tower. It was as though the world had forgotten them, she thought, sadly. The most difficult aspect of her marriage to Thomas was that he was so devoted to the king. She tried to close her ears to her husband's praise of Richard. She did not want to hear that he was in any way a good man, because she did not want to believe it.

But to lose one's child after loving and caring for it for nine years? She could not imagine such heartbreak. A tiny part of her believed that Richard had deserved such sorrow, simply because of the suffering he had caused her. But Anne had done nothing to warrant God's anger, Jane thought. She saw again the slight figure of Anne of Gloucester on her horse passing Jane at the conduit in the Chepe, when Anne's face had held a sweet and happy smile. Now her face must be haggard, her body ravaged by agony, sleepless nights and pointless days. Perhaps she was wondering if her life had been worth living? No mother should have to endure that, Jane decided.

Suddenly a fluttering in her womb arrested her thoughts, and she gave a little gasp.

"What is it, sweetheart?" Thomas asked. "Are you unwell?"

Jane smiled in the dark. "Nay, I have never been better, Thomas. Our babe has just let us know he is alive and growing, 'tis all." And she placed her husband's hand on her belly, although she knew he would feel nothing. How ironic that in that moment of pondering one child's death, the life of another should manifest itself thus. She sent a prayer of grateful thanks to the Virgin for giving her a sign.

It was then she knew she must forgive the king.

Thomas had commissioned a litter to be made for Jane's personal use, and although she was disdainful of his overly protective treatment of her, by the time August came and the heat was unbearable, Jane reluctantly agreed the vehicle was worthwhile. In her seventh month of pregnancy, her belly was threatening to throw her diminutive figure off balance, and Thomas had teased her that she might never see her feet again. He cautioned her about going in and out of the city too much, especially as an outbreak of plague in the overcrowded neighborhood around Billingsgate had forced the temporary removal of the fish market to the area in front of Fishmongers' Hall on the west side of London Bridge. But Jane insisted on a weekly visit to the Lamberts with another stop in St. Sithe's Lane to see Sophie.

One mercifully cooler day in late August, Jane was helped into the awkward litter with Ankarette walking alongside, while two large hired hands carried the boxlike conveyance between them. They picked their way along the hardened rutted mud, doing their best to give their mistress a smooth ride, but at times a loose stone caused a stumble and Jane would be thrown to one side before the duo was able to steady the litter again.

"I cannot help my extra weight, sirrahs," she joked to them, "and I shall soon have to double your pay." But as Jane's legendary generosity always meant a few extra pennies at the end of the day, the men laughed cheerfully as they plodded on.

She loved her days with Sophie, from whom she gleaned much practical information about weathering these last few months and what to expect during the birthing process. Sophie promised to come and be of help after the babe arrived, and Jane was grateful. Seven-year-old Pieter could be cared for by Janneke, who had now married her cordwainer's son and had moved into her in-laws' house. The other two children were old enough to look after themselves.

Jane chose to pay a visit to Sophie first today, and after exchanging their news of that week, Sophie quietly said, "You do not regret your marriage, do you? Thomas is good to you?"

"Silly Sophie," Jane replied teasingly, but then she was serious. "If you had told me a year ago that I would be married to the king's solicitor and expecting a child, certes I would have thought you were ready for Bethlem. Ah, Sophie, I cannot think that I could be any happier. God must have been with me in Ludgate when He sent Thomas to interrogate me, for I would never have met him otherwise."

"And you do not think more on Tom Grey, do you?" She saw a look of sadness flit across her friend's face before Jane shook her head vehemently. Sophie vowed never to bring the man's name into a conversation from that day on. She had simply needed to know.

Next, Amy Lambert greeted her daughter with warmth and a refreshing cup of spring water. She had sent her servant out of the city with John's cart to fetch a bucket of it. "Warm ale does not quench the thirst like fresh water, does it?" she asked, fussing around Jane and giving her more cushions. "Are you managing with the heat, daughter? I must say, you look much too healthy to be so close to delivery. Childbearing suits you, Jane."

Jane drank deeply of the sweet spring water and laughed at her mother's enthusiasm. "I have been fortunate, so I am told. I pray daily that our child will be born whole and healthy." She paused, grimacing. "I cannot say I look forward to the pain, though, Mother. Sophie says the first child is the hardest."

"All will be well, God willing," Amy said with a smile. "After all, women have been birthing children since Adam and Eve." She did not voice the concern she had that Jane's petite frame might make for a long and difficult birth, well remembering her own. "And I shall be there to see you through it. You must have Thomas send for me and Midwife Long as soon as you have the first spasms. She can ride with me."

Jane nodded. "'Tis astonishing to think she brought me into the world, too. She must be as wizened as an old apple now."

"Perhaps, but there is nothing Goody Long does not know about childbirth, Jane. She has brought many a mercer into this world, and the guild pays her well. We can put our faith in her good . . ."

Voices heard in the stairwell stopped Amy's talking. "Who has John brought home with him this time?" she wondered. "Since he has discovered his nicer side, he likes to entertain. I do not mind so much, but I wish he would warn me. We only have mutton pie with peas and spinach from the garden."

"Amy," John called as he mounted the stairs. "You will never guess who came into the mercery today and has agreed to dine with us."

Amy smiled and rolled her eyes at Jane. "Nay, I would not. Who?" she answered.

Both women stared in astonishment as the tall, lanky figure of William Shore walked into the room. Not knowing Jane had chosen today to visit Hosier Lane, poor John's bewilderment caused his mouth to open and shut like a hungry carp, and he looked at Amy to rescue him.

"Mistress Lambert, God's greeting," William said, with a small bow. And then he turned his attention to Jane, forcing his thin lips into a semblance of a smile. "Jane, I hope I find you well."

Jane was, for once, speechless: she had never imagined seeing

William again. She had heard how successful he had become as a merchant adventurer in Antwerp, and she presumed he would remain there until he died. William appeared as disconcerted as she was.

"Aye, she is very well, Master Shore," Amy said, coming to Jane's aid. She could not resist adding, "Can you not see she is with child? She is married to the king's solicitor, Thomas Lyneham, you know. They have a lovely house along the Strandway." Then she took hold of John's elbow and marshaled him out of the room. "Let us go and tell Cook we have one more for dinner, my dear."

Jane lowered her eyes and placed her hands on her belly, aware William was staring at her.

"I am glad you have found the life that suits you, William, as I have found mine." Then she raised her eyes to his. "All I required from you was a child. I suppose now we both have what we wanted."

"We made each other unhappy, did we not, Jane? I have had many years to regret what happened, but aye, I am contented with my lot." He paused, and then without warning his civility vanished. "I always knew you were immoral. I cannot pretend I was not grateful to be out of the country during your debauched liaison with the king. You are a harlot and always have been. At least my reputation stayed intact and my business flourished."

Jane scrambled out of the chair as fast as her condition allowed. Her eyes blazing, she prodded his bony chest and cried, "Aye, your business flourished thanks to the helpful hand from my royal lover. And your lack of manhood pushed me into his arms. Why, you even encouraged me to preen before him, don't you remember?" She turned away in disgust. "I do not think we have any more to say to each other, so either I should take my leave or you should decline dinner."

"Very well. I will make my excuses," William snapped, two spots reddening on his cheeks, and taking two long, purposeful strides, he left the room.

Jane sank back into her chair, feeling the perspiration running down her face and neck, dismayed at the feelings of shame and guilt that his words had reawakened. What quirk of fate brought him here today, she could not imagine, but she had hoped that part of her life was closed now as surely as the door she heard shut behind William below.

She felt the baby kicking as if in protest, and she cradled her belly, whispering: "Hush, sweeting, the odious, spiteful man has gone, and, God willing, gone for good."

After a glorious September, October ushered in a nip in the air, and one morning Jane and Thomas awoke to the sparkling magic of Jack Frost's early visit. Jane's confinement had begun, and a night spent tossing in search of a comfortable position had left her voluminous nightshirt damp with perspiration. For two weeks now, she had experienced false spasms and a nagging backache. She heaved herself out of bed and waddled to the window.

"Come and see, Thomas," she exclaimed. "How beautiful!" The edges of the glass windowpanes were rimed in delicate icy patterns that framed the garden etched with white. Thomas joined her, wrapping his arms around her taut, distended belly, and thrilled to the responding bulge that moved slowly under his fingers, as if the babe were greeting its father. He could not wait to hold his child and prayed it would be a little girl who would have her mother's green-gray eyes—or were they yellow and gray or hazel and green? He could never quite tell. He knew Jane wanted to give him a son, but with so many Lynehams populating the north of England, he really did not care. The baby was to be called Julyan, as the name could be used as much for a girl as for a boy. Thomas told Jane those who carried the name valued truth and justice. "I think we both esteem those characteristics highly. What do you think?" And Jane had been delighted with his choice.

"It seems to me I am having to reach lower to put my arms

around you, my dear," he said softly. "It seems to me the babe has moved down."

"Since when have you learned the language of birthing, husband?" Jane laughed. "Next, you will be demanding to be by my side during the delivery. You know 'tis forbidden. I would not object, in truth, but my mother would. As for Goody Long, from all I have heard of her, she might throw boiling water over you."

"Nay," Thomas said, shuddering at the thought of Jane in pain, "I shall wish to be as far away in the house as I can be with a large jug of wine to numb my nerves. But I shall be downstairs, I promise."

A sudden dull stab caused Jane's belly to tighten, and she gave a little cry. It had a different characteristic this time, she noticed. "It may be that you should send for Mother and the midwife this morning, Thomas," she told him.

Thomas let her go, his face a picture of anxiety. "Now? Today? Are you sure?"

Jane smiled at him. "Aye, now, my dear. And make certain the doors and windows are cracked open. We want to evict all evil spirits, do we not?"

Privately Thomas thought this superstition a waste of time, but he was not about to irritate his wife today, so he assured her all would be as she asked, and making her comfortable back in bed, hurried off to send his servant to Hosier Lane.

Thomas had no sooner left the room, when Jane felt the water gushing between her legs. Sophie had warned her this might be the first sign of the oncoming labor, and she called out for Ankarette and Nurse Isabel to bring clean rags and ready the birthing chair. As the two servants bustled about the chamber, stoking the fire, fetching a pot of water to boil, and piling laundered strips of bed-sheets upon a stool to use as rags, Jane tried to remain calm by picking up the printed book Thomas had recently purchased. She had been intrigued to see that Master Chaucer had included a story about a lawyer in his *Canterbury Tales,* and she became deeply involved with the dramatic story of the Christian daughter of a Roman emperor sent to marry a sultan. She smiled at the lines:

> *Constance, mild and true,*
> *And humble, heavy with her child, lay still*
> *Within her chamber, waiting on Christ's will . . .*

Suddenly, another spasm made her drop the book and clutch her stomach.

"Is the midwife here yet?" Jane asked. She hoped she did not sound as afraid as she was feeling, but she would have been comforted to know help was near.

Ankarette dipped a rag in the tepid water and wiped her mistress's flushed face. "There, there, 'tis too early to be concerned, sweetheart," she cooed, and Jane had to smile. Ankarette was only five years her senior, and yet in times of crisis, the good servant became a mother hen. "This may go on all day, so put your nose back in the book and rest easy. Both Isabel and I have attended births before, so you have naught to fear."

All the same, Jane was much relieved to hear her mother's voice on the stairs an hour later, and when the two newcomers came into the heated room, Jane gave them a wan smile of welcome, although she was dismayed by the number and depth of the midwife's wrinkles. Would this old woman be up to the task? she wondered. For her part, Goody Long was equally dismayed when she looked Jane up and down. "Such a big weight for such a small lass. 'Twill be a long, hard day," she confided to Ankarette.

No one had expected the labor to last so long into the night, and Thomas fell asleep in his chair in the hall after midnight and only awoke when one of the women came hurrying down on an errand. He would then send a new loving message to the weary Jane, giving her courage to persevere.

"You are truly loved," Amy told her, well into the night. "The man has not stopped pacing for hours."

Goody Long might have more wrinkles than a slept-in shift, but she had the stamina of an Araby horse, which Edward had told Jane could run for as many as four hours at a time. The old woman's beard hair could rival a mare's mane, Jane thought to herself as the midwife leaned in close to check Jane's paps. "Plenty there to feed the wee mite," she said, cackling, her surprisingly strong hands expertly working their way down Jane's body as she checked this and that. There was something in the practical, temperate manner that instilled confidence in Jane, and as yet another and stronger wave of pain assailed her, she listened carefully to the woman's instructions as her body prepared to expel the too-large object from the narrow birth canal.

The pains were coming closer together, and each time one tightened its grip on her, Goody Long encouraged her to take quick, short breaths.

"How much longer, Mother?" Jane demanded after night fell, believing she could endure no more. Why had she wanted a child all these years? Why would a woman go through this more than once? And then she remembered: 'Twas all because of Eve's first sin, and during her next pain, she roundly cursed her female ancestor.

"It will not be long now, Jane," Amy soothed when the bell for matins rang. In her weariness, she wondered why someone bothered to ring the bell when only those cloistered communities would heed a call to prayer in the middle of the night.

"Dear God, I want to push. Can I push, goodwife?" she asked. The urge was overwhelming and she began to satisfy it.

The midwife frowned as she inspected Jane's condition, inserting her hand up the widening orifice and feeling for the position of the babe's limbs and head. "Nay, you must not yet. You must fight it," she cried. "Blow hard and keep blowing."

Jane was exhausted but she blew, and Amy and Ankarette blew with her. For more than half an hour Jane blew until she begged to push again. Amy stroked her daughter's damp hair and held her hand. Then Goody Long said, "Come, child, 'tis time to get onto the chair," and relieved, Amy and Ankarette supported the weakened Jane the few steps to the hard, backward-sloping chair. The midwife instructed Amy to sit behind Jane and brace her. As Jane lowered herself onto the broad wooden seat, she screamed as a new and searing pain between her legs now alarmed her, and her tears came unbidden.

"It hurts me too much to sit." She wept, arching her back off the uncomfortable seat and trying to get up.

"She may be torn inside," Goody Long surmised. Her many years of experience and the Mercers Guild's gift to her of Trotula's treatise on *The Sickness of Women* told her that her skills would be put to the test this night. "Let us put her back on the bed." Then she told Isabel to place the large jasper stone between Jane's breasts and start praying to St. Margaret. She put her hand inside Jane, and a scowl informed Amy all was not as it should be. Under her breath the midwife rattled off every curse she could think of: "By Christ and his saints! God blind me! By the nails on the Cross and the Blood on the thorns! Hell's bells! God's truth!"

"What is it?" Amy asked the expert softly. "What is wrong?"

"The babe is facing away," the goodwife mumbled, shaking. "'Tis not a good sign. We must make the bed as hard as we can."

Ankarette tweaked Isabel's sleeve and said, "I know where there is a trestle top. Come with me." The two ran from the room.

Jane was panting again now as the midwife had demanded: "It helps to stay the need to push."

When the soft mattress had been replaced by the hard wooden plank and Jane was lying upon it, her head tipped over the edge, as had been depicted in Trotula's illustration, Goody Long asked Amy for the butter she had brought with her and liberally smeared her right hand and wrist with it. Jane flinched as she felt the probing fingers inside her, but she tried instead to concentrate on the flowers embroidered on the canopy above her head. Giving a grunt of satisfaction, the midwife found what she was looking for and, cradling the back of the baby's head in her palm and with her thumb upon one temple and her fingers on the other, she rotated it with a gentle twist.

"And now you may push, Mistress Jane," she directed as she slowly withdrew her hand, "and as much as you like."

With relieved groans, Jane did as she was told, her strength at its lowest point, and she, too, prayed to the patron saint of childbirth to end the ordeal. Suddenly, a broad grin wreathed the midwife's wrinkled face and the baby was expelled in a gush of blood and birthing fluids.

"You have a daughter, mistress," Goody Long declared, pleased with herself.

Ankarette took the child as the midwife tied off and cut the cord, and holding the infant upside down, she gave it a couple of smacks on the long, thin back. The resulting cry made Jane's eyes fly open and a tired smile greeted her child. After rubbing the protesting babe with salt to clean off the birthing fluid, Ankarette wrapped her in a clean cloth and proudly presented her to Jane, as though she herself were the grandmother.

"Your work is well done, mistress," Goody Long praised Jane, after dealing efficiently with the afterbirth, as the first rays of dawn were filtering through the cracks of the shutters. "There will be more blood, but unless it is bright red and does not stop, 'tis to be expected." She plunged her hands into the basin of hot water and looked around at the others. "God was kind to us today. A backward-seated babe can kill a mother, but this little lass wants to know her ma," she said cheerfully as Amy burst into tears. "This is only the third time I have had success with this kind of birth in all my years. She is a beauty," she said proudly, watching with the others as Jane held the little girl to her breast.

"Her name is Julyan," Jane told them, enjoying the sound of it. "Perhaps someone would be kind enough to let Thomas know he has a daughter."

Amy volunteered and left the room.

"I thank you with all my heart, Goody Long. Your skill is unmatched," Jane said, praising the beaming midwife. "What is your given name?"

"Mary, Mistress," she replied.

"Then my child shall be Julyan Mary," Jane told the woman. "I shall tell her that she came into this world with the same helping hands that brought me here. 'Tis a miracle."

Wiping away a happy tear, Mary Long reached out and stroked the blond fuzz on top of the infant's head. "And you, sweet babe, gave your mother a cartload of trouble today. I've no doubt she will forgive you and will soon have forgotten every last pain. The red mark will disappear as she grows, mistress," she said, indicating the slight bruise where her strong thumb had gripped the tiny head. "It will serve to remind you how fortune smiled upon you this day."

Julyan waved her arms and kicked her legs in protest when Thomas gentled her away from her mother. Weary, Jane watched with delight as the baby settled down at once in the haven of her father's strong arms and broad chest.

"She likes you," Jane rejoiced. "She had no wish to be held by her grandmother. It was a trifle embarrassing. Now that you have your wish, Thomas, are you sure there are no regrets she was not a boy?"

"Not a one, my dearest Jane," her husband replied happily. "She is already my poppet, and I cannot wait to smother her with love."

Jane gave him a baleful look. "You will not forget your wife, will you, and especially now, with my hair scrambled, my eyes swollen, my cheeks reddened, and my body stretched like cloth on a tenter?"

Thomas sat down carefully on the bed and smiled. "No wife will ever be as loved as you, sweetheart. You are more beautiful to me now than you have ever been. No matter how you think on the king, I have thanked God daily in my prayers that his grace sent me to the Ludgate that day in June last year. I never knew a man could know such joy in his life as I have since then."

Jane did not have the fortitude to hold back her happy tears, and she sniffled and laughed at the same time. "The same is true for me, dearest Thomas," she said, and she smiled at the baby, who seemed to be contemplating her father's cleft chin with great seriousness. "See how already she hangs on your every word. Aye, she knows her father, in truth."

A soft knock on the door interrupted an awkwardly managed kiss between husband and wife, and Thomas pulled away guiltily, making them both laugh.

"Come in," he called, rising and carrying the baby with him.

"May we?" Amy called, and clicked open the door. "Jane's father wants to greet his granddaughter."

Jane's contentment was complete when she watched her husband gingerly transfer little Julyan to John's more experienced arms. "You must always hold the head thus," John explained earnestly as Amy winked at Jane. "Praise be to God, she is a marvel," he enthused, "and so quiet for one born of such a clatterer." He turned and beamed at Jane. "I am proud of you, daughter. It has taken you a long time to find your way, but I believe God has guided you home at last. Come, let me kiss you."

Amy bit her lip to stop from weeping. Indeed, God must be smiling on them, for such a scene would have seemed impossible a year ago.

Placing the now whimpering Julyan in her mother's waiting arms, he planted a kiss on Jane's forehead and stepped back, declaring: "So pleased, so pleased, my dear."

"Thank you, Father," Jane said.

John was puzzled. "For what, Jane?"

"For forgiving your prodigal daughter," she replied. "She was lost and now is found."

When Thomas arrived home from his work at Westminster during Advent, he found Jane rocking the baby in her cradle and singing.

> *"Lully, mine liking, my dear one, mine sweeting*
> *Lullay, my dear heart, mine own dear darling."*

He kissed her upturned face, touched the sleeping Julyan, and pulled up his heavy oak chair. Kneeling, Jane pulled off his long, leather boots and wrinkled her nose at his damp, smelly feet.

"Aye, I should have worn my pattens, in truth. It came on to rain on my way home and I fear 'twill turn to snow in the night." He stretched his long legs toward the fire and gave a weary groan.

"Was it a difficult day, my dear?"

Thomas took a deep breath and nodded. "Each time I come face-to-face with Queen Anne, I see a change. It grieves me to say that she looks not long for this world."

Jane stared into the flames and said nothing, but she was thinking first it was Richard's child and now his wife. How much can one man stand? 'Twas no wonder Richard looked so careworn. He had aged greatly since being crowned, she thought, and though much of it must be due to the constant concerns of kingship, she was convinced the crumbling of his little family must hurt him more surely in the heart. Ever generous, Jane felt sorry for him and tried to imagine her heartache should she ever lose Thomas and her precious child.

"Is it certain she will die?"

"The doctors tell his grace that she is afflicted with the same wasting sickness that took her sister all those years ago. The king is advised to eschew her bed now, and it pains me to see my lord so melancholy these days. He is determined to make this yuletide the merriest possible, and with the late king's daughters in attendance on the queen, it will be. They were so long in sanctuary, and they deserve some cheer. The shame of it is that comparisons will be made between the beautiful, healthy Grey girls and frail Anne Neville."

Jane clucked her tongue. "An unfair comparison, in truth." Julyan had awakened and was beginning to fuss, so Jane changed the subject. "There is cold duck and half a rabbit pie awaiting you downstairs, if you are hungry. I must feed the child and will join you anon." She slipped Thomas's velvet slippers on his feet and tilting his chin, kissed him full on the lips. "Perhaps later, I can help you forget your long day, husband," she hinted, smiling seductively, and he pulled her back down onto his lap and kissed her again more passionately.

"Aye, perhaps you can," he murmured, "but not on a empty stomach."

When he had left, Jane unlaced her bodice and picked up the mewling baby, who was making little sucking noises that always melted Jane's heart and gave her a prickling sensation in her breasts.

"All in good time, sweeting," she soothed. "Let me get comfortable."

Feeling the hungry mouth nuzzle for her teat and then latch on with enthusiasm, Jane knew she would never tire of the blissful bond between her and the child. She closed her eyes and rocked her body slowly back and forth as Julyan kneaded her mother's breast with her tiny hand as she suckled. Jane's dream of motherhood had finally been realized, and it was proving to be the most powerful of the many ways she had loved.

First she had wanted her father's love and then transferred it to her brother. She smiled when she thought of William, now a prim priest in a parish that suited him well. And how strange that only after loving many men in different ways, her father's love was at last hers.

Her mind went back to those first tantalizing trysts with Tom Grey. How she had romanticized him, her maturer self now saw. She had clung so foolishly to her youthful fancy. And how thoughtlessly Tom had betrayed her trust, her adoration, and her virtue.

And then there was Edward. Magnificent, strapping, life-loving Edward. How they had reveled in their passionate, uninhibited lovemaking. It was Edward who had aroused her sensuality and taught her how to please a man. When she had been with him, she selfishly thought only of her own and his pleasure. She knew she had sinned with Edward against the queen and against the church, yet she would not have given up her position as his mistress for all the gold in the treasury. Now she opened her eyes and smiled at the thought of Edward, for he had surprised everyone by truly loving her.

She could not remember Edward without thinking of Will. She recalled the time after Edward's death when he had admitted he had had designs upon her that first day she was seated in her father's shop window. Will's love had astonished Jane by its intensity and depth; she had thought of it as a friendship—a deep friendship and perhaps paternal on her side—but she had come to cherish him even more than Edward in those few weeks before his execution. She screwed up her eyes to shut out the vision she had often had of his bloodied head toppling to the ground, and she inadvertently squeezed her infant hard, who came noisily off the nipple, annoyed.

"Hush, greedy one," Jane cooed, smiling and helping her daughter to suckle again, "or your father will be up here in a trice to protect his poppet."

Thomas. How she loved him! He had shown her it was possible to have romance as well as deep friendship in a marriage. Had something about him reminded her of Will? Perhaps. What turn of the wheel of fortune had caused him to be thrown in her path at the very moment when she thought all hope was gone? Had St. Jude intervened? Thomas had fallen in love with her in that first meeting when she was at her worst. She had been a prisoner, accused of harlotry, dirty, unkempt, and rude, and now she smiled at the thought. "Poor, poor Mistress Shore," she chanted to herself. How had the ditty gone that she had conjured on the spot when she had first heard his wonderful, infectious laugh? Ah, yes, now she remembered:

> *The king's whore*
> *She is no more,*
> *For she hath fallen far.*
> *On silken sheets she used to lay*
> *but now her bed it is of hay,*
> *And her fate is in the stars.*
> *Poor, poor Mistress Shore,*
> *Once King Edward's whore.*

She laughed out loud, and Julyan turned unfocused eyes in the direction of her mother's voice while never losing concentration on her hungry task.

"Let us amend the ending, daughter," Jane suggested, pleased with herself.

> "*. . . And her fate is in the stars.*
> *A concubine she is no more,*
> *Forget poor Mistress Shore.*"

While she fervently prayed no one would remember her by that name, the once royal mistress hoped she would not entirely be forgotten.

Her lover was a king, she flesh and blood,
And since she has dearly paid the sinful score,
Be kind at last, and pity poor Jane Shore.

Nicholas Rowe, *The Tragedy of Jane Shore,* 1714

The candle guttered on Sir Thomas More's desk, telling King Henry's favorite councilor that either someone had opened a door somewhere or the wick was faulty. He had lost track of time as he put down on parchment the event that had much moved him that day, his goose quill's busy scratching music to his ears. The words were flowing this night, he thought with satisfaction.

What an extraordinary encounter, he mused, nibbling at the tip of the pen. It was an appropriate addendum to the book he was attempting to write about the last Plantagenet king, Richard III. He doubted the document would ever see the light of day, as some of it was as exaggerated as it was truthful, and the eloquent study about power and corruption of a monarch might be perceived as a criticism of all kings and lose him his favored station with young Henry.

Sir Thomas had been only five when Richard of Gloucester was crowned, yet the story of how the late King Edward's brother came to wear the crown and the disappearance of the princes in the Tower had fascinated him ever since he first heard it as a page from his master John Morton. The wily former bishop of Ely had been rewarded by Henry Tudor with the chancellorship and archbishopric of Canterbury for conspiring to overthrow Richard and place Henry on the throne. Before his death in 1500, Morton had filled Thomas's young ears with venom whenever he talked of King Richard. No one would ever know what really happened to those sons of Edward, Sir Thomas had thought after digesting the information. They had simply disappeared, although Morton had been very convincing in his grisly tale of two little boys murdered on orders of the king and buried at the foot of the White Tower steps. Aye, he had been adamant, Sir Thomas remembered.

Thus Sir Thomas was determined to put down what he recalled being told about the dead king, although some of the details were fuzzy now. Ah, well, if he made up a few myths to create a monster in the process, so much more entertaining the book. Surely no one would believe his statement that Richard had remained in his mother's womb for two years and been born with a mouthful of teeth and headful of long hair? Although, gullible readers did abound, Sir Thomas chuckled to himself. Besides, he had made up his mind not to publish it. He would simply amuse himself, his family, and the king, and so other than adding this intriguing tidbit, he doubted he would even finish it. The former royal mistress had, however, provided him with material to enhance a scanty passage halfway through the manuscript. He could not believe his good fortune when he encountered her that day.

He had already described the involvement of Mistress Elizabeth Shore, known in her heyday as Jane Shore, in the business of Hastings's execution and her penance, but until now, he had had no knowledge of this woman's life other than that she had earned the nickname the Rose of London, presumably for her beauty.

But then a silkwoman, and friend of his daughter, named Janneke had told him the story of the rise and fall of King Edward's mistress, and his sense of justice forced him to include it in his book.

This woman was born in London, worshipfully friended, honestly brought up, and very well married . . . Proper she was and fair; nothing in her body that you would have changed but if you would have wished her somewhat higher.*

Sir Thomas smiled to himself when he recalled having to bend

---

* actual text

down to hear what the old woman was saying. Aye, she was diminutive, he thought. He continued writing.

Yet delighted not men so much in her beauty as in her pleasant behaviour. For a proper wit had she, and could both read
well and write, merry of company, ready and quick of answer,
neither mute nor full of babble, sometimes taunting without
displeasure and not without disport. The king would say that
he had three concubines . . . one the merriest, another the
wiliest, the third the holiest harlot in his realm . . . But the
merriest was this Shore's wife, in whom the king therefore took
pleasure. For many he had, but her he loved, whose favour to
say truth . . . she never abused to any man's hurt.

Where the king took displeasure, she would mitigate and
appease his mind; where men were out of favour, she would
bring them in his grace. For many that had highly offended
she obtained pardon; of great forfeitures she got men remis-
sion; and, finally, in many weighty suits she stood many men
in great stead, either for none or very small rewards, and
those rather gay than rich either for that she was content
with the deed itself well done, or for that she delighted to
be sued until and to show what she was able to do with the
king, or for (to know) that wanton women and wealthy be
not alway covetous.*

As a child, Janneke had known Jane and related to Sir Thomas
that after many happy years married to one Lawyer Lyneham, her
husband had died. During Henry VII's reign his fortunes declined,
and it was whispered he had left many debts, and Jane had been
forced to write begging letters to old friends. Sadly, she was often
seen near the palace at Westminster, hoping for alms from kindly

---

* actual text

passersby or in the hope of encountering someone who would recognize her and give her aid.

It was, therefore, with great curiosity that morning that Sir Thomas had approached the old woman loitering near the palace gate, her clothes worn through, and her white hair straggling from a simple tied-up kerchief. Was this the once-beautiful concubine of King Edward? The words that came to mind as he observed her were *old, thin, withered,* and *dried up.* Nothing left but skin and bone. And yet, he thought, even so, one could recognize that she had been fair. She had smiled at him, and a light suddenly shone from her green-gray eyes. "Sir Thomas More?" she had said, her voice younger than her looks. "I am Mistress Lyneham. I give you God's greeting, sir. 'Tis a fine day for a walk for rich and poor alike." Thomas had bowed and acknowledged the fine day.

"Would you be so kind as to give this letter to my lord Dorset?" she pleaded. "His father, the first marquess, was in my debt and I thought perhaps—" She broke off, her smile fading. Sir Thomas guessed it was not the first missive she had tried to slip to the young marquess, but he took it and promised to see it delivered. Then he drew a rose noble from his purse and pressed it into her hand. "God be with you, Jane Shore," he said, and seeing the anxiety in her face, he assured her, "your identity is safe with me."

"God bless you, sir. You have an old lady's gratitude," Jane replied, her smile revealing her former loveliness. Then, unable to contain her glee, she continued without hesitating,

"Jane Shore met Thomas More,
Both beloved of kings.
She rose and fell;
But he cannot foretell
For him what fate's in store."

The royal mistress and the royal councilor had shared a laugh on the steps of Westminster Hall before Sir Thomas had walked away.

How sad, he thought as he laid down his pen, that, now well into her sixties, the quick-witted, beautiful, generous Jane was reduced to begging. He determined right then that her story would live on in his manuscript, and he prayed that one day history would look upon her kindly.

Author's Note

Sir Thomas More's poignant description of his meeting with Jane Shore is the most detailed information we have of this remarkable woman, who captivated three of England's most powerful men before she settled into marriage and motherhood with the upstanding Thomas Lyneham (or Lynom, as the name is sometimes written). The story of their meeting in Ludgate gaol when Jane was a prisoner is factual, and we know Jane had a daughter, Julyan, because John Lambert's will of 1486 is extant, and he bequeathed the child forty shillings. Julyan Lyneham disappears from the records after that, so perhaps she died long before her mother.

We also do not know for certain what happened to Thomas. There were two Thomas Lynehams that Jane's latest biographer, Nicolas Barker, discovered in his research. One died around 1516, having returned to Middleham after Henry VII came to the throne, and the other went on to have a brilliant career in the reigns of Henry VII and Henry VIII and was still active in 1531. The latter would have been well in his eighties and rich enough to take care of Jane, if he was our man. I think he was the former, and perhaps still being loyal to the White Rose he retired to that part of the country still staunchly Ricardian. Perhaps he and Jane fell on hard times there, and upon his death, she returned to her beloved London to seek aid from her old acquaintances. But these are my conjectures.

The description in my epilogue is taken directly from More's *Historie of King Richard III*, which he probably wrote around 1518 but which was only published after his death (1535). Sir Thomas

spent some of his early life in the household of John Morton, bishop
of Ely and later Archbishop of Canterbury under Henry VII, one
of Richard's bitterest enemies. It is presumed by historians that
Morton is the source of some of Sir Thomas's information on the
events of that fateful June day when Hastings lost his head and Jane
was arrested. No other contemporary source mentions the story,
so famous in Shakespeare, about Richard accusing the queen and
Jane Shore of withering his arm with sorcery. This book formed
the basis of Shakespeare's inaccurate portrayal of Richard, and
much of our present-day layman's understanding of Richard's short,
two-year reign comes from that well-known play, unfortunately.

All texts taken from contemporary documents are marked
with an asterisk.

As always, I like to own up to inventions in my novels, and the
relationship between Jane and her father is one of them. We do know
that John Lambert was involved in a violent argument that caused
him to lose his alderman status when Jane was a young girl, and I
took this piece of information to create his volatile character. The
theme of the novel is the nature of love and how many different
ways a woman can love men. Jane's lack of a loving father figure
was the impetus behind her search for true love. However, we have
proof from the will that Jane was in good standing with her father
at the end of his life: *"To Elizabeth Lyneham, my daughter, a bed of
arras with the vilour* [velvet] *tester and cortaynes, and a stayned cloth
of Mary Magdalene,"* and thus I effected a reconciliation scene to
fit history. I wondered if he purposely chose the latter bequest as
a reminder to Jane of her former reputation!

As well, John must have been pleased with the match with the
king's solicitor and thought so highly of his new son-in-law that he
named Thomas executor of the will and left him a small sum, as
well as a velvet gown to *"Isabel Thomson, Master Lyneham's servant,"*
which is where I found that snippet of information, and so could
add her to the household after the marriage of Jane to Thomas.

I am very grateful to Mr. Barker, the author of an article in *Etoniana* (the scholarly magazine published by Eton College) in June 1972. It is in the lore of Eton that Jane persuaded Edward to finish building the school, and there are three portraits of her (none, however, contemporary) in the Eton archives that I was unable to see, as the archivist was on holiday during my visit. Barker shed new light on Jane Shore's life that was unavailable to one of my favorite authors from the 1960s, Jean Plaidy, whose novel *The Goldsmith's Wife* first introduced me to a rounded portrait of Mistress Shore. We know now that she was born Elizabeth Lambert, not the only child of mercer Thomas Wainstead as previously thought, and that William Shore was a mercer, not a goldsmith. We do not, however, have a date for her birth, and no matter where I look, it is different, so I picked 1453 to make her old enough to be mentioned by More as almost seventy when he met her.

Why Elizabeth Lambert became known as Jane is anyone's guess, and I invented Aunt Elizabeth as a possible explanation. From a brass rubbing, we know that Amy and John Lambert had six children, two of them girls. John's will mentions only three of his sons: John; William, parson of St. Leonard's; and Robert, who inherited his father's Plumstead property in Kent. As the second daughter is not mentioned in the will, I assumed she died before the will was written in 1487. We have no name for her, and with the author's permission, I chose Isabel from Vanora Bennett's novel *Figures in Silk,* in which Jane's sister is the protagonist. However, my account of Bella is as fictional as Vanora's had to be without a scrap of extant historical evidence of her life!

How I wish I could have included so many tidbits I learned about the London guilds or merchant companies, also called mysteries. The Mercers' Company was the richest of the many guilds, and as well as wool, they imported and sold all kinds of rare and luxurious textiles such as silks, lace, velvets, cloth of gold and silver, wall hangings, and bed linens. The merchant guilds of London, of which the Loriners' Company (who made bits and stirrups) was the oldest at two hundred years in 1475, ran the city and because of their wealth had a certain degree of independence from both the Crown and the royal court. After seven years of apprenticeship, a man could set up a business on his own and became a freeman of the city, which meant he did not have to pay tolls at markets and fairs anywhere in England, he could not be pressed into the army, and he could vote in parliamentary and ward elections. He might also become a guild member, although not all merchants did. Jane became a freewoman of London as soon as she married William Shore.

My guides through the records that still exist at the Mercers' Company Hall on Ironmonger Lane in the city, around the corner from Cheapside (modern spelling), were Jane Ruddell and Donna Marshall, who sat me at a desk between them for the best part of the day and plied me with documents and huge ledgers as well as their years of knowledge of the intricate guild system. Guild members of the mercers had a list of rules a mile long that would incur a fine if broken, such as: for being late for a funeral service; for attending fairs outside London; for "conniving" with others; for defective weights and measures; for striking someone, drawing a knife, carrying a dagger, quarreling, fighting or attacking; for not riding in processions; for playing dice; and, my favorite, for bad language. Each company changed their livery every third year, and woe betide if you wore the wrong color in the wrong year, or there was yet another fine.

That Jane Shore, known by her fellow citizens as the Rose of London, became the concubine of Edward IV, William Hastings, and Thomas Grey is fact. I have stayed true to the chronology of those liaisons, even though my imagined Jane should have dumped Tom long before she did! But because of the timing of Richard's proclamation and Jane's second imprisonment (this based on the extant letter from Richard to Chancellor Russell about Thomas

Lyneham), I had to keep Dorset in the picture until Buckingham's pathetic rebellion. Richard's postscript about Buckingham and other extant documents were too perfect to paraphrase, even if the language is a little flowery for our contemporary ears.

Those who have read my other books will know that I have never believed Richard III was responsible for the deaths of the princes in the Tower. I am, however, of the school that believes they were indeed done away with, and I have repeated my Buckingham theory in this book. From mid-April to July 1483 are four of the most confusing and puzzling months in English history. Other than conversations among my main characters, I have meticulously researched and reported every detail of that time as it pertains to historical fact. The timing of the revelation of the precontract—a witnessed pledge between two people that they will marry and which was considered binding—between Edward and another beautiful widow, Eleanor Butler, has had historians bickering for centuries over whether it was real or a ploy by an ambitious Richard to take the crown. These precontracts (or plight-troths) were sometimes used to persuade a reluctant female to succumb to a lover's ardor before a more formal marriage ceremony. I believe this plight-troth existed and that it was very typical of Edward's behavior. After all, he then went on to marry Elizabeth in secret and kept it from the council and the country for six months! Eleanor Butler was a sad figure of history and a victim of Edward's lust. Her father was dead, her noble husband was dead, and she had no man to speak for her who might remind the king that he was pledged to her. She went into a nunnery when Edward tired of her, presumably when his eye lit upon the incomparable Elizabeth, and she died there in 1468, relieving Edward of his guilt, no doubt. We have no idea whether Elizabeth Woodville was aware of this precontract, but I think not.

Those few months in 1483 play out to us like a tragic opera, culminating in the disappearance of the princes and winding down to the execution of one of the key players, Henry Stafford, duke of

Buckingham. I was lucky enough to have a month of sunshine and quiet in a small town in Mexico in which to piece together what happened in what is now referred to as the Year of the Three Kings: Edward IV, uncrowned Edward V, and Richard III. There are many theories about the disappearance of the two princes; mine implicating Buckingham is a popular one. That Bishop John Morton conspired with Margaret Beaufort to put her son, Henry, on the throne is fact, and because we know Buckingham caught up with Richard at Gloucester on the king's progress, and yet was seen very shortly after arriving galloping toward Wales (where Morton was his prisoner), led me to believe this was the beginning, and cause, of why Harry decided to rebel. Morton was there to feed into Buckingham's insecurities. I hope, though, I have elicited enough interest in the time period for readers to do more research and come to their own conclusions. Believe me, there are many variables.

This leads me to explain the most difficult aspect personally of writing *Royal Mistress*. I firmly believe Richard of Gloucester was not the monster Shakespeare created in his brilliant play *Richard III*, but because I was having to look at the man from the point of view of Jane and Will Hastings, both of whom were ill-used by Richard, I became acutely aware of how perception is key in looking at motivation. I do not believe Richard hurried down from the north upon Edward's death in order to seize the crown. He had never shown any inclination to overthrow his brother, as George of Clarence had. If I showed Richard's character as one of duty, piety, and morality, then I could let Richard believe he was doing the right thing every step of the way. Thus he remains true to his character. The extraordinary obsession with morals in his proclamations following Buckingham's rebellion (taken directly from the texts) told me Richard was acting out a fanatical and puritanical desire to clean up his brother's court, and that in order to do God's work, he had no choice but to punish those responsible. It was then clear to me that those who did not understand his character or his motivations would see only ambition and deception. Hence his negative reputation. I hope I have succeeded in creating an enigmatic personality with flaws but one with humanity and empathy as well. Not a monster.

For readers unfamiliar with my first book, *A Rose for the Crown*, I have to confess that Kate Haute is the fictitious mother of Richard's bastard children, John of Gloucester and Katherine Plantagenet, who are not imagined but who did indeed grow up in Richard's household. We do not know with whom Richard had these two children, allowing for my fertile imagination to conjure and use her as a vehicle to tell a more truthful version of Richard's life than Shakespeare did. I could not resist having the two royal mistresses bump into each other in this book and go across the street to the pub for a cup of ale and a chat.

Readers of that first book will remember Kate consulting with a lawyer about proving impotence for an annulment, and I use the same quote in this book from Thomas of Chobham's twelfth-century law book that I found cited in Henrietta Leyser's excellent *Medieval Women*. For though all women were disenfranchised in medieval times, they did have rights, including an expectation of intimacy and the chance to bear children once they were married. Jane's annulment (the word *divorce* did not exist then) from William Shore was granted by three bishops in early 1476 and, very unusually, the cause was impotence. He did not contest it, probably because he knew he would have to prove it by what to us would be very primitive means: allowing several "wise" women to witness the wife try and arouse him and report their findings. I'm surprised more wives did not try it. It is possible he was bought off by the king, as I suggest, because William was given letters of protection from the king to enable him to start a business in Antwerp, where he remained as a merchant adventurer until his documented return to London in 1484. I am sure he was happier as an adventurer, which meant being celibate for the duration of one's time abroad.

Although we know the date that Thomas Grey, Marquess of Dorset, escaped sanctuary, we do not know his whereabouts for the next few weeks of that summer in 1483. He must have been with Jane at that time or she would not have been accused of "lying with him" in Richard's proclamation. We know he was with his uncle, bishop of Salisbury, in Wiltshire at the time of Buckingham's rebellion in October, and he did flee to join Henry Tudor in exile in Brittany and was attainted by Richard. But in an odd turn of events, he deserted Henry when he learned his mother, Elizabeth, had reconciled with Richard. On his way through France to return to his beloved parent, he was captured by the French and held for ransom until Henry repaid a loan from the French government. He was left behind during Henry's invasion of 1485, Tudor having no use for the unstable Dorset, who could not make up his mind which side to support. Eventually, he returned to England but was never again allowed any influence at court. In 1487, when the loyal Yorkists rose in rebellion under a pretender, Lambert Simnel, Henry clapped Dorset in the Tower in case he changed sides again and joined the rebels. A few years later, during the Perkin Warbeck rebellion, he signed a pledge to the Tudor king that he would never again commit treason, and he died at age 45 in 1501, his wife, Cecily Bonvile, having given him fourteen children. One account of him says it all for me: Thomas Grey was a man of "mediocre abilities." He certainly was not worthy of our Jane.

Jane's belief in romantic love was a device to support my theme to show how humans can love in many different ways. Thomas was her first real romance, and I thought it useful to bring back the fashionable idea of courtly love from earlier centuries to better describe her infatuation with him. Knights and nobles would idealize a lady, meet her in secret, pass secret messages back and forth, and write her poems and songs. The lady was supposed to pretend to rebuff the advances, all the while leading the poor man on and occasionally deigning to let him kiss her. It was a courtly dance that may have been born in Aquitaine in the twelfth century, and its rules were set down by Andreas Capellanus. The two rules I chose to have Jane remember were: "When love is made public, it rarely endures"; and "The easy attainment of love makes it of little value; difficulty of attainment makes it prized." Hence Jane is convinced Thomas is obeying the rules by suggesting they meet in secret, and that by not giving in to him, she makes herself more valuable.

I may be a writer, but I am not a poet, and thus I must confess to my paltry prose in the form of Jane's little poems. They were often the hardest writing I tackled! Only the poem on pages 407-408 is borrowed from a popular ballad, *The Woeful Lamentation of Jane Shore*, from the Bagford Collection printed in the first part of the seventeenth century. Each stanza ends with the apt lines:

> *Then maids and wives in time amend*
> *For love and beauty will have end.*

Once again, as with the story of Perkin Warbeck in my third book, *The King's Grace*, I am reminded of how much stranger fact is than fiction in Jane's astonishing rise and fall. It is a tale that has resonated through the centuries in English literature, giving rise to many written works, from plays such as Shakespeare's *Richard III* and Nicholas Rowe's *The Tragedy of Jane Shore* (1714); ballads such as *A New Ballad of King Edward and Jane Shore* (1671) and the seventeenth-century verse *Woeful Lamentation of Jane Shore*, cited above; an *Epistle from Edward the Fourth to Jane Shore* by the Elizabethan poet Michael Drayton; a long anonymous poem published in 1749 entitled "Jane Shore to the Duke of Gloster" (sic); and the poem used to punctuate the four parts of this book, "How Shore's Wife, King Edward the Fourth's concubine, was by description King Richard Despoyled of all her goods and forced to doe open Penance."

These lines from Thomas More's *Historie of King Richard III*, written around 1519, poignantly end my notes on Jane:

But it seemeth to me, she is so much more worthy to be remembered . . . as many other men were in their times, which be now famous only by the infamy of their ill-deeds. Her doings were not much less, albeit they be much less remembered because they were not so evil.

As well as those already cited in the Author's Note, here are a few of the sources I used to write *Royal Mistress:*

Richard III, Paul Murray Kendall, Unwin Hyman Ltd., 1955.

Edward IV, Charles Ross, Eyre Methuen Ltd., 1974.

Richard III, Charles Ross, University of California Press, 1983.

Richard III and The Princes in the Tower, A. J. Pollard, Sutton Publishing, 1991.

The Life and Reign of Edward IV, 2 vols., Cora L. Scofield, Frank Cass & Co. Ltd., 1967.

The Wars of the Roses, Desmond Seward, Penguin Books, 1993.

The Witchery of Jane Shore, C. J. S. Thompson, Grayson & Grayson, 1933.

Medieval Women, Henrietta Leyser, Weidenfeld & Nicolson, 1995.

The Deceivers, Geoffrey Richardson, Baildon Books, 1997.

The Great Chronicle of London, ed. A. Thomas, Humanities Press Intl. Inc., 1983.

Medieval Costume and Fashion, Herbert Norris, J. M. Dent & Sons, 1927.

Food and Feast in Medieval England, P. W. Hammond, Sutton Publishing, 1993.

Anne Easter Smith
Newburyport, Massachusetts
2013

Glossary

arras—tapestry or wall hanging.

attaint—imputation of dishonor or treason; estates of an attainted lord are often forfeited to the Crown.

avise—to look closely, study a person.

bailey—outer wall of a castle.

basse danse—slow stately dance.

butt—barrel for wine.

butts—archery targets.

caravel—medieval sailing ship.

carol—medieval circle dance.

caul—mesh hair covering.

churching—first communion given to a woman following the period of seclusion after giving birth.

curfew—in large walled cities, all city gates were closed when the bell rang; taverns were shut and citizens returned to their houses or inns. Those discovered outside could be prosecuted.

coif—scarf tied around the head.

conduit—drinking fountain in a town or city with piped-in water.

coney—rabbit or rabbit fur.

cote or cotehardie—long gown worn by men and women.

crackows—fashionable long-pointed shoes, said to have originated in Krakow, Poland.

escheator—an officer who manages properties that have reverted to the Crown.

fermail—ornamental buckle.

fox and geese—medieval board game.

fustian—cotton fabric.

garderobe—inside privy where clothes were often stored.

groat—silver coin worth about fourpence.

grosgrain—ribbed worsted wool often mixed with silk.

gipon—close-fitting padded tunic.

gong farmer—man who removes waste from privies and carts it outside the city.

hennin—tall conical headdress from which hangs a veil; steepled hennins were as much as two feet high; butterfly hennins sat on the head like wings with the veil draped over a wire frame.

jakes—privy.

jennet—saddle horse often used by women.

kermes—red dye made from insect of same name.

kirtle—woman's gown or outer petticoat.

madder—dark red-brown dye.

malmsey—kind of wine.

midden—refuse pile in a garden.

motte—artificial mound on which to build the keep of a castle.

murrey—heraldic term for purple-red (plum).

oyer and terminer—commission to act as a circuit judge in the king's name.

palfrey—small saddle horse.

patten—wooden platform strapped to the sole of a shoe.

pavane—a slow stately dance.

pillion—a pad placed at the back of a saddle for a second rider.

pipkin—earthenware or metal pot.

plastron—gauzy material tucked for modesty into the bodice of a gown.

plight-troth—to be engaged or bound to someone, which, if witnessed, was tantamount to a marriage contract.

points—lacing with silver tips used to attach hose to undershirt or gipon.

poppet—a doll.

precontract—see *plight-troth.*

psaltery—a stringed instrument like a dulcimer plucked with a feather.

puling—whining, crying in a high, weak voice.

rebec—a three-stringed instrument played with a bow.

rouncy—a packhorse used by travelers or men-at-arms.

sanctuary—place of protection for fugitives. Safe haven (perhaps in an abbey) usually for noble women and their children, who pay to stay.

sarcenet—a fine, soft silk fabric.

scarlet—a high quality broadcloth usually dyed red with expensive kermes, an insect.

seneschal—steward of a large household.

sennight—a week (seven nights).

settle—high-backed sofa.

shout—a sailing barge carrying grain, building stone, and timbers common on the Thames.

solar—living room often doubling as a bedroom.

staple town—center of trade in a specified commodity (e.g., Calais for wool).

stews—brothel district.

tabbied—moiré effect on grosgrain taffeta.

tabor—small drum.

tasseau—fastening for a cloak.

tester bed—a bed with a canopy overhead and curtains; sometimes a four-posted bed.

tiring woman—a lady's dresser.

trencher—stale bread used as a plate.

tun—barrel.

tussie-mussie—aromatic pomander.

viol—a stringed instrument, the ancestor of the viola da gamba.

wastel—bread.

worsted—spun from long fleece, a smooth, lightweight wool for summer.

TOUCHSTONE READING GROUP GUIDE

ROYAL MISTRESS

As the Wars of the Roses neared its end and Edward IV led England into a period of peace and prosperity, Jane Lambert, a bright young mercer's daughter, cherished hopes of true romance. When she caught the eye of Thomas Grey, son of Elizabeth Woodville and stepson to Edward IV, she believed she had found it. But Grey disappeared from her life, and she married mercer William Shore to find that not only was he emotionally detached, but impotent as well. Determined to have children, Jane searched for a way to end her marriage—and unwittingly came to the notice of Edward IV and his chamberlain, William Hastings.

Despite the antagonism and machinations of Edward's queen, Elizabeth, Jane remained his mistress for seven years and found happiness, stability, and the power to assist her friends. His death in 1483 and her fear for her future threw her into a relationship with Hastings, who had been a friend throughout her life at court. But their affair was doomed to be short-lived—Hastings fell under suspicion of plotting against Richard of Gloucester, protector of Edward's heir and later crowned Richard III. After Hastings's execution, Jane and Thomas Grey were reunited. Still believing him to be her true love, she risked certain punishment by harboring him, only to be abandoned yet again and imprisoned for her troubles. But it was her imprisonment in Ludgate that brought her to her final relationship. There she met the lawyer Thomas Lyneham, who became her husband and the father of her daughter, Julyan.

From a freewoman of London to royal mistress to mother and wife, Jane Shore survived court intrigue, the end of one king's reign and the turbulent start of another, and public shame and imprisonment, and still went down in history as one of the merriest women in England.

For Discussion

1. Jane Shore is remembered for her role in Edward IV's court. What expectations do you associate with the phrase "royal mistress"? How does Jane fulfill her role? In what ways, if any, does she defy expectations?

2. Consider this oft-quoted saying: "Every villain is the hero of his own story." Who are the villains in *Royal Mistress*? What are their motivations?

3. Compare the different ways that Elizabeth Woodville and Jane Shore use their sexuality to gain power, and wield that power once they've attained it.

4. How does the portrayal of Richard III in *Royal Mistress* match up to other accounts with which you are familiar?

5. Did you find yourself wondering about the historical accuracy of a certain character or plot point? How much does accuracy matter to you as a reader of fiction?

6. Jane has very different relationships with Edward IV, William Hastings, Thomas Grey, and Thomas Lyneham. Would you identify one as "true love," above the others? Would Jane?

7. Jane manages to avoid becoming jaded, despite her affairs and their consequences. How does she reconcile her own beliefs and morals with those of her society?

8. Early in Jane's marriage to William Shore, he gives her frequent presents to try and keep her happy, despite their problems. Her friend Sophie has a miserable marriage until Jane is able to help their family financially; then things seem to improve dramatically. What is the author saying about the impact of money on a relationship, and do you agree?

9. Motherhood is very important to Jane, and plays a significant role in the lives of other characters as well. Discuss the different mother-child relationships in the novel, and what it means to be a mother in this era.

10. Edward IV and Richard III have very different approaches to governance and court lifestyle. Both of their reigns end badly; how much of their failure do you believe is circumstance and how much a result of their policies?

11. Richard III and Jane both have strong views on love. Compare their beliefs: where do they match and where do they differ? Do you have more sympathy for one than the other?

12. Have you read other novels about this time period? If so, how would you rank this novel against the others you have read? If not, did *Royal Mistress* inspire you to learn more?

Enhance Your Discussion

1. There are many theories about the fate of Edward V and Richard of Shrewsbury, also known as the Princes in the Tower. The author identifies Buckingham as the murderer in *Royal Mistress*, but there are other possibilities as well. Research the various theories and discuss which the group thinks is the likeliest (Wikipedia or www.r3.org is a good place to start).

2. Have each member name their favorite historical novel, movie, or TV show. Which time periods are the most popular in the group?

3. Throughout the book are funny little verses that Jane composes. Select a few to read aloud as a group, and vote on your favorite.

4. The Wars of the Roses have captured many authors' attention. For other takes on the time period, read the following: Philippa

Gregory's The Cousins' War series; Sharon Kay Penman's *The Sunne in Splendour;* Josephine Tey's *The Daughter of Time;* and Shakespeare's *Richard III.*

A Conversation with Anne Easter Smith

Why do you think modern readers are so fascinated by English history from this time period? By historical fiction in general?
We live in a time of great stress and turbulence. I think readers enjoy leaving the twenty-first century and their troubles behind for a few hours to visit a different time and place. Of course, medieval people had their difficulties and life struggles, too—who today would relish living in such unhygenic conditions; not knowing if their babies would last the week, let alone the first perilous five years; being stretched upon the rack; or being burned at the stake?—but the very slowness in their pace of life is attractive to us in our crazy technological world. Historical fiction is pure escapism, but if I can pass on some knowledge about how people lived back then or what events took place that eventually led us to today, then I have done my job. Ten years ago, all that American readers and TV watchers knew about English history was the Tudors. Yes, it was an exciting period, but I happened to think, earlier than most, that the fifteenth century, when England was transitioning from medieval to Renaissance, had many more intriguing, compelling stories to tell.

Jane's penance walk is incredibly rich in situational and geographic detail. How did you reconstruct what she would have seen and experienced?
All we know of Jane's penance from the chronicles is that she walked the streets of London in nothing but her shift and carrying a heavy taper, ending up in St. Paul's prostrate before the priests. Before I started writing *Royal Mistress,* I walked for hours through today's City of London streets (the square mile of the financial district where most of London was situated in the fifteenth century) just to get a feel for its size, and then I found a medieval street map of the city at the Guildhall Library. I blew it up and it is on my wall, showing tiny alleys and lanes that no longer exist, the exact placement of buildings (especially taverns, noble houses, and the ubiquitous churches), and where each of the many gates led on the outskirts. As Jane was in Ludgate gaol, it made sense to me that she would walk in a large loop

around the huge cathedral (not the one that's there now—the gothic one with its incredible spire burned down in 1665 and was rebuilt by Christopher Wren a few years later), and she would end up back at the front door of the church. Hampered by the rough stones that mangled her feet and the crowds who surged to witness this unusual punishment, I judged it may have taken her more than an hour to make the slow walk.

Jane is historically renowned for her merriness, which is a bit of a surprise given the life she led. What kept her from the bitterness and skepticism shown by other women of the court, like Elizabeth Woodville?
This is difficult to answer because we know very little about her character—except that she had a reputation for being a positive, quick-witted woman. That reputation was cemented in history by chroniclers who only observed her public life with Edward. Certainly we do not know if deep down inside she was unhappy and that, when she lost everything, she did not become bitter and twisted. She would not then have made a very compelling protagonist for a novel, would she? I took the Edward declaration of "merriest mistress" at face value and built my character around it.

In the Author's Note, you mention that there were two historical Thomas Lynehams to choose from: one who died in 1516 and one who was around into the 1530s. Why did you choose the Lyneham, and therefore the ending, for Jane that you did?
Because I could not reconcile Jane begging in her sixties if I had chosen the second, longer-lived, and very successful Lyneham.

While the story centers mostly around Jane, other characters take center stage from time to time. How did you decide when to shift perspective from Jane to another person?
All my other books have been written in third-person limited, meaning that we rarely leave our heroine's head. As Jane was a mistress of the king, she would not have been present at some of the most dramatic events and private conversations at court. She would have to rely on someone relaying information to her, and that becomes tedious reading. How could I write about Edward arguing with Elizabeth on having yet another mistress if Jane could not be there to hear it? Once you make the decision to use the omniscient voice, all sorts of possibilities are open to you. I enjoyed jumping into Will

Hastings's head or even dried-up William Shore's, and I loved being in Richard III's!

You also mention in your Author's Note that writing Richard III, a rather notorious historical figure, was a difficult process for you because of his and Jane's antagonistic relationship. Tell us more! Did you ever consider skipping his viewpoint entirely?

Certainly not! I was a Richard III fan (a Ricardian) from the age of twenty-one when I read Josephine Tey's *The Daughter of Time*. I practically know what he ate for breakfast and lunch on any given day! I read everything there was to read about him and came to the conclusion long ago that he was not the monster Shakespeare led us to believe he was. My first book, *A Rose for the Crown*, was my attempt to get a wide audience to see the real Richard. I have never thought he was guilty of doing away with the princes in the Tower, and I understood why he acted the way he did in those drama-packed four months between Edward's death and Richard's coronation. But if I were looking at him purely from Jane's, Hastings's, or Elizabeth's viewpoints, he would come across as the very usurper, which reputation I had worked so hard to bury in my first book. I truly believe Richard thought he was following his rigid moral code and doing his duty by his brother, his nephews, and his country. Those looking at him from the outside saw him acting contrary to all they had come to expect from Edward, but they weren't in his head. I was! The only decision I will never be reconciled with was the execution of Hastings. I have tried, by looking at all sides, to present a plausible explanation.

Speaking of Richard III, do you think we will ever know the truth about him?

Amazingly enough, after much conjecture and false rumor, Richard's bones may have finally been found under a parking lot in Leicester. The University of Leicester and the Richard III Society (of which I am a member) funded an archeological dig in August 2012 of the site where the medieval Greyfriars Church was believed to have stood. It was there that Richard's bloodied body was deposited after his defeat at nearby Bosworth Field, and where we think it was subsequently buried. Later, when Henry's son, the notorious eighth of that name, ordered the dissolution and destruction of the monasteries, it was thought that Richard's grave had been desecrated and his bones thrown into the nearby Soar River. End of story—until now. Archeologists found the nave and, buried under it, a lone skeleton, its skull caved in, consistent with a battle wound, and an arrowhead lodged in its spine. The backbone also showed that the man had scoliosis. Perhaps this is where the rumor of his having one higher shoulder than the other arises. Hopefully, a DNA test will reveal that this was indeed Richard III, but it will not shed any new light on what happened to the princes in the Tower, unfortunately!

Given that the ideal of romantic love is central to this novel, was it hard to avoid using a modern perspective on love and relationships while writing?

That is the bane of every serious historical novelist, and I have been on several literary festival panels discussing exactly how much modern-day sensibilities we ought to inject into our stories. The answer is that yes, my characters do have many modern-day thoughts, but I am hoping that my readers are relating to those characters, and if the characters' thought processes are too distant from ours, they will make for unlively, if not tedious, people.

You've now written five novels centered on the Wars of the Roses. What originally drew you to this time period? Is there another period you're itching to write about?

Richard III was my draw to the Wars of the Roses initially. As for the second part, I have always enjoyed the Restoration and the Regency periods. I'm not sure if I'll go there, though. I am so enmeshed in the medieval period that I feel I should continue to use my knowledge— and my library—before spending the next dozen years becoming as immersed in another period.

Are there genres aside from historical fiction that you enjoy reading?

I enjoy well-written contemporary novels, but they must be plot-driven, I have come to realize. I have a hard time with sci-fi and fantasy, I'm afraid. I'm very much a factual person.

Which writers and books do you take inspiration from?

For this book, I called upon my favorite of all writers for inspiration: Charles Dickens, the master of omniscient narration. I love Daphne du Maurier's books, too. I aspire to tell a story as well as Ken Follett and Edward Rutherfurd, and to nail characterization like Jane Austen.

"*A*nne Easter Smith has the ability to grab you, sweep you along with the story, and make you fall in love with the characters.... You know you have loved a book when you're sad it ends."

—*Historical Novels Review,* Editors' Choice

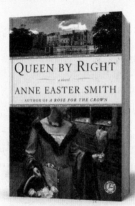

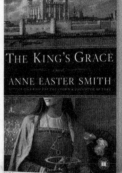

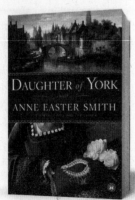

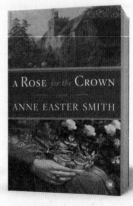

TOUCHSTONE
A Division of Simon & Schuster
A CBS COMPANY

AVAILABLE WHEREVER BOOKS ARE SOLD
OR AT SIMONANDSCHUSTER.COM